Autoboyography

CHRISTINA LAUREN

SIMON & SCHUSTER BFYR

NEW YORK • LONDON • TORONTO • SYDNEY • NEW DELHI

4 6 8 10 9 7 5
The Library of Congress has cataloged the hardcover edition as follows:
Names: Lauren, Christina, author.
Title: Autoboyography / Christina Lauren.
Description: New York : Simon & Schuster Books for Young Readers, [2017] |
Summary: High school senior Tanner Scott has hidden his bisexuality since his
family moved to Utah, but he falls hard for Sebastian, a Mormon mentoring
students in a writing seminar Tanner's best friend convinced him to take.
Identifiers: LCCN 2017005047 (print) | LCCN 2017032074 (eBook) |
ISBN 9781481481687 (hardback) |ISBN 9781481481700 (eBook) |
Subjects: | CYAC: Bisexuality—Fiction. | Authorship—Fiction. | Mormons—
Fiction. | High schools—Fiction. | Schools—Fiction. | Dating (Social customs)—
Fiction. | Family life—Utah—Fiction. | Utah—Fiction.|
BISAC: JUVENILE FICTION / Love & Romance. | JUVENILE FICTION /
Social Issues / Dating & Sex. Classification: LCC PZ7.L372745 (eBook) |
LCC PZ7.L372745 Aut 2017 (print) | DDC [Fic]—dc23
LC record available at https://lccn.loc.gov/2017005047
ISBN 978-1-4814-8169-4 (pbk)

For Matty, because this book would not be here without you.

And for every teen who has ever needed to hear it:
You are perfect, exactly the way you are.

And love is love is love is love is love is love is love is love,
cannot be killed or swept aside.
—LIN-MANUEL MIRANDA

CHAPTER ONE

The end of our final winter break seems almost like the beginning of a victory lap. We're seven semesters into our high school career, with one last—token, honestly—semester to go. I want to celebrate like your average guy: with some private time and a few mindless hours down the YouTube rabbit hole. Unfortunately, neither of those things is going to happen.

Because, from across her bed, Autumn is glaring at me, waiting for me to explain myself.

My schedule isn't complete and classes start up in two days and the good ones fill up fast and *This is just so like you, Tanner.*

It's not that she's wrong. It *is* just like me. But I can't help it if she's the ant and I'm the grasshopper in this relationship. That's the way it's always been.

"Everything's fine."

"Everything's fine," she repeats, tossing her pencil down. "You should have that printed on a T-shirt."

Autumn is my rock, my safe place, the best of my best— but when it comes to school, she is unbelievably anal-retentive.

I roll onto my back, staring up at her ceiling from her bed. For her birthday sophomore year—right after I moved here and she took me under her wing—I gave her a poster of a kitten diving into a tub of fuzzy balls. To this day, the poster remains sturdily taped there. It's a super-cute cat, but by junior year I think the innocent sweetness of it had been slowly sullied by its inherent weirdness. So, over the motivational phrase DIVE RIGHT IN, KITTY! I taped four Post-it notes with what I think the creator of the poster might have intended it to say: DON'T BE A PUSSY!

She must agree with the edit because she's left it up there.

I turn my head to gaze over at her. "Why are you worried? It's *my* schedule."

"I'm not *worried*," she says, crunching down on a stack of crackers. "But you know how fast things fill up. I don't want you to end up with Hoye for O Chem because he gives twice as much homework and that will cut into my social life."

This is a half-truth. Getting Hoye for chem *would* cut into her social life—I'm the one with the car; I chauffer her around most of the time—but what Autumn really hates is that I leave things to the last minute and then manage to get what I want anyway. We're both good students in our own way. We're both high honor roll, and we both killed our ACTs. But where Autumn with homework is a dog with a bone, I'm more like a cat lying in a sunny window; if the homework is within reach and doing something interesting, I'll happily charm it.

2

"Well, your social life is our priority." I shift my weight, brushing away a trail of cracker crumbs stuck to my forearm. They've left a mark there, tiny red indentations in the skin, the same way gravel might. She could stand to spread some of her obsessiveness to room cleaning. "Autumn, my God. You're a pig. Look at this bed."

She responds to this by shoving another stack of Ritz in her mouth, crumbling another trail onto her Wonder Woman sheets. Her reddish hair is in a messy pile on her head, and she's wearing the same Scooby-Doo pajamas she's had since she was fourteen. They still fit . . . mostly.

"If you ever get Eric in here," I say, "he'll be horrified."

Eric is another one of our friends and one of only a handful of non-Mormon kids in our grade. I guess technically Eric *is* Mormon, or at least his parents are. They're what most people would call "Jack Mormon." They drink (both alcohol and caffeine) but are still reasonably involved in the church. *Best of both worlds,* he says—although it's easy to see that the other Latter-day Saints students at Provo High don't agree. When it comes to social circles, Jack Mormon is the same as not Mormon at all. Like me.

A few dry flecks of cracker fly out when Autumn coughs at this, feigning repulsion. "I don't want Eric anywhere near my bed."

And yet here *I* am, lying on her bed. It's a testament to how much her mother trusts me that I'm allowed in her room at all. But maybe Mrs. Green senses already that nothing will happen in here between me and Auddy.

We did that once, over winter break our sophomore year. I'd lived in Provo for only five months by that point, but there was an immediate chemistry between us—driven by a lot of classes in common and a comfort from our shared defector status with the Mormon kids at school. Unfortunately, the chemistry dissolved for me when things got physical, and by some miracle we dodged the post-make-out awkward bullet. I am not willing to risk it again.

She seems to grow hyperaware of our proximity at the same moment I do, straightening and pulling her pajamas down her torso. I push up so I'm sitting, leaning against the headboard: a safer position. "Who do you have for first?"

Autumn looks down at her schedule. "Polo. Modern Lit."

"Same." I steal a cracker, and—like a civilized human—manage to eat it without dropping a crumb. Scanning down my paper with an index finger, I feel pretty good about this last term. "Honestly, my schedule isn't too bad. I only need to add something for fourth."

"Maybe you can add the Seminar." Autumn claps joyfully.

Her eyes are flashlights, beaming their thrill into the dusky room: She has wanted to take this course since she was a freshman.

The Seminar—I'm serious; when the school references it in newsletters or announcements, they even capitalize it like that—is so pretentious it's unreal. WRITE A BOOK IN A SEMES-TER, the catalog cheerfully dares, as if that could happen only in this class. As if the average person couldn't throw together enough words in *four months*. Four months is a lifetime.

Students who apply need to have completed at least one advanced placement English course and have a minimum of a 3.75 GPA for the previous term. Even if that includes seventy kids in our grade alone, the teacher only enrolls fourteen.

Two years ago, the *New York Times* wrote an article and called it "a brilliantly ambitious course, earnestly and diligently directed by the *NYT*-bestselling faculty member Tim Fujita." (I know that direct quote because the piece was printed out, enlarged to about five thousand times the original size, and framed in the front office. My frequent gripe is the criminal overuse of adverbs, which Autumn thinks makes me petty.) Last year, a senior named Sebastian Brother took the Seminar, and some big publisher bought his manuscript. I don't even know who he is and I've heard his story a hundred times: He's a bishop's son! He wrote a high fantasy novel! Apparently, it was amazing. Mr. Fujita sent it to an agent, who sent it to people in New York, and there was some sort of civilized warfare for it, and boom, now he's across the street at BYU and apparently delaying his mission so that he can do a book tour and become the next Tolkien.

Or L. Ron Hubbard. Though I guess some Mormons

might take issue with that comparison. They don't like to be lumped in with cults like Scientology. Then again, neither do Scientologists.

Anyway, now—other than BYU football and the sea of Mormons—the Seminar is the only thing anyone ever talks about anymore when they mention Provo.

"You got in?" I confirm, not that I'm surprised. This class means everything to Autumn, and apart from already meeting the *actual* requirements, she's been devouring novels nonstop in the hope that she'll get a chance to write her own.

She nods. Her smile stretches from sea to shining sea.

"Badass."

"You could, too, if you talked to Mr. Fujita," she says. "You have the grades. You're a good writer. Plus, he loves your parents."

"Nah." I'm expecting acceptance letters to colleges anywhere but here—Mom *begged* me to only apply out of state—and a yes from any one of those schools will be conditional on my grades this last semester. Regardless of how easy I think this might be, this is not the time to be taking chances.

Autumn picks at a beleaguered fingernail. "Because then you'd have to, you know, finish something?"

"I finished your mom earlier. I think you know what I mean."

She pulls my leg hair, and I screech out a surprisingly feminine sound.

"Tanner," she says, sitting up, "I'm serious. It would be good for you. You should take this class with me."

"You say that like I would want to."

Glaring at me, she growls, "It's *the Seminar*, asshole. Everyone wants to."

See what I mean? She's got this course on a pedestal, and it's so nerdy it makes me a little protective of Future Autumn, when she's out in the world, battling her Hermione Nerd Girl battles. I give her my best smile. "Okay."

"Are you worried about coming up with something original?" she asks. "I could help you."

"Come on. I moved here when I was fifteen—which I think we can agree is the worst time to move from Palo Alto, California, to *Provo, Utah*—with a mouth full of metal and no friends. I have stories."

Not to mention I'm a half-Jewish queer kid in a straight and Mormon town.

I don't say that last part, not even to Autumn. It wasn't that big a deal in Palo Alto when, at thirteen, I realized I liked the idea of kissing guys as much as kissing girls. Here, it would be a *huge* deal. She's the best of my best, yeah, but I don't want to risk telling her and finding out she's only progressive in theory and not when a queer kid is hanging out in her bedroom.

"We all had braces, and you had me." She flops back on her bed. "Besides, everyone hates being fifteen, Tanner. It's

7

period emergencies and boners at the pool, zits and angst and unclear social protocol. I guarantee ten out of fifteen students in this class will write about the perils of high school for lack of deeper sources of fiction."

A quick scan through the Rolodex of my past gives me a lurching, defensive feeling in my gut, like maybe she's right. Maybe I *couldn't* come up with something interesting and deep, and fiction must come from depth. I've got two supportive— maybe *overly* supportive—parents, a crazy but wonderful extended family, a not-too-terrible-although-dramatically-emo sister, my own car. I haven't known a lot of turmoil.

So I balk, pinching the back of her thigh. "What makes *you* so deep?"

It's a joke, of course. Autumn has plenty to write about. Her dad died in Afghanistan when she was nine. Afterward, her mom—angry and heartbroken—cut ties with the Mormon Church, which, in this town, is a huge defection. More than 90 percent of the people who live here are LDS. Being anything else automatically leaves you on the outskirts of the social world. Add into the mix that on Mrs. Green's salary alone, she and Autumn barely scrape by.

Autumn looks up at me flatly. "I can see why you wouldn't want to do it, Tann. It's a lot of work. And you're lazy."

She baited me into adding the stupid class, and now, as we drive to school together the Monday after winter break, she's being brittle and clipped because I told her I got in.

I can feel her heated glare on the side of my face as I turn onto Bulldog Boulevard. "Fujita just signed your add card?" she says. "That's it?"

"Auddy, you're insane if you're pissed about this. You get that, right?"

"And . . . what?" she says, ignoring my rhetorical and turning to face forward. "You're going to *do* it?"

"Yeah, why not?" I pull into the student lot, scanning for a spot close to the door, but of course we're running late and there's nothing convenient here. I slip into a spot along the back side of the building.

"Tanner, do you realize what *it is*?"

"How could I attend this school and not know what *the Seminar* is?"

She gives me an aggressively patient look because I've just used my mocking voice and she hates it. "You're going to have to write a book. An entire *book*."

When the end of my fuse appears, it is predictably mild: a rougher than normal shove of my door open into the frigid air. "Auddy, what the hell? I thought you told me to add it."

"Yeah, but you shouldn't do it if you don't *want* it."

I pull out my best smile again, the one I know she likes. I know I shouldn't, but hey, you use the tools you have. "Then you shouldn't call me lazy."

She lets out this savage growl I think *I* like. "You're so lucky and you don't even know it."

I ignore her, grabbing my backpack from the trunk. She is confusing as hell.

"Do you see what I mean, though, that it was so easy for you?" She jogs after me. "I had to apply, and interview with him, and, like, *grovel*. You walked into his office and he signed your add slip."

"It wasn't exactly like that. I went to his office, chatted him up for a bit, updated him on my folks, and *then* he signed my add slip."

I'm met with silence, and when I turn, I realize she's walked in the other direction, toward a side entrance. "I'll see you at lunch, best friend!" I call out. She raises her middle finger.

The warmth inside the hall is heaven, but it's loud in here and the floors are soggy with dirty, melting snow knocked off boots. I squeak down the hall to my locker, sandwiched between Sasha Sanderson and Jack Thorne, two of the best-looking—and nicest—people at Provo High.

Socially, things here are mixed. Even two and a half years later, I still feel like the new kid, and it's probably because most of the students here have gone to school together since kindergarten and live within a handful of wards—meaning, they're in the same congregation and see each other for about a million church activities outside of school. I essentially have Auddy,

Eric, and a few other friends who happen to be LDS, but cool, so they don't drive us too crazy and their parents don't worry we're corrupting them. Back in Palo Alto, my freshman year, I was sort of dating another guy for a few months and had a whole group of friends I'd known since kindergarten who didn't blink when they saw me holding Gabe's hand. I wish I'd appreciated that freedom more at the time.

Here, girls flirt with me, sure, but most of them are Mormon and would never, not in a million years, be allowed to date me. Most LDS parents hope their children will marry in their Temple, and that just can't happen with someone like me, a nonmember. Unless I converted, which . . . is *never* going to happen. Take Sasha for example. I feel something brewing between us; she's super flirty and touchy, but Autumn insists it could never go anywhere. To an even greater extent, the same is true of my chances here with guys, LDS or otherwise; I don't get to test those waters in Provo. I've had a crush on Jack Thorne since tenth grade, but he's off-limits for three important reasons: (1) male, (2) Mormon, (3) Provo.

Before she got pissed at me this morning, Auddy handed me, without comment, a sheet of sparkly dinosaur stickers. So, without question, I pocketed them; Autumn is known to hand me things that will be of use at some unknown point in time, and I roll with it. As I open my locker, I realize her motive: I am notoriously bad about remembering my A and B day schedule—we practice an alternating-day class schedule here, with periods one through four on some days and periods five through eight on others. Each term I need to tape my schedule to my locker, and each term I find myself without any tape.

"You're brilliant," Sasha says, coming up behind me to better see what I'm doing. "And *ohmygod*, you're so cute. Dinosaurs! Tanner, are you eight?"

"I got them from Autumn."

I hear Sasha's reaction to this in her silence, the unspoken, *Are they, or aren't they?* Everyone wonders whether Autumn and I are casually banging.

As ever, I leave it unanswered. Her suspicion is a good thing. Unwittingly, Autumn has been my shield.

"Nice boots," I tell her. They reach a suggestive height: just past her knees. I wonder whose attention she's aiming for the most here: the guys at school, or her parents at home. I give her a dinosaur sticker and a kiss on the cheek as I slip past her down the hall with my books.

Provo High is not by any means a religious school, but sometimes it feels that way. And if there's one thing you learn quickly about Mormons, it's that they focus on the positive: positive feelings, positive actions, happy, happy, joy, joy. So Modern Lit with Mrs. Polo starts out with an unexpected and decidedly *un*happy bang: The first book we're reading is *The Bell Jar*.

I feel a faint murmur around the room as students shift in

their seats to make surreptitious eye contact in such dramatic unison that their covert efforts are wasted. Mrs. Polo—wild hair, flowy skirts, rings on thumbs, you know the deal—ignores the commotion. In fact, I think she's sort of enjoying it. She rocks back on her heels, waiting for us to return to the syllabus and see what else she has in store for us.

Barbara Kingsolver's *The Poisonwood Bible*, Elie Wiesel's *Night*, Milan Kundera's *The Unbearable Lightness of Being*, Jeannette Walls's *The Glass Castle*, and on and on into Toni Morrison's *Sula,* and even James Goddamn Frey's fake memoir. Perhaps most shocking is Sinclair Lewis's *Elmer Gantry*, a novel dealing with fanatical religion and a tent-revival-style creepy preacher. It's pretty on the nose. Mrs. Polo is ballsy, and I for one like seeing their cages rattled.

At my side, and still giving me the silent treatment, Autumn is sitting up, eyes wide. She's read almost every book on this list, and if I know her, I know what she's thinking: *Is there time to transfer to Shakespeare with Mr. Geiser?*

She turns and looks at me, her eyes narrowing as she reads my mind right back. She growls again, and I can't help the laugh it pulls from me.

I've read almost all these books too. Autumn insisted.

I lean back, lacing my fingers behind my head and giving her another good smile.

Piece of cake. I have an easy semester ahead.

CHAPTER TWO

B y the time fourth period rolls around, Autumn is buzzing with nerves. She's excited for the Seminar, but still irritated that I wormed my way into it. I trail just behind her down the hall and try not to let her see me smile when she purposefully evades me inside the door, moving toward a group of desks where only one seat remains free.

"Over here, Auddy." Standing in the back row, I hold out an empty chair for her beside one I plan to claim.

She has the option to come join me, or look mysteriously petulant, so she shuffles over, glowering. "You're a pest."

"I love you, but only a little."

She laughs. "Don't ruin this for me."

And there, right there, it is. I could ruin this by being a total jackass about something she's put her whole heart into. She thinks I'd *want* to?

The way I'm acting, she probably does.

"I won't." I slide my good-luck eraser onto her desk, the one she gave me for Christmas two years ago, with the old-school He-Man illustration printed into the rubber. What used to be a white square is now a gray nub. Present-day Eraser He-Man barely has a face, and only one leg.

Her freckled nose wrinkles as she scowls at me without much commitment. I am forgiven.

Mr. Fujita walks in, arms filled with a teetering stack of books. He slides them gracelessly onto his desk in the center of the semicircle of worktables and ignores them when they slide onto a messy pile. A copy of Stephen King's *The Stand* slaps harshly to the floor, landing facedown and open. He ignores it; in my peripheral vision I can see Autumn sit up straighter, and I know she is now *intensely* worried about the pages of the enormous book growing crumpled under its own weight the longer it sits there.

"Morning!" Mr. Fujita sings, and then looks up behind us at the clock on the wall. "Oops! Afternoon! I'm Tim Fujita. Everyone just calls me Fujita."

I've always really liked Fujita, but the way he hands out his own nickname makes me like him about 7 percent less.

We murmur greetings in return, quiet from intimidation or because we're tired after lunch, and he grins at us, taking in our faces one by one. I glance around too at the class composition: Josh, Dustin, Amanda. Julie, Clive, Burrito Dave. Sabine, Soccer Dave, Asher. Kylie, McKenna, James, Levi.

Every single one of them is Mormon. Trimmed hair, modest sleeves, good posture. In the back row, Autumn and I are a pair of gangly trees looming over a lush, manicured lawn.

Fujita winks when he sees me. He thinks my mom is a superhero. Beside me, Autumn lets out a measured exhale through her nose; because of my mom (a computer genius) and my dad (a highly profiled cardiac surgeon who, according to the papers, saved the governor of Utah), I've received special treatment from teachers since the day I moved here. Fujita adding me to the Seminar is clearly one such perk.

"Welcome, guys." He spreads his hands out and then takes another sweeping glance around the room. "Where is he?"

At our puzzled silence, Fujita scans the room again and then looks at us for answers.

"Who?" Dustin, seated—as ever—right up in the front, finally asks.

Fujita glances at his watch as if to confirm that he's in the right place. "I had hoped this would be a cool surprise, and I assume it will be anyway, but I guess he's running late."

We reply with anticipatory silence as his eyebrows slowly lift skyward. "We'll have a special aide this term," he tells us. I can imagine the drumroll he's intending, but his dramatic pauses give the moment a bewildering, anticlimactic feel instead. "You'll be thrilled to hear that Sebastian Brother will be mentoring each of you!"

A chorus of excited noises pours out of the fourteen other bodies in the room—a Mormon hero, coming to spend time with *us*. Even Autumn has clapped her hand over her mouth. To her—LDS or not—Sebastian is a local celebrity.

With his hands laced together in front of him, Fujita rocks back on his heels. "Seb has a very busy schedule, of course"—I mentally groan. *Seb*—"but he and I both feel that his experience can benefit each of you. *I* believe he will inspire you. After taking this very course, he is only nineteen and on his way toward a prestigious literary career." Leaning in, Fujita adds confidentially, "Of course, I've read his novel. It is stunning. Stunning!"

"Has he heard of Christopher Paolini?" I whisper to Autumn.

She delivers a *shut up* by way of an icy glare.

Fujita grabs a stack of papers from a torn folder and begins handing them out. "I assume we can skip the Why-Are-You-Here. You're here to write a book, right?" Nearly everyone nods enthusiastically. "And you will. Four months isn't very long, it's true, but you will get it done. You will figure it out. That's why *I'm* here.

"We're going to hit the ground running." He makes his way around the room. "I have a suggested reading list, and I have a variety of resources on how to get started and what types of writing processes are out there, but in truth, the only way to write a book is to write it. However you get it done— that is your process."

I look down at the syllabus and proposed drafting schedule he's slipped on my desk and feel my forehead heat, feel that prickle-pin crawl of panic up my neck.

I have this week to come up with an idea.

One week.

When I feel Autumn's attention on me, I turn, giving her an easy smile. But apparently, it isn't as easy as I hope; her own grin falters, cracking at one side.

"You can do this," she says quietly, seeing straight through me.

Ask me to differentiate trigonometric functions and I'll nail it. Give me a molecular modeling kit and I'll build you the most beautiful organic compound you've ever seen. But ask me to pull something straight from my gut and share it with the world? Mental mayhem. I don't particularly relish working, but at odds with this is my other hatred of doing a shitty job at anything. I've never tried to be creative before and realize it only now that I'm sitting here.

To make it worse, Fujita adds, "Now, experience tells me that most of you already have an idea in mind. But over the next week, Sebastian and I will help you hone it. Polish it. And then: You dive right in!"

I can't even enjoy that he's repeated Autumn's inspirational pussy-poster slogan verbatim, because for the first time in . . . well, maybe ever, I feel like I'm in over my head.

Autumn slides my He-Man eraser back onto my desk and uses it as an excuse to squeeze my hand.

The side door opens, and chairs scrape mildly across hardwood as people turn. We all know who it is, but we look anyway.

· · ·

The one and only time I've ever seen Autumn drunk was this past summer, which is also the one and only time she admitted she was in love with me. I thought we'd been on the same page after our make-out session two years ago, but apparently not. Sometime after drinking four Mike's Hard Lemonades but before shaking me awake on her floor and begging me with boozy breath to forget everything she said, she babbled for an hour about the secret feelings she'd been harboring the past couple years. From the haze of my own inebriation and the tangle of her alcohol-fueled incoherence, I remember only three clear sentences:

Your face makes sense to me.

Sometimes I get the weird feeling that I wouldn't be enough for you.

I love you, but only a little.

Being who we are, the only way to move past the potential for profound awkwardness afterward was to joke about it for a solid week.

I love you, but only a little became our new best-friends motto. Autumn tried to explain the logic of my face making sense to her a few times to no real success—something about symmetry of features and how they're pleasing to her on an instinctive level—but it's still one of my favorite non sequiturs when I see her getting stressed about anything. I just say, "Auddy, calm down; your face makes sense to me," and she breaks. Every time, she laughs.

The second sentence—*Sometimes I get the weird feeling I wouldn't be enough for you*—hit too close to home. Although I'd been working up the nerve to come out to her, after she said this, I changed my mind. Auddy's words twanged that dissonant chord inside me, the inner conflict about what it means to be bisexual. There's the devil on one shoulder, the ignorant perception that I get from all sides, both inside and outside the queer community, who say bisexuality is really about *indecision*, that it's impossible for bisexuals to be satisfied with one person and the label is a way to not commit. And then there's the angel on the other shoulder—who the queer-positive books and pamphlets encourage me to believe—saying that no, what it means is I'm open to falling in love with anyone. I'm happy to commit, but the specific parts don't matter as much as the person.

But as I've never fallen in love and never felt that clawing ache for any one person, I never know which of them will end up being right. When Autumn said that about not being enough for me, I let it go and pretended I didn't remember. The problem is, I *do* remember. In fact, I obsess about it, while pretending I'm not painfully waiting for the moment when someone knocks me over, makes me feel sure about them in a way I've never been sure about anything in my whole life.

So when Sebastian Brother walks into our class and he sees me and I see him, I have the sense of falling sideways out of my chair.

I am drunk.

And I know now what Autumn meant about faces.

I've seen him before, in the halls around school, but I never paid much attention: He's one of the perfect, über-LDS kids—the son of a bishop and, as far as I can tell, incredibly devout.

But here I can't seem to drag my attention away. Sebastian isn't a kid anymore. I notice his defined jaw and downturned almond eyes, ruddy cheeks and anxiously shifting Adam's apple as he swallows under the weight of our stares.

"Hey, guys." He gives a small wave, walking haltingly, deeper into the room to shake Fujita's hand. A classroom's worth of eyes track him like crosshairs.

Fujita beams at us. "What'd I tell you?"

Sebastian's hair is shaved on the side, floppy up top. His smile is so wide and bright and pure: He is fucking beautiful. But there's something beyond it, something in the way he moves, that catches my fascination. Maybe it's the way his eyes don't settle on any one person too long. Maybe it's the way I sense he is slightly wary of us.

As he faces the class from the front now, his eyes flash when they meet mine—for a tiny flicker of a second, and then again, like a prism catching light, because he does a double take. That fraction of a heartbeat is long enough for him to register my immediate infatuation. Holy shit, how quickly he recognizes it. This must happen to him all the time—an adoring gaze from across the room—but to me, being so instantly

21

infatuated is entirely foreign. Inside my chest, my lungs are wild animals, clawing at the cage.

"Oh, man," Autumn mumbles from beside me. "His smile makes me stupid."

Her words are a dim echo of my own thoughts: His smile *ruins* me. The feeling makes me uneasy, a dramatic lurch that tells me I need to have him or I won't be okay.

Beside me she sighs in disappointment, oblivious to my own internal meltdown. "Too bad he's Mormon."

CHAPTER THREE

Monday afternoon: We are homework-free, Mom is home early, and she sees it as a sign that she needs to take her children shopping. My sister, Hailey, is thrilled at the opportunity to get more funeral wear. I agree to come, albeit unenthusiastically, mostly because I know if I were left to my own devices, I would spend hours on my laptop, with multiple browser tabs open, trying to learn more about Sebastian Brother.

Fortunately, Autumn is tagging along. Mom's superpower seems to be her uncanny ability to find the ugliest clothing for her children. In this way, Autumn is a great wingwoman. But unfortunately, having all three of them around means any mobile Sebastian investigation needs to be done covertly. Autumn might raise an eyebrow if she caught me googling pictures of our hot male TA. Mom and Hailey know I like guys, but Mom in particular would not be thrilled to know that the object of my current interest is the local bishop's son.

Organized religion isn't something that's regarded too fondly in our house. My dad is Jewish but hasn't been to temple in years. Mom grew up LDS, just north of here in Salt Lake City, but defected from the church at nineteen, when her younger sister, my aunt Emily, came out in high school and her parents *and* the church cut her off. Of course, I wasn't around then, but I've heard some of the stories and see Mom's forehead vein make an appearance whenever any aspect of the church's narrow-mindedness comes up. Mom didn't want to break up with her parents but, like any normal, compassionate human, couldn't justify alienating someone she loved because of a bunch of old rules in a book.

So then, you might ask, why are we here, living in the most LDS-dense place in the world? Also, ironically, my mother. Two and a half years ago, a massive, super-loaded software startup based here lured her away from Google, where she'd been the only senior software engineer with an XX genotype, and she basically cleaned the floor with everyone around her. NextTech offered her the CEO position, but she asked for the CTO job instead, which came with an almost unlimited tech-development budget. Right now her team is developing some 3-D holographic modeling software for NASA.

For any other family with two six-figure incomes still barely cutting it in the South Bay, the decision would have been an easy one. A salary hike in a place where the cost of living could fit in our smallest Palo Alto closet? Done. But because of Mom's past, the decision to move was agonizing. I still remember hearing my parents arguing about it late into the night while Hailey and I were supposed to be sleeping. Dad thought it was an opportunity she couldn't possibly turn down, and one that would feed her imagination. Mom agreed—but worried about how it would affect her children.

In particular, she worried about how it would affect *me*. Two months before the offer came in, I admitted to my parents that I'm bisexual. Well, "admitted" might be taking too much credit. For her graduate school project, Mom created undetectable software that helps employers keep track of what their employees are doing. Turns out it's so user-friendly and has such a pretty interface that a consumer version was created and sold to nearly every household with a working computer in the States. I probably should have put two and two together and realized my parents would also be using it on our home network before I discovered I could stream porn on my phone.

That was an awkward conversation, but at least it resulted in a compromise: I could go to certain sites, and they wouldn't stalk me online as long as I didn't lurk on places that, as Mom put it, "would give me unrealistic expectations about how sex should be or what our bodies should look like."

In the end, my stridently anti-LDS parents moved their emo-scene daughter and queer son back into LDS wonderland. To compensate for their guilt over making sure I protect myself at all costs (read: be very, very careful about who I come out to), my parents have made our home a gay, gay den of pride. Autumn and I spend most of our time together at her house, and Hailey hates almost everyone (and no one from her angry coven ever comes over), so LGBTQ essays, PFLAG pamphlets, and rainbow T-shirts are handed to me at spontaneous moments with a kiss and a lingering look of pride. Mom will slide the occasional bumper sticker into my pillowcase, to be found when the sharp corner meets my cheek at night.

NOTHING WOULD BE THE SAME IF YOU DID NOT EXIST!

COURAGE IS BEING YOURSELF EVERY DAY IN A WORLD THAT TELLS YOU TO BE SOMEONE ELSE.

LOVE KNOWS NO LIMITS.

NORMAL IS JUST A DIAL ON THE WASHING MACHINE!

Autumn has found a few of them here and there over the years but shrugs it off with a murmur of "San Francisco, man."

It's funny to think about these now in the car, surreptitiously scrolling slack-jawed through photos of Sebastian, because I start imagining them read to me in his deep, gentle voice. Even hearing Sebastian speak a mere three times today, the sound of it still hovers like a drunk honeybee inside my head.

Hey, guys.

Oh, the book is out in June.

I'm here to help, however you need me, so use me.

I almost lost it when he said that.

A Web search doesn't tell me anything I didn't already know. Most of the results for "Sebastian Brother" are for a steakhouse in Omaha, links to articles about the Seminar, or announcements about Sebastian's book.

Google Images is where I hit the jackpot. There are photos of him playing baseball and soccer (yes, I save one), and a few of him doing interviews for local papers. When I click through, his answers don't say much about him—they seem pretty canned—but he's wearing a tie in a lot of the photos, and combined with his hair? I'm ready to start the Sebastian Brother Spank Bank folder.

Really, he's the hottest guy I've ever seen in person.

Facebook is a dead end. Sebastian's account is locked (of course it is), so not only can I not see his photos, but I can't see his relationship status, either. Not that I care, or will beyond a few days. He's Mormon eye candy. This flash of infatuation won't go anywhere interesting. I wouldn't let it—we're on opposite sides of a very thick fence.

I close every window on my phone's browser before I fall prey to the worst social media stalking possible: the futile hunt for his Snapchat or Instagram. Even the idea of stumbling upon a sleepy shirtless Sebastian selfie wreaks havoc on my nervous system.

At the mall, Autumn and I follow my mom as she weaves through the racks of the guys' department at Nordstrom. I'm bored putty in their hands. Mom leads me to table of shirts, holding a few up to my chest. She narrows her eyes, asks Autumn's opinion, and the two women confer before wordlessly rejecting most of them. I don't comment; I know how this works.

My sister is off somewhere getting her own things, giving us a nice reprieve from her constant need to bicker with us. Autumn and Mom get along, and when they're together, I get a break from having to pay attention to anything anyone is saying; they keep each other entertained.

Mom holds a hideous Western-themed shirt up to my chest.

I can't let this one slide. "No."

She ignores me and looks to Autumn for her opinion. But Auddy is Team Tanner, and scrunches her nose in distaste.

Hanging the shirt back up, Mom asks her, "How is your schedule this term?"

"I love it." Auddy hands Mom a short-sleeved blue button-down from RVCA. I give her a covert thumbs-up. "I may need to switch Modern Lit to Shakespeare, and calculus is probably going to be my death, but otherwise—good."

"I'm sure Tanner would love to help you with calc," Mom says, and I feel Autumn throw an eye roll in my direction. "What about you, honey?"

I lean against the rack, crossing my arms over the silver bar. "I added biology after lunch, and now I'm sleepy last period."

Mom's blond hair is smooth and pulled into a ponytail,

and she's traded her work clothes for jeans and a sweater. She looks younger dressed like this, and if Hailey would drop her Wednesday Addams thing, she and Mom would look like sisters.

As if on cue, Hailey materializes from behind me, dropping a giant heap of black fabric in Mom's arms. "I didn't like any of the pants, but those shirts are cool," she says. "Can we eat? I'm starving."

Mom looks down at the load in her arms. I can see her mentally counting to ten. As long as I can remember, our parents have encouraged us to be ourselves. When I started questioning my sexuality, they told me their love for me was not dependent on where I stick my dick.

Okay, they didn't use those exact words; I just like saying it.

Last year, when my sister decided she wanted to start looking like a corpse, they bit their tongues and encouraged her to express herself however she wanted. Our parents are saints when it comes to patience, but I'm getting the sense that this patience is wearing thin.

"Three shirts." Mom hands it all back to Hailey. "I told you three shirts, two pairs of pants. You already have a dozen black shirts. You don't need a dozen more." She turns back to me, thwarting Hailey's rebuttal. "So, biology makes you sleepy. What else?"

"Auddy should stick with Modern Lit. It's going to be an easy A."

"Oh. Our Seminar TA is super-hot," Autumn tells her.

As if moving on some protective instinct, Mom's eyes slide to me and then back to Auddy. "Who is he?"

Autumn lets out a distractingly breathy sound. "Sebastian Brother."

Behind us, my sister groans, and we turn, waiting for the inevitable. "His sister Lizzy is in my class. She's always so *happy*."

I scoff at this. "Gross, right?"

"Tanner," Mom warns.

My sister shoves my shoulder. "Shut up, Tanner."

"*Hailey.*"

Autumn works to diffuse this by redirecting us to the point at hand: "Sebastian took the class last year. Apparently his book was really good."

Mom hands me a paisley T-shirt that is so hideous I won't acknowledge it. She thrusts it at my chest again, giving me mom face. "Oh, he sold it, right?" she asks Autumn.

Autumn nods. "I hope it gets made into a movie and he's in it. He has this floppy soft hair and his smile . . . *God*."

"He's a splotchy boy blusher," I say before I can think better of it.

Beside me, Mom stiffens. But Auddy doesn't seem to hear anything odd in what I said. "He totally is."

Mom hangs the shirt back up and laughs tightly. "This one might be a problem."

She's looking at Autumn when she says this, but I know without question she's speaking to me.

My interest in Sebastian Brother's visible attributes hasn't diminished by class on Friday. For the first time since I moved here, I'm struggling to fly under the radar. If it were a female TA I was attracted to, it wouldn't be a big deal for someone to occasionally catch me staring. But here, with him, I can't. And the effort it takes to play it cool is frankly exhausting. Fujita and Sebastian make regular rounds of the room while we jot down ideas in any manner that works for us—outlines, random sentences, song lyrics, drawings—and I'm basically doodling spirals on a blank sheet of paper just to keep from tracking his movement. Beside me, Autumn pounds out what seems like thousands of words per minute on her laptop without coming up for air, and it's distracting and maddening. Irrationally, I feel like she's sucking my creative energy somehow. But when I stand to move to another part of the room for some space, I nearly collide with Sebastian.

Chest-to-chest, we stare at each other for a few seconds before we take a step back, in unison.

"Sorry," I say.

"No, no, it was me." His voice is both low and quiet, and it has this hypnotic rhythm to it. I wonder whether someday he'll give sermons with that voice, whether he'll throw down judgment with that voice.

"Fujita said I should work with you more closely," he says, and I realize now that he was coming over to talk to me. The blush pops in a warm bloom across his cheeks. "He said you seemed to, um, be a little behind on the plotting stage and I should brainstorm with you."

Defensiveness and nervous energy creates a strange brew in my veins. We're only three class sessions in and I'm already behind? And to hear it from *him*? This buttoned-up Bible-thumper I can't get out of my head? I laugh, too loudly. "It's okay. Seriously, I'll catch up this weekend. I don't want you to have to take time—"

"I don't mind, Tanner." He swallows, and I notice for the first time how long his throat is, how smooth.

My heart hammers. I don't want to be this affected by him.

"I need to sort it out in my own head," I say, and then push past him, mortified.

I'd expected Sebastian to be a short fascination, a single night of fantasizing and that's it. But even watching him move through the classroom rocks me. Standing so close to him nearly sent me into a breathless panic. He has command of the space he occupies, but it isn't because he's an imposing jock, or somehow bleeding macho into the room. The light just seems to catch his features differently than anyone else around us.

Autumn follows me over a few minutes later, putting her hand on my arm. "You okay?"

Absolutely not. "Totally."

"You don't have to worry about how far ahead everyone else is."

I laugh, brought back to the other stress: the novel. "Wow, thanks, Auddy."

She groans, dropping her head to my arm, laughing now too. "I didn't mean it like that."

When I glance to the side, I see Sebastian just before he looks away from us. Auddy stretches, kissing my cheek. "Still up for Manny's birthday party tonight?"

Laser tag to celebrate turning eighteen. Only in Utah, man. "I don't know." I like Manny, but in all honesty, I'm merely human. I can stomach only so many nights of laser tag.

"Come on, Tann. Eric will be there. I need someone to hang with so I have something to do besides look awkward in front of him."

High school is such an incestuous little pool. Autumn has a thing for Eric, who is pining over Rachel, the sister of the girl I kissed after homecoming last year and who I'm pretty sure dated Hailey's best friend's brother. Pick almost anyone here and it's like six degrees of second base.

But it's not like there's anything better to do.

The sound of music and electronic chimes seeps through the double glass doors outside Fat Cats. The parking lot is packed. If this were any other town I might be more surprised, but it's Friday night; miniature golf, laser tag, and glow-in-the-dark bowling are about as wild as it gets.

Autumn is at my side, and the light from her phone illuminates her profile as she does her best to type and walk across the icy sidewalk at the same time.

Looping my arm through hers, I guide her around a group of junior high kids with their eyes glued to their own phones and lead us both safely inside.

The year after we moved here, the Scott family drove in Dad's Prius to Vegas for my aunt Emily's wedding to her girlfriend, Shivani. Hailey and I were saucer-eyed the entire weekend: digital billboards, strip clubs, booze, and bare skin . . . There was a spectacle everywhere we looked.

Here, apart from the obvious differences, like sheer size and the distinct lack of scantily clad cocktail waitresses walking around, there's the same kind of frenzy in the air. Fat Cats is like Vegas for kids and teetotalers. Spiral-eyed patrons slide token after token into blinking machines in the hope of winning something, *anything*.

I spot a bunch of people I know from school. Jack Thorne is playing what I'm sure is a rousing game of Skee-Ball with a string of tickets slithering along the floor at his feet. Soccer Dave is playing pinball with Clive and has a soccer ball predictably clamped between his feet. The birthday boy himself, our friend Manny Lavea, is goofing off with a few of his brothers near a row of tables in the back, but much to Autumn's chagrin: no Eric in sight.

I search the silhouettes in front of the giant movie screens suspended above the bowling lanes—sorry, Thunder Alley—before giving up.

"Are you texting him?" I ask Autumn, looking down to find her still staring intently at her phone.

"No."

"Then what has you glued to your phone tonight? You've barely come up for air."

"I was just typing up a few notes," she says, taking my hand and leading me past the ticket redemption center and toward the tables. "For the book. You know, random thoughts that pop into my head or pieces of dialogue. It's a good way to get stuff down. Fujita is going to expect something on Monday."

Stress tightens my gut, and I change the subject. "Come on, Auddy. Let me win you something."

I win her a gigantic tiger, which I'm guiltily aware will soon become landfill, and we wander back over toward the party room as they're bringing out the food. A haggard woman named Liz tries to bring the party to some sort of order before giving up and dropping a tray of veggies and dip on the center table. Truthfully, we've been here so many times, Liz could go out back and smoke a pack of cigarettes and we'd be fine getting through the night.

Eric finds us as Manny's mom is handing out paper plates, and our entire group—about twenty of us in total—moves in a line on either side of the long tables. There's the normal fare of bad pizza and Sprite, but I help myself to some of the dishes his mom has prepared too. Manny's family is Tongan, and when I first moved here in tenth grade from the diverse wonderland of the South Bay, it was such a relief to find a brown person in the smiling sea of white faces. Because of missionary efforts in Hawaii and other Pacific Islands, there's a surprisingly large number of Polynesians in Utah. Manny and his family are no exception, but they're among the LDS families who don't keep only to themselves. Manny is big, and hilarious, and nearly always smiling. I'd probably be into him if it weren't such an obvious waste of time: He is roaringly heterosexual. I would pull out every penny I have and bet that Manny isn't going to be virginal when he marries.

I step up next to Autumn, opening my mouth to tease her about how she's got only a single breadstick on her plate, but the words fall out of my brain. Sebastian Brother is standing across the room, talking to two of Manny's brothers. My pulse takes off in a surging gallop.

I didn't know he was going to be here.

Auddy pulls us over to a bench to sit down, and sips a cup of water, distracted. Now that I look closer, I see she's put more effort into how she looks tonight: She straightened her hair. She's wearing sticky, shiny lip gloss. I'm pretty sure her shirt is new.

"Why aren't you eating?" I ask, unrolling the paper napkin from the plastic utensils.

In an effort to prove she's not looking at Eric, she takes a Snap of her food, examines her handiwork, and then types something before turning her phone to face me. It's a photo of her breadstick on a plain white paper plate with the caption "dinner" written beneath it.

Honestly.

"The pizza looked greasy and the other stuff was weird," she says, motioning to my own plate. "That salad thing has raw fish."

I look up again and subtly glance over her shoulder to see that Sebastian has moved to the table next to us. There's a backpack on the bench next to him. I'm instantly obsessed with the idea of where he's been. School? The library? Does he live on the BYU campus? Or at home with his parents?

I turn back to my food. "It's the same ceviche you had at that place in Park City. You liked it."

"I don't remember liking it." Autumn reaches her fork across the table to steal a bite anyway. "By the way, did you see who's here?"

As if I could miss him.

Eric and Autumn throw out some small talk, and although I'm not really listening, I'm paying enough attention to notice the flashes of awkward every few seconds. Anyone would notice. Autumn's laugh is too loud. The silences stretch and then are broken with a burst of them speaking at the same time. Maybe Eric is into her too, and that explains why they're both acting like a couple of junior high kids. Is it bad that I'm relieved she's into him, even if it could crash and burn, affecting all of us? My friendship with Auddy matters the most to me, and I don't want there to be any residual romantic crumbs between us. If things can go back to normal for good, maybe I can eventually tell her everything.

Maybe I'll have someone to talk to about this Sebastian dilemma.

And with that, the cat ears of my thoughts have turned back around, focusing behind me. It's like Sebastian's mere presence hums. I want to know where he is every second. I want him to notice me.

This plan is prematurely thwarted when Manny drags a bunch of us to the laser tag arena. I go begrudgingly, following them into the briefing room where we await our instructions.

Autumn has opted to watch from the observation area in the next room, so I stand with Eric, wondering if there's a way for me to slip out unnoticed before the game starts. But when I move toward the doorway, I see Sebastian and Manny's brother Kole step into the arena. I nearly choke on my gum.

I'm not even pretending to listen when the instructor comes in. I'm unable to drag my eyes away from Sebastian and the way his jaw and his face and his hair look in this light. He must be having a hard time paying attention as well, because his gaze flickers away to scan the room and he sees me.

For one,

two,

three seconds,

he stares back.

Recognition flashes across his face, and when he smiles, my stomach lurches like the floor has dropped out from under my feet.

Help me.

I smile back, a wobbly mess.

"My name is Tony, and I'm your game master," the instructor says. I blink away, forcing myself to turn toward the front. "Have we chosen the two team captains?" When nobody volunteers, he points to where Sebastian and Kole are standing on the periphery and gestures for us to follow him to the vesting room.

Somehow in the shuffle, Eric winds up at the end of the line, and I'm right next to Sebastian. May God bless Eric. On each side of the room, there are rows of vests outfitted with power packs. Tony instructs us to slip one on and secure it in the front, miming the action like a flight attendant readying us for takeoff.

"Remove a phaser from the charging station and pull the trigger," he says. "You'll see a code name appear on the LED screen. Everyone see theirs?"

I do as he says, and the name "The Patriot" flashes across the small screen. A covert check of Sebastian's shows the name "Sergeant Blue."

"Remember that name. It's how your score will be posted on the boards outside, after the game. To score points and win, you have to take out your opponents on the other team. You can do this in one of six places." Tony reaches for Manny's sleeve and pulls him to his side. "Here's where you should aim," he says, dramatically pointing a finger to each of the illuminated packs attached to the vest.

"If you're hit in the shoulder or back, your vest will flash, and the hit will be counted. Get hit in the chest and your vest will flash, but your phaser will also lock. You can still be hit, but you won't be able to fire back. You'll be a sitting duck until you get to your base or find a place to hide until your gun powers up again."

He lets go of Manny and looks around the room. "There will be two teams playing in the arena, and each team's vest will be lit with that team's specific color." Pointing to Kole's vest, he says, "Team red." And then he points to Sebastian's: "Team blue. Shoot at any color that isn't your own. Each team's base corresponds to your color, and you get triple points for hitting and destroying your opponents'."

Beside me, Sebastian shifts, and I see him look briefly my way, his eyes dropping down to my feet and back up. Goose bumps erupt across my skin.

"Now, before we begin the battle," Tony says, "a few rules. No running; you will run into someone or something. No lying down on the ground. You will be stepped on. No physical contact of any kind, and that includes making out in the dark. We can see you."

I cough, and Sebastian shifts at my side.

Tony finishes up, warning us against beating each other with our weapons or—God forbid—profanity, and it's time to start.

It was dim in the vesting room, but it still takes a moment for my eyes to adjust to the darkness of the arena. Our teams spread out among walls that look like neon brick, and I spot our base in the center. Black lights illuminate the glowing set pieces, but it's hard to make out much else. The sound of phasers powering up one by one moves like a wave across the arena, and a countdown begins overhead.

Five . . .

Four . . .

Three . . .

Two . . .

One . . .

Sirens pierce the air. I race around one wall and then another. It's so dark I can barely see, but the partitions and perimeter of the room are marked with textured neon paint or strips of colored light. A green tank seems to glow in the corner, and I see a flash of red, a rush of movement in front of it.

I fire off a shot and the vest pulses red, registering the hit. My own vest flashes when I'm hit rounding a corner. "Target hit," my gun says, but it must have been in the shoulder because when someone dodges in front of a wall, I'm still able to fire, blasting their chest sensor and ensuring their gun is useless.

Two other players come from opposite sides, and I turn and run, racing toward the base. It's hot in here with absolutely no air movement. Sweat rolls down the back of my neck; my pulse is frantic. Music and sound effects throb overhead, and if I closed my eyes, it would be easy enough to pretend we're all in a rave, instead of rushing around a dark room shooting at each other with plastic laser guns. I take out two more players and manage a series of rapid-fire hits on the red team's base when I'm hit again, this time in the back.

Retracing my steps the way I came, I run into Eric.

"There's a couple of them near the tank," he says. "They're just sitting there waiting for people to rush by."

I nod, able to make him out only by the white of his T-shirt and the packs on his vest.

"I'll go around," I yell above the music. "Try to get them from behind."

Eric pats my shoulder, and I race around a partition.

The arena is a two-tiered maze, with ramps you can jump on to avoid fire, or climb up to get a better shot.

"Target hit. Target hit. Target hit," my gun registers, and

my vest lights up. Footsteps race behind me. When I lift my gun to fire back, there's nothing. I've been hit in the chest. I look around, searching for my team's base or somewhere to hide, when I feel a body crash into mine, whoever it is pulling me into a small corner just as Kole and one of his teammates run by.

"Holy—thank you," I say, wiping my arm across my forehead.

"No problem."

My pulse trips. I'd almost forgotten Sebastian was here. He exhales, out of breath, and a shiver of heat makes its way up my spine.

It's too loud to talk, and we're too close for me to turn and look at him without it being weird, too intimate. So I stand still while my brain goes haywire.

He's holding my vest, and my back is pressed tight to his front. It's less than ten seconds—the time it takes for my gun to unlock—but I swear I feel every tick of the clock. My breath sounds loud in my ears. I can feel my pulse, even above the music. I can feel Sebastian's breath, too, hot against my ear. My fingers itch to reach back and touch the side of his face, to feel whether he's blushing, here in the dark.

I want to stay in this dark corner forever, but I feel the moment my gun powers back up in my hand. He doesn't wait, gripping the side of my vest before pushing me out and shouting at me to follow, toward the red base. Eric rounds the corner, and we sprint across the floor and around the partition. "Go! Go!" Sebastian shouts, and we fire in unison. It takes only a few blasts before the base flashes red and a recorded voice sounds overhead.

"Red base destroyed. Game over."

CHAPTER FOUR

For the first time in my high school career, I don't need my schedule taped to my locker with dino stickers to know where I'm supposed to be. Our first week back, Fujita's Seminar is on Monday, Wednesday, Friday. This week, it's Tuesday and Thursday. It alternates pretty steadily until the end of the year.

I can see three ways this could go:

One, I could love M, W, F weeks because there are three chances to see Sebastian.

Two, I could loathe M, W, F weeks because there are three chances to see Sebastian, but he only attends one class regardless.

Three, I could loathe M, W, F weeks because there are three chances to see Sebastian and he's there all the time but doesn't show me the time of day.

In this last scenario, I grow resentful that I can't seem to shake this crush on an LDS diehard, drown myself in cheese fries and fry sauce, grow a gut, do a crappy job in the class, and lose my admission to the out-of-state school of my dreams.

"What are you thinking?" Autumn appears behind me, tucking her chin over my shoulder.

"Nothing." I slam my locker shut, zipping up my backpack. In reality, I'm thinking that it isn't fair to think of Sebastian as an LDS diehard. I don't know how to explain it, but he seems so much more than that.

She growls in mild irritation, and turns to head down the hall toward the Seminar.

I catch up and dodge a group of juniors having a piggyback race down the hall. I've been trained well by her, and bounce the question back. "What are *you* thinking?" If nothing else, her elaborate answer will keep me distracted from my own spiral into madness.

Autumn hooks her arm through mine. "I'm wondering how your outline is coming."

Ah, right, my outline. The skeletal document with proverbial tumbleweeds blowing across the tundra. "It's fine."

One . . . two . . . three . . .

"Want me to take a peek before we go in?"

I grin. "No, Auddy, I'm good."

She stops right at the entrance to class. "Did you finish it?"

"Finish what?"

From the flare of her nostrils, I know my best friend is imagining me dead and bloody on the floor. "The outline."

A mental image pops into my head of the Word doc with two lonely lines I wouldn't dare show a soul: *A half-Jewish, half-nothing queer kid moves to an LDS-infested town. He can't wait to leave.* "No."

"Do you think you *should*?"

I offer her a single arched eyebrow in response.

This is only our fourth class, and despite the hallowed reputation of this room, already we seem to have a rhythm, a certain comfort being hooligans until Fujita shows up. Soccer Dave, with his ever-present soccer ball, starts kicking it with alternating feet while Burrito Dave counts out the number of times he does it without letting it hit the floor. Julie and McKenna are loudly discussing prom, and Asher pretends to not notice (McAsher—their shipper name, obviously—are a former couple, and his artless breakup with her has left the rest of us a wealth of rubbernecking fodder). Autumn hounds me to show her my outline—remember: dog with a bone—and I distract her with a game of Rock, Paper, Scissors because, on the inside, we are both still ten years old.

A hush comes over the room, and I glance up, expecting to find Fujita, but Sebastian walks in, holding a folder. The effect of seeing him is like a needle screeching across one of my dad's old forty-fives in my brain, and I throw Autumn some unknown hand symbol that roughly approximates a bird claw.

She punches my arm. "Rock beats whatever that was."

"What's up, guys," he says, laughing as he puts down his folder.

The only person not paying intense attention to him

is Autumn, who is ready to keep playing. But I'm back in the laser tag arena with Sebastian pressed up against me. He assesses the room with his calm, remote gaze. "You don't have to stop talking when I walk in."

McKenna and Julie make half-hearted attempts to return to their conversation, but it's hard to be subtly scandalous when everyone else is being so silent, and it's also hard in the face of Sebastian's presence. He's so . . . *present*. He's beautiful, of course, but he also has that air of goodness to him, like he's a genuinely good human. It's one of those things you can tell from across the room. He smiles at everyone, has what I'm sure my mother would call great posture, and I'd bet all the money in my savings account that he's never said—or thought—my favorite word that begins with *F*.

A horrifying thought occurs to me, and I turn to Autumn. "Do you think he wears Jesus jammies?"

If she thinks it's weird that I'm asking her whether Sebastian wears garments, the modest undershirt-and-shorts underwear worn by the majority of faithful adult Mormons, she doesn't show it. "You don't get your garments until you take out your endowments."

"Do *what*?" My mother needs to do a better job educating her children.

She sighs. "Until they go through the Temple."

I try to sound casual, like I'm just making conversation. "So he hasn't gone through the Temple yet?"

"I doubt it, but how should I know?" She bends to dig through her backpack.

I nod, although this doesn't really help me. I can't ask Mom, either, because she'll want to know why I'm asking.

Auddy sits up, clutching a newly sharpened pencil. "He'll go through the Temple when he's about to get married or go on a mission."

I tap my pen to my lip, scanning the room as if I'm only half listening to her. "Ah."

"I doubt he's married," she says, more curious now, nodding to where he stands.

He's reading through something at the front of the room, and for a beat I'm left speechless by the reminder that he *could* be married. I think he's nineteen.

"He's not wearing a ring," she continues. "And didn't he postpone his mission for the book launch?"

"Did he?"

She looks at him and then back at me. To him, then to me.

"I'm not following what you're trying to tell me."

"He's *here*," she says. "You leave for your mission—for two years—usually after high school, or around now."

"So he's not wearing garments?"

"Oh my God, Tanner! Do you really care what kind of underwear he's got on? Let's talk about your goddamn outline!"

You know those moments? The ones where a girl yells

49

in the cafeteria, "I got my period!" or a guy yells, "I thought it was a fart but I crapped my pants!" and the entire room has gone silent? That happens. Right now. Sometime between *So he's not wearing garments* and *Oh my God, Tanner*, Fujita entered the room and everyone but Autumn and I went quiet.

Fujita chuckles, shaking his head at us. "Autumn," he says, not unkindly, "I promise no man's underwear is as interesting as you hope."

Everyone laughs, delighted in this third-grade level of scandal. She opens her mouth to contradict him, to explain that it was *me* asking about underwear, but as soon as Fujita agrees that yes, let's discuss our outlines, the opportunity passes. I'm shoved passively to the left when Autumn slugs my right arm, but I'm distracted, wondering what *he's* thinking about that entire exchange. Of their own volition, my eyes flicker to Sebastian just as his eyes dart elsewhere.

His cheeks are that splotchy, irresistible pink.

Fujita has us pull out our outlines, and I swear it seems like everyone unscrolls these long, highly detailed manuscripts. There's a gentle *thump* as Autumn pulls out a bound packet of paper and drops it on the desk in front of her. I don't even bother opening my laptop to the two skeletal sentences of my outline. Instead, I pull out an empty swath of binder paper and tap it against my tabletop, looking industrious.

"Tanner, want to start?" Fujita calls out, his attention attracted by the noise I've made.

"Um." I glance down. Only Autumn can tell that the pages I'm reading are blank. "I'm still working on the overall idea—"

"That's okay!" Fujita crows, nodding: a beacon of enthusiastic support.

"—but I'm thinking that it will be a . . . coming-of-age novel about a kid"—I don't say queer—"who moves to, um, a pretty religious town from a bigger city and—"

"Great! Great. Still forming, I get you. You should sit down with Sebastian, talk through it, yeah?" Fujita is already nodding at me like I've been the one to suggest it. I can't tell if he's saving me or chastising me. He turns, scanning the room. "Anyone else have an outline they'd like to share?"

Everyone's hand shoots up except Autumn's. Which is interesting, given that her outline is probably the most detailed. She's been working on it for nearly a year. But she's also my best friend, and in this case, I have no question that she's saving me; if she went through hers after that incoherent ramble I just gave, I would look even worse.

The class breaks out into smaller groups, and we bounce ideas around, helping each other plot out story arcs. I'm stuck with Julie and McKenna, and since McKenna's book is about a girl who gets dumped and turns into a witch and exacts revenge on her ex, we spend about ten minutes discussing the actual book before devolving into more prom talk and McAsher breakup processing.

It's so boring I push my chair away from them and curl over my paper, hoping inspiration strikes.

I write the same word over and over again:

PROVO.

PROVO.

PROVO.

It's at once a weird place and an *every*place. Being of Hungarian and Swedish descent, I don't have any features that, anywhere else in the country, would particularly scream *other*—but in Provo, being dark haired and dark eyed is enough to make me stand out. Back in the South Bay, most people aren't just white Middle America anymore, and being LDS wasn't a given, not even close. Also? No one back home had to explain what it means to be bisexual. I have known since I was thirteen that I was into boys. But I knew before then that I was probably into girls, too.

My words slowly morph, turning into something else, a face, a thought.

I DON'T EVEN KNOW YOU.
SO WHY DO I FEEL LIKE
I MIGHT LOVE YOU?
(BUT ONLY A LITTLE)

I look over my shoulder, worried that Autumn might catch me using our line when I'm thinking about something else—*someone* else—but my breath is sliced in half when I see him standing behind me, reading over my shoulder.

Pink cheeks, unsure smile.

"How's the outline coming?"

I shrug, sliding my hand over the four stanzas of insanity on the paper. "I feel like everyone is so far ahead." My voice shakes. "I didn't actually expect to need an outline before I started. I sort of assumed we'd be doing that *here*."

Sebastian nods. Leaning down, he speaks quietly. "I didn't have an outline for a few weeks."

Gooseflesh pricks up my arms. He smells so intensely of *guy*—the tang of deodorant and this hard-to-define maleness.

"You didn't?" I ask.

He straightens, shaking his head. "No. I came in without any idea what I was doing."

"But you ended up writing something brilliant, apparently." I gesture to my mostly blank page. "I'm not expecting lightning to strike this class twice in two years."

"You never know," he tells me, and then smiles. "I felt the Spirit with me when I was writing. I felt inspired. You never know what will call to you. Just stay open to it, and it will come."

He turns, moving on to the next group, and I'm left completely confused.

Sebastian knows—he *has* to know—that I am attracted to him. My eyes are helplessly bouncing around his face, his neck, his chest, his jeans whenever he's in the classroom. Did he read what I'd written? Does he realize that just then *he* was inspiring me? If so, then why throw in mention of the Spirit?

Am I being toyed with?

Autumn catches my eye across the room, mouthing, *What?* because I'm sure I look like I'm struggling to perform some complex mathematical process in my mind. I shake my head and pull my hand back, revealing the words on my page again.

Something lights up in me, the weak flicker of an idea, the thread unraveling from that night in Autumn's room to now.

The queer kid. The LDS kid.

"Sebastian," I call after him.

He looks back at me over his shoulder, and it's like our eyes are connected by some invisible tether. After a couple seconds, he turns and makes his way back over to me.

I give him my best smile. "Fujita seems to think I need your help."

His eyes are teasing. "Do *you* think you need my help?"

"I have two sentences written."

He laughs. "So yes."

"Probably yes."

I expect him to suggest we walk over to the far table near the window, or meet in the library during my free period. I do not expect him to say, "I have some time this weekend. I could help then."

It feels like the rest of the room falls away when he says this, and my heart takes off in a frantic sprint.

This is probably a terrible idea. Yes, I'm attracted to him, but I worry that if I dig deeper, I won't *like* him.

But that would be for the best, wouldn't it? It certainly wouldn't hurt to get some time outside of this class, to get an answer to my question: Could we even be *friends*, let alone more?

God, I have to tread lightly.

He swallows, and I watch as it moves his throat.

"Does that work?" he asks, pulling my eyes back up to his face.

"Yeah," I say, and swallow. This time *he* watches. "What time?"

CHAPTER FIVE

My dad is sitting in his standard green scrubs at the breakfast bar when I get up on Saturday, curled around his bowl of oatmeal like it's the keeper of life's great secrets. It's only when I move closer that I realize he's asleep.

"Dad."

He jumps, knocking the bowl across the counter before he scrabbles for it clumsily. He leans back, clutching his chest. "You scared me."

I put an arm around his shoulder, biting back a laugh. He looks so crazily disheveled. "Sorry."

His hand comes over mine, squeezing. With him sitting and me standing, I feel enormous. It's so strange that I am as tall as he is now. Somehow I got none of my mom's features. I am all Dad: dark hair and towering height and eyelashes. Hailey got Mom's stature, coloring, and sass.

"Did you just get home?"

He nods, digging his spoon back into the bowl. "A patient

came in around midnight with a punctured carotid. They called me in to surgery."

"Punctured *carotid*? Did he make it?"

He answers with a tiny shake of his head.

Oof. This explains the stooped posture. "That sucks."

"He had two kids. He was only thirty-nine."

I lean against the counter, eating cereal out of the box. Dad pretends to not care. "How did he—"

"Car accident."

My stomach drops. Only last year my dad told Hailey and me about how three of his best friends from high school died in a car accident right after graduation. My dad was in the car too, and survived. He left New York to attend UCLA and then moved to Stanford for med school, where he met and married my formerly LDS mother—much to the chagrin of his own mother and extended family back home in Hungary. But because of his time away, whenever he goes back to Upstate New York, the loss of his friends feels fresh all over again.

It's one of the only things he and Mom ever fought about in front of us: Mom insisted I needed my own car. Dad thought I could get by without one. Mom won. The problem with Provo is there is absolutely nothing to do, anywhere, and it's not walkable. But the good thing about Provo is it's incredibly safe—no one drinks, and everyone drives like an octogenarian.

He seems to notice only now that I'm dressed and ready for action. "What are you doing up so early?"

"Going to work on a project with a friend."

"Autumn?"

Crap. Why did I say "friend"?

I should have said "person from class."

"Sebastian." At Dad's unsure expression, I add, "He's the mentor in our Seminar."

"The kid who sold the book?"

I laugh. "Yeah, the kid who sold the book."

"He's LDS, isn't he?"

I look around us as if the room is full of Mormons hanging out, not drinking our coffee. "Isn't everyone?"

Dad shrugs, returning to his cold oatmeal. "We aren't."

"What are we?"

"We are liberated Unitarian Jewstians," Mom says, gliding into the room in her yoga pants, her hair in a high, messy bun. She sidles up to Dad, gives him some disgusting, lingering kiss that sends my face deep into the box of cereal, and then makes a beeline for the coffeepot.

She pours her mug, talking to Dad over her shoulder. "Paulie, what time did you get home?"

He studies the clock again, eyes blinking and squinted. "About half an hour ago."

"Torn carotid," I summarize for her. "Didn't make it."

Dad looks up at me with a disapproving frown. "Tanner," he says, voice low.

"What? I was just toplining it for her so you didn't have to go through it again."

Mom returns to him, quieter now, taking his face into her hands. I can't hear what she's saying, but the low murmur of her voice makes me feel better too.

Hailey is a blur of black pajamas, bird's nest dyed black hair, and scowl as she shuffles into the room. "Why are you guys so loud?"

It's funny that she's chosen the quietest moment to enter with this complaint.

"This is the sound of high-functioning humans," I tell her. She punches me in the chest and tries to talk Mom into giving her some coffee. As expected, Mom refuses and offers her orange juice.

"Coffee stunts your growth," I tell my sister.

"Is that why your penis is so—"

"Tanner is headed out to work on an assignment," Dad interrupts pointedly. "With a person named Sebastian."

"Yeah, the guy he likes," Hailey tells him. Mom's head whips over to me.

My insides turn into an immediate tangle of panic. "I do *not*, Hailey."

She gives me a screamingly skeptical look. *"Hokay."*

Dad leans in, more awake now. "Likes as in *likes*?"

"No." I shake my head. "Likes as in he's a nice person who can help me get an A. He's just my TA."

Dad gives me a wide smile, his enthusiastic reminder that, even if I'm not attracted to the guy we're currently discussing, He's Okay With My Sexuality. The only thing missing in this moment is the bumper sticker.

Hailey sets her glass of juice down on the counter with a heavy *thud*. "He's just your TA who Autumn describes as 'super-hot' and you describe as a 'splotchy boy blusher.'"

Mom steps in. "But he's only helping you with your book, right?"

I nod. "Right."

Anyone watching this exchange might think my mother is getting worked up about the fact that he's a boy, but no. It's that he's Mormon.

"Okay," she says, like we've just cemented a deal. "Good."

Fire ignites in my stomach at the concern in her voice, burning a hole through me. I swipe Hailey's glass, downing her OJ, extinguishing the flames. She looks to Mom for justice, but Mom and Dad are sharing a moment of silent parent communication.

"I'm curious whether it's possible for a super-LDS kid and a super non-LDS kid to be friends," I tell them.

"So, you're viewing this as a sort of experiment?" Dad asks warily.

"Yeah. Kinda."

"Okay, but don't *toy* with him," Mom says.

I groan. This is getting tedious. "You guys." I walk across the room to grab my backpack. "It's for school. We're just going over my outline."

WE'RE JUST GOING OVER MY OUTLINE.
WE'RE JUST GOING OVER MY OUTLINE.
WE'RE JUST GOING OVER MY OUTLINE.

I write it about seventeen times in my notebook while I wait for Sebastian to show up where we agreed to meet: in the writer's alcove at the Provo City Library.

When he scribbled down his e-mail address in perfect penmanship, I'm sure he expected me to ask that we meet at the Shake Shack—not Starbucks, by God—and go over my outline. But the idea of sitting in public with him where anyone from school could see felt too exposed. I hate to admit it, but what if someone saw me and thought I was converting? What if someone saw him and wondered what he was doing with the non-LDS kid? What if it was Soccer Dave, and he noticed my eyes following Sebastian in class, and the bishop asked around with some contacts in Palo Alto who told him I was queer, and he told Sebastian, and Sebastian told everyone?

I'm definitely overthinking this.

WE'RE JUST GOING OVER MY OUTLINE.
WE'RE JUST GOING OVER MY OUTLINE.
WE'RE JUST GOING OVER MY OUTLINE.

Footsteps shuffle up the stairs behind where I'm sitting, and I have just enough time to stand up and knock my notebook onto the floor before Sebastian is there, looking like a Patagonia ad in a blue puffy jacket, black chinos, and Merrells.

He smiles. His face is pink from the cold, but it punches me in the chest how much I like to look at him.

This is so, so bad.

"Hey," he says, just slightly out of breath. "Sorry I'm a couple minutes late. My sister got this giant Barbie house for her birthday, and I had to help my dad put it together before I took off. There were, like, a million pieces to that thing."

"Don't worry about it," I say, starting to reach my hand out to shake his, before pulling it back in because *what the hell am I doing?*

Sebastian notices, extending his hand before pulling it back too.

"Ignore that," I say.

He laughs, confused but clearly amused. "It's like your first day with a new arm."

Oh my God, this is terrible. We're just two dudes meeting to study. Bros. Bros don't get nervous. *Be a bro, Tanner.* "Thanks for meeting me."

He nods and bends to pick up my notebook. I grab it before he can read the lines and lines of me calming myself down about what we're doing here, but I can't tell whether I was successful. He passes it off, avoiding my eyes, and instead looks past me into the empty room.

"We're in here?" he asks.

I nod, and he follows me deeper into the room, bending to look out the window. Snow clouds hover over the Wasatch Mountains in a thick fog, like ghosts looming over our quiet city.

"You know what's weird?" he says, without turning to me.

I try to ignore the way the light coming in the window catches the side of his face. "What's that?"

"I've never been up here. I've been to the stacks, but I've never actually walked around the library."

On the tip of my tongue is a barb: *That's because everything you do outside of school takes place at church.* But I swallow the instinct down. He's here helping me.

"How old is your sister?" I ask.

Blinking back to me, he smiles again. He wears his smile so easily, so constantly. "The one with the Barbie house?"

"Yeah."

"Faith is ten." He takes a step toward me, and another, and in an unfamiliar voice my heart is screaming *YES, COME HERE,* but then I realize that he's indicating we should move to the table, start working.

Be a bro, Tanner.

I turn, and we settle at the table I got here early to claim—though we could have any. There is no one else at the library at nine on a Saturday morning.

His chair drags across the wood floor dissonantly, and he laughs, apologizing under his breath. With him so close to me, I get another drag of his smell, and it feels a little like getting high.

"You have other siblings though, right?"

He glances at me out of the corner of his eye, and I'm tempted to explain my question—I wasn't making a snarky assumption about the size of LDS families; Hailey and Lizzy are in class together. "My other sister is fifteen. Lizzy," he says. "And then I have a brother, Aaron, who is thirteen going on twenty-three."

I laugh too politely at this. Inside, I am a yarn ball of nerves, and I don't even know why. "Lizzy goes to Provo High, right?"

He nods. "Sophomore."

I've seen her around school, and Hailey wasn't wrong: Lizzy is an eternal smiler, often found helping the janitorial staff during lunch break. She seems so full of joy she nearly vibrates. "She seems nice."

"She is. Faith is a cutie too. Aaron is . . . well, he likes to push limits. He's a good kid."

I nod, Tanner Scott, awkward meathead to the end of time. Sebastian turns to look at me; I can almost sense his smile. "Do you have brothers or sisters?" he asks.

See? This is how it's done, Tanner. Make conversation.

"One sister," I tell him. "Hailey. She's actually in Lizzy's class, I think. Hailey is sixteen and the devil's spawn." I realize what I've said and turn to him in horror. "Oh my God. I can't believe I said that. Or *that*."

Sebastian groans. "Great. Now I can't speak to you again after today."

I feel my expression contort into scorn, and too late I realize he's only joking. His smile is gone now too. It vanished as soon as he realized how profoundly confused I was, how easily I believed the worst about his faith.

"Sorry," he says, letting his mouth curl up on one side. He doesn't look at all uncomfortable. If anything, he looks a tiny bit amused by this. "I was kidding."

Embarrassment simmers in my blood, and I struggle to bring back my confident smile, the one that always gets me what I want. "Go easy on me. I'm still learning to speak Mormon."

To my profound relief, Sebastian lets out a real laugh. "I'm here to translate."

With that, we lean in to look at my laptop, reading the paltry handful of letters there:

A half-Jewish, half-nothing queer kid moves to an LDS-infested town. He can't wait to leave.

I feel Sebastian go still beside me, and in an instant I realize my mistake: I never changed my outline. My heart plummets.

I don't mind telling him I can't wait to leave. I don't even

65

feel guilty for using the phrase "LDS-infested," even if maybe I should. Something else overshadows all of that.

I forgot to delete the word "queer."

No one—no one but family, at least—knows about me here.

I try to inconspicuously gauge his reaction. His cheeks are pink, and his eyes jump back to the beginning, rereading.

I open my mouth to speak—to explain—just as he says, "So this is your overall theme, right? You're going to write about someone who is homosexual living in Provo?"

The cold thrill of relief dumps into my bloodstream. Of course he doesn't assume I'm writing something auto-biographical.

I nod vigorously. "I was thinking he'd be bisexual. Yeah."

"And he's just moved here . . ."

I nod again, and then realize there's something sticky in his tone, some awareness. If Sebastian did any Tanner Scott reconnaissance at all, he would know I moved here before tenth grade and that my father is a Jewish physician down at Utah Valley.

He might even know my mother was excommunicated.

When he meets my eyes, he smiles. He seems to be very carefully schooling his reaction to this. I can tell he knows. And now my fears about Soccer Dave telling the bishop and the bishop telling Sebastian seem so overly complicated. Of course it just slipped out of *me* unobstructed.

"No one else knows," I blurt.

He shakes his head once. "It's okay, Tanner."

"I mean *no one*." I swipe a hand down my face. "I meant to delete that word. It's one of the reasons I'm stuck. I keep making the main character bi, and I don't know how I'd write that book in this class. I don't know that Fujita would *want* me to, or my parents."

Sebastian leans in, catching my eyes. "Tanner, you should write any book you want to write."

"My family is very adamant that I don't come out to anyone here, not unless I really trust the person."

I haven't even told my best friend, and now I'm spilling my guts in a flash to the single person I probably shouldn't share any of this with.

His brow slowly rises. "Your family knows?"

"Yeah."

"And they're fine with it?"

"My mom is . . . *exuberant* in her acceptance, actually."

After a pulse of silence, he turns back to the computer. "I think it's a great idea to put this down on paper," he says quietly. Reaching forward, he lets his index finger hover in front of the screen. "There's a lot here in only two sentences. A lot of heart, and heartbreak." His eyes meet mine again. They're a crazy mix of green and brown and yellow. "I'm not sure how much help I can be on this particular subject, but I'm happy to talk it out."

I feel these words as they scrape dissonantly across me,

and scrunch my nose. "You'd be as helpful if I were writing about dragons or zombies, right?"

His laugh is quickly becoming my favorite sound. "Good point."

It takes about twenty minutes for my heart rate to return to normal, but in that time, Sebastian talks. It almost feels like he's aware of my panicked mental bender, like he's intentionally talking me down, but his words seem to fall from his mouth in an easy, mesmerizing cadence.

He tells me it's okay that it's still only an idea, that, as far as he knows, every book starts with something like this—a sentence, an image, a bit of dialogue. What I have to decide, he says, is who the protagonist is, what the conflict is.

"Focus on these two strong aspects of his personality," he says, ticking off on his fingers. "He is anti-Mormon and . . ."

His second finger hovers, unlabeled.

"Queer," I finish for him.

"Right." He swallows, curling his fingers back into his fist. "Does the kid hate all Mormons and plot his escape only to have his parents join the church and disown him once he leaves?"

"No . . ." Apparently, he hasn't read *that* much into my family history. "The family is going to be supportive, I think."

Sebastian leans back, thinking. "Does the kid hate the LDS Church, and he ends up leaving town only to be lured into another 'cultish religion'?"

I stare over at him, at his ability to see his faith from the eyes of a nonbeliever, to actually spin it negatively like that. "Maybe," I say. "But I don't know that I want to demonize the church either."

Sebastian's eyes meet mine before he quickly glances away. "What role does his being, um, bisexual play in the book?" This is the first time he's faltered this entire time—his blush spreads in a heat map across his face.

I want to tell him: *I'm curious whether you could ever like me, whether someone like you could be friends with someone like me.*

But he's already *here*, already being selfless and genuine with *someone like me*. I expected him to show up and be a good TA, to answer a few questions and get me started while I gawked at him. I didn't expect him to ask about me or to be so understanding. I didn't expect to *like* him. Now the conflict seems obvious, and it causes something steady inside me to curl into a tight, anxious ball, because this is something even scarier to write about.

"Think on it," he says quietly, fidgeting with a paper clip. "There are so many ways this could go, and a lot of that depends on his journey, his discovery. He starts out resenting where he is and feeling stifled by the town. Does he find freedom by staying, or leaving? Does he find something that changes his mind about it?"

I nod at my computer screen because I know I can't look at him right now without projecting my feelings across my face. My blood is simmering with the heat of my infatuation.

It begins to snow outside, and thankfully, we move over to a couple of armchairs near the window to watch, letting the book fall away for a while. Sebastian was born here, a few miles down the road. His father is a tax attorney, called to serve as bishop nearly two years ago. His mother was in finance at Vivint before Sebastian was born. Now she's a full-time mother and wife of the bishop, which, Sebastian explains, sort of makes her the mother of their ward. She likes it, he tells me, but it's meant that he and Lizzy have had to step up more with Faith and Aaron. He's played soccer and baseball since he was six. His favorite band is Bon Iver. He plays the piano and guitar.

I feed him the same innocuous details: I was born in Palo Alto. My father is a cardiac surgeon. My mother is a programmer. She feels guilty that she's not around more, but mostly I'm intensely proud of her. My favorite band is Nick Cave and the Bad Seeds, but I'm in no way musical.

We don't rehash the question of my sexuality, but I feel its presence like a third person in the room, sitting in the dark corner, eavesdropping on our conversation.

Silence ticks between us as we watch the icy gray sidewalk just below the window slowly become blanketed in white. Steam rises off the surface of a vent at the curb, and with this weird, frantic lurch of my heart, I want to know more about him. Who he's loved, what he hates, whether it's even possible he's into guys.

"You haven't asked me about the book," he says finally.

He means *his* book.

"Oh—crap—I'm sorry," I say. "I didn't mean to be rude."

"It's not rude." He faces me and grins like we're in on this same, exasperating secret. "It's just that everyone does."

"I think it's pretty cool." I shove my hands in my pockets and stretch back in my chair. "I mean, obviously, it's amazing. Imagine, your book will be here, in this library."

He seems surprised by this. "Maybe."

"I bet you're tired of talking about it."

"A little." He shrugs, smiling over at me. That smile tells me he likes that I haven't asked him about it, that I'm not here for secondhand, small-town fame. "It's added some complication, but it's hard to complain because I realize how blessed I am."

"Sure, of course."

"I've always wondered what it's like to live here when you aren't raised in the church," he says, changing the subject. "You were fifteen when you moved?"

"Yeah."

"Was it hard?"

I take a second to figure out how to answer this. Sebastian knows something about me that no one else knows, and it makes me unsure of my steps. He seems nice, but no matter how nice you are, information is power. "Provo can be suffocating."

Sebastian nods and then leans forward to get a better view out the window. "I know the church *feels* like it's everywhere.

71

It does for me, too. It seems like it seeps into every detail of my life."

"I bet."

"I can see how it might feel suffocating from the outside, but it does a lot of good, too." He looks over at me, and with dawning horror I see this study session for what it is. I understand why he agreed to come. He's *recruiting* me. He knows about me now, and it's giving him even more reason to reach out, to save me. He's not recruiting me to the oiled-up Gay Bliss Club of Northern Utah, but to the LDS Church.

"I know it does good," I say carefully. "My parents are . . . familiar with the church. It's hard to live here and not see both the good and the bad of what it does."

"Yeah," Sebastian says vaguely, not looking at me. "I can see that."

"Sebastian?"

"Yeah?"

"Just . . . wanted you to know, in case . . ." I stop, wincing as I blink away. "I didn't ask you to help me so that I could join the church."

When I look back at him, his eyes are wide in alarm. "What?"

I look to the side again. "I realize maybe I gave you the impression that I wanted to hang out because I questioned something about myself, or wanted to join. I don't have any questions about who I am. I really like you, but I'm not here to convert."

Wind whistles past the window outside—it's chilly this close to the glass—and inside, he studies me, expressionless. "I don't think you want to join." His face is pink. *From the cold. From the cold. It's not because of you, Tanner.* "I didn't think that's why you . . ." He shakes his head. "Don't worry. I won't try to sell you on the church. Not after what you shared with me."

My voice is uncharacteristically timid: "You won't tell anyone?"

"Of course not," he answers instantly. He stares down at the floor, jaw working over something unreadable to me. Finally, he digs into his pocket. "I . . . here."

Almost impulsively, he hands me a small scrap of paper. It's warm, like it's been cupped in his hand.

I unroll it, staring down at the ten digits there. His phone number.

He must have written it earlier, maybe even before he left home, tucking it into his pocket to bring to me.

Does he realize this is like handing me a grenade? I could blow everything up with this, most specifically his phone. I've never been much of a texter, but my God—the way I feel like I want to track his moves when he's in the classroom is like having a demon possession. Knowing I could reach out to him anytime is torture.

"I don't—" he starts, and then looks past me. "You can text me, or call. Whatever. Whenever. To hang out and talk about your outline if you need it."

My chest is painfully tight.

"Yeah, totally." I squeeze my eyes closed. It feels like he's about to bolt, and the need to get the words out makes my insides feel pressurized. "Thanks."

He stands. "You're welcome. Anytime."

"Sebastian?"

"Yeah?"

Our eyes meet, and I can't believe what I'm about to say. "I definitely want to hang out again."

His cheeks pop with color. Does he translate this correctly in his head? And what am I even saying? He knows I'm into guys, so he has to know I'm not just talking about the book. Sebastian scans my face, flicking from my forehead, to my mouth, to my chin, to my eyes, and back down to my mouth, before he looks away entirely. "I should probably go."

I am a tangle of wires; a cacophony of voices shouts out instructions in my head.

Clarify you meant only studying!

Bring up the book!

Apologize!

Double down and tell him you have feelings!

But I only nod, watching him smile stiffly, jog toward the stairs, and disappear around a bend of brilliantly polished oak.

I return to my laptop, open a blank document, and spill it all onto the page.

CHAPTER SIX

Here's my number

Btw it's Tanenr

Um, that should be Tanner.

I can't believe I just typo'd my own name.

Haha! This is how I'm typing in your contact info.

From, Sebatsian

(See what I did there)

I grin down at my phone for the next twenty minutes, reading the text exchange again and again. The phone is stuck to my palm; I'm sure my parents are wondering what I'm doing—I can tell by their concerned looks over the dinner table.

"Put your phone down, Tann," Dad says.

I slide it facedown onto the table. "Sorry."

"Who are you texting?" Mom asks.

I know they're not going to like it, but I don't want to lie. "Sebastian."

They exchange a look across the table. "The TA?" Mom confirms.

"You can read it." I hand her the phone. "You could do that anyway, right?"

Reluctantly, she takes it, looking like she expects to see much more than she will. Her face relaxes when she sees the harmless words there.

"This is cute, but, Tanner . . ." She lets the rest of it fall away and looks to my dad for backup. Maybe she isn't sure how much credibility she'll have while she's still wearing her rainbow PRIDE apron.

Dad reaches for the phone, and his face softens when he reads it, but then a cloud crosses through his eyes. "Are you seeing each other?"

Hailey snorts.

"*No,*" I say, ignoring her. "Jesus, you guys. We're working together on the project."

The table falls into a cloying, skeptical silence.

Mom can't help herself. "Does he know about you?"

"About how I turn into a troll at sunset?" I shake my head. "I don't think so."

"Tanner," she says gently. "You know what I mean."

I do. Unfortunately. "Please calm down. It's not like I have a tail."

"Honey," Mom starts, horrified. "You're deliberately misunderstanding—"

76

My phone buzzes in front of Dad. He picks it up. "Sebastian again."

I hold my hand out. "Please?"

He returns it to me, frowning.

I won't be in class this week. 🙁
Just wanted to let you know.

My chest seems to splinter, a fault line splitting straight down the middle, and it battles with the brilliant sun blooming there because *Sebastian thought to text me with a heads-up.*

Everything okay?

Yeah. I just have a trip to New York.

Are we doing this? Are we casually texting now?

Ooh, fancy.

Haha! I'm sure I'll look lost the entire time.

When do you leave?

Mom sighs loudly. "Tanner, for the love of God, please stop texting at the table."

I apologize under my breath and stand, sliding my phone faceup onto the kitchen counter before returning to my chair. Both of my parents have that surly, aggressively quiet thing going on, and a glance at my sister tells me that she's living her best life watching me get in trouble for once.

Amid the scraping of silverware on plates and the sound of ice clinking in glasses of water, a thick awareness swirls around the table, and the resulting self-consciousness makes my stomach tighten. My parents know I've had crushes on guys before, but it's never been a reality like this. Now there's a guy, with a name and a phone. We've all been *so cool about it*, but I realize, sitting here at this silent dinner table, that there are layers to their acceptance. Maybe it's easy for them to be *so cool about it* when they've all but told me I'm not allowed to date any guys in Provo. Am I allowed to have crushes on guys only once I've graduated and who my parents select from an acceptable pool of intelligent, progressive, non-LDS males?

Dad clears his throat, a sign that he's searching for words, and we look at him, hoping he'll pull this plane up in time. I expect him to say something about the elephant in the room, but instead he lands squarely in the safe zone: "Tell us about your classes."

Hailey launches into a retelling of the injustice of being a sophomore, how she's a midget with a top-row locker, how disgusting the girls' locker room smells, and how globally annoying guys are. Our parents listen with patient smiles before focusing in on the things they actually care about: Mom makes sure she's being a good friend. Dad mostly cares that she's busting her ass in academics. I check out halfway through her braggy answer about chemistry. Having my phone ten feet away means that 90 percent of my brain is focused on wondering whether Sebastian has replied and whether I can see him before he goes.

I feel jittery.

To be fair, meals are a peculiar affair anyway. Dad comes from an enormous family of women whose primary satisfaction in life is the care of their husbands and children. Although the same was true in Mom's LDS household, in Dad's family it centered on food. The women don't just prepare meals; they *cook*. When Bubbe visits, she fills our freezer with months' worth of brisket and kugel and makes quiet, mostly well-intended observations about how her grandchildren largely survive on sandwiches. Over time she has outgrown her disappointment that Dad didn't marry a Jewish woman, but she still struggles with Mom's work hours and our resulting reliance on takeout and packaged food.

And despite her antireligion worldview, Mom was raised in a culture where women are traditionally in the homemaker role too. To her, not packing our lunches every day or joining the PTA is a feminist rallying cry.

Even Aunt Emily struggles sometimes with guilt over not focusing a bit more on the making and keeping of her home.

So Mom's compromise was to let Bubbe teach her how to prepare certain dishes, and she tries to make a huge batch of them every Sunday for us to have throughout the week. It's a questionable endeavor, but we kids are, if nothing else, sporting about it. Dad is another story: He's picky about food. Even if he considers himself as liberal as they come, he still has some traditional holdouts. A wife who cooks is one of them.

Mom watches Dad eat, gauging from how fast he shovels it in how good it is. That is to say, the faster he eats, the less he likes it. Tonight Dad barely seems to chew before he's swallowed. Mom's normally smiling mouth is turning down at the corners.

Focusing on this dynamic is helping distract me, but only barely.

I look over at my phone. Having left it screen-side up, I can tell a call or text has just come through: The screen is lit. I shovel matzo ball soup in, scalding my mouth, until my bowl is clean, and excuse myself, standing before either of them can protest.

"Tanner," Dad chides quietly.

"Homework." I rinse my dish, slotting it into the dishwasher.

He watches me go, giving me a knowing glare for throwing the only excuse at him that he won't debate.

"It's your night for dishes," Hailey calls after me.

"Nope. You owe me because I did bathroom duty last weekend."

Her eyes communicate the mental bird flip.

"Love you too, hellcat."

Running up the stairs, I dive into my texts.

My heart spasms, tight and wild. He's sent me five.

Five.

> I leave Wednesday afternoon.
> I have meetings with my editor and the publisher on Thursday.
> I haven't met the publisher yet. I'll admit I'm nervous.
> It just occurred to me that you're probably eating dinner with your family.
> Sorry, Tanner.

With frantic fingers, I reply.

> No, sry, my parents made me put my phone away.
> I'm so happy for u.

I type my next thought and then—with my breath held high and tight in my lungs—I quickly hit send:

> I hope u have an amazing trip
> but I'm going to miss seeing u in class.

I wait a minute for a reply.

Five.

Ten.

He's not stupid. He knows I'm bi. He has to know I'm into him.

I distract myself by scrolling through Autumn's Snapchat: Her slippered feet. A sink full of dishes. A close-up of her grumpy face with the words "current mood" scrawled beneath it. Finally, I close my social media and open my laptop.

I need to know what I'm dealing with here. Growing up in California, I knew Mom's family was Mormon, but the way she used to talk about it—in the rare moments she even did—made me think they were some weird cult religion. Only once I moved here and lived among them did I register that I knew nothing except the stereotypes. It surprised me to learn that, although other Christian faiths might not agree, Mormons consider themselves to be Christians. Also, a huge portion of their free time is spent performing service—helping others. But other than their no caffeine, no booze, no cursing, and no humping rules, it all still seems like a vague cloud of secret churchiness to me.

As usual, Google helps.

For all my jokes about Jesus jammies, it turns out garments aren't just a modesty thing; they're a physical reminder of the covenants they made to God. Also, the word "covenant" is *everywhere*. In fact, the church seems to have its own language.

Within the LDS Church, the hierarchy is exclusively male.

This is one of the things Mom is spot-on about: Women get screwed. Sure, they're the ones who make babies—according to the church, an integral part of God's plan—and can serve missions if they choose, but women don't have a lot of power in the traditional sense. Meaning they can't hold positions or make decisions that influence official church policy.

The biggest piece on my mind lately—other than the Sebastian/garment question—is the one thing in the world that will make my mom's blood boil: the LDS Church's terrible history concerning gays.

The church has since condemned the practice of conversion therapy, but that doesn't mean it didn't exist, or ruin many, many lives. From the bits I've gathered from Mom, here's the basic situation: An LDS individual would come out to their family, who would quickly ship them off somewhere to be "fixed." This type of therapy involved institutionalization and electroconvulsive shock therapy. Sometimes medication or aversion conditioning, which sounded okay until I realized it meant they would use drugs to make the person nauseated while viewing same-sex erotica. The Internet tells me that more "benign" versions included shame conditioning, or retraining in stereotypical masculine and feminine behaviors, dating therapy, hypnosis, and something called orgasmic reconditioning, which—just no.

When Aunt Emily came out twenty-eight years ago, her parents offered her a choice: conversion therapy or excommunication. Now the Mormon Church's stance on queer stuff is clear as mud.

According to any church statement you can find on the matter, the only sex that should be happening is between a husband and a wife. Yawn. But surprisingly, the church does recognize a difference between same-sex attraction and what they call homosexual behavior. In essence: guys feeling attracted to other guys = we'll look the other way. Guys kissing guys = bad.

The funny part is that, after these lines in the sand that basically insist a gay Mormon put their nose down and be unhappy and unfulfilled their entire life in the name of God, most church statements also say that all people are equally beloved children and deserve to be treated with love and respect. They say that families should never, ever exclude or be disrespectful to those who choose a different lifestyle . . . but to always remind those who choose differently of the eternal consequences of their choice.

And, of course, everyone who lives here knows the big hoopla that made the rounds on the news a couple years ago: a change in a handbook that said members in same-sex marriages would be considered apostates (or defectors from the church—thank you, Google), and that children living in those households should be excluded from church activities until they're old enough to renounce the practice of homosexuality and join.

In summary: love and respect, but only if you're willing to live by their rules . . . and if not, then exclusion is the only answer.

See what I mean? Clear as mud.

From somewhere on my bed, my phone vibrates. Since I'm alone in my room, there's no one to see me actually dive into my covers to retrieve it.

I'm around BYU all day tomorrow.

And then, while the screen is still lit up with his first text, another comes in:

And I'll miss seeing you, too.

Something is happening between us. Something has been happening between us since our eyes met on the first day of class.

I want to see him before he leaves town. I don't care what Mom says. I don't care what the doctrine is.

After all, it's not my church.

Provo High has a closed campus at lunch, but it's an official thing that nobody follows. Campus is surrounded by fast-serve restaurants like Del Taco and Panda Express and Pita Pit. Four days out of five we skip out and grab something easy.

I'll admit that I know Sebastian is an English lit major (it didn't take a huge amount of sleuthing to get there), but I also know—because he told me at the library—that he likes to hang out in the Harris Fine Arts Center because it's quiet.

Today at lunch, I buy enough Panda Express for two.

Before I moved to Utah, I heard a lot about the church from people who, admittedly, have never been a part of it. *They marry their daughters off when they're twelve! They're polygamists!*

They don't and they're not—polygamy has been banned since 1890—but because of my mom, I knew that Mormons were just *people*, and I expected Mormon teens to look like anyone else on the streets of Palo Alto. What's crazy is they don't. Really. They look like the upper end of the bell-shaped curve in terms of polish: They're clean, their clothes are especially modest, and they are exceedingly well-groomed.

I look down at my old Social Distortion T-shirt over a blue thermal and mostly intact jeans. I would not feel more out of place on the Brigham Young University campus even if I put on a purple chicken costume and moonwalked across the quad. It's early in the term, and there is some sort of youth program happening outside the main student center. It's a lot of long skirts and modest shirts, straight trimmed hair and genuine smiles.

A few guys play Frisbee; one of them drops it and yells out a placid "Gosh darn it!"

A trio of girls is playing a hand-slap game accompanied by a song.

BYU is *exactly* like I imagined, and also probably exactly like its founders hoped it would be, even a hundred and forty years later. It's only across the street from Provo High, but it feels like a different world.

Inside the Harris Fine Arts Center it's surprisingly dark, and quiet. Modern architecture makes the space feel more "austere engineering" than "art building," and the upper levels are open in a rectangular frame, looking down on the ground floor. Every sound—my footsteps across the marble, a murmur of voices coming from upstairs—echoes across the entire atrium.

Sebastian isn't at any of the lounge chairs or small desks dotting the second floor, and in hindsight my bag of food seems embarrassingly overconfident. I wonder whether there are cameras tracking my movement, whether the BYU cops will come in, decide I don't belong here, and gently escort me out of the building, wishing me safe travels and promising to pray for me when they leave me at the campus border.

After a few minutes on the third floor, I'm just about to leave and stress-eat two lunches worth of questionably Asian food when I spy a pair of red Adidas peeking out from beneath a desk.

Walking over, I declare, "I have plenty of the world's least healthy lunch to share."

Sebastian startles—and in the time it takes him to turn around, I beg myself to go back in time and never have done this. At the beginning of this school year, a freshman gave me an envelope and then actually *ran off* in the other direction. Bewildered, I opened it. Glitter poured out onto my shoes, and the letter inside was full of stickers and looping handwriting telling me she thought we might be soul mates. I didn't even know her name until I read it at the bottom of the note: *Paige*, with a glittery heart sticker dotting the *i*. I don't think I'd realized until that moment how young fourteen is.

But standing here, waiting for Sebastian to speak . . . I am Paige. I am an emotional infant. It suddenly feels creepy—or absolutely immature—to be here, bringing him food. *What the hell am I doing?*

Slowly, he pulls his headphones off.

I want to fall over in relief: His red cheeks tell me everything I need to know.

"Tanner?" He grins, so wide. "Hey."

"Hey, yeah, I . . ."

Glancing back at the clock on his laptop screen, he makes the obvious observation: "You left campus."

"Doesn't everybody?"

"Actually, no." Blinking back over, he gazes at me in mild confusion.

"I . . . brought you lunch." I glance down at the food in my hand. "But now I feel like I'm breaking the law."

Peering closer at what I'm offering, he says, "Panda Express?"

"Yeah. So gross, I know."

"Totally. But, I mean, since you're already here . . ."

He grins at me. It's the only invitation I need.

I open the bag, handing him a takeout container of noodles and another of orange chicken. "I also have shrimp."

"Chicken is good." Opening it up, he moans, and it causes my entire body to stiffen. "I'm starving. Thank you."

You know those moments that feel so surreal you have a legitimate *Am I really here* feeling? Where you're not just using hyperbole but, for a breath of a second, have an out-of-body sensation? I have that right now. Standing here with him, it's dizzying.

"My dad calls this Fatty Fat Chicken," he tells me as I pull out the chair beside him and sit down.

I blink, working to get my brain and my pulse under control. "I won't tell him if you won't."

Sebastian laughs. "He eats it at least twice a week, so don't worry."

I watch him tuck in, using a fork, not chopsticks, neatly managing to get a pile of noodles in his mouth without greasing up his chin. There's something Teflon about him: He always looks pressed, clean, sanitized. Looking down at myself, I wonder what impression I give off. I'm not a slob, but I don't have the same immaculate sheen.

He swallows, and a million pornographic images fly through my head in the ten seconds before he speaks again.

"What made you come over to campus?" he asks, then neatly maneuvers a forkful of chicken into his mouth.

Is he fishing? Or does he really think I'd come over to BYU for any reason other than to see him? "I was in the neighborhood." I take a bite, chewing, swallowing through my smile. "Came over to campus to dance and sing some songs."

His eyes twinkle. He doesn't seem to mind that I'm not LDS, let alone mocking it a little. "Cool."

I look down the hallway, toward the windows facing the quad. "Are there always people outside just . . . celebrating?"

"No, but it's a pretty happy place."

I lean in, grinning. "Someone actually said 'Gosh darn it' out of frustration."

"What else would they say?"

He's fucking with me again. Our eyes snag, and hold. His are green and yellow, with these razor-sharp flecks of brown. I feel like I've taken a running leap off a cliff and have no idea how deep the water is.

Finally, Sebastian blinks back down to his lunch. "Sorry I left so abruptly the other day."

"It's okay."

I think that's all I'm going to get on the subject, but somehow, the way he can't look back up at me, the way color blooms again across his cheeks tells me so much.

Something *is* happening between us, *holy shit.*

From one of the floors below us, an older man's deep voice rings out. "Hello, Brother Christensen." In turn, this Brother Christensen murmurs a polite reply that drifts up to us, and as they move farther away from the atrium, their voices echo away.

"Wait." I look back at Sebastian, realization dawning. "Are you an elder yet?"

He swallows before answering. "No."

This is amazing. "Sebastian *Brother*. That means you're Brother Brother."

He grins, thrilled. "I've been waiting my whole life for someone to make that joke. People at church are too nice to do it."

I hesitate, unable to read the spark in his eyes. "You're messing with me."

"Yeah." If possible, his smile widens and carves out a space in my chest when he breaks, laughing happily. "But I think it's even better that Lizzy is Sister Brother."

"Does she think it's funny?"

"We all do." Pausing, he watches me for a few seconds longer, like he's trying to puzzle me out and not the other way around, before bending and taking another bite of food.

I think I've screwed this up. I have such a weird impression of Mormons as bland, serious, and secretly evil. It seems impossible to me that they would make fun of themselves this way.

"I'm being an asshole." The word just slips out of my mouth, and I wince as if I've just cursed in a cathedral.

Sebastian shakes his head, swallowing. "What? No."

"I'm not . . ."

"Familiar with the church," he finishes for me. "Most people aren't."

"We live in Provo," I remind him. "Most people *are*."

He looks up at me steadily. "Tanner, I know the world isn't represented in Provo. We all know that. Besides, and I mean this in the kindest way possible, it's likely that the non-LDS kids in town don't share the best side of the church when they talk. Am I right?"

"That's probably fair." I blink down, poking at my mostly untouched lunch. He makes me so nervous, in this giddy, excited way. When I look back up at his face, it almost hurts where my chest pinches. His attention is on his next bite of food, so I'm given a handful of seconds to stare at him without shame.

A weak voice tries to reach me from the back of the crowded room in my head: *He's Mormon. This is doomed! Pull back. Pull back!*

I stare at his jaw, and his throat, and the skin I can see just below, the hint of collarbone.

My mouth waters.

"Thanks again for this," he says, and I snap my eyes back up, catching the glint in his as he watches me realize I'm busted for ogling him.

"You really never snuck off campus?" I ask in the world's most awkward segue.

He chews another bite, shaking his head.

"Part of me wants to hope you misbehave a little."

Holy.

What did I just say?

Sebastian laughs, coughing through a rough swallow, and washes it down with a sip of water from a bottle on the table near him. "I did skip out once."

I nod for him to continue, shoveling some food into my mouth in the hopes that it will calm my uneasy stomach and lunatic mind.

"Last year I had an orthodontist appointment, and when I came back, class was nearly half done. We had an assembly after that, then lunch, and"—he shakes his head, blushing that goddamn blush—"I realized no one would be looking for me. I had three hours to do whatever I wanted."

I swallow a bite of shrimp, and it goes down rough. I want him to tell me he went home and googled pictures of guys kissing.

"I went to a movie by myself and ate an entire box of Red Vines." He leans in, eyes full of that teasing shine. "I had a *Coke*."

My brain is tangled: *Cannot compute. Which emotion to drop into the bloodstream? Fondness or bewilderment?* For the love of God, *this* is Sebastian at his naughtiest.

He shakes his head at me, and in that instant, I realize I'm the naive one here.

When he leans back and lets out a laugh, I'm screwed. Totally ruined.

I can't read him. I can't grasp him.

I have no idea what he's thinking and if he's messing with me or if he really is this good, but never before have I wanted so fiercely to lean forward and put my mouth on someone's neck, begging them to want me.

drive home still in sort of a daze, barely aware of anything that happened after lunch. Classes are a blur. I helped Autumn with her calc homework until late, but I'm not confident I was very helpful—or that her answers ended up being correct.

I've replayed my conversation with Sebastian over and over, and every time I wonder whether he looked as happy to see me as I think he did. We were flirting . . . I *think*? The idea of good, clean-cut Sebastian leaving school for what I suspect was the simple thrill of doing something he wasn't supposed to is causing a serious malfunction in my brain.

I'm also trying to wrestle with the idea that Sebastian will be gone for the next week. I've always liked school, but seeing him in Seminar is pretty much the only thing making this final semester of high school bearable.

A thought occurs to me, and I fumble for my phone.

Can u text me while ur gone?

I regret sending it almost instantly, but figure at this point, what do I have to lose? Thankfully, he doesn't let me spiral too long, and my screen lights up again.

I'll be working with my editor and don't know my exact schedule, but yeah, I'll try.

I climb out of my car and shut the door, still smiling down at my phone when I stumble into the kitchen. Mom is at the sink, already wearing her bright rainbow pajamas, washing dishes.

"Hi, honey."

"Hey," I say, tucking my phone away and slipping out of my jacket. I'm distracted and drop it twice in an attempt to hang it up. "You're home early."

"Let's just say I needed a glass of wine," she says, closing the dishwasher door. She motions to the fridge. "Saved you a plate in there."

I thank her with a kiss to the cheek before heading across the kitchen. It's not that I'm particularly hungry—thinking of my lunch with Sebastian is enough to send my stomach back into roller coaster territory—but if I don't eat, I'll just disappear into my room, where I'll obsessively reread his texts and possibly venture into less-than-wholesome territory. Which—let's be real—is most likely going to happen anyway.

The plate has a Post-it note stuck to the Saran Wrap that

says, YOU ARE MY PRIDE AND JOY. I pull it off and smile, although I can tell I'm too frantic, eyes too wide.

Mom watches me from the other side of the kitchen island. "You look a little . . . wound up. You okay?"

"Yeah, totally." The weight of her attention follows me as I heat my food and pour myself a drink. "What happened at work?"

She steps around the counter, leaning against it like she's going to answer. My phone vibrates in my pocket. As usual for this time of night, there's a text from Autumn.

But there's also a text from Sebastian.

Thanks for lunch btw.
I wasn't having the greatest day and you turned it around.
Night, Tanner.

The roller coaster inside my stomach reaches the top of the hill and goes careening over the edge.

"Tanner?" Mom pulls her hair up into a ponytail, securing it with an elastic from around her wrist.

I tear my eyes from the screen. "Yeah?"

She nods slowly and pours herself that glass of wine before motioning for me to follow. "Let's talk."

Oh, crap. I asked her about her day and then stopped listening. Leaving my phone on the counter, I follow her into the living room.

On the giant easy chair in the corner, my mom tucks her feet beneath her, watching me sit down. "You know I love you."

Inwardly, I wince. "I know, Mom."

"And I'm so proud of the man you're becoming, I could nearly burst."

I nod. I'm lucky. I know I am. But there are times when the declarations of adoration begin to feel . . . excessive.

She leans forward, uses her gentle voice. "I'm just worried about you, honey."

"I'm sorry I didn't listen to what you had to say about work."

"That's not what this is about."

I know this already. "Mom, Sebastian is a Mormon, not a sociopath."

Mom lifts her eyebrow sardonically, as if she's going to crack a joke, but she doesn't. And in a wild rush of relief, I'm *glad* she doesn't. Defensiveness for him rises like heat in my chest.

"But everything between you is still platonic, or . . . ?"

I grow uneasy. Our family talks about everything, but I can't stop thinking about their faces the other night at dinner and the realization that they have a very specific idea of the kind of guy I might end up with someday: someone just like us. "What if I had more than platonic feelings for him?"

She looks pained and nods slowly. "I don't think I'm entirely surprised."

"I went and saw him at lunch."

I can see her swallowing her reaction down like a thick mouthful of cough syrup.

"You're okay with this, right?" I ask.

"About you leaving campus?" She leans back, studying me. "Not really, but I know everyone does it, so I'm willing to pick my battles. About your sexuality? Absolutely. You never have to worry about that with your dad and me, okay?"

Now, I know this isn't the reality for most queer kids. I know I am endlessly lucky. My word comes out a little thick with emotion: "Okay."

"But am I going to be okay with you pursuing an LDS kid, boy *or* girl?" She shakes her head. "No. Tanner, I'm not. This is just me being honest. And maybe it's my blind spot, but it genuinely troubles me."

My gratitude is immediately extinguished. "How would this be any different from his parents saying *guys* are off-limits?"

"It's *completely* different. Among a hundred other reasons, going to church is a choice. Being bisexual is simply who you *are*. I'm protecting you from the toxic messages of the church."

I actually laugh at this. "And his parents are doing it to protect him from hell."

"It doesn't work like that, Tann. The church doesn't threaten fire and brimstone."

My lid blows. "How would I know what the LDS Church says about anything?" I ask, voice rising. "It's not like you give us any level perspective on what they *actually* believe and how they function. All I know from you is they hate the gays, they hate women, they hate, they hate, they *hate*."

"Tanner—"

"I don't actually feel like the Mormon Church hates much of anything. You're the one who hates *them*."

Her eyes go wide, and then she turns her face away, taking a deep breath.

Oh, shit. I went way too far.

If Mom were a violent woman, she probably would have stood up and smacked me just then. I can read it in the stiff line of her shoulders, her deliberately calming breaths.

But Mom *isn't* a violent woman. She's gentle, and patient, and unwilling to rise to my bait. "Tanner, honey. This is so much more complicated for me than you can possibly imagine, and if you want to talk about my history with the church, we can. Right now I'm worried about *you*. You've always led with your heart first and your head second, but I need you to think about this one." Tucking her leg underneath her again, she says, "You and Sebastian come from two very different places, and even though it's not the same thing your dad and I or Aunt Emily went through, it's not completely different, either. I assume his family doesn't know he's gay?"

"*I* don't even know if he's gay."

"Well, for argument's sake, let's assume he is and your feelings are reciprocated. You know the church thinks it's okay to have same-sex attraction but you aren't allowed to act on it?"

"Yeah, I know."

"Would you be able to be with him without touching him?" It's rhetorical, so she doesn't need me to answer. "If not, how would you feel being a secret? Would you be okay going behind his parents' backs? What if his family is as close as we are? How would you feel if his parents cut him off because of his relationship with you?" This time she waits for me to reply, but I don't honestly know what to say. This feels like putting the cart before horse—hell, before the entire stable. "How would you feel if he lost his community, or if the two of you genuinely fell in love, but in the end he chose the church over you?"

I deflect with a joke. "We're barely texting. I'm not ready to propose just yet."

She knows what I'm doing and gives me a patient, sad smile. "I know. But I also know I've never seen you this intense about someone before, and in the excitement of all the firsts, sometimes it's hard to think about what comes after. It's my job to look out for you."

I swallow. Logically I know she has a point, but the stubborn part of my brain insists that the situations aren't exactly the same. I can handle this.

. . .

Although Mom means well, my thoughts about Sebastian are a runaway train: The engineer is gone and the engine is basically on fire. My attraction is beyond control.

But once I'm up in my room, thinking about what she said, I calm down enough to realize that she's shared more with us than I gave her credit for. I know how devastated Aunt Emily was when she worked up the courage to come out to her family and her parents told her she was no longer welcome at home. I know she lived on the street for a few months before she moved into a shelter, and even there it wasn't very welcoming; she tried to commit suicide.

This was the final straw for Mom. She dropped out of school at the University of Utah and took Emily with her to San Francisco. There, she enrolled at UCSF and worked night shifts at a 7-Eleven to support them both. Mom went on to get a master's at Stanford. Emily eventually got her own master's from UC Berkeley.

Their parents—my grandparents, who I know live somewhere in Spokane now—cut both of their daughters out of their lives *and* their will, and have never tried to find them.

Mom tries to pretend like it doesn't still hurt, but how can that possibly be true? Even though they make me insane sometimes, I would be lost without my family. Would Sebastian's really kick him out? Would they *disown* him?

Jesus, this is getting more intense than I expected. I

thought it would be a short crush, a curiosity. But I'm in it now. And I know that Mom isn't wrong that my pursuing Sebastian is a terrible idea. Maybe it's a good thing he's going to be gone from class when he's in New York.

I head up to visit Emily and Shivani for the weekend and—strangely—don't even feel the desire to text him. I'm sure Mom told Emily all about what's going on, because she tries to talk to me about my "love life" a couple of times, but I skirt the issue. If Mom is intense about it, Emily is nearly vibrating.

They take me to see some weird art-house movie about a woman who raises goats, and I fall asleep in the middle somewhere. They refuse to let me have wine with dinner, and I ask them what the hell having two heretic aunts is good for anyway, but Emily and I play pinball in the garage for about four hours on Sunday, and I eat about seven plates of Shivani's chickpea curry before driving home, feeling pretty damn great about my family.

It's amazing how a bit of distance and perspective seems to help clear my head.

But then Sebastian comes to class the following week wearing a dark gray henley with the button open at the throat and his sleeves pushed halfway up his forearms. I'm faced with a landscape of muscle and vein, smooth skin and graceful hands, and how am I supposed to handle *that*?

Besides, he seems more than happy to come over and look at my first few pages. He even laughs about the reference to Autumn's pussy poster and asks me with thinly veiled curiosity whether the book is autobiographical.

As if he didn't already know.

The question hovers in his eyes—*Am I in it?*

That depends on you, I think.

Obviously my "distance" and "perspective" didn't last very long.

I had a fleeting thing for Manny when we first met—even had a moment or two of *alone time* imagining what it might be like with him—but it didn't last, and my attention was snagged by the next person who came along. Kissing boys feels good. Kissing girls feels good. But something tells me kissing Sebastian would be like a sparkler falling in the middle of a field of dry grass.

Outside of school and a few Snaps of her meals, I haven't seen much of Autumn lately. When she stops by around dinner one night, my mom doesn't even try to hide how excited she is to see her and invites her to stay. Afterward, we disappear into my room and it's just like old times.

I lie on my bed, trying to organize the day's worth of Post-it notes into something coherent for my next chapter, while Autumn goes through my clothes and gets me up to speed on school gossip.

Did I know that Mackenzie Goble gave Devon Nicholson

a blow job on the balcony of the gym during the teacher basketball game last week?

Did I hear that some kids went through the ceiling tiles in one of the bathrooms and made their way to the area above the girls' locker room?

Did I hear that Manny asked Sadie Wayment to prom?

This gets my attention, and I blink up to see her standing in one of my T-shirts. My parents have a strict door-open policy whenever anyone is over—boy or girl—but it doesn't seem to apply to Autumn. Which is honestly hilarious, because in the time I've been staring at my notes, she's been undressing and trying on my clothes. "I forgot people are already talking about prom."

She gives me the look that tells me I'm being slow. "It's less than four months away. I brought it up in the car last week."

I sit up. "You did?"

"Yeah, I did." She looks at herself in the mirror, tugging on the shirt. "It's like you don't hear anything I say anymore."

"No, I'm sorry. I've just . . ." I push my pile of Post-its away and fully face her now. "I'm sucked into my project and distracted. Tell me what you said."

"Oh," she says, annoyance extinguished for the moment. "I asked if you wanted to go together so we didn't have to make it a big thing."

Wow. I am a jerk. She essentially asked me to prom and

I didn't say anything. I haven't given it any thought at all. It's true Autumn and I have gone to dances when neither of us had dates, but that was before.

Before Sebastian?

I am an idiot.

She studies me in the mirror. "I mean, unless there's someone else you wanted to take?"

I look away so she can't see my eyes. "No. I guess I just forgot."

"You forgot about prom? Tanner. It's our senior year."

I grunt, shrugging. Abandoning my closet, she sits on the edge of the bed next to me. Her legs are bare and my shirt hits her about midthigh. It's in moments like these I realize how much easier my life could be if I felt for her the way I feel about Sebastian. "You sure you don't want to ask someone? Sasha? What about Jemma?"

I wrinkle my nose. "They're both LDS."

Oh, the irony.

"Yeah, but they're *cool* LDS."

I tug her closer. "Let's see how it goes before we decide. I haven't lost hope that Eric will pull himself together and make an honest woman out of you. Like you said, it's our senior year. Don't *you* want it to be a big deal?"

"I don't want to—" she begins half-heartedly, but I pull her down over me and then roll her into a ball, tickling her. Autumn squeals and laughs and calls me names, and it's only when Hailey is pounding on my wall and Dad is yelling at us to keep it down that I finally move, satisfied that the subject of prom has been forgotten.

Life here gets easier when the seasons change and the days grow longer. Other than the occasional hike or day of skiing, none of us have spent much time outdoors in months. It's left me stir-crazy, with too much time to think. By the middle of February I'm so sick of my room and my house and the inside of the school that when the first real warm day comes, I'm willing to do just about anything as long as it happens *outside*.

The snow pushes away from the sidewalks a little more each day, until there are only a few patches left on the lawn.

My dad left the truck, the trailer, and a to-do list with my name on it taped to the fridge Saturday morning. I tow our boat from the side of the house to the driveway and pull off the tarp. Silverfish scamper away; it's musty and dark inside, and I survey how much work I have ahead of me. We're still months away from being able to *use* it, but it needs some serious TLC.

There are puddles of melting snow everywhere on the driveway. With the oil from the street and the tangle of leaves and branches, it looks disgusting, but I know where it leads: sunshine and outdoors and the smell of barbeque all weekend long. We're having the seats reupholstered and the marine carpet replaced this April, so I start pulling the old stuff out along with the adhesive. I wouldn't categorize any of this as *enjoyable*, but since I don't have an actual job and gas doesn't buy itself, I do what my dad tells me.

I get out everything I need, laying another large tarp down on the grass to make hauling it away easier. I've just pulled the driver seat out when I hear brakes squeaking mildly, hear tires coming to a stop on the driveway behind me.

I swing around to see Sebastian standing next to a bike, squinting up into the sun.

I haven't seen him outside of class in two weeks, and it causes a weird ache to push through me. Straightening, I walk over to the edge of the deck. "Hey."

"Hey," he says back, smiling. "What are you doing up there?"

"Earning my keep, apparently. I believe you call this 'service,'" I say, using my hands to form air quotes around the words.

He laughs, and my stomach clenches. "Service is more"—finger quotes—"'helping others' and less"—more finger quotes—"'fixing my dad's fancy boat,' but okay."

Holy crap, he's teasing me. I motion to the mess at my feet and strewn across the tarp. "Do you see this monstrosity? This is not fancy."

He peers over the side. "Keep telling yourself that."

Kneeling down, I bring my face within a few inches of his. "What are you doing here anyway?"

"I was tutoring in the neighborhood. Thought I'd stop by."

"So you go to school, write, work as a TA, and tutor? I am *lazy*."

"Don't forget all the church service." Stepping back, he looks away, cheeks burning. "But I wasn't really in the neighborhood."

It's taking my brain a moment to get from point A to point B, and when it finally connects the dots—that he came here specifically to see me—I almost jump over the side and tackle him.

Of course I don't. I can see by the way he's gripping the handlebar that he's not entirely comfortable with the admission, and a pang of hope blooms inside me. This is how we reveal ourselves: these tiny flashes of discomfort, the reactions we can't hide. In some ways, it's why it's so terrifying to live here and have my sexuality safely known only behind my front door. Outside, I could give myself away by a twitch of my lips at the word "faggot," by staring at someone too long, by letting a guy friend hug me and doing it wrong.

Or, by being nervous simply because he wanted to stop by.

I'm probably just projecting, probably seeing this out of my own hope, but still, I want to climb down, gently pry his hands from the bike, and hold them.

I crack a joke instead. "I notice you didn't disagree with the lazy part. I see how you are."

The line of his shoulders eases, and he lets go of the

handlebar. "I mean, I didn't want to say anything, but . . ."

"You could stop hassling me and come up here and help."

Sebastian pushes his bike to the grass and slips off his jacket, surprising me when he easily hops onto the trailer and up onto the stern. "See, now you're getting what service is all about."

I know there's a joke in there about servicing, but I manage to keep it to myself.

With his hands on his hips, Sebastian looks around. "What needs to be done?"

"I need to pull out the seats and rip up the old carpet. Oh, and scrape up the adhesive. Bet you're sorry you're such a good person now." I hand him my gloves and give myself three seconds to stare at him. There's not a wrinkle, or a stitch out of place. He's been outside in the sun lately too. His skin is a warm brown.

"You don't need to give me those," he says, pushing them away.

"I think there's another pair in the garage."

Sebastian concedes, and I hop down, taking a second to breathe as I slowly make my way toward the garage and back to the boat again. If I were taking Mom's advice, this would be the perfect opportunity to lay out a boundary about things, to clarify that although he knows something about me that no one else knows, nothing between the two of us could ever happen.

Soon, I tell myself. *I'll tell him soon. Probably.*

We manage to get the other front seat out, along with the bench, and even though it can't be above sixty degrees—a record for this time of year—we're both sweating by the time we tackle the carpet.

"So don't take this the wrong way," he says, "but why is your dad having you do this instead of . . . I don't know"—with a guilty tilt of his head, he glances over at my house—"paying someone?"

I follow his attention to my house. Our neighborhood is arguably the nicest in this part of Provo. Houses have curved driveways and long, rolling lawns. Everyone has a finished basement, and many of us have in-law quarters over our garages. It's true that my parents make good money, but they are anything but spendthrifts. "Mom will save a penny any-where she can. Her reasoning: She already let Dad buy a boat. She's not going to let him hire someone to maintain it."

"Sounds a lot like my mom too." Sebastian tightens his grip on a particularly tough section of carpet and pulls. A satisfying *rip* moves through the small quarters. "The saving a penny part, anyway," he clarifies. "Her motto is 'Use it up, wear it out, make it do, or do without.'"

"Please never tell my mom that. She'll put it on a shirt."

Or a bumper sticker.

With the carpet finally pulled free, Sebastian stands and throws it over the side, where it lands on the tarp with a *whack* and a plume of dust. Using the back of his arm, he wipes his forehead.

It feels like a crime the way I have to force my eyes away from his torso.

Looking around us, he surveys the damage. "Still. Old or not, this is a pretty nice boat."

"Yeah, it is." I push to stand, climbing down onto the driveway. Both of my parents are still gone, and inviting him in seems tantalizingly criminal. "You want something to drink?"

"Sure."

Sebastian follows me through the garage and into the house. In the kitchen, I open the fridge, grateful for the refrigerated air on my face, and survey what we have. Dad is at the hospital and Mom and Hailey are shopping.

I'm grateful, but also *acutely aware* that we're alone.

"We have lemonade, Coke, Diet Coke, Vitaminwater, coconut water—"

"Coconut water?"

"My mom likes to drink it after she works out. Personally, I think it tastes like watery sunscreen."

Sebastian steps up behind me to peer into the fridge, and my breath catches in my lungs. "It's a wonder they don't put that on the package." When he laughs, I can feel the way it moves through his chest.

I am not okay.

He clears his throat. "Vitaminwater is fine."

I pull out two bottles and hand him one, pressing the other against my face when his back is turned.

"Your dad's a doctor?" he asks, taking everything in. I watch as he untwists the cap and puts the bottle to his lips for a long drink. My heart beats in time with each swallow . . .

. . . one

. . . two

. . . three

. . . and I'm pretty sure I don't breathe again until he does.

"Yeah, up at Utah Valley." I turn back to the fridge, hoping my voice doesn't crack. "You want something to eat?"

Sebastian walks toward me. "Sure. Do you mind if I wash my hands?"

"Yeah, good call."

Side by side, we stand at the sink, lathering our hands and rinsing them under the tap. Our elbows knock together, and when I reach across him for the towel, my hip bumps into his. It's just a hip, but my mind goes from hips to hip bones to what's in between in a fraction of a second. My perving is nothing if not efficient.

Realizing I can't just stand there at the sink and think about his hips, I hand him the towel and return to the fridge. "Sandwiches okay?"

"Yeah, thanks."

I pull out lunch meat and cheese and whatever else I can find and snag plates and a few knives from the dishwasher.

113

Sebastian has taken a seat on one of the kitchen stools. I slide the bread across the counter toward him.

"So how's the project coming?" He untwists the plastic bag, placing bread on the plates.

"Project?"

He laughs, leaning forward to meet my eyes. "You know, the book? For the class you're in?"

"The book, right." The lunch meat is new, so it requires a little of my attention to open, which means I get at least ten seconds to stall. It's still not enough. "It's great."

He lifts a brow, surprised. "Great?"

Everything I've written lately is about you, but it's cool. No need for things to be awkward between us.

"Yeah," I say with a shrug, unable to come up with anything more articulate under the weight of his attention. "I feel pretty solid."

Sebastian rips a piece of lettuce off the head and places it neatly on the center of his bread. "You going to let me read more?"

"Yeah, totally," I lie.

"Now?"

My answer comes out too sharply: "Not yet. No."

"You could come by after school next week, and we could look through it."

A mouthful of water seems to solidify in my throat. With effort, I swallow. "Really?"

"Sure. How about Friday?"

It gives me nearly a week to edit the book. "Okay."

"Bring me the first few chapters." His eyes twinkle.

I have just over five days to triage my book. Change the names, at the very least. Maybe take this book out of diary territory and into *novel* territory.

Lord, give me strength.

We eat in silence for a few minutes, passing the bag of chips back and forth and finally cracking open a few caffein-ated Cokes—so scandalous!—when Sebastian stands, walk-ing over to a photograph stuck to the fridge. "That's a great picture," he says, leaning in to get a better look. "Where was this? This building is *insane*."

It's a photo of me the summer after tenth grade. I'm stand-ing in front of a towering, elaborately constructed church. "That's the Basilica of the Sagrada Família, in Barcelona."

Sebastian blinks over to me, eyes wide. "You've been to Barcelona?"

"My dad had a big conference and brought us along. It was pretty cool." Moving to stand just behind him, I reach over his shoulder and touch part of the photo. "It looks differ-ent on each side. Where I'm standing is the passion side, and it's simpler than the others. And in these towers"—I point to the stone spheres that seem to stretch into the clouds—"you can take a lift to the top."

"Your expression." He laughs. "You look like you know

something the person taking the picture doesn't."

I look down at him, so close I can see the freckle he has on the side of his nose, the way his eyelashes practically touch his cheeks when he blinks. What I want to tell him is that I'd made out with a guy on that trip, only the second guy I've ever kissed. His name was Dax, and he'd been visiting with his parents. We snuck off during a dinner with a bunch of the other doctors and their families and kissed until our lips were numb.

So yeah, I guess I did know something the person taking the picture didn't know. But I told Dad and Mom about Dax a few months later.

I want to tell Sebastian that he's right, if only to see his reaction when I explain why.

"I have this thing about heights," I say instead. "And nearly lost it when my parents explained we had tickets to go to the top."

Lifting his chin, he looks up at me. "Did you go?"

"Yeah, I did. I think I held my mom's hand the entire time, but I made it. Maybe that's why I look a little proud."

Sebastian steps away, sitting at the counter again. "We drove forty miles to Nephi once," he says. "I think it's safe to say you win."

I cough out a laugh. "Nephi sounds pretty cool."

"We visited the temple in Payson and watched a handcart reenactment along the Mormon trail. So . . . yeah."

116

We both laugh now. I cup a sympathetic hand on his shoulder. "Okay, maybe you'll win the next one."

"I don't think that's going to happen," he says, grinning at me over the top of his Coke. His smile dumps endorphins into my veins.

"Maybe when we get the boat finished we can take it out."

He sets his can down next to his plate. "You've done that before?"

"I mean, I've never pulled the trailer by myself, but I'm sure I can handle it. You could even come when we go to Lake Powell in July."

Sebastian's face falls for a fraction of a second before his standard perfect persona slips back into place. "Sounds good."

"Maybe we'll get lucky and it'll warm up soon," I say. "An early summer."

I wonder if he can see the way my heart is banging against my ribs. "I hope so."

spend all of my free time every weeknight frantically doing a find and replace for the names "Tanner," "Tann," and "Sebastian." Tanner becomes Colin. Sebastian becomes Evan. Everyone I go to school with gets a new, generic name. Autumn becomes Annie. Fujita becomes Franklin, and the class becomes an honors chemistry lab.

I realize it's an exercise in futility. Even when I save the book in a new version, where "Colin" is actually interested in "Ian," one of the LDS students in the class, I know my changes are sloppy and unconvincing at best.

Friday after school, with the first four chapters printed and tucked under my arm, I walk from my car to the front door of Sebastian's house. I would swear under oath that their doorbell is the loudest in existence. At least, it feels that way as soon as I've depressed the button. My pulse takes off without looking both directions; my nerves get slammed by an eighteen-wheeler.

But there's no going back now. I am about to enter Sebastian's house. The *bishop's* house.

This isn't *really* my first rodeo. I've been inside Eric's house before, but his place is more LDS-lite. Eric's senior photo now hangs where the portrait of the Savior used to be. They still have a framed photograph of the temple on the wall, but they also have a coffeemaker, like civilized people.

This all means that part of the anticipation I'm feeling is the same way an archaeologist might feel before a big dig in Egypt: There's going to be a lot to unearth here.

Heavy footsteps land on the wood floors inside. They're heavy enough to make me wonder whether it's Mr. Brother on the other side of the door, and then I panic in a burst because I got my hair cut and put on my best clothes and what if instead of looking passably Mormon I look super gay?

What if Sebastian's father immediately sees my intentions for what they are and sends me away, forbidding his son from ever talking to me again?

My panic spirals. I'm clean but don't look particularly clean-cut; I'm obviously in lust with Sebastian; my dad is Jewish—is that bad? There aren't a whole lot of Jews in Provo, but since we don't really practice anyway, I never considered how that might make me *more* of an outsider. God, I don't even know how to use the word "covenant" correctly. I feel sweat pricking at the back of my neck, and the door is swinging open. . . .

But it's only Sebastian, with a kid in a headlock under his arm.

"This is Aaron," he says, spinning slightly so I can see his brother better. "This is Tanner." His brother is lanky, smiling, and has a head of dark floppy hair: a miniature version of his big brother. Well done, genetics.

Aaron pushes away and stands, extending a hand for me to shake. "Hi."

"Nice to meet you."

He's thirteen, and here I am wondering whether my handshake is sufficient. Mormons just seem so fucking good at these things.

I let go and smile, resisting the urge to apologize. The cursing is going to have to stop, even if it's only in my head.

Almost as if he can tell there is a silent Chernobyl happening inside me, Sebastian ushers Aaron back inside and then tilts his head for me to follow him.

"Come in," he says, and then grins. "You won't catch fire."

Inside, it is immaculate. And very, *very* Mormon. It makes me wonder how similar this is to Mom's childhood home.

Up front, there is a living room with two couches that face each other, an upright piano, and an enormous framed picture of the Salt Lake Temple. Beside it is a framed painting of Joseph Smith. I follow Sebastian down the hall, past a curio cabinet with a white statue of Jesus with his hands outstretched, framed photos of their four kids, and a wedding photo of his parents dressed completely in white. The two of them look like they're barely out of puberty, if I'm being honest, and the wedding dress nearly climbs all the way to her chin.

In the kitchen, as expected, there is no coffeemaker on the counter, but to my eternal delight, on the wall just by the kitchen table is a huge eight-by-ten photo of Sebastian standing on a brilliant green lawn, smiling from ear to ear and casually clutching a copy of the Book of Mormon.

He catches me studying it and clears his throat. "Want something to drink? Root beer, Hi-C . . . lemonade?"

I break my attention away from the photo to look over at him in the flesh—somehow so different here in front of me: eyes more guarded, skin clear even without photoshopping, stubble shadowing his jaw—and as ever my eyes are drawn to his splotchy cheeks. Is he embarrassed, or excited? I want to learn each and every one of his blushes. "Water's fine."

He turns, and I watch him walk away before returning my attention to each of the framed wonders in this house. Such as a document in a heavy, gilded frame, entitled THE FAMILY: A PROCLAMATION TO THE WORLD.

I never see stuff like this. In our house, you'd be much more likely to see a liberal manifesto nailed to the wall.

I've read to the fourth paragraph, where the LDS Church proclaims that "the sacred powers of procreation are to be employed only between man and woman, lawfully wedded as husband and wife," when Sebastian presses a cold glass of water into my hand.

I'm so startled, I nearly knock it onto the floor.

"So, this is interesting," I say, working to keep my tone neutral. I'm torn between wanting to finish reading it and to somehow unread everything I've already absorbed.

I'm starting to understand what Mom means about protecting me from the church's toxic message.

"There's a lot packed into that one page," Sebastian agrees, but from his voice I can't tell how he feels about it. I knew all of this before I came over here—that is, sex is for heterosexuals; parents are obligated to teach their children these values; no sex before marriage; and above all, pray, pray, pray—but seeing it here in Sebastian's house makes it feel more real.

Which makes everything I've been feeling a little more *un*real.

I'm left momentarily dizzy by the realization that Sebastian's family aren't just enjoying the nice *idea* of this. They're not just visualizing an idealized world; they're not playing a game of Wouldn't-It-Be-Nice-If. They genuinely, truly *believe* in this God, in these doctrines.

I look over at Sebastian. He's watching me, eyes unreadable.

"I've never had someone over before who wasn't a member," he says. The mind reader. "I'm just watching you take it all in."

I decide to go for pure honesty: "It's hard to understand."

"I wonder if you opened the Book of Mormon and just

read a bit of it, whether it would speak to you." He holds up his hands. "I'm not recruiting you. I'm just curious."

"I could try." I don't really *want* to try.

He shrugs. "For now, let's go sit down and talk about *your* book."

The tension of the moment snaps, and only after it's gone do I realize I've been holding my breath, muscles clenched all over.

We head into the family room, which is much cozier and less sterile than the living room up at the front of the house. Here, there are countless framed photos of the family: together, in pairs, alone leaning against a tree—but in every single one, they're smiling. The smiles look real, too. My family is as happy as they come, but during our most recent photo session, my mom threatened Hailey with a closet full of colorful sundresses from the Gap if she didn't stop sulking.

"Tanner," Sebastian says quietly. I look at him, and a slow grin spreads over his face until he breaks, laughing. "Is it that fascinating?"

The way he's teasing me makes me realize I'm acting like early man emerging from a cave. "Sorry. It's just so adorably wholesome."

He shakes his head, looking down, but he's still smiling. "Okay, so about your book."

Yeah, Sebastian. About my book. My book about you.

My confidence bolts, leaving the scene of the crime. I hand

over the printed pages. "I don't think it's great yet, but . . ."

This makes him look up at me, interest lighting his eyes. "We'll get it there."

Well, at least one of us is optimistic.

I lift my chin, gesturing that he should dig in. He smiles, holding my gaze and offering a teasing "Don't be nervous" before he blinks down to the pages in his hand. I watch his eyes flicker back and forth, and my heart is a grenade in my throat.

Why did I even agree to this? Why did I try to rewrite the class sections? Yes, I wanted to spend time with Sebastian today, but wouldn't it be so much easier to keep this a secret from him until I know where he and I stand?

As soon as I have the thought, I realize my subconscious has already won: I wanted him to look for himself in it. So much of this is taken from our conversations. I'm here because I want him to tell me which love interest he wants to be: Evan or Ian.

He nods as he finishes, and it seems like he goes back and reads the last section again.

I do not expect him to say, "I have some time this weekend. I could help then."

This is probably a terrible idea. Yes, I'm attracted to him, but I worry that if I dig deeper, I won't *like* him.

But that would be for the best, wouldn't it? It certainly wouldn't hurt to get some time outside of this class, to get an answer to my question: Could we even be friends, let alone more?

He swallows, and I watch as it moves his throat.

"Does that work?" he asks, pulling my eyes back up to his face.

"Yeah," I say, and swallow. This time he watches. "What time?"

He grins, handing it back to me. "Wow."

Wow? I wince. Obviously, that means it's horrible. "I feel like an idiot."

"Don't," he says. "Tanner, I really like it."

"Yeah?"

He nods and then bites his lip. "So . . . *I'm* in your book?"

I shake my head. The pin is pulled from the grenade. "No one we know. Well, except Franklin is a stand-in for Fujita, obviously. I'm just using the class as the structure."

Running a finger under his bottom lip, Sebastian watches me for a few quiet seconds. "I think . . . I mean, I think this is about us."

I feel the blood drain from my face. "What? No."

He laughs easily. "Colin and . . . Ian? Or is it Evan, the TA?"

"It's about Colin and *Ian*. Another student."

Oh God. Oh God.

"But," he starts, and then looks down, blushing.

I struggle to hold my cards close to my chest. "What?"

He flips to a page and puts his index finger there. "You had a typo in Tanner here. Right where I think you mean to put 'Colin.' It didn't pick up on your search and replace."

ARGH.

The same stupid typo in my name I *always* make. "Okay, yeah. Originally it was about me and some theoretical person."

"Really?" he asks, eyes lit with curiosity.

I fidget with the binder clip I'd used to hold the pages together. "No. I know you're not . . ."

He flips to another page and hands it to me.

I curse under my breath.

> With his hands laced together in front of him, Franklin rocks back on his heels. "Seb has a very busy schedule, of course"—I mentally groan. *Seb*— "but he and I both feel that his experience can benefit each of you. *I* believe he will inspire you."

Seb. I never did a search and replace for the nickname.

Sebastian's about to say something else—his expression is impossible for me to read, but it doesn't look like horror—when a voice rises from the doorway.

"Sebastian, honey?"

We both turn and look up at the sound. I want to kiss the woman who has derailed this awkward hellhole. His mother, I recognize from the photos, steps into the room. She's petite, with dark blond hair pulled back in a ponytail, wearing a simple long-sleeved shirt and jeans. I don't know why I was expecting some frumpy, floral sister-wife dress and a giant Molly Mormon bow in her hair, but my synapses quickly rearrange themselves.

"Hey, Mom," Sebastian says, smiling. "This is Tanner. He's in the Seminar this term."

His mother smiles at me, walking over to shake my hand and welcome me to the house. My heart is still jackhammering around inside my ribs, and I wonder if I look like I might pass out. She offers me something to drink, something to eat. She asks what we're working on, and we both mumble out something blah, blah book-related without looking at each other.

But apparently our answers were sufficiently wholesome because she turns to Sebastian. "Did you call Ashley Davis back?"

As if on their own steam, Sebastian's eyes flicker to me and then back. "Remind me again who she is?"

Her clarification makes my stomach plummet to my gut: "The activities coordinator." She pauses, adding meaningfully, "She organizes the singles ward."

"Oh. Not yet."

"So," she says, smiling warmly, "make sure you do, okay? I've told her you'll be calling. I just think it's time."

It's time? What does that mean? Does it bother his parents that he's nineteen and doesn't have a girlfriend? I thought he wasn't supposed to be in a relationship when he left on his mission.

Do they suspect he's gay?

He starts to speak, but she gently cuts in, answering some of my questions. "I'm not saying you should grow attached to anyone. I just want you to know some . . . people . . ."—*Ugh, she means girls*—"so that when you come home—"

"Okay, Mom," Sebastian says quietly, blinking to me and away again. He smiles at her to remove the insult of his interruption.

She seems satisfied with this answer and moves on. "Have we received your promotional schedule from your publicist?"

Sebastian winces, shaking his head. "Not yet."

His mom's smile droops, and a furrow takes up residence on her brow. "I'm worried we won't have time to coordinate everything," she says. "We still need to do your paperwork and coordinate with the MTC. If you leave in June, you'll be cutting it close. We don't know where you'll be going, so we assume you need three months at the center before you leave."

In any other house, this detailed planning would have me making a crack about spies and Agent Q and pens that turn into machetes. Not here.

But then something clicks. My brain suddenly feels like Mom's old Buick. She would always push the accelerator before the motor turned over, and the engine would flood, needing a few extra seconds to clear. It takes me the same amount of time to realize Sebastian and his mom are talking about *this summer*.

As in, when he'll leave Provo for two years.

The MTC is the Missionary Training Center. He's leaving in four months.

Four months used to feel like an eternity.

"I'll ask her," Sebastian says. "I'm sorry. When I last checked in, they told me they would be getting me an itinerary with my tour stops as soon as it was done."

"We have so much to do before you go," she says.

"I know, Mom. I'll follow up."

With a little kiss to the top of his head, she leaves, and the room seems to be swallowed by tense silence.

"Sorry about that," he says, and I'm expecting his face to be tight, but when I look at him, he's smiling broadly. The awkward conversation between us is gone. The awkward conversation with his mom, too. "So much to coordinate. I need to get her this stuff soon."

"Yeah." I pinch my lower lip, trying to figure out how to ask what I want to ask, but the move distracts him, and his smile slips as he watches me touch my mouth.

I don't know what it is about that tiny break, but—much

like his reaction when he admitted coming to see me that day with the boat—it says so much.

It says so much because the smile seemed real until he looked at my mouth, and then it just totally shattered.

The room is full of unspoken sentiments. They hang over our heads like rain clouds. "Where are you going?" I ask.

He looks back up at my eyes, and the smile is nowhere to be seen now. "Oh. After my book tour? I'm going on my mission."

"Right, right." My heart is a hundred marbles rolling on the floor. I don't know why I needed him to say it out loud. "And you're not sure where you'll be assigned?"

"I'll find out in July, I think. As you heard, we still need to send in my papers, but I can't do that until the book comes out."

Missions, from the outside, are hard to understand. Young men—and women sometimes, but not as often—leave their homes for two years to be sent to a location anywhere in the world. Their job? Make new Mormons. And not the sexy way, at least not yet. Missionaries make new Mormons the *baptizing* way.

We've all seen them, walking or riding bikes in their clean trousers and pressed, short-sleeved white shirts. They come to our doors with bright smiles, tidy hair, and glossy black name tags and ask whether we'd like to hear more about Jesus Christ, our Lord and Savior.

Most of us turn them away with a smile and a "No, thank you."

But my mother never says no. No matter how she feels about the church—and trust me, she doesn't let them talk about the Book of Mormon to her—they're far from home, she said back when we lived in Palo Alto. And it's true; many of them are, and they're on their feet all day, pounding pavement. If we invited them in, they'd be as gracious and lovely as you can imagine. They'd take lemonade and a snack, and their gratitude would be effusive.

Missionaries are some of the kindest people you will ever meet. But they will want you to read their book, and they will want you to see the truth the way their church sees it.

While they're gone, they aren't allowed to watch television, or listen to the radio, or read anything beyond a few church-sanctioned texts. They're there to dive deeper into their faith than they ever have, to be alone and become men, to help grow the church and spread the Gospel. And they aren't allowed to leave a girlfriend behind. Of course they aren't allowed to engage in any sexual behavior—certainly not with members of the same sex. They want to save you, because they think you need saving.

Sebastian wants to be one of them.

I can't get the thought out of my head, and we're sitting here in his house, surrounded by the truth of it—of course he wants to be one of them. He *is* one of them. The fact that he so easily saw himself in my book, that he knows I have feelings for him, doesn't change that one single bit.

I don't even care about the farce of my novel anymore; I'd let him see the original version, the version where I clearly can't stop thinking about him, if he would promise me to *stay*.

He wants to go on a mission? He wants to leave here and commit two of his best, hottest, wildest, most adventurous years to the church? He wants to give his life to this—really *give* his life?

I stare at my hands and wonder what the hell I'm actually doing here. Glitter-heart Paige has nothing on me. I am the King of Naive.

"Tanner."

I look up at him. He's staring at me, and it's clear he's said my name more than once.

"What?"

He tries to smile. He's nervous. "You got quiet."

Quite frankly, I have nothing to lose. "I guess I'm still stuck on the part where you're going on a mission for two years. Like, it just hit me now that's what you're doing."

I don't even have to break it down further for him. He totally gets it. He gets the subtext, the *I'm not Mormon; you are.* The *How long can we really be friends?* The *I don't just want to be your friend anyway.* I see it in his eyes.

And instead of brushing it aside or changing the subject or suggesting I learn the art of prayer, he stands up, tugging down the hem of his shirt when it rides up on the side. "Come on. Let's go for a hike. This is a lot to digest, for both of us."

There are a million trails headed up the hill, and when it's nice out, you'll usually pass someone on each one of them, but Utah weather is unpredictable, and our warm front is long gone; no one is hiking.

We have the outdoors to ourselves, and we trudge up the sludgy hillside until the houses in the valley are just tiny specs and we're both out of breath. Only when we stop do I realize how hard we've both been pressing up the trail, exorcising some demons.

Maybe the same one.

My heart is pounding. We are clearly headed somewhere to capital-T *Talk*—otherwise why not just put away the schoolwork and turn on the Xbox?—and the possibilities of where this could go make me feel a little insane.

It's going nowhere, Tanner. Nowhere.

Sebastian sits down on a boulder, bending to rest his arms on his thighs and catch his breath.

I watch the rise and fall of his back through his jacket, the solid muscle there—but also the straight posture, the unique *poise* of him—and absolutely defile him in my head. My hands all over him, his hands all over me.

I *want* him.

With a small growl, I look away and into the distance at

the BYU Y monument embedded in the distance, and it's honestly the last thing I want to see. It's made of concrete, and in my mind is a total eyesore, but it's revered in town and on the BYU campus.

"You don't like the Y?"

I look over at him. "It's fine."

He laughs—at my tone, I think. "There's an LDS story that the Native Americans who lived here many years ago told the church settlers that angels had told them whoever moved here would be blessed and prosperous."

"Interesting that the Native Americans don't live here anymore because of those settlers."

He leans forward, catching my eye. "You seem really upset."

"I *am* upset."

"About my mission?"

"I'm certainly not this upset about the Y."

He falters, brows flickering down. "I mean, didn't you know that's what most of us will do?"

"Yeah, but I guess I thought . . ."

I look up at the sky and cough out a laugh. I'm such a moron.

Was there a time I could have stopped this train of feelings from barreling into my bloodstream?

"Tanner, I'll only be gone two years."

My laugh is so dry it's dusty. "'Only.'" I shake my head,

blinking down to the ground at my feet. "Well, in that case, I'm totally not upset anymore."

We fall into silence, and it's like a block of ice has been dropped between us. I am an enormous jerk. I'm being such a baby right now; I'm making this endlessly awkward.

"Can you at least call me when you're gone?" I ask. I don't care anymore how crazy I must sound.

Sebastian shakes his head.

"E-mail, or . . . text?"

"I can e-mail family," he clarifies. "I can go on Facebook but . . . only for church-related stuff."

I feel when he turns to look at me, and the wind whips across my face so hard it hurts, but it also feels like the sky trying to slap some sense into me.

Wake up, Tanner. Wake the hell up.

"Tanner, I don't . . ." He rubs a hand on his face, shaking his head.

When he doesn't finish the thought, I press. "You don't what?"

"I don't understand why you're so upset."

He's fully staring at me, brows pulled down low. But it isn't confusion there; at least I don't think it is. I mean, I *know* he knows. Does he just want me to say it? Does he want me to say it so he can explain gently why us being together is impossible? Or does he want me to admit how I feel so he can . . . ?

I don't actually care why. The words are this heavy boulder in my thoughts, *in every waking thought*, and if I don't just let it roll straight out of me, it's going to crash around and break everything delicate inside.

"I like you," I say.

But when I look over, I see that these words aren't enough; they don't clear away the expression on his face. "And I know your church doesn't allow that kind of feeling."

He waits, so still, like he's holding his breath.

"It doesn't allow for guys to have feelings like this . . . for other guys."

He breathes out a barely audible "No."

"But I'm not LDS," I say, hardly any louder than him now. "In my family, it isn't a bad thing. And I don't know what to *do* about how I feel or how to stop feeling this way about you."

I was right. This doesn't surprise him at all. His face clears, but only long enough to cloud in a new way. Every feature grows tight. I wonder if maybe he wishes that I hadn't said anything at all, or that I'd just pretended that he was my new favorite dudebro and I would miss platonic hanging out and fumbling through this stupid book project with him for the next two years.

"I . . . ," he starts, and then exhales in a controlled stream, like each molecule of air is coming out single file.

"You don't have to say anything," I tell him. My heart

is racing. It's a fist punching, and punching, and punching me from the inside. Stupid, stupid, stupid. "I only wanted to explain why I was upset. And," I add, wanting the ground to open up and swallow me, "also why my book is basically about how it feels to fall for you."

I watch his throat as he swallows thickly. "I think I knew."

"I think you knew too."

His breath is coming out so hard and fast. His cheeks are pink. "Have you always . . . liked guys?"

"I've always liked whoever," I tell him. "I really *am* bi. It's about the person, not the parts, I guess."

Sebastian nods, and then he doesn't stop. He just nods, and nods, and nods as he stares at his hands between his knees.

"Why wouldn't you just be with a girl, then?" he asks quietly. "If you were attracted to them? Wouldn't it be so much easier?"

"That's not something you get to choose."

This is so much worse than I ever would have guessed. This is even harder than telling my dad. I mean, when I came out to him, I could tell he was worried about how the world might treat me and what kinds of obstacles I would meet that he would be unable to help me navigate. But I saw that reaction masked beneath the firmest discipline. He wants me to be accepted and does everything he can to hide his fears from me.

But here . . . I was so wrong about this. I shouldn't have

said anything to Sebastian. How can we even be friends after today? I have the melodramatic thought that this is what it's like to have a heart broken. There's no shattering; there's just this slow, painful fissure that forms straight down the middle.

"I think . . . I've *always* liked guys," he whispers.

My eyes fly to his face.

His lower lids are heavy with tears. "I mean, I know I have."

Oh my God.

"I'm not even attracted to girls. I envy you that. I keep praying I will be at some point." He puffs out a breath. "I've never said that out loud." When he blinks, the tears slide down his cheeks. Sebastian tilts his face up, looking at the clouds and letting out a sad laugh. "I can't tell if this feels good or terrible."

My thoughts are a cyclone; my blood is a river overrun. I scramble to think of the best thing to say, what I would want someone to say to me right now. The problem is, him admitting this to me is huge. It's not the same as anything I've ever faced, even with my family.

I go with my first instinct, the thing my dad said to me: "I can't tell you how good it feels that you trust me."

"Yeah." He looks over to me, eyes wet. "But I've never . . ." He shakes his head. "I mean, I've . . . wanted to, but never . . ."

"You've never been with a guy?"

He shakes his head again, quickly. "No. Nothing."

"I've kissed guys, but honestly . . . I've never felt like . . . this."

He lets this sink in for a beat. "I tried to change. And"—he squints—"to not even let myself *imagine* how it would feel . . . being with . . ."

This is like a punch to my solar plexus.

"But then I met you," he says.

His meaning hits me even harder.

I've been pulled out of my own body, and it's like watching this from across the trail. We're sitting on a rock, side by side, arms touching, and I know this moment will be seared into my history forever.

"The first time I saw you," I start, and he's already nodding, like he knows exactly what I'm going to say.

"Yeah."

My chest squeezes. "I never felt that way before."

"Me either."

I turn to him, and it happens so fast. One second he's staring at my face and the next second his mouth is on mine, warm and smooth and it feels so good. Oh my God. I make some guttural sound I can't control. He makes it back, and the growl turns into a laugh because he pulls away with the biggest smile the sky has ever seen, and then he's coming in to kiss me more and deeper, his hands on my neck.

His mouth opens, and I feel the tentative sweep of his tongue.

Light bursts behind my closed eyes, so intensely I nearly hear the popping sound. It's my brain melting, or my world ending, or maybe we've just been hit by a meteor and this is the rapture and I'm given one last perfect moment before I'm sent to purgatory and he's sent somewhere much, much better.

It isn't his first kiss—I know that—but it's his first real one.

CHAPTER NINE

On the walk back down the mountain, I don't even know what to do with my hands, let alone the gnarled tangle of my emotions. What just happened back there is tattooed onto every synapse I have; I'm sure I'll remember the sensation of every touch, even four decades from now.

Mom always tells me to take an accounting of my feelings. So, other than dizzy with lust, I'm feeling

Nervous.

Hesitant.

Desperate for that to happen again, and soon.

But the more queasy emotions are paled by the elation.

I

Kissed

Sebastian.

I felt his *mouth* on mine, and his tongue, and his laugh reverberating in the space between us. We kissed over and over. All kinds of kisses too. Fast and messy, and the slower deep ones that make me think of sex and long afternoons safely hidden in someone's bedroom. He bit my lip, and I did it back, and then he let loose a sound that I'll hear echoing around the frenzy of my thoughts for the rest of the weekend. It felt . . . so fucking right. Like, whatever I did before, with someone else, wasn't really kissing. Maybe it sounds dumb, but it was like every cell in my body was engaged. It makes everything else I've ever done feel sort of whitewashed and hard to remember. We kissed until the chill started crawling beneath our clothes.

Actually, now that I think about it, we kissed until Sebastian pulled away when my hand was flirting with the hem of his shirt.

He said he's never done anything with a guy, but it's clear the mechanics of this weren't new to him, and I'm betting he's had girlfriends. Still, we were both literally shaking with the same manic hunger, so maybe for him this was as different as it was for me.

Has he . . . had sex before? I'm guessing he hasn't—I'm sure Autumn would laugh and say that some of the LDS kids are the dirtiest kids at school, but something about Sebastian tells me he's different in that way, like, other than what we did today, he honors those sorts of rules.

But would he? With me?

The question triggers anxiety and heat in my blood.

Clearly I am getting way ahead of myself, but I'm worked up and high and don't know how this proceeds. Are we . . .

dating, or something? Even if only on the down low?

Will he see me again?

In my thoughts, my Mom taps a foot in the background, urging me to take a closer look at this. But the thought immediately evaporates. The feel of Sebastian is still too fresh.

When we stood up and dusted ourselves off, it felt a little like puncturing a bubble. Even out in the open up there, we seemed to be genuinely alone. But every step we take down the hillside dissolves more of that protective film. Provo spreads out, vast and tidy, below us.

I don't want to go back down there. I don't want to go home; no matter how much I love my house and my family and my bedroom and my music, I like being with him more.

Sebastian is predictably quiet. He's walking a safe distance away, out of reach, with his eyes on the spot his feet land before him on the trail. I'm *sure* he's more of an internal mess right now than I am, but I'm pretty messy, and it makes it hard to figure out what to say, whether we should be talking about what we just did.

In this type of post-make-out situation with girls—my only Provo experience to date—we'd be holding hands, and I'd be working to get my body under control as we walked back to town. No doubt with guys the same would apply, but not *Mormon* guys who—our silence and lack of touching seems to suggest we've realized this in unison—would be in for a heap of discussion and prayer if found walking down the mountain holding hands.

Still . . . despite it all, I hope this silence isn't a bad thing. Every now and then he looks over at me and smiles, and it makes me glow inside. But then I remember his easy smile (despite his stress) after his mom left the room, his easy smile when girls talk to him at school (but he only likes guys), and his easy smile in the photos of him on the wall at home (where he has to hide one of the biggest things about himself), and it feels like a shallow knife wound to wonder whether I could tell the difference between an easy smile that's real and one that's fake.

"You okay over there?" My voice gives an awkward waver.

The smile barely falters. "Yeah."

I dread what happens in five minutes when we reach the sidewalk outside his house. If there were some way to take him out of this town and drive until we ran out of gas and spend the night talking about this and helping him work through it, I would. I know what he's going to do, because it's a more dramatic version of what I did when I first kissed a guy: go back to his room and tell himself over and over the reasons why what happened can be explained by simple curiosity, nothing more.

"What are you doing this weekend?"

He inhales sharply, as if answering the question first requires putting himself back together. "I have a soccer tournament tomorrow, and then Lizzy and I are headed to Orem to help a family move in."

Ah, service. And Orem. Oof. The houses there are sometimes nicer but, if possible, it's quieter than Provo. "Where are the poor sacks moving from?"

The look he gives me is bewildered. "From Provo."

"You say that like no one would move to Orem from anywhere else."

This pulls a real laugh out of him, and I drink up the sight of his crinkly eyed smile. "No. I just mean . . ." He considers this and then laughs again. "Yeah, okay, I don't think anyone would move to Orem from anywhere but Provo."

"Heyyy, Sebastian?"

His cheeks flush at my tone, and his smile is somehow both shy and seductive. "Yeah?"

"Are you okay with what we just did?"

He blanches, and his answer comes too readily for my liking: "Yeah. Totally."

"You sure?"

Shy and seductive gives way to magnanimous, and I feel like we're talking about whether he genuinely liked my mom's overdone pot roast. "Of course."

I reach out, intending to touch his arm out of some instinctive need to connect, but he flinches and then looks around us in a momentary panic. "We. I, no. We can't." His words come out so choppy, like clumsy hacks at a tree trunk.

"Sorry."

"Not so close to town."

Clearly I'm not as good at schooling my emotions on my face as he is, because he winces, whispering, "I'm not trying to be a jerk. It's just reality. I can't . . . talk like that . . . not down here."

I avoid Mom all night when she gives me that lingering *wanna-talk* look, and claim I'm swamped with homework, which is true, but it's a Friday night and I'm not fooling anyone. Autumn calls. Manny calls. Eric calls. Everyone is headed somewhere, planning to do something, but it's the same nothing-something we've been doing for almost three years. Drinking three-two beer or root beer and watching people peel off to go make out in the dark corners doesn't sound like what I want to be doing tonight.

I want to be alone—but not so I can scroll through my Instagram feed full of hot male models. I want to replay the hike over, and over, and over. All but the end.

It's just reality.

Not down here.

I could spiral into this depressing truth, except Sebastian texts me before bed with a simple snowy mountain-top emoji and it's kerosene dumped on the flickering candle in my chest.

Standing, I pace my room, grinning down at the screen.

A mountain. Our hike. He's in his room, maybe, thinking about our hike.

My brain takes a detour. Maybe he's in bed.

A tiny voice raises orange flags, working to get my thoughts back on track.

I resist replying with a rainbow, or eggplant, or tongue and instead send the one of a sunset over the mountain. He replies with a soccer ball. Ah, his weekend. I reply with an emoji of a boat—a reminder of what we could do this summer . . . if he's around.

My phone buzzes in my palm.

Can we talk more about your book?

Yeah, of course.

My heart takes off running. In the flurry of our anxiety and admissions and kisses, I'd forgotten that he read my chapters and knew they were about him. I'd forgotten—though clearly he hasn't—that I have to turn this book in, eventually.

I can fix it.
I can change it so it's not so obvious.

We can talk about it in person, if that's okay.

I wince, cupping my forehead. *Be more careful, Tanner!*

Sure, of course.

After that, he sends a simple

Good night, Tanner.

I reply the same way.

And I remember something he said earlier today: *I can't tell if this feels good or terrible.*

"I have around fifteen thousand words," Autumn says Monday afternoon, in lieu of a greeting. She sits down at her place in the Seminar room and looks over at me expectantly.

I scratch my chin, thinking. "I only have about seventy Post-its."

It's a lie. I have chapter upon chapter written. Despite what I promised Sebastian, the words pour out of me every night. I haven't changed anything. I've *added*, wanting to capture every second.

"Tanner." She sounds like a schoolmarm. "You need to think of this in word count."

"I don't think of anything in word count."

"I am so surprised," she deadpans. "A book is around sixty to ninety thousand words. You're writing on a pad of Post-its?"

"Maybe I'm writing a children's book?"

She glances down, eyebrows raised. I follow her attention to the space in front of me. A Post-it sticks out from the bottom of my notebook, and the only words visible are

LICK HIS NECK

"I'm not writing a children's book," I assure her, tucking it back in.

She grins. "I'm glad to hear it."

"How many words are on a page, anyway?"

Autumn's sigh is long-suffering, and she probably comes by it honestly. I would drive me crazy too. "About two hundred and fifty, for twelve-point, double-spaced font."

I do some quick mental math. "You've written sixty pages?"

I've written more than a hundred.

"Tanner." She repeats my name with more emphasis this time. "We need to have the book done in May. It's late February."

"I know. I'm fine. I promise." I want her to believe me. But I don't want her to ask to see. Even showing my fake version to Sebastian was mortifying. If he was already anxious about the transparency of "Colin," and "Evan," and "Ian"— imagine if he read what I wrote Saturday night where *Tanner* and *Sebastian* made out on the mountain?

"Where were you Friday?" she asks, absently poking her pencil into a groove created in the top of her desk by a hundred other students doing exactly what she's doing.

"Home."

This gets her attention. "Why?"

"I was tired."

"Were you alone?"

I give her a flat stare. "Yes."

"I saw you and Sebastian walking up Terrace on Friday afternoon."

My heart takes off sprinting out of the room and down the hall. It doesn't even look back. Until now, it hadn't even occurred to me that anyone would see us, or anyone would *care*. But Autumn cares about nearly everything I do. And she saw us walking off onto a hike together—a hike, of course, where we ended up making out like the teenagers we are.

"We just went for a hike."

She smiles widely, like of course it was just a hike. But do I see something beneath the surface there, some suspicion?

Maybe I'm not playing it as cool as I thought.

"Auddy," I whisper. Just then Sebastian walks in with Mr. Fujita. My entire body seems to burst into flames, and I hope no one notices. Autumn stares straight ahead, and Sebastian's eyes meet mine before he looks away. His face flushes.

"*Auddy.*" I tug at her sleeve. "Can I borrow a pencil?"

I think she can sense some panicky edge to my voice because she turns, expression softening. "Of course." When she hands it to me, we register in unison that I'm already holding a pen.

"It doesn't matter to me that you're thinking what you're thinking," I whisper, now acting like I asked for the pencil just to get her to lean closer to me. "But it would matter to *him*."

She makes a screwball face of confusion. "What would I even be thinking?"

My heart unclenches.

When I look to the front of the class, Sebastian quickly turns his attention away from us. We haven't seen each other in six days. I'd wanted our first interaction after the hike to carry a secret, precious weight, but instead it's loaded with weirdness. He probably saw Autumn and me huddled together talking and then looking over at him. Is he worried I told her something? Is he worried she's read my book— the *real* version? I try to shake my head to communicate that everything is fine, but he's not looking at me anymore.

And he doesn't look at me for the rest of the class. When we break into smaller groups, he spends the entire time with McKenna and Julie, who flutter and fawn all over him. When Fujita goes to the front of the room and talks to us a bit about character development and narrative arc, he stands to the side of the class, reading through some of Asher's book.

When the bell rings, he simply turns and walks out, down the hall. By the time I get my things shoved into my bag and follow him out, all I see is his back as he pushes out of the exit and steps into the sun.

Over lunch, I pace and pace and pace, trying to figure out what to text him to let him know—without being obvious—that there's nothing to worry about.

"You're acting insane," Autumn says from the concrete block where she's spread out her tray of hummus and veggies. "Sit."

I plop down at her side to appease her, stealing one of her carrots and eating it in two crunching bites. But anxiety over Sebastian is a rubber band pulled tight around my rib cage. What if he's really upset about this book thing? Can I start over? Yes.

I can start over. I *should*.

I begin jiggling my leg in a new type of panic.

She doesn't seem to notice. "You should ask Sasha to prom."

"Prom again." I shove my thumbnail between my teeth, gnawing it. "I don't think I want to go."

"What! You have to."

"I don't, though."

She kicks my foot with hers. "So . . . Eric asked me."

I turn and gape at her. "What? How did I not know this?"

"I have no idea. I posted it on Instagram."

"Is this how we're sharing information now? Random posts on social media?" I pull out my phone. Sure enough there's a picture of her garage door covered in colored Post-its arranged to form the word "Prom?"

Super creative, Eric.

"You should ask Sasha. We could go as a group."

My breath seems to be lodged in my windpipe, and I take her hand. "I can't, Auddy."

She tries to hide the way her face falls. This is all good and terrible.

I mean, it's not like Sebastian would go with me, not in a million years. But my heart belongs to him right now, and until he decides what he wants to do with it, I can't take it back.

Autumn watches me, and we breathe in and out in this weird unison for a few quiet seconds.

I pull out of her grip and take another carrot, this time without any guilt. "Thanks."

She stands, leaving her lunch for me to finish and kissing the top of my head. "I've got to meet Mrs. Polo before sixth. Text me later?"

With a nod, I watch her disappear into the building before I grab my phone from where it lies beside me. Typing out a few efforts at fixing this, I settle on

How was your weekend?

He begins typing immediately. Blood rushes too fast in my veins.

The dots are there for a while, and then they disappear, and I'm expecting some dissertation on soccer and moving houses from Provo to Orem, but all I get, after about five minutes, is

Good! ☺

Is he kidding me?

I stare at my phone. My heart isn't just in my windpipe now. It seems to be beating in every organ, every empty space in my body. If I closed my eyes, I could hear it. I don't even know what to say. So, I just send a thumbs-up and put my phone away.

Four more carrots later, I check.

Sebastian replied with a mountain emoji and, a few minutes later, something else.

My grandparents are coming down from Salt Lake this weekend. Mom told me to invite you to dinner. I'm sure it sounds terrifying to you, but I promise they're nice.
And I'd like to have you there.

CHAPTER TEN

I assume there is some secret code buried in Sebastian's invitation to dinner. Maybe this is his way of reminding me that we have to be careful. Maybe this is the only way he can express his anxiety about my book and its potential to out him. Because, seriously, nothing gave me as clear-cut a picture about how different our home lives are than going to his house did; even he witnessed my fascination.

But then there's the matter of what we did on the mountain. We kissed, and it wasn't a simple kiss or accidental peck, but *a kiss*, with tongue and hands and lips and *intent*. I can't even think about it without feeling like I've been submerged in warm water. He could barely look at me without blushing as we walked on the trail. Is this dinner plan complete insanity?

What is he *doing*?

I scrutinize my reflection in the mirror across the room. My clothes are new, so they fit at least—I grew so fast for a few years that my sleeves were always a touch too short, my pants hovering just above my ankles. I've changed my shirt seven times, and with my haircut, I think I look pretty good.

I'm worried I'm too casual in a short-sleeved Quiksilver button-down. Still, to dress up in a shirt and tie would feel sort of presumptuous, like this is a date or *meeting the parents*.

Which it isn't. At least, I don't think . . .

"So, are you two like . . . *together*?"

Hailey leans against my doorway, arms folded over her chest as she judges me from across the room.

I look down at my shirt again. "Who the hell knows."

She clucks her tongue at me, pushing away from the door to flop gracelessly on my bed. "They won't like that kind of language."

I swear under my breath because, dammit, she's right. I have to be better about that.

"You don't know if you're together, but you're having dinner with his family? That's weird."

"How did you know about it?"

"If it was supposed to be a secret, you might want to rethink talking about it with Mom and Dad in the middle of the house."

"It's not really a secret, but . . ."

But it is.

Hailey nods. Apparently she doesn't need me to explain, and it's nice to see a flash of her not being a self-absorbed brat. When we decided to move here, my parents sat her down and made it very clear that her discretion is everything. Even I could see Mom's panic as she tried to explain to Hailey that outing me in a fit of rage somewhere would be disastrous. The rest of the world wouldn't always be as understanding as we were raised to be, especially here in Provo.

Bending to pick up the rest of my clothes, I remember that Hailey and Lizzy are in the same grade. "I'll get to hang out with Lizzy tonight. I'll tell her you said hi."

Hailey wrinkles her nose.

I laugh, putting T-shirts back in drawers and hanging up the rest. "You'd be surprised to hear that they're all like that."

Hailey rolls onto her back and groans. "She's always smiling and saying hi to everyone in the halls."

"What a monster."

"How can someone be that happy being *Mormon*?" In her words, for the first time, I hear our blind bias. "I'd want to punch myself."

I haven't spent any time with Lizzy, but I feel a prickle of protectiveness toward her anyway. "You sound like an ignorant dumbass."

Seeing my phone charging on the nightstand, she picks it up and types in my passcode. "Bet she wouldn't be so happy if she knew you wanted in her brother's pants."

"Shut up, Hailey."

"What? You think they'd still be inviting you to dinner if they knew? To them you're the devil trying to lure their son to hell."

"They don't really believe in hell," I say, grabbing for my phone. "Don't say that kind of stuff."

"Oh, is Sebastian tutoring you in Mormon, too?"

"Actually, *Mom* told me that. I'm just trying to get to know him better, and that means understanding where he comes from."

Hailey sees right through my self-righteous act. "Of course, of course, that's what I mean. Is he sharing the part where they're on the verge of accepting gay marriage? Or where they've admitted what a cruel and horrible mistake conversion therapy was?" she asks, laden with sarcasm. "He's not going to miraculously realize he likes you more than God or Jesus or Joseph Smith. This is a bad idea."

Her words poke at some vulnerable thing in my chest. I lash out, grabbing my phone from her hands. "You're a dick."

Sebastian's house isn't any less intimidating the second time around. From the outside, you can tell everything you need to know about the family inside: It's white and tidy, scrupulously maintained but not overdone. It looks welcoming and safe but also like I might mess it up somehow, break something, leave fingerprints *somewhere* . . . perhaps, for example, on their eldest son.

The Brothers' Suburban sits inside the open garage, and a newer Lexus is parked farther down. It must belong to the grandparents. I see my reflection in the passenger window as

I pass, and the tension in my nerves doubles. How will I make it through dinner with the most clean-cut family in Provo without outing myself as the lovesick boy I am?

Maybe Hailey was right: This is a really bad idea.

I brace myself before pressing the doorbell. It echoes through the house before Sebastian's voice rises from inside: "I got it!"

Thrill kick-starts in my chest.

The door swings open, and the sight of him sucks up every bit of oxygen on the porch. I haven't seen him since class, when things were weird and silent. He wouldn't look at me then, but he's definitely looking at me now. Any neuron in my brain that worried whether I should be here melts into gray matter goo.

Pulling the door closed behind him, Sebastian steps out onto the porch. He's in dress pants and a crisp white shirt that he's unbuttoned at the collar. I see smooth throat and collarbone and the suggestion of his chest just out of sight. My mouth waters.

I wonder if he had a tie on. Did he take it off for me? "Thanks for coming," he says.

Desperation takes over my pulse, and the thought of doing something to lose this pushes a blade of pain between my ribs. I want to immediately reassure him that I plan to rewrite my entire book, but go with "Thanks for inviting me" instead.

"Okay," he says, taking a step forward and motioning to the door. "So this is probably going to be boring. I just want to warn you up front. And I'm sorry if they start talking about church stuff." He pushes one hand into his hair, and it makes me think about how it felt to do that on the mountain. "They can't help it."

"Are you kidding? Look at me. I love church stuff."

He laughs. "Sure you do." With a deep breath, he smooths his hair down, straightens his shirt, and reaches for the doorknob.

I stop him with a hand on his arm. "Is this weird, or is it just me?"

I know I'm fishing for some indication that he remembers what we did, that he liked it.

His answer makes my whole goddamn week: "It's not just you." His eyes meet mine, and then his face breaks into the most amazing smile I've ever seen. No family portrait inside has been a witness to this one, not for a second.

On impulse, I blurt: "I'm starting over with my book."

His eyes go wide. "You are?"

"Yeah." I swallow thickly, choking on my pulse. "I can't stop thinking about . . . *that* . . . but I know I can't turn it in." Anxiety about the prospect of starting over and the thrill at seeing him bubble together in my stomach. The jittery sensation makes it easier to lie. "I've already started something new."

I can tell this is what he wanted to hear, and he brightens

instantly. "That's good. I can help you." He gives himself three seconds to look at my mouth before pulling his gaze back up to mine. "Ready?"

When I nod, he opens the door, giving me one last encouraging look before we step inside.

The house smells like fresh bread and roast turkey, and because it's slightly colder outside than in, the windows are steamy with a layer of condensation fogging up the glass. I follow Sebastian past the small living room in the front—*Hello again, picture of hot seventeen-year-old Sebastian. Hello, multiple Jesuses. Hello, oppressive plaque*—and down the hall to where the space opens into the family room on one end and the kitchen on the other.

A man I can only assume is Sebastian's dad is watching TV.

He stands when he sees us. He's taller than Sebastian by maybe only an inch or two, but with the same light brown hair and easy way about him. I'm not sure what I was expecting—a more intimidating posture, maybe?—but I'm unprepared when he reaches out to shake my hand and hits me with the same knee-buckling smile.

"You must be Tanner." His blue eyes are bright, and they twinkle with an easy sort of contentment. "I've heard a lot about you."

He . . . what now?

I shoot a questioning glance to Sebastian, who is pointedly looking the other way.

"Yes, sir," I say, quickly correcting with, "I mean, Bishop Brother."

He laughs and places a hand on my shoulder. "I'm only Bishop Brother in church. Call me Dan."

My dad wouldn't approve of me calling a parent by their first name, ever, but I'm not about to argue. "Okay. Thank you, Mr.—Dan."

An older man descends the stairs. Dark hair curls over the tops of his ears, and despite the austerity of his suit and the beginning of gray at his temples, it makes him look younger, even mischievous. "Aaron needed some Lego assistance. When he asked how I knew what I was doing, I told him it was because I have an engineering degree. Now he's set on getting an engineering degree to build Legos forever. Whatever works, I guess."

Sebastian steps up to my side. "Grandpa, this is Tanner. A friend from the Seminar."

He inspects me with the same bright blue eyes. "Another writer!" he says, and reaches out to shake my hand. "I'm Abe Brother."

"Nice to meet you, sir," I say. "And Sebastian's the writer. I'm closer to a monkey given free access to a keyboard."

Dan and his father laugh, but Sebastian stares at me, brows drawn. "That's not true."

I mumble some laughing version of "If you say so," because—honestly—the fact that I could only write about what was literally happening to me day to day and then let him read a badly bastardized version of my book is still mortifying.

In the kitchen, Sebastian introduces me to his grandmother, Judy, who asks me if I live nearby. I think it's code for *What ward are you in?*

"He lives over by the country club," Sebastian explains, and asks if there's anything we can do to help. When they say no, he tells them we're going to work on my manuscript.

Panic dumps ice water over my skin.

"Okay, honey," his mom says. "Dinner will be ready in about fifteen minutes. Could you ask your sisters to start washing up?"

With a nod, he leads me back down the hall.

"I didn't bring my new manuscript," I whisper, climbing the stairs behind him and doing my best to keep my eyes on my feet and not on his back.

At the top, the hallway splits off in two directions.

Bedrooms.

I watch as he stops in front of Faith's room. Inside, it's a fluffy pink and purple monstrosity with signs of preteen angst bleeding through at the edges.

He knocks and leans in. "Dinner soon, so wash your hands, okay?"

She says something in reply, and he steps out.

"Did you hear me?" I whisper, a little louder now. "I didn't bring my new manuscript."

Have I made a huge mistake by implying that I'm already working on something new? Is he going to want to see it soon?

He glances over his shoulder at me and winks. "I heard you. I didn't invite you here to work."

"Oh . . . Okay."

Sebastian's grin is wicked. "I guess I should give you the tour?"

I can already tell there's not much to see—upstairs it's a dead end with four doorways—but I nod.

"My parents' room," he says, pointing to the largest of the rooms. Another photo of the Salt Lake Temple hangs above the bed, along with a framed print that says FAMILIES ARE FOREVER. School photos and vacation snapshots line the walls; smiling faces beam from every direction.

"Bathroom, Faith, and Aaron. My room is downstairs."

We descend to the main floor, before turning the corner and starting down another set of stairs. Our footsteps are muted by the thick carpet, and the voices from upstairs grow quieter with every step.

For a basement, it's pretty bright. The stairway opens to another large carpeted family room with a TV, a couch, and beanbag chairs at one end, a small kitchenette at the other. A few doorways sit off to the side, and Sebastian points to the first. "Lizzy," he tells me, and moves on to the next one. "This is me."

My heart is in my throat at the possibility of seeing Sebastian's room.

Where he sleeps.

Where he . . .

I'm disappointed to find it's so neat. I'll have to file away my thoughts of Sebastian and rumpled sheets for another time. A row of soccer trophies line a shelf above a BYU Cougars flag. A bright blue foam finger emblazoned with a giant *Y* sits propped in a corner. I imagine him at one of the games, screaming along with the crowd, grin wild, heart hammering.

Sebastian stands near the door as I make a short circuit around his room, not touching anything but peering closer at photographs and the spines of books.

"I'm sad I didn't do more snooping at your house," he says, and I look back at him over my shoulder.

"Next time," I say with a grin. I'm struck momentarily dumb by the awareness that there *will* be a next time. "I'll admit I was surprised to be invited over for dinner with your family, after . . ." I search for the right words, but know he gets my meaning when a flush rises from his neck to his cheekbones.

"Mom likes to be involved in who is coming and going," he explains. "I don't have a lot of friends over."

"Oh."

"I think she wanted to get to know you better." He quickly holds up his hands. "No recruiting. I promise."

Another question pushes its way out of me. "Do you think she thinks I'm . . . ?" I let my rising eyebrows finish the sentence for me.

"I don't think it would ever occur to her. I think she just wants to know my friends, especially if she doesn't know them through church."

The way he's watching me sets off a game of pinball inside my stomach. Breaking away, I look around. There are books everywhere: on shelves and stacked near his bed, in small piles on his desk. Alongside his computer I see a leather-bound Bible in a zip-around cover. His initials are embossed in gold on the top.

"Um, those are for church," he explains, taking a step closer. He slips it free of its case and flips through the delicate pages.

"It's huge."

He lets out a small laugh. "It's called a quad," he says, and I take it from him again, feel the heft in my hand.

"That is a lot of rules."

"When you put it that way, yeah. I guess it is." He leans across me to open it, pointing to a table of contents. "But see? It has more than one book. There's the Bible, the Book of Mormon, the Doctrine and Covenants, and the Pearl of Great Price."

I blink up, surprised to find him so close. "Have you read it all?"

"Most of it. Some of it more than once."

My eyes go wide. Without question, these books would put me to sleep. I would be the worst Mormon. I would Rip Van Winkle my way through life if I had to endure it.

"When I have a question," he says, "I know the answers will be there."

I glance back down to the book. How can he be so sure? How can he have kissed me on the trail and still agree with what's in here?

"So, how is this different from just the Bible?" I feel like I should know this already. I mean, I'm not familiar with the Bible, either, but I am pretty confident they're not the same.

"You don't really want to hear this, do you?" His posture is self-conscious, a little unsure.

"Maybe just give me the Mormons for Dummies version."

Sebastian laughs and takes the book from my hands, turning to the right page. We're standing so close, and I'm thinking about moving closer, realizing that if anyone came in and saw us like this, they'd simply think we were reading Scriptures together.

"The Book of Mormon is another testimony that Jesus lived, that he was the son of God." He blinks over to me, checking to see that I'm listening. Seeing that I am, he bites back a smile and returns his attention to the book in his hands.

"It would be what came after the Bible, and outlines our Heavenly Father's plan for His children." Looking up at me again, he says quietly, "His children being us."

I laugh. "I got that part."

His eyes flicker to mine for a moment, amused. "The Doctrine and Covenants contains the revelations Joseph Smith and other prophets received from God. It's a way to receive guidance from modern prophets in modern times. This one," he says, flipping to the back, "is the Pearl of Great Price, which is said to be a record of the prophet Abraham in Egypt as a young man. As the church grew, they saw a need to put the stories and translations and history in one place, so more people could learn from it. These books are tools, in a way. If you read and sincerely pray, you'll find answers and guidance and know beyond a shadow of a doubt that the words are true."

I don't realize how intently I'm listening until I look up to see him watching me again. It's not that I agree with any of this, but there's something about his voice and the strength with which he believes it that has me hanging on every word.

"You're good at this," I say, but my mouth has gone dry. "Have you considered . . . I don't know, going on a mission and teaching this stuff? Get yourself a sign that says 'gone baptizing'?"

He laughs like I'd hoped he would, but now that we've

touched on the subject of his mission, I want to ask more. Where does he think he'll go? What will he do there? Who will he be with? Are there any loopholes in this no-contact thing? Will there be any space for me in his life at all?

"Briefly," he says with a grin. The moment grows quiet and his eyes flicker down to my mouth.

Has he thought about our hike as much as I have? It's the last thing I think about before I go to bed and almost the first thought in my head when I open my eyes. I want to kiss him so badly, and if the look on his face, the way his breathing has picked up is any indication, I think he wants it too.

Everyone is at the table when we reach the dining room. There are four chairs on each side and one at each end for his parents. Sebastian takes the empty seat nearest his dad, with me to his left, Lizzy and Aaron next to me, and his grand-parents and Faith on the other side.

The table is covered in plates and bowls of food, but nobody is eating. I realize why when Sebastian taps his foot against mine, nodding to where his hands are clasped in front of him.

Right. Prayer.

"Dear Heavenly Father," Dan begins, eyes closed and chin bowed to his chest. I quickly mimic the action. "We are thankful for this food and the bounty You have once again placed before us. We are thankful for the loved ones and new friends You have brought to our table. Please bless this food to nourish and strengthen our bodies and minds so that we may do right by You. Please bless those who cannot be here, and may they find their way safely back. We thank You for this, Lord, and ask that You continue to bless us. In the name of Jesus Christ, amen."

A hushed wave of *amens* move around the table, and just like that, the quiet is gone. Silverware scrapes across dishes, and plates are passed in a rush as everyone dives in. Faith wants chicken nuggets, and Aaron wants to know if his dad will play catch with him after school tomorrow. Lizzy is chatting about Young Women's Camp coming up.

I inspect the drink choices on the table in front of me: water, milk, strawberry kiwi Shasta, and even worse, root beer. Absolutely no caffeine. I pour myself a glass of ice water.

Dan hands Sebastian a platter full of turkey, and smiles over at me. "So, Tanner, Sebastian tells us you're originally from California?"

"Yes, sir. Palo Alto."

Sebastian takes some meat, and holds the platter for me, giving me an encouraging smile. My pinky finger grazes against his. I'll feel that brush of contact for hours.

Abe leans in, catching my eye. "California to Utah? That must have been quite a change."

I laugh. "It was."

Tanner's mother looks at me sympathetically from her

end of the table. "I can't imagine going from sun almost all year long to gloomy winter and snow."

"It wasn't so bad," I say. "The mountains are beautiful here, and we would get a lot of fog at home, anyway."

"Do you ski?" Judy asks.

"A little. We usually go up to Snowbird or the Canyons at least once a year."

His mom jumps back in. "With your whole family?"

I nod, reaching for a bowl of cheesy potatoes and scooping some onto my plate. "Yeah. There's just the four of us; I have a younger sister, Hailey."

Sebastian's mother hums. "Beautiful name."

"My parents are both pretty outdoorsy," I tell them. "My dad loves to bike and my mom runs."

Sebastian's dad swallows his food before asking, "What do they do, exactly? Sebastian said you moved here for your mom's job?"

That Sebastian has been chatty.

I take a sip of ice water and set down my glass. "Yes, sir. She is the CTO for NextTech."

Various sounds of interest pass around the table.

"When they opened a satellite office here, they wanted her to run it." More pronounced sounds of interest. "She writes computer software. She'd worked for Google in California, and left to come here."

"Wow," Dan says, impressed. "It must be quite a job

for her to have left Google. I hear they're very good to their employees."

"And his dad is a physician at Utah Valley," Sebastian adds. I look over at him and grin. He sounds braggy, like he's *proud*.

Judy's eyes go wide. "I volunteer there every Wednesday! What's his name?"

"Paul Scott. He's a cardiac surgeon."

"I know exactly who he is! I don't spend much time on that floor these days, but he is the nicest man. The Jewish cardiologist, right?" she asks, and I nod, surprised that she knows him but also that her identifier is that he's Jewish. "So attentive, and the nurses love him." She leans in and whispers dramatically, "And quite handsome, if I do say so."

"Grandma! Do you love Tanner's dad?" little Faith asks, scandalized, and the entire table laughs.

"Now, you know I only have eyes for your grandpa. But I'm not blind, either," she says with a wink.

Faith giggles into her cup of milk.

"That's right," Abe says. "She saw me at a church dance and hasn't looked away since."

"Mommy, you and Daddy met at a dance, too, right?" Faith asks.

"We did." Sebastian's mom looks across the table at Dan. "I asked him to Sadie Hawkins."

The little girl shoves a bite of food in her mouth before asking a garbled, "What's Sadie Hawkins?"

172

His mom goes on to explain, but all I can think about is what she just said. When she's finished, I turn to his dad. "You guys dated in high school?"

"We did," Dan says, nodding. "We met when we were seniors and married shortly after I came home from my mission."

My brain screeches to a halt. "You can do that?"

"We're told not to keep a girlfriend while we're on our missions," he says, smiling at his wife, "but there's no rule against writing letters once a week."

"As if you could tell these two anything." Judy looks at the younger children and adds, "Your dad won't like me telling you this, but you should have seen the love notes he used to write your mom. He'd leave them in his pocket and I'd always find them in the wash. They were crazy about each other."

The rest of the conversation blurs around me. All the other complications aside, if we could keep in contact while he's gone, that wouldn't be so bad. Two years isn't that long, and I'll be at school anyway. Maybe by then the prophet will have had a revelation.

It could work, couldn't it?

For just a moment, I feel hope.

Dan pulls me out of my fog. "Tanner, does your family attend synagogue in Salt Lake?" He looks over to Abe. "I'm trying to remember where the closest one is."

This is awkward. *I* don't even know where the closest synagogue is.

"Well, let's see now," Abe says. "There's Temple Har Shalom in Park City—"

"Too far." Dan shakes his head as if he's decided himself it's unsuitable for us.

"Right, and the city has a handful—"

I decide to nip this in the bud. "Actually, no, sir. Sirs," I amend, to include Abe. "We don't attend temple services. I would say my parents are more agnostic at this point. Mom was raised LDS, and Dad isn't very Jewish anymore."

Oh my Jesus, what have I said?

Silence swallows the table. I'm not sure which gaffe was more artless: that I admitted my mom is ex-LDS, or that I so casually referenced dropping a religious faith like a hot potato.

Sebastian is the one to break into the quiet. "I didn't know your mom was LDS."

"Yeah. She was raised in Salt Lake."

His brow is drawn, his mouth a gentle, wounded line.

His mom jumps in brightly. "Well, that means you have family locally! Do you see them?"

"My grandparents are in Spokane now," I tell them. I have the foresight to not mention that I've never met them in my eighteen years, and mentally high-five myself. But it means my mouth is left unattended and is off running: "But my aunt Emily and her wife live in Salt Lake. We see them at least once a month."

The only sound at the table is the vague shifting of uncomfortable people in their chairs.

Oh my Jesus, what have I said again?

Sebastian kicks me under the table. When I look at him, I see that he's struggling to not laugh. I barrel on: "My dad's mother comes to stay with us a lot. He's also got three siblings, so our family is pretty big." I lift my water, fill my mouth with it so I'll shut up. But once I swallow, one more bit of mania manages to escape: "Bubbe still attends synagogue weekly. She's very involved. Very spiritual."

Sebastian's heel lands on my shin again, and I'm sure he's telling me to calm the hell down, maybe even that I don't need to be connected to religion to be accepted. Who knows. But it certainly feels that way. Everyone here is so put together. They eat neatly, napkins in lap. They say "Please pass the . . ." and compliment their mother's cooking. Table posture is across-the-board impressive. And, maybe more importantly, rather than asking me more about my parents' backgrounds or about Emily, Sebastian's grandparents deftly move away from my verbal diarrhea, asking about specific teachers and upcoming sports events. The parents offer gentle reminders to their kids to keep their elbows off the table (I swiftly pull mine back too), to go easy on the salt, to finish their vegetables before they ask for more bread.

Everything stays so aboveboard, so safe.

Our family seems almost savage in comparison. I mean, we aren't knuckle-dragging, monosyllabic oafs, but Mom has been known on occasion to tell Hailey to "knock it the hell off" at the dinner table, and once or twice Dad has taken his meal into the living room to get away from the sound of Hailey and me bickering. But an even more noticeable difference is the closeness I have at home that I only really understand now that I'm here with this warm but docile group of strangers. Over spaghetti and meatballs, the Scott family has been known to have an in-depth conversation about what it means to be bisexual. Over Bubbe's kugel, Hailey actually asked my parents if you can get AIDS from giving a blow job. It was horrifying to me, but they answered it without hesitation. Now that I'm thinking about it, if Sebastian came over for dinner, I'm pretty sure Mom would send him home with some bright, affirming bumper sticker.

Maybe those kinds of dinner conversations—minus the blow job talk—happen here behind closed doors, but I don't think so. Where my parents might dig a little deeper in an effort to understand Sebastian and his family, I'm not really surprised that nobody asks why my mom left the church or why Dad no longer goes to synagogue. Those conversations are hard, and I'm but a lost sheep passing through their obedient flock, most likely impermanent. And this is *the bishop's house*. Happy, happy, joy, joy, remember? Everyone is on their best behavior, and nobody will pry or make me feel uncomfortable. It wouldn't be seen as polite. From my experience, Mormons are nothing if not polite. *This* is who Sebastian is.

CHAPTER ELEVEN

Mom and Dad are waiting up for me when I get home, mugs of tea that have grown cold in front of them and tight, expectant smiles in place.

Of course I couldn't lie to them on my way out the door about why I'd be eating elsewhere, but it wasn't an easy exit, either. They'd stood on the porch and watched me drive off, wordless. I honestly felt like I'd been stealing something.

"So?" Dad asks, patting the barstool beside him at the counter.

The chair scrapes across the tile, and we wince. For some reason, I find the jarring cacophony hilarious, because it's already a pretty loaded moment—me, home from dinner at the house of the bishop, whose son I'm sort of falling in love with, my parents disapproving vehemently—and the horrible screech seems to only lend more weight here.

My parents have their own kind of secret language; an entire conversation happens in their single shared look. I work to swallow the hysteria bubbling up in my throat.

"Sorry." I sit down, slapping my hands on my thighs. "So. Dinner."

"Dinner," Mom echoes.

"It was good. I think?"

They nod. They want more.

"His family is super nice." I widen my eyes meaningfully. *"Super. Nice."*

Mom laughs a little unkindly at this, but Dad still seems more concerned than anything.

"But it wasn't, like, a date," I clarify. "I mean, obviously. This wasn't me *meeting the family*. It was just dinner."

Mom nods. "They like knowing his friends, especially if they don't know you from church."

I stare at her for a few beats. "That's exactly what Sebastian said."

"Think about it," she tells me. "Everyone they know goes to their church. Having your son—especially if you're a bishop around here—spending time with someone who isn't LDS? You want to make sure they're okay."

"Except I'm *not*, at least not as far as they're concerned."

I can tell Mom doesn't like this answer, but she waves her hand, like she wants me to keep going. So I tell them about the evening and how his parents met in high school. I tell them about my gaffes about Emily, and Mom's past. Mom makes a face—because these shouldn't be gaffes at all. I tell them that we talked about his mission again, for only a second though, and they listen the entire time, rapt.

Still, I can see the worry etched into tiny lines in their faces. They are so genuinely afraid I'm going to fall for him, and it will end in heartbreak for one or both of us.

"So . . . you liked them?" Dad asks, ignoring the way Mom turns and stares at him like he's a traitor.

"Yeah. I mean, they didn't feel like my *tribe*, but they were nice enough."

Now it's Dad's turn to make a face. Family is everything to my parents, but maybe especially to my father because, obviously, Mom's parents aren't in the picture. My dad's family makes up for it in spades. His mother comes to live with us for three months every year and has since I was a newborn. Since my grandpa died six years ago, she doesn't like being home alone, and Dad is happier when she's here under his roof. After she's with us, she goes and stays with his brother and sisters in Berkeley and Connecticut, respectively, taking turns with the grandchildren.

If I could have Bubbe here year-round, I would. She is amazing, and witty, and brings a certain type of comfort into the house that we can't seem to muster when it's just the four of us. My parents are great—don't get me wrong—but Bubbe makes things feel warmer somehow, and over the last two decades my parents have been married, Bubbe and Mom have grown very close. Dad wants a relationship like that with us when he's older, and for us to have it with our in-laws, too.

Honestly, it probably bothers him more than it bothers Mom that she doesn't talk to her parents anymore.

I can see these thoughts pass over Dad's face as I'm talking, and I reach out, patting his shoulder. "You look stressed, Dad."

"I haven't often seen you . . . invested in someone before," he says carefully. "We worry this isn't the ideal first choice." His eyes move away, to the window.

Taking a deep breath, I try to think of the best thing to say. Even if what he says is true, that truth feels like a sticker on the surface of my emotions: easy to peel off. I know Sebastian isn't right for me. I know how likely it is that I'll get hurt. I simply care more about trying than I do about protecting myself.

So I tell him what I think he wants to hear: "It's just a crush, Dad. He's a nice guy, but I'm sure it will pass."

For a second, he lets himself believe this. Mom, too, stays notably silent. But when he hugs me good night, he holds me tight for three deep breaths.

"Good night, guys," I say, and jog upstairs to my room.

It's only eight on Friday night, and I know I won't be tired for hours still. Autumn texts that she's going over to Eric's. I'm relieved that I won't feel guilty for bailing on something with her yet again and send a long string of eggplant emojis to which she replies with a long string of bird flip emojis.

I wonder if Sebastian updated his emoji keyboard and

what he feels about having that crude gesture on his phone, whether he's even noticed it, whether he'd ever *use* it.

Everything, everything circles back to him.

Mom is on a run, Dad is at the hospital, and Hailey is stomping around the house, complaining that no one does any Saturday-morning laundry anymore.

I point out that her hands aren't broken.

She punches me in the side.

I put her in a headlock and she screams bloody murder, trying to reach up to claw at my face, screaming, "I hate you!" loud enough to shake the walls.

The doorbell rings.

"Good job, asswipe," she says, shoving away from me. "The neighbors called the cops."

I reach forward, swinging the door open with my best *she-did-it* smile.

My world stops spinning.

I didn't know what "bemused" meant until I looked it up last year. I always thought it meant something like "coyly amused," but in fact it's more like "bewildered," which is exactly how Sebastian looks standing on my porch.

"What the—?" My surprised grin spreads as far as it can, east to west.

"Hey." He lifts his hand to scratch the back of his head and his bicep pops, smooth and tan.

I am goo.

"Sorry." I step back, gesturing him inside. "You walked in on a murder in progress."

He laughs, taking a step forward. "I was going to say . . ." Blinking up past me, he smiles. I can only assume Hailey is standing there, shooting death rays at my back. "Hi, Hailey."

"Hi. Who are you?"

I want to shove her into the wall for being so rude but resist because with this one bitchy question she's made it seem like I'm not walking around gushing about this guy constantly. "This is Sebastian."

"Oh. You're right. He *is* hot."

And there it is. Turns out I do want to shove her into the wall.

With a small laugh, he reaches out to shake her hand. To my horror, she stares at it for a breath before taking it. When she looks at me, I lift my eyebrows in an *I'm-going-to-finish-killing-you-later* gesture. If Mom or Dad were here, she would be nothing but manners. With just me, she's prime asshole.

"Want to come upstairs?" I ask him.

He glances at Hailey, who has already stomped back down the hall to the laundry room, and nods. "Where are your parents?"

"Mom's on a run. Dad's working."

I think he gets the subtext here. The air between us crackles.

Beneath our feet, the wood stairs creak, and I'm hyper-aware of Sebastian behind me. My bedroom is the last at the end of the hall, and we walk down there in silence; my blood feels like it's bubbling up to the surface of my skin.

We're going to my room.

He'll be in my room.

Sebastian walks in, looks around, and doesn't seem to flinch when I gently click the door shut behind me—breaking Mom and Dad's open-door policy. But hello: kissing might happen here, and Hailey is in beast mode. That door is getting s-h-u-t.

"So this is your room," he says, taking it in.

"Yeah." I follow his gaze, trying to see it through his eyes. There are a lot of books (none of them religious), there are a few trophies (most of them for academics), and a few pictures here and there (I'm not holding a Bible in any of them). For once I'm glad that Dad makes me keep my room clean. My bed is made; my laundry is contained in the basket. My desk is empty except for my laptop and . . .

Oh shit.

Sebastian wanders over, thumbing the stack of blue Post-it notes. It's already too late to say anything. I know what the one on top says.

WE LEAVE EACH OTHER
CUTTING SHORT AT THE USUAL STALEMATE.

I IMAGINE WHERE HE GOES THERE'S A QUIET
DINNER
SECRETS STUCK LIKE GUM BENEATH THE DINING
TABLE.
HE IMAGINES WHERE I GO THERE'S SOMETHING
DIFFERENT.
AT BEST: RIOTOUS LAUGHTER, GIDDY FREEDOM
AT WORST: CURSING, VAGUE SIN.
MAYBE I'M GIVEN SIPS OF WINE.
BUT EVEN IF THIS IS WHAT HE THINKS
HE ISN'T JUDGING ME
I HOPE SOMEDAY HE LOVES ME
GOOD NIGHT, HE SAYS
I WANT TO KISS, AND KISS, AND KISS HIM.

"What is this?"

"Um." I walk over, pulling it off the top to read it as if I'm not sure what it is. In fact, I couldn't be more sure; I wrote it just last night. "Oh. It's nothing."

I count to five, and five, and five again. The whole time, we're just staring at the bright blue Post-it note in my hand.

Finally, he takes it back. "Is this about me?"

I nod without looking at him. Inside my chest, feet stomp and animals roar.

His hand comes up my arm, from my wrist to my elbow, tugging gently so I'll turn to look at him.

"I like it," he whispers. "But it's not going in your new book, right?"

I shake my head. Lie number two.

"Are there more?"

I nod.

"Use your words, Tanner," he says, laughing at the end.

"There are more, but I'm, um, writing about something else now."

He nods. "What's the new one about?"

I blink over to the window, making this up on the fly. "Same idea, but he doesn't fall in love with the bishop's son."

I watch as the words "fall in love" roll over him. His mouth twitches. "So you'll let me read it?"

"Yeah." I nod quickly. "When there's enough to read." The implication of this makes me queasy, but I know at some point I'll have to stop writing about Sebastian, write something else, and let him and Fujita read it. The weirdest part? I don't want to stop writing about Sebastian. It's almost like I need to keep writing it in order to find out how it ends.

He lets go of my arm and walks over to my bed, sitting down on it. My heart dumps fuel everywhere; there's drag racing happening in my veins.

"I got my author copies today. I want you to read my book too," he says, fidgeting with a hangnail. "But I'm worried you'll think it's terrible."

"I'm worried I'll think it's amazing and I'll be even more obsessed with you than I am."

Thankfully, he laughs at this like I hope he will. "I'm nervous."

"About the book coming out?"

He nods.

"Are you writing a second one?"

Another nod. "It was a three-book deal. And I really love it. It feels like what I'm supposed to be doing." He looks up at me, and the light coming in the window catches his eyes in a way that seems nearly divine. "After the hike," he says, and then nods to me for confirmation, as if I would somehow not know what he's referring to, "I went home and . . ."

Jerked off? "Freaked out?"

He laughs. "No. I prayed."

"That sounds like freaking out."

Sebastian shakes his head. "No. Praying is calming." He stares at my wall, where I have a framed photograph of the Golden Gate Bridge that Dad took a few years before we moved. "I haven't felt guilty about it," he says, quieter now. "Which is unexpected."

I didn't realize how much I needed to hear him say that until he did. I feel like a pool raft, lazily deflating in the sun.

"Guilt is sort of a sign that I'm doing something wrong," he says, "and when I feel peaceful, I know God approves of what I'm doing."

I open my mouth to reply, but turns out, I have no idea what to say to that.

"Sometimes I wonder whether it's God or the church that feels the strongest about these things."

"My opinion?" I say carefully. "A God worthy of your eternal love wouldn't judge you for who you love while you're here."

He nods at this for a few seconds and finally smiles shyly up at me.

"Will you come over here?" he asks, and this is the first time I've ever seen him wearing an unsure smile.

I ease down next to him on the bed, and not only can I feel how much I'm shaking, but I can *see* it. I clamp my hands between my knees to keep them from flapping across the mattress.

I'm around six foot three. He's probably five foot ten, but right now his emanating calm seems to loom over me like the shade of the big willow tree out back. He twists, planting his right fist at my hip, and his left hand comes up to my chest, pressing gently until I realize he's urging me to lie back. Having lost all voluntary muscle control, I essentially collapse onto the mattress, and he hovers over me, looking down.

He got a haircut this morning, I realize. The sides are cut close to his scalp again, and the top is soft and floppy. His dancing lake-in-the-sun eyes stare down at me, and I'm possessed by heat, and need to feel, and feel, and feel.

"Thanks for coming to dinner last night," he says, and his gaze is doing a full circuit of my face. Over my forehead and down my cheeks, hovering near my mouth.

His eyes flicker down, watching me swallow before I say, "Your family is nice."

"Yeah."

"They probably thought I was a lunatic?"

He grins. "Only a little."

"You got a haircut."

His eyes go unfocused, staring at my mouth. "Yeah."

I bite my lip, wanting to roar because of how he's looking at me. "I like it. A lot."

"Yeah? Good."

God, enough small talk. I pull him to me, my hand on the back of his neck, and he comes down immediately, mouth over mine, weight partially on me, breath leaving his lips in a relieved gust. It starts so slow, this relieved, leisurely kissing. First through self-conscious smiles and then with the confidence that this—*us*—is so good it aches.

And it ramps up from there, like a plane at takeoff, and we're infected at the same time with something wilder and more desperate. I don't want to think that we're hungry like this because there is a ticking clock. I am unwilling to play the chess game too many moves ahead. Instead, I think we're hungry like this because we feel something deeper. Something like love.

His chest rests on mine and his hands are in my hair and he makes these small, deep sounds that slowly unravel me until the only word I can think, over and over, is *yes*.

Everything feels yes.

His mouth is yes, and his hands are yes, and over me, on top of me now, he's moving and yes, yes, yes.

I run my hands down his back and under his shirt to the warm skin of his torso. Yes. There's no time to appreciate that I've answered my own garment question because then his shirt is off, yes, and mine comes off; skin to skin is

Y

E

S

and I've never been on bottom like this, never wrapped my leg around someone's hip, never felt this kind of shifting and friction, and he tells me he thinks about me every second

yes

and tells me he's never felt this way, he likes to suck on my bottom lip, he wants to pause time so we can kiss for hours

yes

and I tell him truthfully that nothing ever felt as good as this does, and he laughs into my mouth again because I'm sure it's obvious how into this I am. I am a monster beneath him, with arching hips, an octopus with hands everywhere at once. I don't think anything in the history of time has felt this good.

"I want to know everything about you," he says into me, frantic now, his mouth moving over my jaw, stubble scraping my neck.

"I'll tell you anything."

"Are you my boyfriend?" he asks, and then sucks my bottom lip before laughing at himself, as if this isn't the most amazing thing anyone has ever said to me in the history of my life.

"Um, *yes*."

Boyfriend. Yes.

"Even if I'm your boyfriend now, I won't tell anyone about this," I whisper.

"I know."

His hand comes over me, between us—oh my God—and through my track pants it seems so innocent and so dirty at the same time, but the dirty is washed away when I look up and realize he's watching my face, awestruck.

And I get it. I've never done that either.

In a daze, I reach down too. His eyes roll back before they fall closed.

It doesn't feel real. How can this be real?

He moves forward once, and again, and this is the most amazing thing I've ever done—

I don't even hear the footsteps or the door before I hear my dad's mortified "Oh!" and the door slam shut.

Sebastian vaults off me, turning to face the wall, his hands pressed to his face. In the ringing silence, I'm not sure what's just happened.

I mean, I *know* what happened, but it went so fast that for a few pounding heartbeats I think I can pretend that he and I just shared the same hallucination.

This is so bad on so many levels. No longer do I get to play the *We're just friends!* angle with the grown-ups downstairs. Now we're *in* it, and I'm going to get an earful from one or both of my parents.

But without a doubt, this is so much more humiliating for Sebastian.

"Hey," I say.

"This is bad," he whispers. He doesn't drop his hands, doesn't turn back to me. His back is bare, and a map of muscle. I'm drowning in dueling reactions: giddy that I have a hot boyfriend now, and terrified that this one moment has ruined everything.

"Hey," I say again. "He's not going to call your parents."

"This is so bad."

"Just come here, okay?"

Turning slowly, he walks back over, lowering himself onto the bed without looking at me.

He groans. "Your dad walked in on us."

I take a beat to find the best response, settling on, "Yeah, but he's probably more mortified than we are."

"I highly doubt that."

I knew he wouldn't go for that line of reasoning, but it was worth a try. "Look at me."

After about ten seconds, he does. I see how he softens, and the relief of that makes me want to stand up and pound my chest. "It's okay," I whisper. "He isn't going to tell anyone. He's probably just going to talk to me later."

As in, he will *for sure* talk to me later.

With a defeated exhale, Sebastian closes his eyes. "Okay."

I lean forward, and I think he senses my proximity even if he doesn't open his eyes because his mouth twitches in a suppressed smile. Pressing my lips to his, I offer up my bottom lip, the one he likes to suck, and wait for him to respond. Slowly, he does. It's nothing like the heat of before, but it's real.

He pulls away, standing and reaching for his shirt. "I'm going to head home."

"I'm going to stay *right here*."

Sebastian fights another grin at the implication of this, and then I watch as the mask slowly slips into place. His forehead relaxes, and a vibrant light comes into his eyes. The easy smile I'm learning to distrust spreads across his face. "Walk me out?"

It takes Dad only fifteen minutes after Sebastian has left to come to my room. His knock is tentative, almost apologetic.

"Come in."

He steps in, shutting the door carefully behind him.

I'm not sure whether I should be angry or remorseful, and the combination sends prickly static across my skin.

Dad walks to my desk chair and takes a seat. "First, I should apologize for not knocking the first time."

I place my open book facedown on my chest, looking over at him from where I'm lying on the bed. "Agreed."

"I don't know what to say beyond that." He scratches his jaw and then reconsiders. "No, that isn't quite true. I know what I want to say, but not where I should start."

Pushing to sit up, I swivel to face him. "Okay?"

"I know how you feel about Sebastian. And I'm pretty sure it's reciprocated."

"Yeah . . ."

"I also know that you feel this genuinely, and not out of some curiosity or rebellion."

How do I even respond to this? I nod, aware that my expression is mostly one of vague confusion.

"Does Autumn know?"

I blink, confused. "Auddy?"

"Your best friend, yes."

"I'm not *out* to Autumn, Dad. I'm not out to anyone, remember? Like Mom wants?"

"Look," Dad says, resting a hand on my knee. "Two other things I want to say. I'll start with the easy one. It's tempting, when you fall for someone, to ignore everything else in your world."

"I'm not *ignoring* Audd—"

"I'm not finished," Dad says, voice gently stern. "I need you to promise me that you are taking care of your other relationships. That you are spending time with Autumn and Eric and Manny. That you are still being a role model for Hailey. That you are being an attentive and helpful son to your mother."

I nod. "I promise."

"The reason I say that is because it's important you keep your life full, regardless of how deep your relationship with Sebastian becomes. This is independent of his religion. If it continues, and works out somehow, then you'll want friends who accept and support you. And if, for whatever reason, it does not work out, you'll need to have people you can turn to."

I stare at the floor, feeling an odd warring reaction inside. He's right. It makes sense. But I hate the implication that I don't know this already.

"The other thing I wanted to tell you . . ." Dad scratches his jaw, looking away. "I don't share your mother's history with the church, so my reaction to your relationship is drastically different from hers." He meets my eyes again. "That said, I don't think she's wrong. I don't necessarily agree with each of her reasons for warning you off, but I do agree that it's complicated. I assume his parents wouldn't approve?"

"I think it goes a shade beyond disapproval."

Dad is already nodding at this. "So anytime you're with him, you're going behind his parents' backs."

"Yeah."

"I don't love that," he admits quietly. "I like to think that if the situation were reversed, you would either be open with us, or not betray our wishes while you lived at home."

"The difference, Dad, is I can be open with you."

"The thing is, Tann, you're eighteen, and what you do with your body is your choice. But what you do under my roof is still something I have a say over."

Oh.

"I love you and your sister and your mother more than anything on this planet; you know that."

"I know."

"And I know you are attracted to girls, and boys. I know you're going to experiment, and I never, for one second, begrudge you that." He meets my eyes. "The complexity here is not that Sebastian is male. If I had walked in on you with someone outside the church, I probably wouldn't have even said anything, and we'd exchange a knowing look across the dinner table and that would be that."

My desire to curl into a ball and rock in the corner rises. This is so awkward.

"But I don't want you and Sebastian using our house to sneak around behind his parents' backs."

"Dad," I say, face hot. "We don't have a lot of other options."

"Sebastian is an adult. He can move out if he wants his own space with his own rules."

This, right here, is essentially Dad closing the door on any discussion. I know this opinion comes from experience. And sitting here, staring at the face I know nearly as well as my own, I realize how hard it is for Dad to say this to me.

After all, according to his family, he fell in love with the wrong woman twenty-two years ago.

CHAPTER TWELVE

Autumn's mom answers the door, stepping back to let me in. She gave her daughter the dimpled smile genes, but that's about it. Auddy is all red hair and freckled nose and bright blue eyes. Mrs. Green has black hair, brown eyes, olive skin. I wonder what it's like to every day look at a daughter who is so similar to Mrs. Green's dead husband. It's either wonderful, or heartbreaking. Most likely it's a combination of both.

We have a routine: I kiss her cheek hello, and she tells me she has some Yoo-hoos in the fridge, and I act excited. They're the weirdest thing, like watery chocolate milk in juice boxes. I mentioned I liked them one time to Mrs. Green, my first summer here, and she's been buying them for me ever since. Now I always feel obligated to take one with me on my way up to Auddy's room, but, actually, I can't stomach them anymore. We've been doing a small science experiment with a plant on her shelf: Can African violets survive solely on Yoo-hoo?

Princess Autumn is sprawled on her floor with a draft of

her chapters in front of her. She's even marking it up with a red pen; I can't make this shit up.

"Auddy, you are the cutest, nerdiest person I have ever met in my entire life."

She doesn't even look up when I enter. "Don't be patronizing."

"Don't you know that red pen can be viewed as harsh and can hurt students' esteem? Better to use purple."

Blue eyes turn up to my face. "I like red."

Her long ginger hair is piled in an enormous bun atop her head. "I know you do."

Pushing off her elbows, she moves to sit up, cross-legged now. "What are you doing here?"

This hurts a bit, because it tells me Dad is right. Before Sebastian, it wouldn't be weird for me to just come over here anytime. Now I see Auddy maybe once a week outside of school, and spend so much more time alone, writing words and words and words about him, no matter how much my brain screams at me to start the new book. "I can't stop by and hang with my best girl?"

"You've been busy."

"So have you." I give her a meaningful eyebrow waggle. "Did you have fun with Eric the other night?"

"If by 'fun' you mean 'make out until our faces fell off,' then yes."

My jaw drops. "Seriously?"

She nods, blushing through her freckles.

"And how many 'your mom' jokes did he make?"

Laughing, she sings, "None!"

"I don't believe you." To Eric, everything is an opportunity for a *your mom* or *that's what she said* joke. It doesn't matter how many times we remind him it's no longer 2013.

"It was fun," she says, leaning back against her bed. "I like him."

I reach forward, pinching her cheek. There's something tight inside me. It isn't jealousy exactly, but it's some weird sense of loss, like it isn't Tanner and Autumn versus everyone else anymore. We both have other people now.

Even if we don't know it yet.

"What's that face?" She draws a circle in the air in front of me.

"Just thinking." I pick up her red pen, doodle on the sole of my sneaker. "I wanted to talk to you."

"This sounds serious."

"It's not." I narrow my eyes, thinking. "No, it is, I guess. I just wanted to say I'm sorry."

She doesn't say anything, so I look up at her, trying to read her expression. I know Autumn better than I know almost anyone, but right now I can't decipher what she's thinking.

"For what?" she says finally.

"For being so distracted."

"It's a busy term," she says. She leans back and tugs at a

loose thread at the hem of my jeans. "I'm sorry I haven't been the best friend lately either."

This surprises me, and I look up at her. "What do you mean?"

"I know you've become friends with Sebastian, and I guess I was jealous."

Oh. Alarm bells go off in my head.

She swallows, and it's awkward and audible, and her voice wavers when she says, "I mean, he's getting some of your time that I usually get. And there's something so intense about it when you guys are talking, so I feel like he might be taking something that's mine." She looks up at me. "Does this make sense?"

My heart jackhammers up and down in my chest. "I think so."

Her face goes red, telling me that this conversation is more than just about friendship. If she were just staking her bestie territory, she wouldn't blush; she would be brass. But here it's something else. And even if she doesn't know the extent of things between me and Sebastian, she feels the intensity of it. There's some awareness she can't name yet.

"I'm jealous," she says, and tries to look brave with her chin in the air. "For a lot of reasons, but I'm working on some of them."

It feels like I've been knocked in the chest with a hammer. "You know I love you, right?"

Her cheeks flush bright pink. "Yeah."

"Like, you're one of the most important people in the world to me, okay?"

She looks up, eyes glassy. "Yeah, I know."

In truth, Autumn has always known who she is and what she wants. She's always wanted to be a writer. She's white; she's straight; she's beautiful. She has a path she can follow that will lead her to these things, and no one will ever tell her she can't or shouldn't want them. I'm good at the physical sciences but am ambivalent about following my dad down the doctor trail, and have no idea what else I could be. I'm just a bisexual half-Jewish kid who's falling in love with an LDS guy. The path for me isn't as clear.

"Come here," I say.

She crawls onto my lap, and I wrap her up in my arms, holding her as long as she'll let me. She smells like her favorite Aveda shampoo, and her hair is soft on my neck, and I wish for the hundredth time to feel something like desire for her, but instead it's just a deep, desperate fondness. I see now what Dad meant. It's easy to say that I'll keep my friendships, but I need to do more than that. I need to protect them too. More than likely we aren't going to be going to the same college next year, and now is the time to make sure we're solid. If I ever lost her, I'd be devastated.

· · ·

The Warriors are playing the Cavs in a rematch, and Dad is planted on the couch. Every line of his body is tense. The degree to which he despises LeBron James eludes me, but I can't fault him for his loyalty.

"I saw Autumn today," I tell him.

He grunts, nodding. He's clearly not listening.

"We eloped."

"Yeah?"

"You need a beer, and a beer gut, if you're going to be this zoned out at the television."

He grunts again, nodding.

"I'm in trouble. Can I have five hundred dollars?"

Finally, Dad looks at me, horrified. "What?"

"Just checking."

Blinking a few times, he exhales in relief as the game goes to commercial break. "What were you saying?"

"That I saw Auddy today."

"She's well?"

I nod. "I think she's dating Eric."

"Eric Cushing?"

Again I nod.

He processes this the way I expected him to. "I thought she was into you?"

There's no way to answer this without sounding like a dick. "I think she is, a little."

"Did you tell her about Sebastian?"

"Seriously? No."

The game comes back on, and I feel bad for doing this now, but it's like termites eating at a wooden beam. If I don't get it out of me, I will be riddled with anxiety. "Dad, what happened when you told Bubbe that you were dating Mom?"

He gives the television a last, reluctant glance before he reaches for the remote, muting it. And then he turns, pulling one leg up on the couch to face me. "This was a long time ago, Tann."

"I just want to hear about it again." I've heard the story before, but sometimes we hear things as kids and the details sort of wash over us—what sticks isn't always what is meant to. The story of my parents' courtship is one of those things; it was romantic when they first told us about it, and the reality of how hard it was on Dad and his family—and Mom, too—was lost in the greater narrative that they got their happily ever after.

I was thirteen, Hailey was ten, and the story they gave us was abbreviated: Bubbe wanted Dad to marry her best friend's daughter, a woman who was raised in Hungary and moved here for college. It was normal, they told us, for the parents to be hands-on with the matchmaking. They didn't explain the other bits that I learned over time, talking to aunties and cousins, like how having the family involved makes sense in a lot of ways: Marriage is forever, and infatuation wears off. Finding someone that comes from the same community and has the same values, in the end, is more important than being with the person you want to have sex with for a few months.

But Dad met Mom at Stanford, and, as Mom says, she knew. He fought it, but in the end, he knew too.

"I met your mom my first day in med school," he recounts. "She was working at this funky sandwich shop near campus, and I came in, frazzled and starving. I'd moved only the day before classes started, and the reality of being away from home was so different from my expectations. It was expensive, and busy, and my workload was unbelievable already. She made the most perfect chicken sandwich, handed it to me, and asked if she could take me to dinner."

I've heard this part. I love this part, because usually Dad slips in a joke about the bait and switch with Mom's cooking. This time, he doesn't.

"I thought she meant it to be friendly because I looked so overwhelmed. It never occurred to me that she would think we could date." He laughs. "But when she showed up, it was clear what her intentions were." And now his voice lowers. I'm no longer given the surface version of the story. I'm given the version a grown man gives to his grown son.

Mom is beautiful. She's always been beautiful. Her confidence makes her nearly irresistible, but combined with her brilliance, Dad never stood a chance. He was only twenty-one, after all—young for a med student—and that first night, at dinner, he told himself it wouldn't hurt to spend some time with her. He'd had a couple of girlfriends before, but nothing serious. He always knew he would eventually return home and marry someone from the community.

Mom and Dad dated in secret, and for two years together, even while he was staying at her place, he still insisted he would marry a Jewish woman. Every time he said this, she would hide her hurt and say, "Okay, Paul."

When Bubbe and Dad's sister Bekah came to visit for three weeks, Mom never once met them. He didn't tell them anything about her, and the entire time they were in town, she never once saw him either. It was like he disappeared. He didn't call or check in. She broke up with him after they left, and Dad never argued. He told her he wished her well and watched her walk away.

Whereas Dad has always been mute on the subject of their time apart, Mom has jokingly referred to it as the "Dark Year." Joke or not, I've seen photos of them from this time, and the images always made me mildly uneasy. My parents are capital *I,* capital *L In Love.* Dad thinks Mom is brilliant, beautiful; he thinks she hung the stars. She thinks he is the smartest, most wonderful man alive. I'm sure their time apart made them grateful for what they have, but it's clear they felt this way even before the breakup. In those photos, they both have this sort of carved-out, hollow look. The bluish circles under Dad's eyes seem like dark phases of the moon. Mom is already on the thin side, but in the Dark Year, she was skeletal.

He admits to me now that he couldn't sleep. For nearly a year, he slept only a couple hours a night. It wasn't rare to find med students who were up all night studying, but Dad is an organized, dedicated guy and had no problem staying on top of his work. He couldn't sleep because he was in love with her. That year, it had felt like he was a widower.

He went to her old apartment and begged her to take him back.

I never knew this. I've always heard that they just happened to run into each other on campus one day and Dad knew from then on he couldn't stay away from her.

"Why did you tell us that you ran into Mom on campus?"

"Because that's what I told Bubbe," he says quietly. "It hurt her for a long time that I married Jenna. But to think that I had sought her out and begged her to come back to me would have been a more active betrayal."

My heart aches when he says this. Every time I go see Sebastian feels like an active betrayal of Mom. I'd just never had a name for it before now.

"Jenna sat me down," Dad says, "and yelled at me for an hour. She told me how much it hurt to be put in a position where she had no power. She told me that she would always love me, but she didn't trust me." He laughs. "She sent me away and told me to prove myself to her."

"What did you do?"

"I called Bubbe and told her that I was in love with a

woman named Jenna Petersen. I bought a ring and went back to your mother's apartment and asked her to marry me."

Apparently, Mom said, "When?" and Dad said, "Whenever you want." So they were married at the courthouse the next morning, another detail I'd never heard. I've seen countless photos of their official wedding: the signing of the ketubah, Mom obscured from view beneath her veil, waiting to walk down the aisle, my Dad breaking the glass under the chuppah, the row of photos of honored friends and family members giving the *sheva brachot*—the seven blessings, my parents being lifted on wide wooden chairs while their friends danced around them. Their wedding photos line the upstairs hallway.

I had no idea they were legally married nearly a year before.

"Does Bubbe know that you were married earlier?"

"No."

"Did you feel guilty?"

Dad smiles at me. "Not for a single second. Your mom is my sun. My world is only warm when she is in it."

"I can't imagine what that was like for you." I look down at my hands. "I don't know how to stay away from Sebastian, or if I even could." I need to ask, as much as I dread the answer. "Did you tell her that you walked in on me and Sebastian?"

"I did."

"Was she mad?"

"She wasn't surprised, but she agreed with what I said to you." He leans closer, kissing my forehead. "What Jenna learned with me was that she always had power, even when she felt like I didn't acknowledge her. You are not helpless here. But you need to be clear about what you are and are not willing to tolerate." He tucks a finger under my chin, lifting my face to his. "Are you willing to be a secret? Maybe you are for now. But this is your life, and it will stretch out before you, and you are the only person who can make it whatever you want it to be."

CHAPTER THIRTEEN

Sebastian texts me before bed every night and first thing every morning. Sometimes they're as simple as **Hey**.

Other times they're longer, but barely. Like the Wednesday after dinner at his house, he sent me a note that said simply, **I'm glad we agree on the situation.**

I take it to mean we're definitely together.

I also take it to mean we're definitely a secret.

Ergo . . . we're a little homeless. My house is now out of the question. His house is *definitely* out of the question. We could hang out in my car, but not only does that feel too shady, it feels dangerous, like we'd be inside a fishbowl with a sense of privacy and no real walls.

So—beginning the weekend after we're busted in my room by Dad—at least twice a week, we hike. Not only does it allow us to get away from prying eyes during a time of year when no one else is out on the mountain, but—at least for me—it helps burn off the extra energy I seem to be carting around. It's cold as hell some days, but worth it.

Things we have done in the two weeks after he whispered the word "boyfriend" into a kiss:

- Celebrated our one-week and two-week anniversaries, in the cheesiest way possible—cupcakes and handmade cards.
- Stealing knowing glances in every Seminar class we're in together.
- Passing off letters as subtly as we can—usually under the guise of handing him pages of "my book" to read and him handing them back. (Sidenote: My book is flying out of me, but it's still not the one I'm supposed to be writing. Thinking about it sends me into a spiraling panic. Moving on.)
- Rereading the letters until the paper is practically falling apart.
- Finding creative use for emojis in texts.

Things we have *not* done since he whispered the word "boyfriend" into a kiss:

Kissed.

I know it's hard for both of us to be able to feel closer without *feeling closer*, but everything else is so good right now,

I won't let the lack of groping pull me down off cloud nine.

Autumn takes a page off the stack of handouts going around the room and drops the pile onto my desk, pulling me out of my fog. Sebastian is at the front of the room, bent over a notebook with Clive and Burrito Dave. It doesn't matter that Clive is dating Camille Hart and Burrito Dave is dating half the junior class. Jealousy spikes sharply between my ribs.

As if he can sense the fire of my stare, Sebastian glances up and then quickly away, blushing.

"Do you . . . ?" Autumn starts, and then shakes her head. "Never mind."

"Do I what?"

She leans in, whispering, "Do you think he *likes* you? Sebastian?"

My heart trips over her question, and I force my attention back down to the laptop in front of me, typing the same word over and over again:

Thursday
Thursday
Thursday
Thursday

Thursday is three days from now, and when we're going on our next hike.

"How would I know?" I ask. Casual. Unconcerned.

Maybe I *should* ask Sasha to prom.

Fujita makes the rounds, checking in on us to see how we're progressing with word count, character arcs, plot development, pacing. It's March 10, and we're supposed to have twenty thousand words written, as well as our critique buddies picked out. I have more than forty thousand words written, but they're all this—and I can't turn *this* in.

Autumn didn't want to work with me—everyone but me was surprised by this—so I lack a partner and am going to fly under the radar with this as long as possible. I should have known better though. Despite his hippie, messy-literary-dude vibe, Fujita is on top of the details.

"Tanner," he says, coming up behind me so stealthily that I jump, slamming my laptop closed. Laughing, he bends in close, stage-whispering, "What kind of novel are you writing, kid?"

If I had my way, it would go from young adult to pornography, but I'm pretty sure that's not going to happen. See also: secret, homeless relationship.

See also: must start new book ASAP.

"Contemporary," I tell him, adding in case he saw my string of *Thursday*s, "I'm just a little stuck today."

"We all have days when it flows and days when it doesn't." He says this loud enough for the benefit of the entire class, and then leans in again. "You're on track otherwise?"

"Surprisingly," I say, "yes."

Depending how you look at it.

"Good." Kneeling down, Fujita comes eye to eye with me. "So, it looks like everyone else is paired up for critiques. Since you're on track but struggling today, I'm going to have Sebastian give you feedback." My pulse trips. "I know he's been talking to you a bit about your idea, and in the absence of an even number of students in the class anyway, that seems like the easiest way to go." He pats my knee. "Work for you?"

I grin. "Works for me."

"What's this?"

Fujita and I both look up as Sebastian materializes at our side.

"I was just letting Tanner know that you'll be his critique buddy."

Sebastian smiles his easy, confident smile. But his eyes dance over to me. "Cool." A pair of perfect, dark eyebrows rise. "That means you'll have to show me what you've got so far."

I lift my brows in return. "It's pretty bare."

"It's okay," he says breezily. "I can help you find the shape of it."

Autumn clears her throat.

Fujita claps us both on the back. "Great! Onward!"

Sebastian slides a folder onto my desk. "Here are some of my notes from our last meeting."

My pulse sprints out of the starting gate, and my voice shakes when I try for a casual, "Awesome, thanks."

I feel Autumn's attention on the side of my face the second he walks away.

Without looking over at her, I ask, "What's up, Auddy?"

She leans in, whispering. "You and Sebastian just had an entire conversation in sexual innuendo."

"We did?"

She goes quiet, but her intentional pause is a living, breathing thing between us.

Finally, I meet her eyes, and before I look away, I wonder whether she sees it all there. I know it's written on my face as clearly as it would be on a banner in the sky:

SEBASTIAN + TANNER = A BOYFRIEND THING.

"Tanner," she says again, slowly, like she's nearing the end of an Agatha Christie novel.

I turn in my seat to face her. My skin is on fire beneath my shirt, chest hot and prickly. "I think I'm going to ask Sasha to prom."

T,

How was your weekend? Did your family
end up going down to Salt Lake?
This weekend at the Brother house

was insane. It seemed like our doorbell was constantly ringing. We had a few Primary activities at church on Saturday. Lizzy and I were helping run it, and trying to get twenty six-year-olds into a single-file line is like trying to work with feral cats. Plus, I think Sister Cooper gave them candy when she finished her activity with them before ours, so they were wild.

I got home late on Saturday and went up to my room and thought about you for about two hours before I could fall asleep. Well, I thought about you, and prayed, and then thought about you some more. Both activities make me feel amazing—the more I pray, the more confident I am that what we're doing together is right—but then I'm also lonely. I wish we could be together at the end of days like this, talking about it in the same space rather than through these letters. But we have this, at least.

And we have Thursday. Is it crazy I'm so excited? You might have to control me. All I want to do is kiss, and kiss, and kiss you.

When are you going to let me read the new book? You're good, Tanner. I'm dying to see what you're writing now.

I'm heading off to campus and will be in class for the Seminar today to give this to you. When you finish reading it, just know that I was thinking about kissing you while I was writing this sentence (and all the ones that came before it, probably).

Yours,
S

I read it about seventeen times before tucking it into the deepest pocket in my backpack, where I will hold it until I get home and can put it in a shoe box on the top shelf of my closet. (Now that I think about it, if I die today, a shoebox on the top shelf of my closet is where my parents will probably look first for clues about what happened to me; I should find a better hiding place.)

I let these meandering thoughts distract me from the uneasiness I feel regarding Sebastian's curiosity about my book.

Don't get me wrong: I actually love what I have so far.

But I have to face reality: At this point, I'm not going to have a book I can turn in. So far, that truth has been this repellent magnet, and my thoughts bound freely away from it. I've told myself again and again that I can demonstrate that I did it, give Fujita some sample pages before Sebastian appears in the narrative—under the request of confidentiality—and ask him to grade me on what he sees. Fujita is a pretty laid-back guy; I think he'd actually do this for me. Or, I can admit to Sebastian that this book is still about us and have him press to grade some of the projects, mine included, under the guise of taking some of the work off Fujita's hands.

But what if Fujita doesn't go for it? What if he won't give me a passing grade based on the first twenty pages or so? I've been writing in a fever. Since I crap-edited the first four chapters for Sebastian, I haven't changed any details, not even our names. In the present version, it's all there in stark black-and-white for the world to see, and I don't *want* to change it. The Seminar. Bishop Brother. Our hikes on Y Mountain. My parents, my sister, our friends. I know Sebastian needs me to, but I don't want to hide.

He's waiting for me at the trailhead at three on Thursday. We have only a few more hours of daylight, but I'm hoping we can stay out later tonight, stretch this into the darkness. I know he doesn't have any classes until after lunch tomorrow, and I'm happy functioning on little sleep.

"Hey." He shakes his head, flipping his hair out of his eyes. My skin hums. I want to press him up against a tree and feel his hair slip through my fingers.

"Hey."

God, we are idiots, grinning like we just won a gold medal the size of Idaho. His eyes are impish, and I love this side of him. I wonder who else sees it. I want to think what I see right here in his eyes is his one, pure truth.

"You brought water?" he asks.

I turn halfway to show him my CamelBak. "The big one."

"Good. We're going up today. You ready?"

"I'll follow you anywhere."

With an enormous grin, he turns, charging up the path and into the thick, rain-damp brush. I follow close behind. The wind picks up as we climb, and we don't bother with small talk. It reminds me of going to a seafood buffet with Dad when he took me to a conference in New Orleans. Dad got this intensely focused look on his face. *Don't eat the filler*, he said, meaning breadsticks, tiny sandwiches, even the beautiful, tiny-but-flavorless cakes. Dad made a beeline for the crab legs, crawdads, and seared tuna.

Breathless small talk right now would be breadsticks. I want to feel Sebastian's body right up against mine the next time he says anything.

Most people hiking Y Mountain stop at the enormous painted *Y*, but after we arrive there a half hour into our hike, we continue, leaving the town sprawling below us. We head where the trail narrows and continues south, then turns east into Slide Canyon. Everything is more rugged here, and we watch our step more carefully to avoid stinging nettle and scratchy brush. Finally, we reach the area of the mountain where there is pine tree cover. We need it less for shade—it's getting colder, in the high twenties now, but we're bundled in jackets—and more for privacy.

Sebastian slows and then sits under a thatch of trees overlooking Cascade Mountain and Shingle Mill Peak. I collapse beside him; we've been hiking for well over an hour. Any question I had about whether we'd be here together at night has been put to rest. This is farther than we've hiked together on a weekend, let alone a weekday, and it will take us at least another hour to get home. The sun hangs low in the horizon, turning the sky a heavy, seductive blue.

His hand slides into mine, and he leans backward, pressing our joined fists to his chest. Even through his puffy jacket I can feel his body heat. "Holy . . . that was a hike."

I stay seated, leaning back on my other hand to balance and stare out at the canyon. The mountains are dramatically green with patches of white snow. Their sharp peaks and smooth rock faces are dotted with trees. It's so unlike the valley below us, where everything seems to be dotted with TGIFridays and convenience stores.

"Tann?"

I turn, looking down at him. The temptation to crawl over him and kiss him for hours is nearly impossible to resist, but there's also something pretty great about being able to just sit here and hold hands

with

my

boyfriend.

"Yeah?"

He brings my hand to his mouth, kissing my knuckles. "Can I read it?"

It came at me so fast. I was expecting it, but still. "Eventually. I'm just . . . It's not *done*."

He pushes to sit. "I get that. You just started it, right?"

The lie is starting to turn me black inside.

"Actually," I say, "I'm having a hard time beginning. I want to write something new. I do. But every time I sit down at my laptop, I write about . . . us."

"I get that, too." He goes quiet for a few breaths. "I meant what I said. What I read was really good."

"Thanks."

"So, if you want, I could work on editing it? Making it less recognizable?"

I'm sure he'd do an amazing job, but he's busy enough as it is. "I don't want you to worry about it."

He hesitates, and then squeezes my hand. "It's hard not to, though. You can't turn that book in to Fujita. But if you don't turn in something, you'll fail."

"I know." Guilt flashes cold across my skin. I'm not sure what would be worse: asking for his help here, or trying to start all over.

"I like thinking about us, too," he tells me. "I think I would *like* editing it."

"I mean, I could send you what I have in chunks to work on, but I don't want to send it to your BYU e-mail."

I can tell that a separate e-mail address had never occurred to him. "Oh, right."

"You can make a new Gmail account, and I can send it there."

He's already nodding, and it accelerates as the implication of this seems to hit him more fully. I know exactly what he's thinking: We could write e-mails to each other *all the time*.

He's so adorable, I hate to burst his bubble.

"Just be careful what you do at home," I tell him. "My mom created the Parentelligentsia software. I know better than most how easily they could track every move you make."

"I don't think my mom and dad are that tech savvy," he says, laughing, "but point taken."

"You'd be surprised how easy it is," I say, half proud, half deeply apologetic to those in my generation who've been hosed by my mother's first invention. "It's how my parents found out about me . . . and my interest in guys. They installed the software in our cloud and could see everything I'd searched, even if I cleared my history."

His face goes ashen.

"They came to talk to me about it, and that's when I admitted I'd kissed a boy the summer before."

We've alluded to this but never spoken about it freely.

Sebastian shifts, facing me. "What'd they say?"

"Mom wasn't surprised." I pick up a rock, tossing it over the edge of the cliff. "It was harder for Dad, but he wanted it to be easy. He deals with his feelings on his own time, I think. The first conversation, he asked me if I thought it was a phase, and I said maybe." I shrug. "I mean, I honestly didn't know. It's not like I'd been through this before. I just knew that I felt the same when I looked at pictures of naked guys as I did when I looked at pictures of naked girls."

Sebastian flushes bright red. I don't actually think I've seen his face this heated before. Has he never looked at naked pictures? Have I embarrassed him? Amazing.

His words come out a little garbled: "Have you had sex?"

"I've been with a few girls," I admit. "Only kissed guys."

He nods, as if this makes sense.

"When did you know?" I ask.

His brow furrows. "Know what? About you being bi?"

"No." I laugh, but bite it back because I don't want it to come off as mocking. "I mean, that you're gay."

The confusion on his face deepens. "I'm not."

"Not what?"

"Not . . . *that*."

Something seems to catch in the spinning wheel of my pulse, and it trips. For a breath, my chest hurts. "You're not gay?"

"I mean," he says, flustered, trying again, "I'm attracted to guys, and I'm with you right now, but I'm not gay. That's a different choice, and I'm not choosing that path."

I don't even know what to say. The sensation inside me feels like sinking.

I let go of his hand.

"Like, you're not gay, you're not straight, you're . . . *you*," he says, leaning forward to catch my eyes. "I'm not gay, I'm not straight, I'm *me*."

I want him so much it's nearly painful. So when he kisses me, I try to make the feel of him sucking my bottom lip block out anything else. I want his kiss to be the clarification, the reassurance that a label doesn't matter—*this* is what matters.

But it doesn't. The entire time we kiss, and later—when we stand and hike back down—I still have that sensation that I'm sinking. He wants to read my book, the book about falling in love with him. But how can I send my heart to him when he's just said, in no uncertain terms, that he doesn't speak its language?

CHAPTER FOURTEEN

Late Saturday afternoon, Autumn jogs after me, down my driveway. Finally we are free of my house, and she lets loose her barrage of questions.

"Were you talking to him when I got here?"

"Yeah."

"You're telling me he doesn't like you? Tanner, I *see* how he looks at you."

I unlock the car, opening the driver's side door. I'm 100 percent not in the mood for this. Even after talking to him this morning, Sebastian's words from Thursday still bounce around my head.

Not . . . that.

I'm not gay.

"You don't see how he looks at you?"

"Auddy." It's not a denial; it's not a confirmation. It'll have to work for now.

She climbs in after me, clicking her seat belt in, and then turns to face me. "Who is your *best* friend?"

I know the right answer to this one: "You. Autumn

Summer Green." I turn the ignition, and laugh despite my dark mood. "Still the best bad name ever."

Auddy ignores this. "And who do you trust more than anyone in the world?"

"My dad."

"After him." She holds up her hand. "And after your mom, grandmother, family, blah, blah."

"I don't trust Hailey as far as I could throw her." Turning, I look over my shoulder to back out of the driveway. Dad won't let me rely solely on the backup camera in the sensible Camry I drive.

Autumn slaps the dashboard. "I'm making a point! Stop thwarting me."

"*You* are my best friend." I turn the steering wheel and set out of our neighborhood. "I trust you the most."

"So why do I feel you aren't telling me something important?"

A dog with a bone, this one. My heart is a hammer again, *tap-tap-tapping* against my sternum.

I *was* on the phone with Sebastian when Auddy got to my house. We were talking about his afternoon away at a church youth activity.

We were *not* talking about how un-gay he is.

We were also not talking about my book.

"You're with him *all the time*," she needles.

"Okay, first of all, we're honestly working on my book,"

I say, and a metaphorical knife pokes my conscience in reprimand. "You chose to work with Clive—which is fine—but now I'm paired with Sebastian. We hang out. Second, I don't know if he's gay, or what"—and that's certainly not even a lie—"but third, his sexuality isn't our business."

The only reason it's mine is because . . .

Only now does it register that giving this relationship oxygen outside our Sebastian + Tanner bubble would be amazing. Even the idea of talking to someone other than Mom and Dad about this makes me feel like I can take a full breath for the first time in weeks. I want more than anything to talk with someone else—Auddy, especially—about what happened on Thursday.

"If he *is* gay," she says, chewing a nail, "I hope his family isn't too terrible about it. It makes me sort of sad." She holds up her hand. "I know you aren't gay, but shouldn't the bishop's son be allowed to like dudes if he wants to?"

This conversation makes me feel mildly queasy. Why *haven't* I come out to Auddy yet? Yes, Mom's panic before we moved was mildly traumatizing to me, and Auddy's friendship is my bedrock. I guess I've never wanted to risk it. But still. Autumn Summer Green is the least closed-minded person I've ever known, isn't she?

"Someone needs to have a revelation," I say, glancing at her. "Call the prophet; let him know it's time to accept the queer folk into his heart."

227

"It's gonna happen," she says. "Someone is going to have a revelation. Soon."

Revelations are a big part of the LDS faith. It's a pretty progressive idea: The world is changing, and the church needs God to help guide it through these times. After all, they are the *Latter-day* Saints. They believe anyone can have a revelation—that is, a communication directly from God—as long as they're seeking it with the intention of doing something good. But only the current living prophet—the church president—can have revelations that make their way into church doctrine. He (always a he) works with two counselors and the Quorum of the Twelve Apostles (also men) "under the inspiration of God"—to determine what the church's position is on any given matter and whether rules get changed.

For example, the hot button: Polygamy was okay back in the day. Autumn's mom once explained it to me that, at the time of early LDS settlements, there were many women and few men to protect them. By taking on multiple wives, men could better provide for the women in the community. But in my own digging, I read how the US government didn't love this aspect of the church and wouldn't grant Utah state rights. In 1890, Church President Wilford Woodruff declared that plural marriage was no longer acceptable to God—apparently, he'd had a revelation about it.

Conveniently, it was what the US government needed to hear; Utah became a state.

The idea of a revelation about wholly accepting openly LGBTQ members in the church is pretty much the single golden thread I hang on to for hope whenever I let myself think past today or tomorrow with Sebastian. Brigham Young himself said, in essence, he hopes that people in the church don't just take what the leaders say as God's truth; he wants them to pray and find that truth within themselves, too.

No doubt Daddy Young wasn't talking about homosexuality, but there are those of us who live in the modern world, who are not LDS, and who sincerely hope that a revelation about homosexuality *not* being sin is just a matter of time.

And yet even with the legalization of same-sex marriage, it still hasn't happened. Autumn taps her fingers on her thighs in time with the music. I hadn't been listening to what's been playing, but now it's a song I love. It has this slow, building beat, and the singer's voice is throaty, scratchy. The lyrics seem innocent at first, but it's clear it's about sex, just like nearly every song on the radio.

It makes me think about sex, and what that would be like with Sebastian. How it happens. How we'd . . . be. It's this vast unknown, both thrilling and terrifying.

"Did you talk to Sasha?" Autumn asks me out of the blue.

"About what?"

She stares at me. "About *prom*."

"Seriously, Auddy. Why are you so hung up on this?"

"Because you said you were going to ask her."

"But why do you *care*?"

"I want you to go to your senior prom." She smiles winningly at me. "And, I don't want to go alone with Eric."

This sets off an alarm bell in my brain. "Wait, why?"

"I just want to take things slow with him. I like him, but . . ." She looks out the passenger window, deflating when she sees that we've arrived at the lake.

"But what?" I ask, pulling into a parking spot.

"No, nothing like that. He's good. I just want you there." She holds my eyes for one . . . two . . . three. "Are you sure you don't want to go with me?"

"Do you *want* to go with me? Dude, Auddy, I'll go with you if that's what you need."

She slumps. "I can't back out with Eric now."

Relief floods my blood. Sebastian would understand, surely, but the idea of dancing with Autumn when I'd rather be with Sebastian doesn't seem fair to either of them.

Turning off the ignition, I lean back, closing my eyes. I don't feel like being here with Manny or any of the other kids from school, messing around in the parking lot with remote-controlled cars. I feel like going home and writing out this tangle and heat in my head. I'm upset with Sebastian, and hate that he's gone for the entire day when I feel so twisted inside.

230

"How many girls have you been with?"

I blink over to her, startled by the abrupt question. "What?"

Even in hindsight, I feel this weird twinge of disloyalty to Sebastian for having slept with anyone else.

Autumn is blushing. She looks sheepish. "Just curious. Sometimes I wonder if I'm the only virgin left."

I shake my head. "I promise, you're not."

"Right. Like, I'm sure you have a whole bunch of stories I don't even know about."

God, she's making me uneasy.

"Auddy, you know who I've been with. Three. Jessa, Kailley, and Trin." I reach for her hand. I need air. "Come on."

Utah Lake used to be gorgeous. It was full, and splashy, and a great place for all kinds of environmentally irresponsible water sports that positively horrified my parents when we first moved here. If you ask my dad, Jet Skis are the devil's work.

Now the water level is low and the algae cover is so thick that even if it were swimming weather, we probably wouldn't venture in. Instead, we just lurk between the parking lot and the shore, eating the pizza Manny brought and throwing stones as far out into the horizon as we can.

I dream about college life and living in a big city where I can spend a day in museums or at a bar watching soccer, or doing any number of things that don't involve sitting around, talking about the same crap we talk about every day at school. I dream about convincing Sebastian to move with me and showing him that being gay isn't a bad thing.

Kole brought a few of his college friends I've never met, and they're flying radio-controlled helicopters near the parking lot. They're big, footbally, and the kind of loud, frequently swearing guys that have always made me mildly uncomfortable. I'm no Manny, but I'm not small by any stretch, and I know there's a certain calm to me that's often interpreted as threatening somehow. One of them, Eli, sizes me up with a frown before looking at Autumn as if he's going to roll her up in a slice of pizza and eat her. He's muscular in a suspicious way, with a thick neck and splotchy, acne-scarred skin.

She shuffles into my side, playing the girlfriend role. So I immediately take on the boyfriend role, tucking my arm around her, meeting his gaze. Eli looks away.

"You don't want to experiment with that?" I joke.

Auddy grunts out a *"No."*

After our call this morning was cut short by Autumn's arrival, Sebastian left for an activity at some park in South Jordan. I know he isn't going to be home until after six, but it doesn't stop me from obsessively checking to see if I have any cryptically suggestive emojis in my text box.

I don't.

I hate the way we left things—with a casual "Talk later"—and I especially hate that he doesn't seem to have any sense how his words on Thursday affected me. It's something I've read about in the pamphlets Mom has left out—how queer kids sometimes feel this hovering sense of doubt, knowing someone could reject us not only for who we are specifically but *who we are* more deeply—but I've never really felt it before now. If Sebastian doesn't think he's gay, then what the hell is he doing with me?

I pull Autumn closer, calmed by the solid weight of her against me.

Manny recruits a few guys to help him build a huge radio-controlled Humvee, and when they're done, they take turns hurling it over the uneven ground, the path down to the lake, small boulders bordering the parking lot.

Our attention is drawn away by a scuffle in the distance, near my car. Kole's friends are wrestling, laughing, and we watch as a big guy I think is named Micah takes down Eli. Beneath him, Eli bucks and shoves, but he can't get up. I don't know what he's done to get wrestled to the ground, even if it's clearly good-natured, but I can't help enjoying the sight of him pinned down there. We've exchanged zero words; he just has that asshole vibe about him.

"Get off me, *faggot!*" he yells, noticing how much attention they're getting now.

Absolute zero: Everything stops moving inside me. Every particle of energy is focused on schooling my expression.

Beside me, Auddy freezes too. The word "faggot" seems

to echo across the surface of the lake, but the only people it seems to have hit somewhere tender is the two of us.

Micah gets up, laughing harder, and helps Eli to his feet.

"I bet you just got the biggest boner, you fucking homo." Eli brushes off his jeans. His face is even redder than it was before.

I turn away, acting like I'm just going to squint across the horizon at the beautiful mountains in the distance, but when I catch a glimpse of Auddy, she looks like she wants to rip Eli's balls off with her bare hands. I can't really blame her—I'm horrified to realize that people still talk like that . . . *anywhere*.

Wandering off, Micah seems unconcerned. The rest of the group turns to walk over to where Micah is picking up his fallen remote control toy, and the moment seems to pass as easily as a wave breaking on the rocky shore.

"Gross," Auddy whispers. She looks up at me, and I try to smile through my repressed rage. I try to channel Sebastian, and for the first time, I understand his amazing fake smile. He's had so much practice.

She stands, swiping the dried grass from her jeans. "I think we should head out."

I follow her. "You okay?"

"Yeah," she says. "Just not my crowd. Why would Kole hang out with these douche bags?"

Not my crowd either. I'm relieved. "No idea."

Manny follows, protesting. "Guys, you just got here. Don't you want to race these cars?"

"I told Tanner I wasn't feeling great this morning," Auddy lies. "I feel worse."

"I'm her ride," I say, shrugging as if she's dragging me out of here against my wishes. But remote-controlled vehicles and homophobia just aren't my cup of tea, I guess.

He walks us to my car, stopping me at the driver's side. "Tanner, what Eli said back there . . ."

Heat pricks at the back of my neck. "What did he say?"

"Aw, man, come on." Manny laughs, looking to the side in a *don't-make-me-say-it* gesture. "Whatever, Eli's an idiot."

I move to get in the car.

This is so weird.

This is *so* bad.

It's like he knows about me. *How* does he know?

Not to be detoured, Manny pushes his sunglasses up on his head, squinting at me in confusion. "Tann, wait. Just so *you* know, we're cool. Yeah? I would never let someone say that crap to you."

I don't resist when he pulls me into a hug, but I feel like a two-by-four against him. Reels and reels of memories are flying past. Somewhere in my brain a poor, underpaid theater geek is trying to find the footage of Manny realizing I'm into dudes. I can't locate the memory, the possibility anywhere. "Manny, dude. We're cool. I don't even know what this is about."

He pulls away and then looks at Autumn, who is standing very, very still. Manny looks at me again. "Hey, no, man, I'm sorry. I didn't realize."

He backs off and turns, leaving Auddy and me in a cloud of silence and wind.

"What was *that*?" Auddy asks, watching him walk away.

"Who knows?" I look at her, preparing some easy explanation in my head. I mean, this is what I do. I'm fast on my feet. I'm usually *so* fast. But today, I don't know, maybe I'm tired. Maybe I'm sick of protecting myself. Maybe I'm leveled by Sebastian's denial. Maybe the hurricane of my feelings and the lies and the half-truths just knocked the covers off my windows and Auddy sees straight through, inside.

"Tanner, what is going *on*?"

It's the same voice Sebastian used on the mountain. *I don't understand why you're so upset.*

Just like Sebastian, she does understand. She just wants me to say it.

"I'm . . ." I look up at the sky. A plane flies overhead, and I wonder where it's headed. "I think I'm in love with Sebastian."

CHAPTER FIFTEEN

Auddy smiles, but it's this weird, bright, robot-girl smile. I nearly laugh, because the first thought I have is how much better Sebastian is than Autumn at fake smiling, and how that would be the worst possible thing to let slip out of my mouth right now.

"Let's talk in the car?" I say.

She turns and walks around to the passenger side just as robotically. I'm in a weird state of shock, where Manny's words and expression are looping in my head, and I know this conversation with Autumn is about to happen, but I've been waiting for it for so long that more than anything, I just feel insane relief.

Her door slams shut. I climb in beside her, sticking the keys in the ignition just to turn on the heat. "So."

She turns to face me, tucking a leg beneath her. "Okay. What just happened?"

"Well, apparently Manny figured out that I'm into guys."

She blinks. I know that Autumn is pro-gay rights—she adores Emily and Shivani, she rails about the LDS policy about queer members, and she helped put up flyers for the Provo High Gay-Straight Alliance party last spring. But it's one thing to support it in theory. It's another to have it right there, in her life. In her best friend.

"Technically, I'm bi. I've known probably forever, but I've been sure since I was thirteen."

She points to her own face. "If I look anything other than fine with this, please understand I'm only upset that you didn't tell me sooner."

I shrug. I don't really need to point out that the timing of me sharing this information isn't up to her. "Okay. Well, here we are."

"This feels like a big deal."

This makes me laugh. "It *is* a big deal. I'm describing how my heart beats."

She blinks, confused. "But you made out with Jen Riley sophomore year. I *saw* you," she says. "And what about Jessa, Kailley, and Trin? You've had *sex*. With girls."

"I also made out with *you*," I remind her. She flushes, and I point to my chest. *"Bi."*

"Wouldn't it be weird if there was a girl at school—a girl we had talked about, who we both thought was insanely hot, and sweet, and perfect—and I was in love with her and dealing with that on my own and I didn't say anything to you about it?"

I hadn't really thought about it this way, and even that

hypothetical makes me feel the tiniest bit sad, like all this time I was there, available, invested, and Auddy didn't come to me because she didn't trust me. "Yeah, okay, I get that. But in my defense, it's *Provo*. And you know my mom. She is, like, militant about this stuff. There's no room to be anything but one hundred percent on my side. I didn't want to risk that you'd have any conflict or issue with me."

"Oh my God. So much makes sense now." She exhales, long and slow, turning to blow her breath on the window. A cloud of condensation appears, and Autumn draws a heart in it and then takes a Snap, typing an enormous red "WOW" before posting it.

"So, Sebastian," she says.

"Yeah. Sebastian knows," I say, intentionally misunderstanding her. "He found out by accident, though. The summary of my book . . . I forgot to take the word 'queer' out, and it's pretty obvious it's autobiographical."

Her eyes widen at the way the word slips so easily from my mouth, and I forget not everyone lives in a household where a parent sleeps in a MY QUEER KID RULES nightgown. "Your book is about him?"

"It started out being about who I am, in this town. And then Sebastian came along and . . . yeah. It's about falling for him."

"Is he . . . ?"

"He's never told me he's gay," I say. Technically, I'm not

lying. It is not my place to out him, no matter what. "And he's still going on his mission, so I assume . . ."

She smiles and takes my hand. "That doesn't mean he's not gay, Tann. *Lots* of Mormons are gay. Lots of missionaries, lots of married men, even."

"I guess. I'm just . . . bummed."

Autumn squeezes my fingers. Her cheeks flush just before she asks, "Have you had sex with a guy?"

I shake my head. "Kissed. I had a boyfriend for a few months back home."

"Wow." She bites her lip. "The idea of you and Sebastian kissing is . . ."

A laugh bursts out of my throat, and it sounds like relief. "And there she goes. Autumn is back."

She peppers me with questions, and we decide to drive to the mall.

How did my parents react?

What does Hailey think of it?

Are there other guys at school I've liked?

How many guys have I kissed?

Is it different from kissing girls?

Which do I prefer?

Do I ever think I'll be totally out?

I answer everything—almost. I obviously can't tell her that kissing Sebastian is better than anything I've done, ever.

And, of course, I tell her that as soon as I get to college, I plan to be out. I was out in Palo Alto. The second my wheels hit the state line, I am going to roll down my window and wave my flag.

There's an undercurrent to the conversation that's impossible to ignore, an edge of hurt that I didn't tell her sooner. Luckily, Autumn is easily distracted with hugs, and jokes, and ice cream. A spring inside seems to uncoil.

Autumn knows.

We're okay.

Spending the rest of the day under the heat of her gentle grilling has the added benefit of not allowing me to obsess over Sebastian being gone, Sebastian *not* being gay, and—maybe especially—what Manny said back at the lake. It's great that he's supportive, I guess, but it still irks me that I'll probably spend most of my life dividing the people I know into two groups: the people who support me without question and the ones who should. I'm glad that Manny ended up on the right side, but I can't let myself dive into the rabbit hole of wondering *how* he knew. I hop between being relieved that it seems obvious to someone and still not a big deal, to worrying that it's going to be obvious to more people . . . and become a big deal. Please let me just get out of Provo before the shit hits the fan.

We lick our ice-cream cones and meander through the thick Saturday evening crowd. Everyone shops on Saturdays; Sundays are for worship and rest. Mormons aren't supposed to do anything on Sundays that require someone else to work, so most of the time, they stay home after church services. It means the crowds today are dense and exuberant.

The other thing that's easy to notice is that prom is on the horizon: Storefronts at every clothing shop proclaim they have dresses, tuxes, shoes, earrings, flowers. Sale, sale, sale. Prom, prom, prom.

With Eric having manned up and asked Autumn, I get to be Supportive Best Friend again, which apparently means waiting patiently while she tries on dress after dress in the brightly lit fitting room.

The first one is black, floor-length, and fitted, with cap sleeves and a neckline that dips questionably low. It also has a slit that runs clear up her thigh.

"It's a bit much . . ." I wince dramatically, keeping my eyes in the general vicinity of her face. "It's a *lot* much, actually."

"A lot as in *good*?"

"Can you wear that to a school dance in Utah? It's . . ." I pause, shaking my head. "I don't know . . ." I motion to the lower half of her body, and Autumn leans forward to see what I'm looking at. "I can practically see your vagina, Auddy."

"Tanner, no. Don't say 'vagina.'"

"Can you even sit down with that on?"

Autumn moves to a fuzzy pink chair and crosses her legs as if to demonstrate.

I look away. "Thank you for proving me right."

"What color are my underwear?" she asks, grinning like she thinks I'm lying.

"Blue."

Autumn stands, tugging the dress back down. "Damn. I like this one." She moves to stand in front of the mirror, and a tiny spark of protectiveness hums in my chest as I imagine Eric and his hands and eighteen-year-old hormones all over her. She meets my eyes in the glass. "So you don't like it?"

I feel like a dick for making her think she's anything less than perfect and shouldn't wear whatever she wants, but it's in direct conflict with some big-brother-like instinct to tie Eric's hands behind his back. "I mean, you look hot. It's just . . . a *lot* of skin."

"I look hot?" she asks, hopeful, and I feel my brows come together.

"You know you are."

She hums as she considers her reflection. "I'll put it in the maybe pile."

Autumn disappears back into the dressing room, and from the bottom of the louvered door I see the black fabric pool around her feet before being kicked aside. "How's the book coming, by the way? Now that I know a little more about it, I'm even more curious."

I groan as I scroll through Instagram. "I like it, but I can't use it."

She peeks around the curtain. "Why not?"

I keep it vague: "Because it's obvious that it's about me falling in love with Sebastian, and I don't think the bishop's son would particularly appreciate being the star in a queer love story."

Her voice is momentarily muffled as she slips into a new dress. "I can't believe it's about him. I could beta read it for you?"

The suggestion sends a panicked shiver across my skin. I'd feel less exposed sending a roll of naked selfies to the Provo High LISTSERV right now than I'd feel sending this book off to someone. Even Autumn.

The curtain parts again, and she steps out in a dress that's a third of the size of the one before, and I feel like I'm missing something here. Autumn's changed in front of me before, but it's been in more of a rushed my-boobs-are-coming-out-so-if-you-don't-want-to-see-them-you-better-make-a-run-for-it-now kind of way. But this feels different. A little . . . flaunty.

God, I feel like a douche for even thinking it.

"It looks like a bathing suit," I say.

Undeterred, she flips her hair over her shoulder and adjusts the tiny skirt. "So can I read it or not?"

"I'm not quite there yet. Soon." I watch her shimmy in the dress, not happy with either direction this conversation is going, but knowing the dress is the safer route. "I like this one. It'll get you grounded till graduation, but I think that's the fun part."

She looks in the mirror again, turns around to see it from the back. "It might be too short," she says, considering. Her ass is just covered by the fabric. If she bent over to adjust her shoe, the entire dress would climb up her back. "But I'm not buying anything today. Just getting a feel for what's out there so I can start an idea book."

"Like you'd do for a wedding dress?"

She gives me the finger before moving back to the changing room. "Are you sure you're not going to prom? It won't be the same without you there."

When she peeks out of the curtain, I give her a flat, patient face.

"Yeah, yeah. I know," she says, slipping from view again. "I mean, you could *ask* him."

It's strange that this is reality now: talking about my sexuality to someone besides my parents. Talking about him.

"I'm pretty sure it would be a hard pass."

I watch her feet as they climb into her jeans. "That sucks."

I'm worried she's starting to assume that something is happening with me and Sebastian even though I haven't indicated it. "Let's list the reasons it's unrealistic: I don't know if he's gay. He's LDS. He graduated last year. He leaves soon on his book tour and then his mission. I swear the last thing he would want to do is go to prom with me."

Somewhere in my monologue, Autumn has emerged from the dressing room, but now she's looking wide-eyed over my shoulder. I turn just in time to see Julie and McKenna leaving the store, madly typing on their phones.

Autumn doesn't think they heard anything, but how the hell would she know? She was in the dressing room the whole time. I'm trying not to freak out, and as nice as it is that I think this brings it home for Autumn how precarious it can be to be queer here, her sweet babble in the background of my blender-brain isn't helping calm me down.

Despite blowing up his phone nearly constantly, I haven't heard from Sebastian. Now, for the first time, I'm relieved he's out of cell range and I won't be tempted to spill the events of the day with Manny, Autumn, Julie, and McKenna. I have to do some damage control or he is going to *Lose. His. Mind.*

"Do you think I should text Manny and find out what he was talking about?" I ask Autumn, turning onto her street.

She hums. "Or I could?"

"No, I mean, I would do it, but . . . I wonder if it's better to just leave it alone. Pretend nothing is different."

I pull up at the curb and put my car in park.

"How did Manny know, anyway?" she asks.

This right here is what I can't figure out. And if Manny knows, maybe everyone knows. And if everyone knows and they see me with Sebastian . . . they'll know about him, too.

. . .

I'm stress-watching an episode of *Pretty Little Liars* when the first text from Sebastian comes in. I almost bolt off the couch.

Just got home. Is it cool if I come over?

I look at the empty house around me. Hailey is at a friend's and my parents are enjoying a rare night out together. It's nearly nine, but no one will be home for a few hours. I know what my dad said about using this place to sneak around, but he can at least *come over*, right? We'll hang on the couch, watch some TV. There's nothing wrong with that.

Yeah, it's just me here. Come over whenever.

His reply comes almost immediately.

Cool. See you in a few.

I run upstairs and change my shirt. I grab the kitchen garbage and clean up my soda cans and chip crumbs and throw the leftover pizza box away. I'm just coming in from the garage when the doorbell rings and I have to stop, take a few calming breaths before I cross the room, and open the door.

He's standing there, wearing a black T-shirt, worn jeans with a rip in the knee, faded red Converse. Even lacking some of his normal polish he's . . . breathtaking. His hair has fallen in his eyes, but it doesn't mask the spark I see there.

I smile so wide my face hurts. "Hey."

I step back so he can follow me in. Inside, he waits just long enough for me to move away from the door before he's pressing me to the wall. His lips are as warm as his hand on my hip, where his thumb presses into the skin just above my jeans. That tiny touch is like a starter pistol in my blood, and I rock forward, so worked up by the thought of his hand and its general proximity to other parts that I can't even remember why he's not supposed to be here. I want him to tug the denim down. I want to take him to my room and see if he blushes everywhere.

A few more kisses and Sebastian sucks in a breath, moving to drag his teeth along my jaw. My head falls back with a mild *thud*, and only then do I see that I never got around to closing the door.

"Let me just . . . ," I start, and Sebastian takes a step back. He looks around for the first time, in a mild panic as if only just realizing where he is.

Following the path of his attention, I tell him, "It's just us."

I can tell it shocks him how he just came in here and kissed me without any regard to what was going on deeper in the room. I won't pretend it doesn't surprise me, too. It's the sort of impulsivity I'm known for, but he's always seemed so much more measured. I like that I can break down his manufactured borders though. It makes me feel powerful, and hopeful.

Tugging him down onto the couch, I watch him fall back

next to me. That's right. I bet he was working his ass off all day building houses or digging ditches or something equally servicey. "How was your day?" I ask.

He loops his arm around my shoulder and pulls me closer. "It was fine." I tilt my head back enough to see a splotchy blush bloom just beneath his skin. "I missed you."

That sound you hear is my heart running full speed and jumping out of a plane. It's flying. I don't think I knew until he said that how much I needed to hear it. It lifts an eraser, rubs across the "Not . . . *that*."

"I missed you, too, in case you couldn't tell by the unending texts."

A few moments of comfortable silence pass.

"Tann?"

I hum, looking over to see him squinting at the screen, confused. "What is this?"

"Oh. *Pretty Little Liars*. It's the teen equivalent of a soap opera with dead-end plot twists and red herrings, but oh my God, I can't look away. How many people have to die before you call the police?" I pick up a bag of chips and offer him one. "I'm shocked you haven't seen it, Brother Brother, in all your spare time."

He laughs. "What did you do today?"

My heart punches me from the inside. "Hung out with Autumn."

"I like Autumn. She seems nice."

My stomach clenches, and I wonder if I should tell him that she knows about me now, and then reject the idea immediately. She doesn't know about *this*, right? It'd be cool for the three of us to hang out at some point, but I don't think he's anywhere near ready for that yet.

"Autumn is the best."

The rest of what happened today trails like a stalking shadow: Manny, Julie, McKenna.

But Manny doesn't know about us either. And if Julie and McKenna did overhear me at the store, all they would have heard is that Sebastian isn't gay and won't go to prom with me. He should be okay, right?

Sebastian's phone goes off on the table, and he reaches for it. When he settles back, he pulls me closer. If I turned my head, I could kiss him again.

He types in his code and frowns down at the screen.

"Everything okay?" I ask.

"Yeah. I just . . . my mom." He tosses his phone to the other side of the couch. I sit up, getting some distance for the first time since he walked in the house. His eyes are puffy and bloodshot. It doesn't look like he's been crying, but it does look like he's been rubbing them an awful lot, something I've seen him do when he's stressed.

"Oh, man. What now?" On top of school and tutoring and drafting his second book, he has his upcoming mission stuff to juggle.

"No, it's fine." He waves it off. "She wants to talk about what happened at the camp."

This sets off some tiny alarm bell in my brain. "What happened at the camp?"

"We did an activity and it sort of got to me."

I look over at him. "What kind of activity?"

I can see the flickering of the TV reflecting in his eyes, but I know he isn't watching it; his head is somewhere back up on the mountain. "We do this thing called Walk to the Light. Have you heard of it?"

My expression must be largely bewildered, because he laughs and doesn't wait for an answer. "They blindfold us as a group and have us line up, telling us to hold on to the shoulder of the person in front of us."

Blindfolds in the woods? It sounds more horror movie than church activity.

"The group leader gives us instructions. 'Go left,' 'go right,' 'slow down,' and it's fine because you can feel the person in front of you, feel the weight of a hand on your own shoulder." He takes a breath, eyes flickering to the floor and back up to the screen. "Until you don't. One minute you feel a hand on your shoulder, and then it's gone. And it's your turn to let go and follow directions."

"That sounds terrifying," I say.

Sebastian takes my hand, lining our fingers up. "It's not too bad. Most of us have done the exercise before and know what to expect, but . . . it felt different this time."

"Different like more confusing?" Because, honestly, that sounds awful.

"I don't know how to describe it. The person who leads you off the trail takes you to a spot and tells you to sit and seek diligently for the Spirit, just like they always do. But it was different. I *felt* different."

I sit up, fully turning to face him. "They leave you in the woods alone?"

"I know it sounds bad, but I'm sure if we could see we'd realize we're not that far away from each other, and only barely off the trail. But we can't look, so we sit quietly with our eyes closed, and wait, and pray."

I look down to our hands and twist my fingers with his. "What do you pray for?"

"For whatever I need." He looks down at our hands. I see a small quiver in his chin. "So I'm sitting there on the ground, and I can't see, and after a while I hear something through the trees. Someone is saying my name—my dad. It's quiet at first, but then gets louder as he gets closer. He's calling my name and telling me to come home."

A tear slips down his face. "I've done it before and it's always a little scary. I mean, you can't see, so of course it is, but this felt different—to me. Urgent in a way it's never been before. So I stood up and followed his voice. My eyes were still closed, and I was tripping down this hill, hoping that I wasn't about to fall off a rock or walk into a tree. But I kept going, knowing my dad wouldn't let me get hurt but feeling like I had to hurry. When I finally got to him, he hugged me so hard and said 'Welcome home,' and that he loves me and he's proud of the man I'm becoming. And all I could think was 'Are you really? Would you still be if you knew about Tanner?'"

My chest goes tight. "Sebastian . . ."

He shakes his head, wiping tears away with the back of his hand. "You know, I have this dream where I've told them everything, about how I had a crush on a guy in eighth grade, and a handful of guys after that, and no one ever knew. In the dream I tell them how I've never wanted to kiss a girl—not once—and I can't promise that I'll ever want to get married. Then I'm waiting in the woods, and nobody ever comes. Everyone else peels off, heading out with their family, but I'm sitting there with my eyes closed, just waiting." He blinks up to the ceiling. "I was so relieved that Dad was there this weekend that I almost promised myself I wouldn't ever do anything to jeopardize that. But what if I never want what he wants for me? What if I can't do it?"

My throat feels like it's full of wet sand. I don't even know what to say. Instead, I pull him to me, pressing his face to the crook of my neck.

"I'm just thinking about this so much lately," he says, his voice muffled by my skin, "and trying to figure out what it means, but there aren't any answers anywhere. There are all kinds of essays written for us about falling in love, and getting married, and becoming a parent. Even losing a child or questioning your faith. But there's nothing about this, nothing helpful at least. Everywhere, it's like 'Same-sex attraction is just a technical term; it's not who you are. You might not be able to control the feelings, but you can control how you respond,' and it's such a lie. We're taught to turn our life over to Christ and he'll show us the way. But when I pray? The Heavenly Father says yes." He rubs his eyes with the heels of his hands. "He tells me he's proud of me and that he loves me. When I kiss you, it feels right, even if everything I read says it shouldn't. It makes me feel crazy."

He turns in, and I kiss his temple, struggling to not lose it with him right now. No wonder he's "not . . . *that*"—a label would take away everything he's ever had. I want to be strong. I have it so easy. I have so much support. It aches to see that he has none of that.

"Babe, I'm so sorry," I whisper.

"We're supposed to pray, and listen—so I do. But then, when I turn to others, it's like . . ." He shakes his head. "It feels like I'm pushing through the dark and I know that what's ahead is safe, but no one is following me there."

I'm still shaken up when I park outside Sebastian's house a few days later.

After his confession, he stood up to use the bathroom,

and when he came back and sat down next to me, he smiled and it was like nothing even happened. I've never met someone who is so good at switching gears and filing their feelings away so they can sort through them later. I'm not sure whether it's the most impressive thing I've ever seen, or the most depressing.

We held hands as we watched TV, but when his phone went off again, he said he needed to get home. He kissed me at the door and looked back over his shoulder as he walked down the driveway, and e-mailed me that night to let me know that everything was fine.

Sebastian is really good at being *fine*.

The church *has* changed some of their wording lately, and just like Sebastian said, it emphasizes acceptance and kindness—always with the kindness—to those who are struggling with their sexuality. But it's not *actually* a change in position; it's a way to counter arguments that say the church isn't welcoming to the LGBTQ community. In reading, I found it's only recently spoken out against conversion therapy, saying a change in attraction should not be expected or demanded as an outcome by parents or leaders. So Sebastian could technically say that he was gay and not be forced from the church, but he couldn't be *with* me. Having a boyfriend would mean he was actively pursuing a homosexual "lifestyle," and that would still be against the rules.

Basically, it changes nothing.

I put my car in park and hop out. Sebastian's mom is out front unloading groceries, and even though I really want to ask her who the hell would embrace a religion that excludes people for who they love, I jog up the driveway to help instead.

"Oh my gosh, Tanner. You are so sweet. Thank you," she says, reaching for her purse.

I follow her into the house, setting the bags on the counter before going back outside for more. I don't see Sebastian anywhere, but Faith is in the front room, stretched out on the carpet, coloring.

"Hi, Tanner," she says, flashing me a toothless grin.

"Hey, Faith." I look down at her drawing and realize it's some sort of Ten Commandments coloring book. Don't these people have anything that isn't church-related? She's halfway through the current page, on which a blue-haired Jesus is standing on a mountain addressing a rainbow-colored crowd. I sort of love this kid. "That's a pretty great picture." I point to a camel she's embellished with wings. "Very creative."

"I'm going to glue some glitter on it later, but I'm only allowed to do it in the kitchen. Are you looking for my brother?"

"I am," I say. "He's going to help me with my book."

He's not, but this remains an excellent alibi.

Mrs. Brother steps into the living room and smiles at both of us. "Wow," she says to Faith. "Blue hair?"

"Jesus can have blue hair." Her crayon scratches defiantly over the paper, and I want to tell her to remember that, to remember the things she believes and not let someone's rules change them.

"Yes, I think he most definitely can." Mrs. Brother turns to me. "Tanner, honey, I think Sebastian's downstairs in his room."

"Thanks," I tell her. "Nice drawing, Faith."

"I know," Faith says, aiming her grin up at me.

"Tanner, there are some cookies on the counter." Mrs. Brother straightens and motions toward the kitchen. "Can you take them down with you? He's working on something and has barely come up for air."

Yes, Mrs. Brother, I can definitely take cookies down to your hot son's room. My pleasure.

"Of course." I gather up my things and follow her into the kitchen.

"I'm taking Faith to dance soon, so if you two need anything else, just help yourself."

A plate with six chocolate-chip cookies sits on the granite countertop. I'm just about to turn toward the stairs when something outside catches my eye, a flash of blue near the swing set. Sebastian had a blue shirt on today. It stretched across the defined expanse of his chest and showcased his biceps. I barely paid attention to anything else. I wonder whether he dresses every morning to torture me.

The sliding glass door slips silently across the track, and I step outside and onto the patio. I can see him from here, head down as he sits on one of the swings, drawing large swaths of yellow highlighter across lines of text in his book.

I cross the grass, and he looks up when he sees me. "Hey, you," he says, eyes dropping to the plate in my hand. "You brought me cookies?"

"Technically, they're your mom's cookies. She just gave them to me."

"She likes you," he says, dragging his feet across the grass. "They all do. I knew they would."

I laugh. "I have no idea why."

"Come on, everyone likes you. Girls, boys, teachers, parents. My grandma called you the adorable one with the hair."

"Your grandmother thinks I'm adorable?"

He looks up at me, squinting into the sun. "I think you know you're adorable." I want him to write those words down so I can read them over and over and over. "Are you going to give me a cookie?"

I hold his gaze for a moment before handing him one from the plate. They're still warm. "She told me to take them to your room," I say with a suggestive lift of my brow. "That's where she thinks you are, by the way."

He looks so much better today—happy—church-activity trauma apparently behind him. His mental and emotional resiliency is some kind of superpower.

When he grins, my heart does a little hiccup in my chest. "If she thinks I'm inside, I vote we hide out here."

"She's taking Faith to dance."

"Still, it's nice out." Sebastian picks up his things, and I follow him to the shade of a giant tree. To anyone in the house we'd be invisible, completely hidden by the canopy of new, bright green leaves overhead.

I take one of the cookies and break it in half. "What are you working on?"

"Psych." He flops the book closed and stretches out in the grass. I work to keep my focus on his face, but when he turns to me, I can tell he knows I was just checking out his happy trail. "How was it working in a group with McAsher today?" he asks.

I love that he seems so above the gossip cloud but totally isn't. Sebastian sees everything. "She nearly fell out of her chair trying to show off her cleavage."

"I caught that." He laughs, taking a bite of cookie.

"How was the rest of your day?"

"Economics quiz." He takes another bite, chews, and swallows. Watching his jaw work is mesmerizing. "Latin quiz too. Choir practice."

"Wish I could have seen that."

"Maybe next time you can cut school and watch." He opens one eye to look at me. "I know how much you like flipping the bird to authority."

"That's me, four-point-oh student and juvenile

delinquent." I lick chocolate from my thumb and catch the way his eyes follow the movement now. A shiver moves down my spine. "Autumn is almost done with her book."

He considers this. Maybe he sees the tightness in my eyes. "That's good, but not necessary. I mean, you still have a month. Some people need more time to revise. Some people need less. You just need a finished draft by the end of term. Not a polished manuscript."

I avoid his gaze, and he ducks down, catching my eye. "Are you going to send me chapters?"

I hate the idea of making him fix my book.

I also hate the idea of him seeing my fears and neuroses laid out so plainly.

So, I divert: "When did you finish writing yours?"

"Um." He squints up at the branches overhead. "I finished in May—right before the deadline, if I'm remembering correctly—and turned in a draft a week later. I still wasn't sure it was any good."

"But apparently it was."

"People like different things. You could read my book and hate it."

"I highly doubt that."

"You could. My mom's probably already promised most of my author copies away, but I'll snag you one. That way we'll be even because you're going to give me *your* book." He offers up his most charming smile.

I tap the bottom of his shoe with the toe of mine. "A fancy New York editor has already read and bought yours. You know it's not crap."

"Your book isn't crap, Tanner. It isn't possible. Sure, details need to be changed to protect the innocent, but it isn't crap. You're too thoughtful, too sensitive." He grins. "Yeah, I said 'sensitive' . . . despite your outward flippant thing."

"My 'outward'—" I start with a grin, but clap my mouth shut at the sound of voices overhead.

"What are you doing here?" Sebastian's mom asks, and we duck lower, as if we've been caught doing something wrong. "I wasn't expecting you home until dinner."

When I lean forward, stretching to see, I see an open bathroom window just above our tree. She's not talking to us.

Sebastian starts stacking his books. "Let's go inside," he whispers. "I don't want to—"

"Brett Avery married his boyfriend in California last week." We both freeze at the sound of his dad's deep voice, and the tenor of hardened disapproval there.

Sebastian looks over at me, eyes wide.

I can only imagine the stricken expression his mom must be wearing, because his dad sighs, saying sadly, "Yeah."

"Oh no," she says. "Oh no, *no*. I knew he moved away, but I had no idea he was—" She stops short of saying the dreaded G-word, and lowers her voice. "How are his parents?"

For the briefest moment, Sebastian's face falls, and I want

to reach out and cover his ears, pull him into my car, and take off driving.

"They're managing, I suppose," he tells her. "Apparently Jess took it more calmly than Dave did. Brother Brinkerhoff is praying with them, and added them to the temple roll. I told them I'd stop by, so I just ran home to change."

Their voices fade as they move to another room. Sebastian is staring mildly off into the distance, and the thunder of my silence rolls through me as I struggle to think of what to say.

How are his parents?

It can't have escaped Sebastian's notice that his mom didn't ask about *Brett* or whether he was happy; she asked about his parents, almost like having a gay son is something they have to manage, to explain, to *deal with*.

He's gay; he didn't *die*. Nobody is *wounded*. I know Sebastian's parents are good people, but holy hell, they just inadvertently made their own son feel like there's something about him that needs to be fixed. So much for acceptance. So much for *welcoming*.

"I'm sorry, Sebastian."

He looks up from where he's gathering his highlighters, a tight smile on his face. "What's that?"

A few seconds of bewildered silence tick between us.

"Isn't it weird to hear them talk like that?"

"Talk about Brett being gay?" When I nod, he shrugs. "I

don't think anyone is surprised his parents are reacting the way they are."

I search his face, wondering why he seems so resigned. "I don't know. . . . Maybe if enough people get angry, things will change?"

"Maybe, maybe not." He leans in, trying to get me to hold on to his gaze. "It's just the way it is."

Just the way it is.

Is he resigned, or realistic?

Does he even feel any of this is about *him*?

"It's just the way it is?" I repeat. "So you'll go off to wherever and preach the Gospel and tell more people that being gay is wrong?"

"Being gay isn't wrong, but it's not God's plan, either." He shakes his head, and I think this moment, right here, is when it really hits me that Sebastian's identity isn't queer. It's not gay. It's not even soccer player or boyfriend or son.

It's *Mormon*.

"I know this must not make any sense to you," he says carefully, and panic squeezes my gut. "I'm sure you have no idea what you're doing with me or what I'm doing with you, and if you—"

"No." I squeeze his fingers, not caring that someone could see. "That's not what I'm saying. I want you. But I hate to think that your parents would ever look at us and think we are something to be fixed."

It's a long time before he answers, and I can tell he doesn't entirely like what I've said because he pulls his hand away, tucking it between his knees. "I don't presume to know why Heavenly Father does the things He does, but I know in my heart that He has a plan for each of us. He brought you into my life for a reason, Tanner. I don't know what that reason is, but I know that there's a purpose for it. I *know* that. Being with you isn't wrong. The way I feel about you isn't wrong. Somehow it'll work out."

I nod down at the grass.

"You should come along next weekend," he says quietly. I hear it in his voice, the way he begs for this to be solved by me joining the church. The way he lifts the corner of the rug and capably sweeps this inconvenient dirt pile underneath. "We have a youth activity, and it should be pretty fun."

"You want to bring your *boyfriend* to a church activity?"

His brows flicker down at this before he clears his expression. "I want to bring *you*."

don't think Sebastian really expected me to take him up on the offer. Even Autumn stared at me in blank shock when I mentioned I was going to tag along on a church activity. And yet here we are, Sebastian and Tanner, parking beside the soccer field at good ol' Fort Utah Park.

We climb out of my car, and I follow him down the small hill to where everyone has gathered in a circle around enormous cardboard boxes, still unopened. For mid-April, it's gorgeous out. I'm sure it means everyone will get sick when the temperature dips down into the thirties again, but right now it's in the midsixties, and no one under the age of twenty is wearing long pants. There are pasty white legs peeking out of shorts everywhere.

But let's be real: Unlike the teeny ass-baring cutoffs Hailey wears, the shorts on display here are pretty tame. It's not even weird here how modestly everyone dresses, but it does make me wonder briefly what it's like for LDS kids living in towns where they aren't the majority.

Girls stare and fidget when Sebastian approaches. I can

see a few guys, too, gazing at him just a touch longer than normal. Does he notice the effect he has on people? He's not even leading the event, but it seems like everyone's been waiting for him to arrive.

A few people come up, greeting him with handshakes. I'm introduced to a Jake, a Kellan, two McKennas (neither are the McKenna from school) and a Luke before I stop bothering to learn the names and instead greet every smile with my own grin and a hearty handshake. A guy around our age, maybe a bit older, comes out from a cluster of people at the back and introduces himself to me. His name is Christian and he's thrilled I'm here to join the group. Clearly, he's leading the exercise.

With that, we get started.

"We're doing some service today," Christian says, and a hush falls over the small crowd. The six enormous boxes become the focus of everyone's attention as he walks over and leans against one. "The amenities in this park are getting old, and it seems time to spruce it up a bit." He pats the box at his side. "This box, my friends, contains everything you need to build a table or a bench." A grin spreads across his face. "The twist is that there are no directions, no tools."

I look around at the group. No one else seems surprised by these rules in the least. No directions, okay, but no tools?

My mind yells a panicked *But—splinters!*

"We're going to break into six teams." When Christian

says this, I feel Sebastian casually sliding away from me, and I glance over at him, but he shakes his head. "First, we need to move the existing tables and benches over to the parking lot, where they'll be picked up by Brother Atwell's crew. Then we build. We'll have some pizza in a bit. Drink water when you need to. Remember, it isn't a race. Take your time and do it right. This is how we give back." He smiles, and something inside me suddenly feels very, very out of place here when he adds, "Now, let's somebody say a prayer."

This part takes me by surprise, and I catch the apologetic look Sebastian gives me just before he lowers his head.

An older teen across the circle from us steps forward. "Heavenly Father, thank you for bringing us together on this beautiful spring day. Thank you for our many blessings, for the strong bodies we will use today. Bless that we can remember this lesson and apply it in our daily lives, that we remember it is only through you that we can find salvation. Please guide Brother Davis's aim straight and true that we may not have a repeat of last week's emergency room visit." A wave of giggles moves through the group, and the boy tucks his smile away before finishing. "Bless that we travel home safely. We say this in the name of Jesus Christ, amen."

When we straighten, Sebastian's distance quickly makes sense as Christian has us count off, one through six. My boyfriend has just ensured that we're on the same team, getting the same splinters.

As threes, we are joined by two giggling thirteen-year-old girls, a freshman named Toby, and a junior named Greg. Toby, Greg, Sebastian, and I join the other male forces hauling away the old picnic tables. The girls stand and watch; mostly they're watching Sebastian.

I try to imagine Hailey in this situation. She would lose her goddamn mind if we started doing some sort of manual labor without expecting her to help.

Having expected the building exercise to be pretty straightforward, I'm surprised when there are about seventy pieces of wood in the box and no clear indication what part goes where. It's obvious that Sebastian and Greg have been doing this their whole lives. They quickly get to work sorting the pieces by size and shape, while Toby and I act as the muscle, moving the pieces where they direct us.

Sebastian reels in the girls, Katie and Jennalee. "Can you find every piece this size?" He holds up a wooden pin, approximately four inches long. They're scattered all over the grass where we overturned the box. "And make sure there are as many dowels as there are holes in the boards, see?" He points to the place where the dowels fit into the boards, and the girls immediately get to work, glad to have a task.

"Tann," he says, and the familiarity in his voice makes a shiver break out along my skin. "Come help me line these up."

We work side by side, arranging the boards meant to be the table, the boards meant to be the legs. We figure out that we'll have to use one of the shorter, heavier boards as a mallet to get the pieces in, and then we'll use Greg's boot to get that final board in place. The problem-solving is a blast, if I'm being honest, but it doesn't hold a candle to the thrill of crouching beside Sebastian, feeling his body move next to mine.

Seriously, if he meant for me to come here and find religion, mission accomplished.

We are the first group to finish, and we split off, helping other groups that are struggling with the arrangement and how to use the various parts as tools. I'd be exaggerating if I said it was backbreaking work, but it's not easy, either, and when the pizza arrives, I'm glad to see a huge stack of boxes because I am *s-t-a-r-v-i-n-g*.

Sebastian and I collapse against a tree, a bit away from the group. With our legs splayed out in front of us, we devour the food like we haven't eaten in weeks.

I love watching him eat—it's usually so fascinating to realize how well mannered he is—but here he's all brute construction worker: The pizza gets rolled in half, and he shoves most of it in his mouth in one bite. Still, nothing gets on his chin or shirt. I take one bite and have a smear of pepperoni grease on my T-shirt.

"Motherfucker," I hiss.

"Tann."

I look over at him, and he smiles, but then tilts his head, like *Language!*

I give him a sheepish "Sorry."

"I don't mind," he says quietly. "Some of them would."

We're far enough away that I have this sense of privacy, even if it's not entirely real. "How long have you known everyone here?"

"Some of them their whole lives," he says, looking out at the group. "Toby's family moved here only two years ago. And some of the kids here are more recent converts. I think this is Katie's first service activity."

"I would never have guessed," I tease.

"Come on, she's sweet."

"Her being sweet is totally unrelated to the fact that it took her twenty minutes to count forty dowels."

He acknowledges this with a quiet laugh. "Sorry about the prayer earlier. I always forget."

I wave him off and look around the field of teens with new eyes. "You ever dated anyone here?"

He lifts his chin, indicating a tall girl on the other side of the soccer field, eating near the goal. "Manda."

I know who he means. She graduated with Sebastian's class, and was in the student council. She's pretty, and smart, and I never heard a single bit of gossip about her. I'm sure she would be the dream match for Sebastian.

"How long?" I ask. Wow, that question came out sharp.

He heard it too. "You jealous?"

"A little."

I can tell he likes this. His cheeks pop with a blush. "About a year. Sophomore year to just before junior."

Wow. I want to ask what he did with her, how much they kissed, how close they came . . . but I don't. Instead, I say, "But you knew, even then . . ."

He looks up sharply and then around, his features relaxing once he confirms we're out of earshot. "Yeah, I knew. But I thought, maybe if I tried . . ."

This is like a hundred pins pushed slowly into my skin. A year-long relationship is a lot of trying.

I'm not . . . that.

"You didn't sleep with her though, right?"

He takes another huge bite of pizza, shaking his head.

"So you think you might marry a Manda someday?"

I can see exasperation in his expression when he looks up at me, chewing. Swallowing, he looks around meaningfully. "Do you think this is the best place for this conversation?"

"We can do it later."

"I want *you*," he says quietly, ducking to take another bite. When he's swallowed again, he looks straight ahead, but adds, "I don't want anyone else."

"Do you think the church will change their mind about us?" I ask. I nod toward the crowd of his peers across the field. "Do you think *they'll* eventually come around?"

Sebastian shrugs. "I don't know."

"But you feel happy with me."

"The happiest I've ever been."

"So you know it isn't wrong."

His eyes clear and finally he looks at me. "Of *course* I do."

Emotion rises, thick in my throat. I want to kiss him. His gaze drops to my mouth and then he blinks away, his face red again.

"You know what I'm thinking," I say. "What I'm always thinking."

He nods, leaning forward to reach his water bottle. "Yeah. Me too."

The sun is hanging low in the sky when we put everything back in place and test to make sure it's safely assembled. People are laughing, playing tag, tossing a Frisbee around. It's so much better than the wrestling, name-calling of the trip to the lake the other day. There's an undeniable layer of *respect* to everything we do here. Respect for the community, for each other, for ourselves, for their God.

Most everyone piles into a large van to head back to the church parking lot, but Sebastian and I hang back, waving as they retreat from view.

Sebastian turns to me, and his smile slips. "So? Was it terrible?"

"I was just thinking it wasn't bad," I say, and he laughs at this. "I mean, actually it was pretty cool. Everyone is so nice."

"'Nice,'" he repeats, shaking his head a little.

"What? I'm serious. It's a *nice* group of people."

I like being with his community not because I think this would be a good fit for me, but because I need that window into his head. I need to understand why he would ever say things like "I felt the Spirit so strongly this weekend," or how he'll pray to find answers. The reality is, this is the language he was born with and he was raised hearing. The LDS Church has an entire vocabulary that still sounds so stilted to me, but which rolls right out of them, and I'm coming to understand that it essentially just means things like "I'm trying to make the best choice," and "I need to understand if what I'm feeling is wrong."

The only sounds left in the park are of birds in trees overhead and the distant hum of tires on asphalt.

"What do you want to do?" I ask.

"I don't want to go home yet."

My whole body vibrates. "Then let's stay out."

We climb in my car with the weight of an anticipatory silence all along my skin. I pull out of the lot and drive. I just drive. I don't even know where we're going or what we'll do when we stop, but when we're miles from home, Sebastian's hand slides onto my knee and slowly inches up my thigh. Houses fall away, and soon we're on a quiet two-lane road. On instinct, I pull down a dirt road leading to a restricted-access side of the lake.

Sebastian looks back over his shoulder as we pass through

the open gate with the sign NO ACCESS mostly obstructed by overgrown foliage. "Should we really go down here?"

"Probably not, but it doesn't look like that gate has been closed for a long time, so I'm guessing we're not the first to try it."

He doesn't reply, but I feel his uncertainty in the stiff shape of his hand on my leg, the rigidity in his spine. I have to trust that he'll relax once he sees how truly isolated it is down here after dark.

The mud grows thicker, and I pull off into a firm patch of grass, shutting off my lights and then, finally, the ignition. My car engine ticks in the silence. Outside, it's almost completely dark except for the shimmering reflection of the moon on the lake surface. Dad always insists I keep some emergency supplies in my trunk—including a thick blanket—and although it's getting chilly with the sun gone, I have an idea.

Opening my door, I look over at him. "Come on."

Reluctantly, he follows.

I pull the blanket from my trunk and spread it over the still-warm hood of my car. Using a few spare jackets and a random beach towel, I make some pillows for us up near the windshield wipers.

Like this, we can lie back and stare up at the stars.

When he sees what I'm doing, he helps me arrange it all, and then we climb up, lying back and letting out, in unison, a satisfied moan.

He bursts out laughing. "It *looked* so comfortable."

I shift a little closer, and the hood protests with a metallic rumble. "It's not so bad."

Above us, the moon hangs low on the horizon, and stars seem to hold it up by strings.

"One thing I like about this place," I tell him, "is you can see stars at night. We never could in Palo Alto. Too much light pollution."

"*One* thing you like about this place?"

I turn, leaning forward to kiss him once. "Sorry. Two."

"I know nothing about stars," he says when I look back up at the sky. "I keep meaning to learn, but there never seems to be time."

Pointing, I say, "Up there is Virgo. See the top four that form that lopsided trapezoid? Then there's Gamma Virginis and Spica—they form, like, kite strings below?"

Sebastian squints, sliding closer to better see what I'm pointing to. "That shape there?"

"No . . . I think you're looking at Corvus. Virgo is . . ." I move his hand so it's hovering over my chest. My heart is going to climb right up my throat and out of my body. "Right there."

"Yeah, yeah," he whispers, smiling.

"And that bright one, that's Venus—"

He inhales, excited. "Right, I remember—"

"And just beside it, that tight cluster? That's the Pleiades,"

I tell him. "They'll move closer and closer together."

"Where'd you learn all this?" he asks.

I turn to look at him.

He's looking at me, too, so close.

"My dad. There's not much to do after dark when we're camping, other than make s'mores, tell ghost stories, and look at constellations."

"Left to my own devices, I can only ever find the Big Dipper," he says. His eyes drop to my mouth.

"I would be pretty useless out here without my dad."

He blinks away, looking back up. "Your dad seems cool."

"He is."

An ache builds in my chest because my dad is the best, in part, because he knows me and loves all of me. And yet there is this entire side of Sebastian that his dad knows nothing about. I could go home and tell Dad everything that happened today—could even tell him about lying here with Sebastian on the hood of Mom's old Camry—and it wouldn't change anything between us.

Apparently Sebastian has the exact same train of thought, because out of the silence, he says, "I keep thinking about my dad the other day, hugging me so tight. I swear my whole life, the only thing I wanted was to make him proud of me. It's so weird to say this out loud, but I feel like if Dad is proud of me, it's this external confirmation that God is proud of me too."

I don't know what to say to this.

"I can't even imagine what my dad would do if he knew where I was." He laughs, sliding a hand over his chest. "Down a dirt road with a no-access sign, lying on a car with my boyfriend . . ."

The word still sends a jolt through me.

"I used to pray so hard to not be attracted to guys," he admits.

I turn and look at him.

He shakes his head. "I always felt so terrible afterward, like I was asking for something so minor when other people have these huge problems. But then I met you, and . . ."

We both let it trail off. I'm choosing to think the end of that sentence would be . . . *and God told me you were the right choice for me.*

"Yeah," I say.

"So nobody at school knows you like guys, then," he says.

I notice the way he avoids the words "gay," "bi," "queer" again. This would be the perfect time to have the Autumn/Manny/Julie/McKenna conversation, but it's easy to skip it here. I mean, who knows what the girls heard, Manny has kept his knowledge pretty quiet so far, and Autumn promised on penalty of death to never say anything. Sebastian has his secrets; I guess it's okay for me to have this one.

"No. I think because I've dated girls, most people just assume I'm straight."

"I still don't understand why you wouldn't just choose to have a girlfriend if you could."

"It's about the person, not what I can do with them." I take his hand, linking my fingers with his. "It's not my choice. No more than it is for you."

I can tell he doesn't like what I've just said. "But you think you might tell more people one day? Like if you ended up with a guy, would you . . . be *out*?"

"Everyone would know if you came to prom with me."

Sebastian looks horrified. "What?"

My smile feels wobbly at the edges. I hadn't actually meant to say that, but I hadn't *not* meant to either. "What would you say if I asked?"

Conflict crashes across his features. "I mean. I . . . couldn't."

A tiny bit of hope deflates in my chest, but I'm not surprised. "It's okay," I tell him. "I mean, of course I would take you, but I didn't expect you to say yes. I'm not even sure I'd be a hundred percent ready yet."

"Are you going to go?"

Turning my face back up to the sky, I tell him, "Maybe with Autumn if she bails on Eric. We're sort of default plus-ones. She wants me to ask Sasha."

"Sasha?"

I wave my hand like *Not worth explaining.*

"Were you ever *with* Autumn?" he asks.

"We made out once. It wasn't magical."

"For you, or for her?"

Grinning, I look back at him. "For me. I don't know how it was for her."

His gaze slides across my face, landing on my lips. "I think she's in love with you."

I don't want to talk about Autumn right now. "Are *you*?"

At first I can tell he doesn't know what I mean. A tiny line forms between his brows, marring the smooth landscape of his forehead.

But then it clears. His eyes widen.

Later, I'll look back on this and wonder whether he kisses me right now because he doesn't want to answer, or whether his answer was so obvious he had to kiss me. But in the moment when he leans forward, rolling over me, his mouth hot and familiar on mine, emotion becomes a liquid; an ocean fills my chest.

I find the true impossibility in writing when I think back on this moment right here, when he's touching me and his palms are branding me, his fingertips tiny spots of heat on my skin. I want to capture it somehow, not only so I'll remember, but so that I can *explain*. There's almost no way to put into words that frantic transition, the deranged tangle we become, except to think of it like a wave on a beach, the physical force of water unstoppable.

The only thing I'm sure of in the moment his touch goes

from exploratory, to determined, to purposeful, and his eyes hold steady on my face, full of thrill as I fall, is we are both thinking how good this is, how right. This moment, and the quieter moments afterward, can't be edited. They can't be rewritten. They can't be erased.

CHAPTER SEVENTEEN

Dad is still up when I get home, mug of tea in his hand, and the *you're-cutting-it-a-bit-close-for-curfew* frown weighing down his features.

I feel the curl of apology begin to tug down the edges of my smile, but no, this smile is bulletproof. I am in an echo chamber and Sebastian's touch is reverberating all around me.

Dad's brows twitch, like he's puzzling out my grin. "Autumn?" he asks, but sounds unsure. He knows I don't look like this when I've been hanging out with Autumn. Or anyone.

"Sebastian."

His mouth makes the *Ahh* shape, and he nods again and again as his eyes move across my face. "You're being safe?"

Oh my God.

The smile wobbles under the weight of my mortification. *"Dad."*

"It's a legitimate question."

"We're not . . ." I turn to the fridge, opening it to grab a Coke. Warring images flash through my thoughts: Sebastian on top of me, over me. Dad sitting here, eyes tight and invested. "You know Mom would murder you for that, for your semi-unintentional blessing that I deflower the bishop's son."

"Tanner." I can't tell if he wants to laugh or smack me. To be honest, I don't think *he* knows either.

"I'm kidding. We're not there yet."

Dad puts his mug down, and the ceramic scrapes across the countertop. "Tann, eventually you might be. I just want to know you're being careful."

The top to my soda cracks open with a satisfying hiss. "I promise I won't get him pregnant."

His eyes roll skyward, and Mom chooses this exact moment to walk in, stopping short just inside the doorway.

"What?" Her voice is flat, eyes wide. I take a moment to appreciate that she's wearing a nightgown that says LIFE GOES BY TOO QUICKLY, with rainbow-colored words highlighting the LGBTQ acronym.

Dad laughs. "No, Jenna. He was out with Sebastian, but it's not what you think."

She looks between us, brows furrowed. "And what do I think?"

"That he and Sebastian are . . . *serious*."

I blink over to Dad. "Hey. We *are* serious."

"Serious as in love?" Mom asks. "Or serious as in sex?"

I groan. "Which would be a bigger problem?"

"Neither would be a problem, Tann," Dad says carefully, eyes on Mom.

Based on this silent exchange, I'm convinced my parents spend more time talking about me dating the bishop's son than they do talking about everything else combined right now.

"You're lucky, you know," I tell them, walking over to envelop my mom in an enormous hug. She melts into me, wrapping her arms around my waist.

"How's that?" she asks.

"I've never freaked you guys out before."

Dad laughs. "You've given us a few heart attacks, Tanner. Don't kid yourself."

"But this one seems to really have thrown you."

His expression sobers. "I think this has been harder for your mom than she's let on." Mom makes a noise of agreement into my chest. "It's brought up a lot of feelings, a lot of anger. Probably some sadness, too. She wants to protect you from all that."

My ribs seem to grow too tight around my lungs, and I squeeze her tighter. "I know."

Her words come out muffled. "We love you so much, kiddo. We want you in a more progressive place."

"As in, as soon as I get my college acceptance letters, I should run and never, ever look back," I say with a grin.

Mom nods against me. "I'm praying for UCLA."

Dad laughs. "Just be safe, okay? Be careful?"

I know he isn't just talking about the physical stuff. I walk over to him next, wrapping an arm around his shoulder. "Will you quit worrying about me? I'm fine. I really like Sebastian, but I'm not unaware of the complications."

Mom shuffles over to the fridge to get a snack. "So, putting aside his parents and their feelings, you know he could be kicked out of school for just being with you tonight? The church might be more accepting than when I was growing up, but you're aware the BYU honor code doesn't allow him to do whatever it is that you did tonight?"

"Mom, when does it get to just be this exciting thing I have?" I swear, the last thing I want to do right now is analyze every little bit of how this could go wrong. I do enough of that all day long anyway. "The problem isn't with Sebastian and me; it's with the rules."

She looks over her shoulder at me, frowning. Dad jumps in. "I get what you're saying, but it isn't that simple. You don't get to say just because the rules are wrong that you can do whatever you want."

My high over Sebastian's touch, over what we did, starts to fade, and I want to get out of the room as fast as I can. It sucks feeling this way with my parents. I like that I tell them everything. I like that they know me so well. But every time we talk about this, their concern becomes this dark shadow that slides in front of the light. It eclipses everything.

So I don't reply. The more I argue, the more they'll

calmly reason. Dad sighs before giving me a small smile and lifting his chin like *Go.* Like he can see I need to escape and pour this night out somewhere.

I kiss Mom, and then run upstairs to my room. The words are bursting out of my head, my hands. Everything that happened, everything I feel pours out of me, liquid relief.

When the words are gone but the feeling still fills my chest—of seeing Sebastian collapse back on the hood of my car, wearing that lazy revelation of a grin—I pick up my Post-it pad and climb into bed.

WE SPENT THE AFTERNOON BUILDING
"FOR SERVICE," HE SAID.
NEW PIECES, NEW PLACES, NEW PARTS
TO BE PUT THERE AND TAKEN FOR GRANTED.
BUT IT FELT GOOD, AND I TOLD HIM THAT.
HE RESTED A PLANK ON HIS SHOULDER
LIKE A BAYONET.
AND I NEARLY LAUGHED, THINKING,
IS THIS WHAT IT FEELS LIKE TO FALL IN LOVE
WITH A SOLDIER ON THE OTHER SIDE?

I close my eyes.

I should probably have predicted this. After Saturday night, I should have known that things would be awkward in class on

Monday, because in between those two days was a whole lot of time back at church.

Sebastian doesn't look up from what he's reading when I walk into the Seminar on Monday afternoon, but I know he senses me the way I sense him, because his shoulders pull back a little, his eyes narrow, and he swallows thickly.

Even Auddy notices. At my side, she shuffles her books onto the table and tilts her head to mine. "What's that about?" she asks under her breath. "Are you guys okay?"

"What?" I look at him like I don't know what she means, and shrug it off. "I'm sure he's fine."

But inside I'm tripping over my own heartbeat. He didn't text me yesterday. Won't look at me now.

Something feels off, and the flippant way I brushed aside my parents' concern feels like it's about to bite me in the ass.

Asher rips into the classroom with a shrieking McKenna on his back, and the entire room goes still as he lets her down in the lewdest way possible. She slides down his back, all giggly, and his hands are basically glued to her ass. Their entrance is so preposterous, so attention-whorey, even Burrito Dave lets out a bewildered, "Dude, *seriously*?"

They kiss in front of the entire class, announcing their reunion.

"Okay, then," I say. Anger spikes in my chest. McAsher can PDA it all over campus and, outside of a little eye rolling, no one cares. They're both Mormon, by the way, and if I'm not mistaken, shouldn't be engaging in this kind of behavior anywhere, let alone in the middle of school, but will they be ridiculed or shunned or threatened? No. No one is going to report them to their bishop. They can't get kicked out of school. And yet they're chaos fodder, getting back together because they're probably so bored with the lack of gossip they're subconsciously making something for people to talk about. I'm willing to bet that McAsher has had sex in every conceivable manner, and yet Asher will still go on his mission and come home and marry a good Mormon girl—maybe even McKenna—and be as self-righteous about LDS values as any of the rest of them. Meanwhile, Sebastian can't even look at me in class, probably because he's beating himself up over our comparably innocent touches on Saturday.

My stomach turns sour and then starts to boil.

"I think the impending prom made them feel amorous," Autumn says beside me.

"Or desperate." I pull my laptop from my backpack and glance back up at Sebastian. He still hasn't turned around to even look at me.

I wish I could throw something at the back of his head or shout an unashamed "HELLO, REMEMBER ME?" in front of everyone. Instead I just pull out my phone and, beneath the table, send him a quick **Hey, I'm over here** text.

I watch as he reaches for his pocket, pulls out his phone, reads.

And then he turns, offers me a wan little smile over his shoulder without actually making eye contact—his eyes swim somewhere above my head—and turns back.

My brain is a blender. Mom's voice pushes to the surface again, calming, reminding me that Sebastian is leaving soon and has pressures I'll never understand. What if this was the first time he prayed and felt worse afterward?

The class ticks by in enormous, redwood-size chunks while I continue to spiral. Almost everyone is done drafting, and Fujita is giving us tips on revisions. At least I think he is. I'm glad Autumn is taking meticulous notes because I'm not catching a word of it. Instead, I bend, crouching over my Post-it, writing,

THE MOON WAS GONE,
LEAVING ONLY THE YELLOWING GLOW OF THE
LAMPS BEHIND US.
DIRT ROAD STRETCHED BACKWARD FOR ETERNITY
AND FOR ONCE WE WERE ALONE.
I'D TAKE THE HEAT OF YOU ON THIS TINY CAR
EVERY DAY
OVER THE MEMORY OF YOU IN MY BED.
IN MY HAND, SO HEAVY.
A LIFETIME OF WANT, FILLING MY PALM.
YOU BIT MY NECK WHEN YOU CAME
AND THEN KEPT YOUR EYES CLOSED WHEN YOU
KISSED ME.

And doing everything I can to not stare at him.

I grab my things and am out the door seconds after the bell rings. Autumn calls after me, but I keep going. I'll text her later and explain. I'm at the end of the hall when I hear my name. It's not Autumn.

"Tanner, wait up."

My feet slow, even though I don't want them to.

"Hey." I keep my eyes glued to the span of lockers near me. I shouldn't do this right now; I'm hurt and mad and embarrassed by his avoidance, and afraid of what I might say.

"'Hey'?" he says back, obviously confused. And it's no wonder; I think this is the first time he's been the one to come after me.

Standing in the middle of the hall, we're like a stone in the river, a steady stream of students moving to make their way around us. I wouldn't describe this spot as *inconspicuous*, but if he's here, I'm here.

"Were you headed to class?" he asks.

I don't know why the storm is choosing this second to build inside me. Why this moment? Why now? Everything was so good this weekend. We had one day of silence and one weird interaction in class and *boom*—my brain is taking this to DEFCON-1 levels of panic.

I'm back on the mountain, hearing him say, *Not . . . that. I'm not gay.*

And there's something today, some set in his jaw, some weird lean in his posture away from me that tells me Saturday did more harm than good. He's fighting something, and he doesn't even know it. He's so far buried in his own dogma and his own world of *shoulds* that he can't admit to himself that he's into dudes, that he'll always be into dudes, that it's a piece of him, a perfect part of him, and it deserves admiration and respect and space the same way anything else about him does.

"It's the end of the day," I tell him. "I was going home."

He shakes his head. "Right, I knew that. Tanner, I'm s—"

Sebastian never gets to finish that thought, because Manny is coming toward us. "Hey, guys," he says, smiling in our direction.

But he doesn't just say "Hey," he says "Hey, *guys.*" Not like we're two people, but like we're two people *together.* Like we're a couple. When I look over to gauge Sebastian's reaction, I know he made the distinction too.

Jesus, Manny. Would it be possible for you to be supportive more *quietly*?

"Manny, hi," Sebastian says.

I blink away and nod toward Manny's letterman's jacket. "Game tonight?" I'm careful to keep my voice conversational, despite feeling like a constellation of small explosions have started inside my chest. I never told Sebastian about the conversation with Manny. I never told him that he knows.

"Yeah, basketball. Listen, we're opening my pool this weekend, and I wanted to invite you both over. It'll be a few kids from here, some of my brother's friends . . ." He pauses, eyes going from me, to Sebastian, to me again, and if I had to guess what we look like based on his expression, it's bad. He turns to me. "But, Tanner, it's not the guys from the lake. Everyone will be cool, so you don't have to worry or anything."

Sebastian's head tilts slowly to the side before he asks, "What do you mean?"

The air leaves my lungs in a rush.

Manny's eyes go wide, and the only way this would be more awkward would be if Manny opened with *You guys are the cutest couple.* "I just mean . . ." He looks to me for help. "Sorry, I saw you guys on a hike the other week and thought . . ."

All the blood drains from Sebastian's face.

"Manny—" I start, but he waves me off.

"Nah, guys, I get it. Whatever. You're both invited, or— either of you, separately, whatever works." He's such an easygoing guy, and I hope it comforts Sebastian that he clearly couldn't care one way or another what we do together, but Sebastian is like a statue beside me. With a quick glance over his shoulder, Manny is gone, and Sebastian turns on me.

Oh, shit.

"What did you tell him?"

291

I hold up my hands. "Whoa—I didn't *tell* him anything. He just said he saw us on a hike."

God. Which hike? There are so many now, and over time we just got so comfortable being on the mountain, kissing like we were behind closed doors. The idea that Manny saw some of that . . . that maybe someone was with him . . . My stomach feels like a bubbling cauldron.

Sebastian turns, and his profile is a portrait of tight anger. This is probably the first second I feel like we're actually a couple. How ironic, too, that it's happening while we're at school, the halls thinning out but for a few stragglers here and there who have no idea we're together, that we've kissed, that I've seen what he looks like when he's lost to pleasure, that I've watched him cry and held his hand. That I've seen his generosity and felt that pride I feel when I realized he's mine. None of those moments feel as real, as coupley, as this one right here, where I know we're about to start arguing in earnest.

"What happened at the lake?"

"Some guys were being dicks, and he came up to me and Autumn after and said—"

His voice rises several pitches. "Autumn knows too?"

Someone passes, and Sebastian startles to attention, rearranging his features into the mask and giving her a mild, "Hi, Stella."

When she's gone, I lead him out the door next to us, to

the parking lot. It's dead out here—like, there are no students in this lot, no teachers, barely anyone walking down the sidewalk—but even still, Sebastian keeps a healthy distance from me. *A Mormon distance*, my mind sneers.

"I mean, clearly Manny saw us. He came up to me and Autumn when we were leaving the lake—because someone called someone else a faggot—and told me he was sorry. It was awkward—like that," I say, gesturing back to the hallway, "and Autumn grilled me for, like, two hours."

"Tanner, this is so bad." Sebastian glares at me and then blinks away, exhaling slowly. I imagine a dragon and fire.

"Look. Manny saw us. Not just me—*us*. I'm not exactly waving the rainbow flag here. *I don't tell people I'm bi.* Autumn—my best friend—didn't even know until a week ago, and I didn't tell her about *you*. I told her I had feelings for you, not that they were reciprocated."

"I just thought . . . after Saturday night . . ." He shakes his head. "I thought maybe you said something to Eric or Manny."

"Why would I do that?" I know I shouldn't say this next part; it's childish and petty, but my mouth doesn't get the memo: "Unless, you know, I wanted contact with someone about this important emotional event in my life."

His head snaps up. "What does that mean?"

"Just that it would have been nice to hear from you yesterday and get some acknowledgment from you today that you *saw* me and you weren't freaking out."

Sebastian's expression screws up into irritation. "Tanner, I was *busy* yesterday."

Oh, that just feels like a slap. Palm open, handprint to my cheek. "Tons of church to do, I guess."

Sebastian picks this right up and runs with it. "It's what we do on Sunday. Have your mother educate you on how we operate. If she remembers."

One . . .

Two . . .

Three . . .

Four . . .

Five . . .

I keep counting. I remember that he's just scared. I remind myself that he's confused. If I take a step back from this second, I know I would want to tell myself, *This is not your battle. This is Sebastian's battle. Give him space.* But isn't it mine, too? Even a little bit? Are we in this as a team, navigating this first together?

He's turned away from me, hand pulling at his hair as he paces the small corner of the parking lot. He looks like he's ready to run. It's funny to realize that's probably *exactly* what he wants to do, because it's not just that he doesn't want to have this discussion here; he doesn't want to do this *anywhere*. He wants to be together without any expectation or discussion. It's a cloud formation—here for now, gone sometime in the nebulous future, undefined.

So I ask him, "Do you ever imagine telling your parents that you're gay?"

He's not even surprised I've gone here so quickly, I can tell. There's no startle, no double take. His scowl deepens, and he takes a step even farther away from me. "I would need to figure out a lot of things about myself before I'd have that kind of conversation with them."

I stare at him. "Sebastian? *Are* you gay?"

I mean, of course he is.

Right?

He looks at me like he doesn't even know me. "I don't know how to answer that."

"It's sort of a yes or no thing."

"I know who I want to be."

"Who you want to be?" What the fuck does he even mean?

"I want to be kind, and generous, and Christlike."

"But what does that have to do with my question? You're *already* that person. You're also good, and thoughtful, and loyal. All those qualities that make you the person I love. You *are* him already. Being gay doesn't change that."

And I can see the moment that it hits, the moment that the word settles into his skin, when it's absorbed. I said it. Not gay. I said "love."

He says my name under his breath and then looks to the side.

He's not even looking at me, and I just told him that I love him.

Somehow this next question feels so much more important than the one that came before it. "Sebastian, did you hear what I said? I love you. Did that register at all?"

He nods. "It registered."

He's blushing, I notice the blush still, and I know it's a happy blush. I can see it; now I know the different colors of emotions; how weird is that?

He likes hearing that I love him, but he doesn't, too. "It's too much for you," I say. "Isn't it?"

"Yeah," he says. "I mean, honestly, that's a lot to hear right now. And it isn't even about what you asked before"—his voice drops then, and he looks around furtively—"whether I'm gay. It's a lot to say to me right now because I have a book coming out, and I'm going on a mission, and there's so much going on."

"So it's *inconvenient* to hear me say I love you?"

He winces. "Tanner. No. I just mean, I don't know that I can give you the same thing that you want to give me."

"It isn't a matter of wanting to *give* you my feelings." I actually laugh at this. "It's just *how I feel.*"

He looks at me like I'm insane.

Like, maybe, he doesn't believe me.

"I love you because of who you are, not because of your blush, or your eyes, or the things you make me feel when you touch me," I say, and he blushes again. "The things that I love about you aren't going to go away when you go on your book tour, and they're not going to go away when you go on your mission. I'll still be here, and I'll still be thinking about all those things. I'll still be working on being a better person, a better friend, a better son. I'll still be wondering what it would be like to be a better boyfriend for you. And you will be on your mission, thinking about how much you wish you weren't gay."

He's mad, I can tell. My first instinct is to wish I could take the words back, but it vanishes like smoke as reality hits me: I meant every single one of them.

"I won't wish . . . ," he starts, but then turns away, jaw ticcing in anger.

"So this is it?" I ask him. "We've reached the limit of what you're willing to give?"

He shakes his head but says, "You want me to be something I'm not."

Something. Not someone, some*thing*.

"I just want you to be okay with who you are *now*. I know I'm not the only one who has feelings here."

He aims, and shoots, his face a mask of calm. "I think we should break up." Sebastian pauses, watching while my organs turn to bricks and crumble inside me. "This isn't right anymore."

The rest of today is going to be hard to explain.

I left right after those words fell from his mouth, and

even now I don't really remember what I did. I went out to the lake, maybe. Drove around, and around, and around.

When it's dark and my phone is lit up with a million texts from Auddy and none from Sebastian, I turn my car around, land softly at the curb near her house.

I never noticed before that her room smells like vanilla candles and that her lamp casts a calming blue light. I never noticed before how she hugs in phases. Like, she'll take me into her arms and then squeeze, and then she'll squeeze harder, and in my head we're moving through different levels of comforting, from *Hey, what happened*, to *Tanner, talk to me*, to *Oh my God, what's wrong?*

And then we hit some other level, because she's coaxing me down. Her hands are on my face—I'm crying; I didn't know—and she's kissing away tears, and I'm babbling. I'm admitting that Sebastian and I were together. I'm telling her about what happened, how he ended it, how small I feel.

Her mouth is near mine, on mine, opening in surprise and then something more.

I fuck it up right here.

This is where I ruin everything.

don't know what I'm doing. I definitely shouldn't be here. My eyes are red, and my hair is a mess. I'd still be in the clothes I slept in except (a) I showered the second I got home and (b) I didn't sleep anyway. I'm a mess.

My eyes scan the hall on my way to her locker. She's usually easy to pick out of a crowd; her hair is a spark of fire in a sea of navy and denim, and her voice can carry from one end of school to the other like nobody I've ever known.

Nothing.

I spin the dial on her locker, turning it right and left and then right again, only to see her coat and backpack aren't here either.

Fuck.

The bell rings, students siphon into classrooms, and the halls slowly drain to empty. Adrenaline mixes with dread as I stand alone in the hall, anticipating the gentle *click* of our principal's shoes on the linoleum. I should be in Modern Lit— with Auddy, who never actually transferred to Shakespeare. I walk to the class, peek inside just enough to see her chair is empty, and turn around. I'll take the truancy and whatever comes along with it, because I am too restless and frantic to sit and discuss James Frey and his fake drama.

But I don't want to go home. My dad is off this morning, and even though I'll have to talk to my parents eventually, I'm not ready to see that look—disappointment softened with pity—that tells me they knew this was going to happen, that it was just a matter of time before this all blew up in my face. I deserve every *I told you so* because they were right, about everything.

There's a bench at the top of the stairs, out of the line of sight of teachers and administrators trolling the halls for the dumb truants like me who aren't smart enough to leave school grounds. I grip my phone in my hand, praying for a few breaths that there'll be something there when I turn it on. But nope. There aren't any new notifications.

Auddy hasn't answered her cell since last night. Feeling desperate, I open her contact info and press the number listed next to the word "home." It rings twice before a voice fills the line.

"Hello?"

"Hi, Mrs. Green." I sit up straighter, clear my throat. I used to speak to Autumn's mom nearly as much as my own, but I'm suddenly nervous. Has Autumn told her what's happened? Does she know what I did?

"Tanner, hi."

"Is Autumn there by chance?" I wipe my free palm across the denim over my thigh.

There's a blink of silence, and I realize that I don't know what I'll say even if she does come to the phone. That I love her—even if it's not in the way she needs? That we made a mistake—*I* made a mistake—but I need her in my life anyway? Will any of that be enough?

"She is. Poor thing woke up with some kind of stomach bug and needed to stay home. Didn't she text you?"

An exit sign glows green at the top of the stairs, and I squeeze my eyes shut. I climbed out of Autumn's bed last night and left without a backward glance. When I finally got my head together, she wouldn't answer. I've texted and called and e-mailed.

I swipe at my eyes with the back of my hand. "I must have missed it."

"I'm sorry, Tann. I hope you weren't waiting outside for her this morning."

"I wasn't. Is she awake? Would it be possible to speak to her?" My voice is pure brittle desperation. "There's a test in calc, and I was hoping she had the notes in her locker."

"She was asleep last time I checked. I can wake her if you need me to."

I hesitate. "No. No, that's okay."

"I'm just leaving for work, but I'll put a note on her door. She'll see it when she wakes up."

I keep my voice even long enough to finish the call and tuck my phone back in my pocket.

The bell rings and the halls fill and empty again, but I don't move. I don't even know what time it is.

I imagine I look like a statue, sitting on the bench, framed by the big window behind me. I'm bent at the waist, elbows on my knees, staring at the floor, and I start to force myself into complete stillness. My brain is chaos, but as I sit here, unmoving, things start to settle there, too.

It's easy to acknowledge that I'm an asshole, that I acted impulsively—like I always do—and that I potentially broke another heart to distract myself from the tattered state of my own. I sit here and start to pretend I was carved out of something cold and unfeeling. I'm not sure if people don't notice me or if they can just tell I should be left alone, but I see feet pass in front of me and no one speaks.

Until someone does.

"Tanner."

I look up, startled, to see Sebastian standing halfway up the stairs. He takes one tentative step up and then another as students jog past him, hoping to make it into third period before the late bell.

He looks like crap too, for the first time ever. It strikes me that in the middle of this, I've barely thought of him at all. Do I tell him about Autumn? Despite what he said yesterday, he's here—are we still together?

"What are you doing here?"

He makes his way toward me, hands pushed into the pockets of his hoodie, and stops when he reaches the top stair. "I went by your house."

"I'm not there," I deadpan. I don't mean it to sound the way it comes out. The statue seems to be cracking more slowly than expected. Maybe I am this cold and unfeeling.

"Yeah, I figured that out when your dad answered." Sebastian hasn't seen my dad since the afternoon he walked in on us, and he must be thinking about that too, because a blush spreads high in his cheeks.

"You talked to my dad?"

"For a minute. He was nice. Told me you were at school." He looks down at his feet. "Not sure why I didn't put that together myself."

"Shouldn't *you* be in school?"

"You'd think so."

"Cutting school." I try to smile, but it feels like a grimace. "So perfect Sebastian isn't that perfect."

"I think we both know I'm not that perfect."

I don't even know how to navigate this conversation. What are we talking about? "Why did you come here?"

"I didn't want to leave things the way they were yesterday."

Just the mention of it makes my stomach drop. "Breaking up, you mean?"

Autumn's face floats in my thoughts, the feel of what we did, and nausea rises in my throat. I genuinely worry I'm going to be sick, and tilt my head up to the ceiling, sucking at the air.

"Yes," he says quietly. "I'm sure it felt terrible to say what you said and have me respond that way."

I blink back down to him, aware of the weight of tears on my lower lids. *What I said?* I want him to acknowledge the words. "Yeah. It felt pretty terrible to tell you I love you and have you break up with me."

There's that blush again, and I can almost see the elation he feels when he hears those three words. It's childish, but it's so unfair that he should get joy out of something that feels like a rope tied around my chest that tightens every time I say it.

He swallows, and a muscle tics in his jaw. "I'm sorry."

He's *sorry*? I want to tell him what I did—because it was two betrayals—but I don't actually think I could get through the words without breaking. Right now, we're speaking quietly enough that no one can hear. But if I broke down and started crying? It would be obvious to anyone watching what kind of conversation we're having. I'm not ready for that, and even after everything, I want to protect him, too.

His face is arranged in a perfectly patient expression. I can see in this moment what a great missionary he'll be. He looks attentive and completely sincere, but somehow . . . peacefully removed.

I meet his eyes. "Did you ever picture me in your life after this semester?"

He looks confused for a beat. I know it's because what came next was always an abstract thought. He had plans, of course—book tour, mission, returning home, and finishing school, probably meeting some sweet girl and following God's plan—but I never figured into any of it. Maybe early in the morning or in some secret, dark corner of his mind, but not in any real way that mattered.

"I don't think I pictured much of anything," he says carefully. "I don't know how the book tour will be—I've never done it. I don't know what leaving on a mission will be—I've never done it. I've never done this, either." He gestures between us with his index finger, and it feels somehow accusatory, like it's something I hoisted onto him.

"You know what I don't get?" I say, running a hand down my face. "If you never had any intention of anyone knowing, or of it meaning anything, why did you dangle me in front of your family and your church? Did you *want* to get caught?"

Something flashes across his face, and the calm, disconnected mask is gone. Has the thought never occurred to him? His mouth opens and closes again. "I . . . ," he starts to say, but there's no more room for easy answers or sound bites from a church manual.

"I know you said you prayed, and prayed, and that God told you that being with me wasn't wrong." At this, Sebastian breaks eye contact to look behind him, making sure we're still alone. I bite down my frustration—he followed me here, for crying out loud—and push on. "But when you did that, did you actually take time to think about how this fit into your future, and who you are, and what it means to be gay?"

"I'm not—"

"I know," I growl. "I *get* it. You're *not gay*. But did you ever look inside yourself while you prayed and try to find the seed of who you are in there, instead of just asking God over and over for *permission* to look?"

He doesn't say anything else, and my shoulders sag. I just want to go. Without any idea why he came to find me, I can't fix this for either of us. Sebastian is going to go, and I have to let him.

I stand for the first time in what feels like hours. I get light-headed as blood flows to my legs, but it feels good to be moving, to have a goal again: Autumn.

I move to pass him and stop, leaning in to whisper and getting caught in the familiar smell of him. "I don't actually care if you break my heart, Sebastian. I went into this knowing it could happen and I gave it to you anyway. But I don't want you to break your own. You have so much space in your heart for your church, but does it have space for you?"

I hear the music as soon as I get out of my car. The windows of Autumn's small, two-story house are closed, but the pounding bass of her screaming death metal rattles them in their frames. She's moved from sad and hiding under her covers to death metal.

All in all, this is a good sign.

I'm usually the one who cuts the grass in the summer, and right now it's in need of a good mowing; unruly tufts of green creep along the edge of the sidewalk. I make a mental note to bring the mower over later this week . . . if Autumn lets me. We might not even be speaking.

With a steadying breath, I ring the bell, knowing she'll probably never hear it over the music. There's no movement in the house. I pull out my phone and dial her number again. My head snaps up when—for the first time since last night—it actually rings instead of going to straight to voice mail. She doesn't answer, though, and it goes to voice mail anyway. I leave yet another message: *Autumn, it's me. Please call me back.*

Stuffing my phone in my pocket, I try the bell again before sitting down on her front steps for the long haul. I know she's in there; I'll just have to wait.

I'm up to twelve cars, two dog walkers, and one mailman passing by before I finally hear something. The music cuts off so quickly that the sudden silence leaves my ears ringing.

I twist around in time to see a red-eyed Autumn peeking her head around the door. In my rush to stand I almost pitch myself off the porch, and the corner of her mouth twitches up into a smile.

My chest grows carbonated with hope.

"I saw you pull up," she says and, squinting into the bright afternoon, steps out onto the porch. It means she's known I've been here for nearly an hour. "Figured I better come out before the neighbors call to report a squatter."

"I tried to call."

"I saw." With a sigh, she looks out into the yard before squinting up at me again. "Maybe you should come in?"

I nod eagerly. She pulls the door open wider and steps back into the darkness, waving me in with a pale hand.

Her living room is a literal blanket fort, the way it always is when she needs to hide out from the world: The curtains are pulled shut, and the TV is on but muted. Pillows and blankets engulf the couch, and in the corner is a package of Chips Ahoy! that looks like it's been torn open by a band of ferrets. Her phone is sitting placidly on the coffee table. The screen is lit with notifications. I bet they're all from me.

I've been in this house a thousand times, had dinner here, done homework, watched countless movies on this very couch, but I've never stood here like this, with a mountain of awkward between Autumn and me. I don't know how to scale it.

I watch as she moves to the couch, kicking the majority of the blankets to the floor before waving me over. We hardly ever *talk* out here. We'll watch movies quietly on the couch, eat food in the kitchen, but always—for as long as we've been best friends—our conversations happen in her bedroom.

I'm not sure either of us is ready to go back in there yet.

My stomach is in knots. What was the point of sitting at school, calming my thoughts all morning if, now that I'm here, I can't think of a single thing to say?

I look at her and try to focus. When I came over last night, she had on a pair of pink-and-black pajamas. A flash of color pops in my head, chased by the question: Did she get dressed? Or did she climb immediately into the shower?

Did she try to wash away what happened as quickly as I did?

She's wearing a pair of sweats now, and a U of U shirt we got at a game last summer. They were playing BYU, and we wanted U of U to beat them so badly we were scouring the ground for lucky pennies and making wishes in fountains. It feels a hundred years away from where we are now. Her hair is pulled to the side and twisted into a single braid. It looks wet. Why am I relieved that she showered? My thoughts trip down another tangent: I remember how Sebastian's hair felt against my face as he kissed down my jaw to my chest, but I have no recollection of whether Autumn's hair was up or down last night, whether I felt it at all.

This seems to pull my guilt right up to the surface, and the words tumble out. "When I came over, I never meant . . ." I swipe at a tear and try to start over. "I didn't mean for . . . that to happen. I was hurt and not thinking straight, and I never meant to take advantage of you and—"

Autumn holds up her hand to stop me. "Wait. Before you go all noble on me, I get to talk."

I nod. I'm breathing so hard, like I just ran ten miles to get here. "Okay."

"When I woke up this morning, I thought it had been a dream." She says this with her eyes fixed on her lap, her fingers toying with the ribbon tie at her waistband. "I thought I'd dreamed you came over and that we did that." She laughs and looks up at me. "I've dreamed about it before."

I don't know what to say. It's not that I'm surprised exactly, but Autumn's attraction to me was always some abstract concept, nothing solid, no foundation to make it last.

"Oh."

Which is probably not a great response.

She reaches up and twists the end of her braid around her finger until the skin turns white. "I know you're going to tell me that you took advantage of me, and I guess . . . in a way, you did. But it wasn't only you. I wasn't lying when I said this whole thing with Sebastian was hard for me, Tann. For a few reasons. I think a part of you has always known some of it. Has known *why*."

Autumn looks to me for confirmation, and I get this sick, slithering feeling in my chest. "I think that's why it feels so terrible," I say. "That's the *definition* of taking advantage."

"Yeah, okay"—she shakes her head—"but it's not really that simple. Our relationship has changed so much these past few months, and I think I was still trying to figure it out. Figure *you* out."

"What do you mean?"

"When you told me you were bi—and God, this makes me such a terrible person, but since there are literally no more secrets between us, I need to get it out. Okay?" I nod, and she pulls her legs to her chest, rests her chin on her knees. "I'm not sure I believed you at first. I had a moment where I thought, great, now I have to worry about girls *and* boys? But then I also thought maybe I could be the one to change your mind."

"Oh," I say again, not knowing how else to respond. She's obviously not the first one to think bisexuality is about choice and not about the way you're made, so I have a hard time faulting her for that. Especially now.

"You were so upset and just . . . I *know* you. I know how you react when you're hurt. You dive into me, into your best friend safe space, and last night . . ." She bites a lip, chewing it as she thinks. "I pulled you over me. Maybe I took advantage too."

"Auddy, no—"

"When you said that Sebastian didn't love you, it's like some fuse burned down in my chest." Tears fill her eyes, and she shakes her head, trying to blink them away. "I was so mad at him. And then the worst part, how could you let him hurt you? It was so *obvious*."

I don't know why—I honestly don't—but this makes me laugh. My first genuine laugh in what feels like days.

She reaches for me, pulling my head onto her shoulder. "Come here, idiot."

I lean against her, and with the smell of her shampoo and the feel of her arm around my neck, a filmstrip of images blurs past me, and a quiet sob escapes. "Autumn, I'm so sorry."

"I'm sorry too," she whispers. "I made you cheat."

"We broke up though."

"There has to be a mourning period."

"I want to love you like that," I admit.

She lets the words hang there, and I keep expecting it to thicken, to grow weird, but it doesn't. "This will be in our rearview mirror soon." She kisses my temple. It's something her mother has said to her probably a thousand times. Right now Auddy sounds like a girl trying on wisdom, and it makes me squeeze her tighter.

"Are you okay?"

I feel her shrug. "Sore."

"Sore," I repeat slowly, trying to follow.

And then she laughs, self-consciously, and the brakes lay down a long scar of black in my mind.

How.

How did I forget?

How did it not even pop into my head for one goddamn second?

A sensation like my chest crumpling causes me to fall forward. "Auddy. Holy shit."

She pushes back, trying to trap my face with her hands. "Tann—"

"Oh my *God*." I duck down, putting my head between my knees so I don't pass out. "You were a virgin. I knew you were. I knew, but—"

"No, no, it's fi—"

I make some ghoulish moan, wanting—basically—to die on this couch, but Auddy smacks my arm, jerking me upright.

"Knock it off."

"I am Satan."

"*Stop* it." She looks pissed, for the first time. "We were sober. You were upset. I was at home, doing homework, reading. I wasn't out of my mind. I wasn't intoxicated. I knew what was happening. I wanted it."

I close my eyes. *Come back, Statue Tanner. Listen to what she's saying and nothing else.*

"Okay?" she says, shaking me. "Give me some credit, and give yourself some while you're at it. You were so sweet to me, and we were safe. That's what matters."

I shake my head. I remember tiny flashes. Most of it is this weird, emotional blur.

"I wanted it to be you," she says. "You're my best friend, and in some twisted way, it made sense that it would be you. Even if you were doing it to get out of your own head for a half hour"—I actually snort at this; it was definitely not a half hour, and she smacks me again, but I can see she's smiling—"I'm the one you make that kind of mistake with. That person is *me*."

"Really?"

"Really," she says. Her eyes turn into these shining beacons of vulnerability, and I want to punch my own face. "Please don't say you regret it. That would feel terrible."

"I mean," I begin, wanting to be honest, "I don't know what to say to that. Do I sort of like that I was your first? Yeah." She grins. "But that's shitty, Auddy. It should be with . . ."

She raises an eyebrow, waiting skeptically.

"Yeah, not Eric," I admit. "I don't know. Someone who loves you like that. Who takes their time and stuff."

"'Who takes their time and stuff,'" she repeats. "Honestly, you're so smooth, I have no idea why Sebastian broke up with you."

I bark out a laugh that seems to die out into silence almost immediately.

"So we're okay?" I ask, after a minute or so of quiet.

"*I* am." Auddy runs her fingers through my hair. "Have you talked to *him*?"

I groan again. It's like a revolving door of suck. I pass through the lobby of Terrible Best Friend Behavior and into the room of Heartache and Religious Bigotry. "He came by today to apologize."

"So you're back together?" I love her for the seed of hope in her voice.

"No."

She makes a small sound of sympathy that reminds me how easily everything happened yesterday.

I think we both realize it at the same time. Autumn pulls her arm away, tucking her hands between her knees. I shift so that I'm sitting up. "I think he just wanted to own the way that he was sort of shitty about it. As much as I want to hate him, I don't think he set out to hurt me."

"I don't think he set out for a lot of this to happen," she says.

I lift my chin to see her. "What do you mean?"

"I think he was intrigued at first. Sometimes you actually can be as charming as you think you are. I think he saw you as a way to rule something out, and then the opposite happened."

"God, that's depressing."

"Is it terrible that I sort of feel sorry for him?" she asks. "I mean, I know it hurts and feels like it will never be okay again, but it will. Someday. You'll wake up and it will hurt a little less and a little less, until some boy or girl is smiling at you and it makes you stupid all over again."

It does sound impossible. "My whole book is about him," I tell her. "He was going to help me edit it, to cut out himself in it, make it someone else. I never sent it to him. That's out the window now, and I honestly don't know what I'm going to do."

quickly learn that just because things feel fine after a conversation like the one Auddy and I have, it doesn't mean things are *normal*.

Whatever the hell normal is anymore.

Autumn is back at school on Wednesday, but there's a shorthand between us that seems to have been elongated. We climb out of my car, and she makes a joke when she points out that my zipper is down; we both turn into awkward robots as I reach for it, zipping it up. I throw my arm around her as we walk down the hall, and she stiffens before leaning into me, and it's so forced I want to laugh. One look at her face—anxious, hopeful, eager to make everything okay—and I try to pull her into a bear hug, but we are crashed into by a couple of students running down the hall. It's going to take some time to find our way back into an easy, physical space.

I wonder if it's because, after the chaos of mutual apologies, the reality has settled in that *we had sex*. These are the kinds of things we would normally dissect together. If it were anyone else, I could complain to Auddy how it changed everything, but you see the obvious issue there.

I can't talk to Mom or Dad about it either, because no matter how much they love me, knowing I did something like that would change the way they see me. I know it would. All they know is that Sebastian broke up with me and I'm a basket case.

Mom's bumper sticker drive is out in full force. In the past three days, I've received deliveries in my pillowcase from, ostensibly, Morgan Freeman, Ellen DeGeneres, and Tennessee Williams. For as much as I tease her about it, I can't deny it helps. I let out a long breath when I walk into the house. I'll never shy away from her hugs. We don't always need to speak out loud for them to know what I'm feeling.

The clock ticking down to graduation is both welcome and dreaded—I can't wait to get out of here, but graduation signals the time when I'll need to get this book in, and my only strategy right now is to offer Fujita the first twenty pages, tell him that the rest is too personal to share, and hope he understands.

Also contributing to the dreaded column: Auddy and I were stupid and didn't apply to any of the same schools. So while I've been accepted to UCLA, University of Washington, Tufts, and Tulane, Autumn has been accepted at the U of U, Yale, Rice, Northwestern, and the University of Oregon. She's going to Yale. I'm going to UCLA.

I say it over and over again.

Autumn is going to Yale. I'm going to UCLA.

We almost couldn't be moving farther apart. It's a few months away and I'm already dreading the pain of this good-bye. It carves out a hollow pit inside me, like I'm losing more than just a geographical anchor. I'm losing an era. Is that lame? Probably. Everyone seems to be getting deep about finishing high school. And then our parents listen to us and laugh, like we're still so young and don't know anything.

Which is probably true. Though, I do know some things.

I know that my feelings for Sebastian don't seem to dim over the next two weeks. I know that the book I'm writing feels like an enemy, a chore. It has no heart, and no end. I realize now that what I thought was easy—writing a book—really *was* easy. Reasonably speaking. Anyone can start one. It's finishing that's impossible.

Autumn suggests changing the names and the places, but I assure her that didn't work out so well before. *Tanenr* can attest to that. She's quick to offer suggestions: I can rewrite it, she can, or we can work together. She thinks there are a million ways I can make it work without outing Sebastian. I'm not so sure.

Looking back, this book is so basic it's almost embarrassing: It's just one guy's story, the lamest autobiography ever of falling in love. Love fails for a million reasons—distance, infidelity, pride, religion, money, illness. Why is this story any more worthy?

It felt like it was. It felt important. Living in this town is suffocating in so many ways.

But if a tree falls in the woods, maybe it makes no sound.

And if a boy falls for the bishop's closeted son, maybe it makes no story.

Sebastian's been in class only once in the past two weeks. Fujita informs us that he's taking a break to finish up his own school year and will be back in time to see us turn in our papers.

The last day Sebastian was in class, he sat in the front, ducked low over a table with Sabine and Levi, going over their final chapters. His hair fell over his eyes, and he would flip it out unconsciously. His shirt stretched across his back, and I remembered seeing him shirtless, seeing the treasure map of muscle and bone. Being in the same room with him after the breakup was actually painful. I mean, I wonder about that, how I can be sitting there and no one is touching me and still, I *hurt*. My chest, my limbs, my throat—everything aches.

The whole time, Autumn sat beside me, her spine curled with guilt, and tried to listen to what Fujita was telling us about copyedits. Every time she looked at Sebastian, she'd glance at me, and I could see the question in her eyes: *Did you tell him?*

But she knows the answer. I'd have to talk to him to tell him anything. We haven't texted, or e-mailed, or even passed notes in folders. I won't lie; it's killing me slowly.

I saw a movie when I was a kid, something that was probably way too mature for me at that age, but there's one scene that stuck with me so intensely that sometimes it rushes into my thoughts and actually makes me shiver with dread. In it, a woman is walking across the street with her child, and the child runs ahead and gets hit by a car. I don't even know the plot that comes after this, but the mother starts screaming, tries to walk backward, to undo what just happened. She's so frantic, so tortured, that for a minute her mind splits and she thinks there's a way she can take it all back.

I'm not comparing my breakup to the death of a child—I'm not that melodramatic—but that feeling of helplessness, of being totally unable to change your fate, is so dizzying, sometimes it makes me nauseous out of the blue. There's nothing I can do to fix this.

There's nothing I can do to get him back.

I've told my parents that we crashed and burned, and as much as they try to cheer me up, and as much as Auddy and I work on finding a way back to the easy comfort we had before, that rain cloud follows me everywhere. I'm not hungry. I sleep a ton. I don't care about this stupid book.

Three weeks after we broke up and eight days before my novel is due, Sebastian is sitting on my front steps when I get home.

I'm not proud to admit it, but I immediately start crying.

It's not like I break down and crumple onto the sidewalk, but the back of my throat gets tight, and the sting spreads across the surface of my eyes. Maybe I'm crying because I'm terrified that he's come here to do more damage, to reactivate what I feel only to let me down easy again, missionary style.

He stands, wiping his palms on his track pants. He must have come right after practice.

"I skipped soccer," he says by way of greeting. He's so nervous, his voice is shaking.

Mine shakes too: "Seriously?"

"Yeah." He smiles, and it's the kind of smile that starts on one side, unsure, more like a question. Are we smiling? Is this cool?

It hits me like a slap across my cheek that I'm his safe space. I get his real smiles.

He's never had an Autumn, or a Paul and Jenna Scott, a Manny, or even a Hailey, who hates him but accepts him.

I give up the battle and smile back; Sebastian has become quite the truant. God, it feels so good to see him. I missed him so much it's like there's an animal inside me, a beastly puppeteer, trying to direct my arms around his shoulders and my face into his neck.

The question hangs like a cloud over my head. "What are you doing here?"

He lets out a tight cough and looks down the street. His eyes are puffy and red, and I think this time he has been crying. "I'm not doing so great. I didn't know where else to go." He laughs now, squeezing his eyes closed. "That sounds so lame."

He came to *me*.

"It doesn't." Reeling, I move closer to him, close enough to touch if I wanted, to check him everywhere and make sure he's okay. "What happened?"

Sebastian stares down at our feet. He's got on indoor cleats, and I love them on him. They're black Adidas, with orange stripes. I'm wearing some scuffed-up Vans. While he figures out his answer, I imagine our feet moving at a dance, or our shoes side by side at the front door.

My brain is such a traitorous beast. It immediately goes from *Ouch, Sebastian is sitting right there* to *happily married dudes*.

"I talked to my parents," he says, and the world comes to a screeching stop.

"What?"

"I didn't come out," he says quietly, and it's such a revelation to even hear him say this much that my knees want to buckle. "But I gave a hypothetical."

Gesturing that we walk around to the backyard for more privacy, I turn, and he follows.

I wish I could describe what happens inside my chest when I feel his hand slide into mine as we move past the trellis of ivy along the garage. There's a party in my blood, riotous and electric; it vibrates my bones.

"This okay?" he asks.

I look down at our hands, so similar in size. "I don't know, actually."

Autumn's voice pushes into my head: *Be careful.* I shift her voice to the front, but I don't let go of his hand.

We find a spot under Mom's favorite willow tree, and sit. The grass is still wet from the sprinklers, but I don't think either of us cares. I stretch out my legs, and he follows, pressing the length of his thigh to mine.

"What should we do first?" he asks, staring at our legs. "My apology, or my story?"

His *apology*? "I don't know if my brain has caught up yet."

"Are you okay—*have* you been okay?"

I let out a single dry laugh. "About us? No. Not at all."

"Me either."

I count out my heartbeats. One, two, three, four. A bird shrieks overhead, and wind moves through the leaves. This tree always reminded me of Mr. Snuffleupagus on *Sesame Street*. Lumbering and unobtrusive and gentle.

"I didn't end things because I was over you," he says.

"I know. That made it worse, I think."

He turns, cupping my neck in both palms so I look him in the eye. "I'm sorry."

His hands are so warm, and they're shaking. I bite my lip so I don't lose it. Sebastian moves closer, ponderously, never closing his eyes even when his mouth touches mine. I don't even think I kiss him back. I just sort of sit there, mouth hanging open in shock.

"I love you too." He kisses me again, this time longer. *This* time I kiss him back.

I pull away because maybe I need to lose it a little, bending and pressing my hands to my face. Of course, this moment is playing out almost exactly like I wanted it to in every iteration of the fantasy. But there's a lot of scar tissue there, and I'm not sure how or whether I can cleanly remove it with him sitting there watching. I need about a half hour to figure out how to react to what he's said that's slightly more measured than pulling him on top of me on the lawn.

"I need a minute to process this," I say. "Tell me what happened."

He nods, cheeks hot. "Okay, so, remember that guy Brett my parents mentioned?" he says. "When we overheard them?"

The guy who married his boyfriend, and Sebastian's mom worried for the well-being of the parents. "Yeah. I remember."

"He and his husband moved from California to Salt Lake. I guess there's some drama in the ward about it." Sebastian turns our hands over, tracing the tendons under my skin with his index finger. "Is *this* okay?"

"I think so." I laugh, because the tone of my voice is the acoustic equivalent of a tail wagging, but I can't even bother being embarrassed about it.

"So, he moved back, and my parents were talking about it at dinner. My grandparents were there." He laughs, and looks over at me. "I chose a bad time to do this, I know, but it just sort of . . . came out."

"So to speak."

He laughs again. "So at dinner, they're talking about Brett and Joshi, and I just put my silverware down and asked them point-blank what would happen if one of us was gay."

"You did?"

"Yeah." He nods, and keeps nodding like he almost can't believe it. "I haven't been okay the past few weeks. I don't know that I can go back to thinking that it will go away. I tried out all these hypotheticals with myself, like what if you moved on from this, would I stop being attracted to guys? Would I be able to marry someone like Manda one day? But the truth is, I wouldn't. I felt right with you. In part because you're you, but in part because . . ."

I point to my chest. "Guy."

Sebastian smiles his real smile. "Yeah." He pauses, and I know what's coming before he even says it, and it's like the sun chose this moment to press through the dense branches of the tree. "I'm totally gay."

A gleeful laugh rips out of me.

I throw my arms around his neck, tackling him.

Beneath me, he laughs, letting me kiss all over his neck and face.

"I mean this in the least patronizing way possible: It makes me so proud to hear you say that."

"I've been practicing," he admits. "I said it into my pillow. Then I'd whisper it while I rode my bike. I've been saying it every day since we broke up. It doesn't feel weird anymore."

"Because it isn't." I let him up, and remember that he was in the middle of a story. "Okay, so you asked them the hypothetical . . ."

"Mom got really quiet," he says, and both of our smiles fade because no, this isn't silly, wrestling fun anymore. "Dad and Grandpa looked at each other, like 'Oh, here we go.' Grandma focused on cutting her steak into tiny, tiny pieces. Lizzy stood up and gathered Faith and Aaron and walked them out of the room." He looks at me, pained. "Lizzy, my closest friend, wanted to remove them from the conversation. Like, I don't think *anyone* was surprised by this."

This, I think, is what it feels to have a heart broken. I let out some garbled sound of sympathy.

"Finally, Dad said, 'Do you mean attraction or behavior, Sebastian?' And he never uses my full name." He swallows, with effort. "I told him, 'Either. Both.' And he went on essentially to say that our family believes that the sacred acts of procreation are to be shared only between a man and his wife, and anything else undermines the foundation of our faith."

"So, basically what you expected," I say carefully. I mean, it's a testament to how messed up the situation is that I'm hearing this and thinking, *Could be worse!* "Do you think they're open to the conversation at least?"

"This was a week ago," he whispers. When he looks up at me with tears in his eyes, he adds, "No one has spoken to me in a week."

A week.

A week!

I can't even fathom not speaking to my parents for a week. Even when they've been on work trips, they call and check in nightly and require detailed updates that go far beyond the scope of their mildly distracted at-home check-ins. But Sebastian has been living in a house with a family that moves around him as if he's a ghost.

I don't know when exactly we move on, but it's not long after he tells me this. It's like there's nothing I can say that makes it less terrible. I try, but I fail, and eventually just focus on making him lie back next to me, staring up at the tree, and telling him all the stupid gossip Autumn has told me.

Oof. Autumn. I need to go there at some point.

But not yet. Right now we're holding hands and lying side by side. Our palms grow slippery and clammy, but he doesn't let go, and I won't either.

"What have you been doing?"

"Moping," I tell him. "School. Mostly moping."

"Same." He reaches up with his free hand, scratches his

jaw. It's stubbly for once, and I'm into it. "Well, and church. I've been practically living there."

"What are you going to do?"

"I don't know." He rolls his head to look at me. "I leave on tour three weeks from today. Honestly, I don't think my parents are going to be able to keep this up when the book comes out. I know they're proud. They'll want to share that pride with everyone."

I'd forgotten about the book. It's like the tour just sort of bled into his mission and stopped having any legitimate purpose. I am a brat. "And they won't want anyone to see them being assholes."

He doesn't say anything to this, but that means he doesn't disagree, either.

"I'm sorry," I say. "I don't want to bad-mouth your parents because I know you guys are super close. I'm just pissed."

"Me too." He shifts, putting his head on my shoulder. The next eight words come out thin, like he's run them through his thoughts so many times, they're worn down, frayed: "I don't think I've ever felt this worthless."

This is a knife to my gut, and in a heated flash, I want him to get the fuck out of Provo. I hope his book sells a million copies in a week and everyone loses their mind over how great he is. I hope his ego gets enormous and he becomes unbearable—anything but that shaking tenor of his voice saying those words again.

I pull him to me, and he rolls to his side, letting out a choking sob into my neck.

So many platitudes pile onto the tip of my tongue, but they'd all sound terrible.

You're amazing.

Don't let anyone make you feel worthless.

I've never known anyone like you.

And on and on.

But we've both been raised to care greatly what our family thinks about us—their esteem is everything. On top of that, Sebastian has the looming judgment of the church, telling him wherever he looks that the God he loves thinks he's a pretty foul human being. It's impossible to know how to undo the damage they're doing to him.

"You're amazing," I say anyway, and he chokes out a sob-laugh. "Come on, kiss me. Let me kiss that amazing face."

Mom finds us like this—crying-laughing-crying in a heap under the Snuffleupagus tree—and one look at our faces sends her into triage mode.

She claps a hand over her mouth when she sees Sebastian, and tears rise to the surface of her eyes nearly immediately. Mom pulls us up, hugs me, and then wordlessly takes Sebastian into her arms—he gets the longer hug, the one with the soft Mom words spoken into his ear—and something breaks loose in me because it makes him cry harder. Maybe she's just saying things like "You're amazing. Don't ever let anyone make you feel worthless." Maybe she tells him she understands what he's going through and that it will get better. Maybe she's promising him weekly deliveries of bumper stickers. Whatever it is, it's exactly what he needs because the tears eventually stop, and he nods down at her.

The sun is starting to set, and there's no question he's staying for dinner. We wipe the grass from our pants and follow Mom inside. It's late spring, and even though it gets pretty warm during the day, the temperature drops like a rock once the sun goes away, and it's only now that I realize how cold it was out under the tree. Inside, my parents have a fire going in the living room. They're blasting Paul Simon from the stereo. Hailey is sitting at the kitchen table, carving out her chemistry homework with dark, resentful scrapes of her pencil.

It's suddenly impossible to get warm. We laugh, clutching each other in this sort of surreal, high way—he's here, in my house, with my family—and I pull Sebastian down the hall with me, handing him one of my hoodies from the coat hooks near the front door. It's deep red, with the S-T-A-N-F-O-R-D stamped across the front in white letters.

He patiently lets me zip it for him, and I admire my handiwork. "You look good in those colors."

"Unfortunately, I'm already enrolled at a local university."

For now, I think. God, his decision to embrace this—*us*—impacts so many things. If he wants to stay at BYU, he can't be out, period. Even being here he's essentially breaking an honor code. But there are other schools. . . .

This is unreal. I look down the hall at where my parents are bent over, laughing over my dad's hysterical distaste for touching raw chicken. They both seem to have put their worry away for the night, realizing that we need this—a few hours where we can just be together like any other couple. The only instruction they give us is to wash our hands before dinner.

"Speaking of college, though."

I startle when he says this because it hits me: It's been only a few weeks that we've been apart, but so much has happened, future-decision-wise. He doesn't know where I'm moving in August.

"I assume you've heard back from most places?"

"Yeah." I reach forward, zipping down his sweatshirt just enough to get an eyeful of throat and collarbone. His skin is this perfect kind of smooth and tan. I want to get him shirtless and have my own photo shoot.

I'm stalling.

"So?"

I meet his eyes. "I'm going to UCLA."

Sebastian falls wordless for a few tense seconds, and the pulse in his neck picks up pace. "You're not staying in state?"

Wincing, I admit, "No." I hope the grin I give him takes the edge off my words: "But neither are you, most likely."

He deflates a little. "Who even knows." His hand comes

up to my chest, sliding flat-palmed from my shoulder to my stomach. Everything tenses. "When do you move?"

"August, I think."

"How's your book coming?"

My stomach spasms, and I gently guide his hand away from my navel. "It's fine. Come on. Let's get something to drink."

He sends a text to his parents, telling them he'll be home late. It goes unanswered.

I think I'll remember this night for the rest of my life, and I don't say that to be flippant or hyperbolic. I mean, my parents are charged up on something—together, they are being hilarious. Hailey is actually crying she's laughing so hard. Sebastian nearly loses a sip of water when my dad tells his favorite terrible joke about a duck walking into a bar and ordering raisins. When we finish eating, I take Sebastian's hand on the table and my parents stare at us for a few beats with a mixture of adoration and concern. Then they offer us dessert.

It's what I want for us. And whenever I look over at him and he meets my eyes, I try to say, *See? It could be like this. It could be like this every day.*

But then I see his own words pushed back to me, high and tight in his thoughts: *It could. But I'd lose everything I know and everyone I have.*

I can't honestly blame him if it's not enough yet.

. . .

Mom and Dad head up to bed only about twenty minutes into *Spectre*. They lift a snoring Hailey off the chair and help her up the stairs too. Dad looks back over his shoulder at me, giving me a single half encouraging, half reminding-me-not-to-have-sex-on-the-couch look, and then disappears.

Then we're alone, in the living room, with the strange blue glow of the television and a giant mostly untouched bowl of popcorn in front of us. At first we don't move. We're already holding hands under a throw blanket. I keep having these flashes of realization—I wonder if it happens to him, too—where I can't actually believe he's here, we're back together, my parents are just hanging out with me and my boyfriend like it's something we can do, no problem.

But that voice that's been in my thoughts all day clears its throat, and I know I can't put it off anymore.

"I need to tell you something," I say.

He looks over at me. The left side of his face is glowy from the television, and combined with his sharp jaw, cheekbones, and mildly concerned expression, he looks a little like the Terminator. "Okay."

"I messed up." I take a deep breath. "After you broke up with me, I was a mess. I don't actually remember a lot of the day. I know I drove around for a few hours, and then I went to Autumn's. I was crying, and not thinking very clearly."

I can tell he *knows* the minute I say this because he does this sharp inhale through his nose, like he's saying, "Oh."

Nodding, I let out a slow, remorseful, *"Yeah."*

He nods, turning back to the TV.

"She's okay. I'm okay. We talked about it, and obviously it's weird, but she and I will get through it. I just . . . didn't want to keep it from you."

"Just to make sure I understand: You had sex with her?"

I pause, guilt and shame pressing down on my shoulders like a weight. "Yeah."

His jaw tics. "But you don't want to *be* with her?"

"Sebastian, if I wanted to be with Auddy, I'd be with Auddy. She's my best friend, and I went to her because I was heartbroken. I realize this sounds completely insane, but we got into a weird comfort spiral that turned into sex."

I think this makes him laugh in spite of himself. But he looks back at me. "This doesn't feel great."

"I know."

He reaches up, absently rubbing his sternum with his fist. I lift his hand to kiss his knuckles.

"I know I messed up," he says quietly. "I guess I can't have the kind of reaction that I want to have."

"You can. I get it. I would be losing my mind right now if the situation were reversed."

"But you wouldn't be able to tell me what to do after you break up with me." Apparently, his calm demeanor wins out. I'm not sure whether I'm relieved, or wish he would show a small flash of jealous rage.

"I guess not."

"But if we're together, you're with *me*, right?" he asks. "Even if I go away?"

Pulling back, I study him for a second. "I thought you couldn't be in a relationship when you leave."

He ducks his head. "I'm going to have to figure out what rules I follow and what rules I don't."

"While keeping everything about you a secret?"

Sebastian turns to me, pressing his face into my neck, and lets out a cute growl. "I don't know yet." His words come out muffled: "I love so many things about the church. Speaking to God feels like instinct, like it's wired into me. I can't imagine what I'd do if I left. It's like standing in an open field and trying to point to the four walls. There's just no framework to my life without the church."

I wonder if he has to leave, if his choice is binary like that. "Maybe things are more relaxed in wards in other cities," I say. "Like LA, for example."

He laughs, and bares his teeth against my collarbone.

Things go wordless for a while.

I keep one ear open for the sound of footsteps on the stairs and the other open for the sounds Sebastian makes next to me.

CHAPTER TWENTY

A word to the wise: Don't try to be the little spoon while sleeping on a couch. You'll fall off, for one, and wake up with a cramp in your neck, for two. And most likely, when you wake up alone on the floor with your father staring down at your shirtless body sprinkled with the detritus from an overturned bowl of popcorn, you'll be grounded.

"Sebastian *slept over*?"

"Um . . ." I sit up when Dad asks this, looking around. Without even looking in a mirror, I can tell my hair is standing straight up. I pull a sharp kernel of popcorn away from where it is dangerously close to my nipple. "I don't actually know. I think he's gone."

"Kind of like your shirt?"

"Dad—"

"*Tanner.*"

It's hard to take his gruff tone seriously when he's wearing the Cookie Monster pajama pants Hailey got him for Chrismukkah two years ago.

"You're running late," he says, and turns. I catch a glimpse of a grin. "Get dressed and eat something."

I grab a bowl of cereal and sprint straight to my bedroom. I have a lot to write down.

Sebastian doesn't answer the chicken/popcorn/beach landscape emoji text I send him just before school starts, and he isn't in the Seminar this afternoon. I send his private e-mail a short note when I get home.

> Hey, it's me. Just checking in. Everything okay? I'm around tonight if you want to stop by. —Tann

He doesn't answer.

I try to ignore the familiar sinking ache that takes residence in my stomach, but at dinner, I'm not hungry. Mom and Dad exchange worried looks when they ask if I've talked to Sebastian today and I answer in a grunt. Hailey even offers to do the dishes.

I send our old standby—the mountain emoji—the next day, and get nothing in return.

At lunch, I call him. It goes straight to voice mail.

From there, my texts to him pop up in a green bubble, as though his iMessage has been turned off.

. . .

Nothing today.

Nothing today.

It's been four days since he was here, and I heard from him, an e-mail.

> Tanner,
> I'm so sorry if I miscommunicated anything to you about my feelings, or my identity. I hope my lack of clarity hasn't brought you too much pain.
> I wish you nothing but the best in your upcoming adventures at UCLA.
> Kindest regards,
> Sebastian Brother

I don't even know what to say or think after I finish reading it. Obviously, I read it about ten times, because the first nine times, I can't believe that I'm reading it right.

I go to my folder, the one with the letters from him. I read different phrases, totally blown away by the distance and formality in the e-mail.

Is it weird that I want to spend every second together?

Sometimes it's hard to not stare at you in class. I think if people saw me looking at you for even a second, they would know.

I can still feel your kiss on my neck.

But no, he miscommunicated his feelings.

I send my official acceptance letter to UCLA, but my hand shakes when I sign the acknowledgment that my acceptance is dependent on my grades this term. The plan is for me to move August 7. Orientation is August 24. I text Sebastian and tell him, but he doesn't answer.

I counted today: In the past six days, I've sent him twenty emoji texts. Is that crazy? It feels like nothing compared to how many real ones, with words, I've started and deleted. I have Auddy and Mom and Dad ready to listen anytime I need them. Manny and I had lunch, and it was quiet, but actually pretty easy just to hang in silence. Even Hailey is being sweet.

But I just want to talk to *him.*

My book is due tomorrow, and I have no idea what I'm supposed to do. Sebastian shows up in chapter two. Fujita told me I need to turn in at least a hundred pages to get a grade, but he knows I have more. If I gave him even the first hundred, he would get right to the part where Sebastian told me he's attracted to guys. He would get to where we kiss.

The funny thing is, if you've watched me for more than two minutes in that class, it wouldn't matter what changes I make. I could move it to an alternate universe on a planet called SkyTron-1, rename him Steve and myself Bucky, and give us both superpowers, and it would still be obvious what this book is about. I can't hide anything when he's in the room, and my heart is on every page, regardless of the details.

If I get a D in this class—what I'd get if I didn't turn in the final book or only gave Fujita twenty pages—I would still graduate, but would lose my honors ranking. I think UCLA would still take me. I think.

I realize the end of this book sucks, and I'm barely trying to make it anything worthwhile, but this is the end I have. What kind of idiot was I to start a book about writing a book and just assume the ending would be happy? That's my framework—happy endings, easy life. But I guess it's better that I learn this lesson now instead of later, down the road, when I'm not living at home and the world isn't so kind.

I have been a lucky asshole, one with no idea how the world really works.

I stand outside Fujita's office. He's in with a student—Julie, I think—who is crying and probably stressed about turning in her book, but I feel oddly numb. No, that's not entirely true. I feel relieved, like both of my looming fears—the fear of Sebastian ending things again, the fear of having to deal with the book—have come to pass and at least I don't have to worry about either of them anymore.

When it's my turn, I walk inside. Fujita looks at the laptop in my hands.

"You didn't print me a copy?"

"No."

He stares at me, puzzling this out.

"I don't have anything I can turn in."

There's something almost electric about hearing a teacher say *"Bullshit."*

"I don't." I shift on my feet, uncomfortable with the intensity of his attention. "I wrote something, but I can't turn it in. I can't even give you a hundred pages."

"Why?"

Even that I can't explain. I look past him, at his messy desk.

"What do you expect me to do?" he asks quietly.

"Fail me."

"Sit down," he says. "Take five minutes and think this through. Have you lost your mind?"

Yes, I have. What other explanation could there be?

So my laptop is open on my lap, and I'm typing words

words

words

words

SEBASTIAN

At night, when Sebastian lies awake, he stares up at his blank white ceiling and feels like there is a hole slowly burning through his torso. It always starts right beneath his breastbone and then expands downward, black and curling, like a match held to cellophane.

The first night he thought it was indigestion.

The second night he knew it wasn't.

He dreaded it the third night, but by the fourth he went to bed early, anticipating the way it started with a tiny poke and then grew into a piercing burn that spread, roiling and salty, into his gut. Oddly, it happens just after that first moment of contact between his head and his pillow, which used to trigger a swarm of images of Tanner: his smile and his laugh, the curve of his ear, and the lean set of his shoulders, the way his eyes would narrow just before his humor turned biting, chased by the immediate remorseful dilation of his pupils. Now, instead, the moment Sebastian lays his head on his pillow, he remembers that Tanner isn't his anymore, and then after that he feels nothing but the ache.

He doesn't like to be melodramatic, but the ache is better than guilt; it is better than fear, it is better than regret, and it is better than loneliness.

When he wakes, the ache is gone, but the smell of breakfast is there, and that triggers its own routine: Get up. Pray. Eat. Read. Pray. Run. Shower. Write. Pray. Eat. Write. Pray. Eat. Read. Pray. Ache. Sleep.

Final grades are due in two days, and in a fit of desperation, Fujita gave Sebastian three of the books to read and grade. Apparently, it was a prolific term: Every student turned in more than sixty thousand words. Turns out, nearly a million words is too much for one person to get through in five days.

But he wasn't given Tanner's book, and although it occurred to Sebastian a thousand times to request it, in the end, he put it out of his head. He read Asher's indecipherable manifesto, Burrito Dave's ham-fisted mystery, and Clive's exceptionally well-plotted CIA thriller. He wrote summaries of the strengths and weaknesses of each work. He suggested grades.

He turns it all in two days early, giving Fujita time to go through them himself if he needs to before turning in final grades. And he returns home, ready to catch his routine at the next meal, only to find Autumn standing on his doorstep.

She's wearing a Ravenclaw sweatshirt, jeans, and flip-flops.

She's also wearing an uncertain smile and holds something in her cupped hands.

"Autumn. Hey."

Her smile grows more uncertain. "I'm sorry to just . . . show up."

He can't help but grin back at her. Has she so quickly forgotten that people *just show up* all the time?

But seeing her is also a little painful because she gets to see *him* whenever she feels like it.

"Should we go inside?"

He shakes his head. "It's probably better to talk out here." The house feels like the inside of a giant, fuzzy microphone. It's too hot in there, too tense and silent. In his rare flashes of free time, Sebastian goes online and searches for spacious, unfurnished apartments in Atlanta, New York, Seattle, Los Angeles.

"Okay, well, first," Autumn begins quietly, "I want to apologize. I know Tanner told you what happened between us. I hope you know what a mess he was. I took advantage, and I'm sorry."

A muscle clenches in Sebastian's jaw. The reminder of what happened between Tanner and Autumn isn't great, but at least it answers one question he had: *Are they together now?* "I appreciate that, but it's not necessary. Nobody owes me an explanation."

She studies him for a few breaths. He doesn't even have

to wonder what he looks like from the outside. Of course, Autumn has seen grief before, and now Sebastian knows too, how it can take up residence in the tiny spaces on a face where muscles can't force a smile. Beneath Sebastian's eyes there are blue smudges. His skin isn't pale exactly, but it has a sallow tint, like he's not getting much sunlight.

"Okay, well, I wanted to say it anyway." Autumn opens her hand, exposing a small pink USB drive. The flush of betrayal climbs up her neck. "And I wanted to give you the book."

"Didn't you turn it in to Fujita?" The due date was days ago; Autumn knows this.

She looks at him, confused. "This isn't *my* book."

Sebastian has never felt the ache in daylight before, but there it is. Out in the sun, it spreads faster, fed like wildfire whipped to a frenzy in the wind. It takes him a moment to remember how to speak. "Where did you get that?"

"From his laptop."

His heart does a weird fist-clench in his chest, and then begins pounding against his breastbone. "I'm guessing he doesn't know you took it."

"You would be correct."

"Autumn, you have to take it back. This is a violation of his privacy."

"Tanner told Mr. Fujita he didn't have anything to turn in. You and I both know that's not true. *Fujita* knows it's not true."

Heat drains from Sebastian's face and his words come out as a whisper. "You want me to turn it in for him?"

"No. I would never ask you do to that. I want you to *read* it. Maybe you can talk to Fujita, ask if you can grade it. I heard you're grading a few others. He knows Tanner didn't feel comfortable turning it in but will probably be happy to hear that you've read it. I don't have the clout to do that. But you do."

Sebastian nods, staring at the drive in his hand. His desire to read what's there is nearly blinding. "It's a bit of a conflict for me. . . ."

Autumn laughs at this. "Uh, *yeah*. But I don't know what else to do—if he turns it in, you're outed to a teacher without your consent. If he doesn't turn it in, he fails the assignment that makes up most of his grade and jeopardizes his standing at UCLA. You and I both know there's no easy way to just swap names here."

"Right."

"Personally, I don't know what he was thinking." Autumn looks up at him. "He knew he'd have to turn *something* in eventually. But that's Tanner for you. He feels before he thinks."

Sebastian sits on the front step, his eyes on the sidewalk. "He said he was writing something new."

"Did you honestly believe that, or did it make it easier? He couldn't think about anything else."

Sebastian is filled with this clawing sense of irritation; he wants her to leave. Autumn's presence is like a thumb pressed to a bruise.

Autumn sits next to him on the step. "You don't have to answer because it's probably none of my business. . . ." She laughs and then hesitates. Sebastian focuses on trying to find the ache again. "Do they know about Tanner?"

His gaze darts to her face and quickly away.

Do they know about him?

It's such an enormous question, and the answer is an obvious *no*. If they knew about him—truly *knew* about his capacity for tenderness, for humor, for quiet and for conversation—he would be *with* Tanner right now. He genuinely believes that.

"They know that I was interested in someone and that it was him. I didn't tell them everything, but it didn't matter. They lost it anyway. . . . That's why . . ."

Why he sent the note.

"We used to have all these inspirational quotes and photos around my house," she says. "I remember one that said 'Family is a gift that lasts forever.'"

"I'm sure we have that one somewhere."

"There was no asterisk though, saying, 'But only under these specific conditions.'" She picks a piece of invisible lint from her jeans and looks up him. "My mom got rid of most of it. I think she kept the one of them on their wedding day in front of the Temple, but I'm not sure. She was pretty angry;

it could have gone in the trash with everything else."

Sebastian looks at her. "Tanner told me a little about your dad. I'm sorry."

"I didn't understand Mom's reaction at the time, but it makes sense now. I know those sayings are supposed to be inspirational, but they mostly feel like someone standing over your shoulder, passive aggressively reminding you where you fall short or why your tragedy is for the greater good, all in God's plan. Mom had no use for any of it."

He blinks, eyes trained on his feet. "Understandable."

She bumps his shoulder with hers. "I'm gonna wager a guess that things aren't great right now."

He leans forward, wanting to get away a little, and rests his elbows on his knees. It isn't that he doesn't want to be touched; it's that he wants it so intensely it nearly burns. "They're barely speaking to me."

Autumn growls. "Sixty years ago they would have been just as unhappy if you'd brought home a black girl. She'd have had the right things inside but the wrong skin color. Do you see how ridiculous that is? That's not independent thinking; that's deciding how to love your *child* based on some outdated teaching." She pauses. "Don't stop fighting."

Sebastian stands and brushes the dirt from his pants. "Marriage is eternal, is between a man and a woman, and leads to an exalted, eternal family. Homosexuality denies that plan." He sounds completely detached, like he's reading from a script.

Autumn stands slowly, giving him an unreadable smile. "What a great bishop you'll make."

"I should. I've heard it enough."

"They're upset, but at some point they'll figure out you can be right, or you can be loved. Only a handful get both at the same time."

He runs a finger along the thumb drive. "So it's on here?"

"I haven't read it all, but what I have . . ."

He waits, one, two, three beats of silence between them, before he finally breathes.

"Okay."

Sebastian's not used to avoiding his family. He's the son who helps his mother clean so she has time to relax before dinner, who goes to church early for some extra time with his dad. But lately he's treated more like a tolerated houseguest. As Autumn's car backs out of the driveway and disappears down the street, he wishes he didn't have to go back inside at all.

Things have been strained since he asked his parents—hypothetically—what they would do if one of their children were gay. Apparently, his lack of blatant heterosexuality had been noticed already, and discussed. He dropped a match straight into a pool of gasoline.

That was a couple weeks ago. His mom is talking to him again, but just barely. His dad is never home because it seems he always needs to be somewhere else, helping some other family in crisis. His grandparents haven't stopped by in weeks. Aaron is mostly oblivious; Faith knows something is wrong but not what. Only Lizzy understands the specifics and—to his desperate heartbreak—is giving him a wide berth as if he's Patient Zero, infectious.

What's terrible is that Sebastian isn't even sure he deserves to be heartbroken. *Heartbroken* implies that he's innocent in this, the victim in some tragic romance and not largely responsible for his own pain. He's the one who went behind his parents' backs in the first place. He's the one who fell in love with and then broke up with Tanner.

Seeing Autumn shook something loose in him, and he can't go inside and pretend that everything's fine, that hearing what Tanner did to protect him didn't just turn his world upside down.

He's always been good at pretending, but he doesn't know if he can do it anymore.

When the curtains have opened and closed for the third time, Sebastian finally goes back in. His mom doesn't waste any time, and as soon as the door shuts behind him, she's on his heels.

"Autumn left?"

He wanted to go straight back to his room, but she's blocking the staircase. He walks into the kitchen instead, grabbing a glass from the cupboard and filling it with water.

The USB drive burns a hole in his pocket. Sebastian's hands are practically shaking.

He drains the glass in a few seconds and places it in the sink. "Yes," he says. "She left."

His mom circles the kitchen island to turn on the mixer, and the scents of butter and chocolate fill the air. She's making cupcakes. Yesterday it was cookies. The day before it was biscotti. Her routine hasn't shifted at all. Their family isn't falling apart. Nothing is different.

"I wasn't aware you two were friends."

He doesn't want to answer questions about Autumn, but knows it will only bring more if he doesn't. "I was only a mentor to her in class."

There's a heavy silence. In theory he was only a mentor to Tanner, too, so that answer doesn't hold much reassurance. But his mom doesn't press; he and his parents don't *converse* anymore—they exchange pleasantries like *please pass the potatoes*, or *I need you to mow the lawn*—and Sebastian feels like they're losing that muscle. He always expected his relationship with them to shift over time as he had more experiences, was able to relate to them as adults in ways he never understood before. But he didn't expect to see his parents' sharp edges and limitations so soon, and so quickly. Like discovering the world really *is* flat; suddenly there is no other side of wonder and adventure to explore. Instead, you disappear over the edge.

With the mixer off, she watches him from across the counter. "I've never heard you mention her before."

Does she not realize he's never really talked about *any* girl before, not even Manda? "She dropped off something for Fujita."

Sebastian watches as she connects the dots. Her suspicion rises like a dark sun across her face. "Autumn knows him, doesn't she?"

Him.

"They're friends."

"So she wasn't coming by about *this*?"

There's only one reviled "him," just as there is only one unmentionable "this."

Irritation flares in his chest that they won't even use his name. "His name is Tanner." Saying it makes his heart itch in his chest, and he wants to reach in, claw at it roughly.

"You think I don't know his name? Is that a joke?"

Suddenly her face is red from her hairline to her collar; her eyes are glassy and bright. Sebastian has never seen his mom so angry. "I don't even know how we got here, Sebastian. *This*? What you're going through?" She stabs the air with savagely curled finger quotes around the words "going through." "This is your own doing. Heavenly Father is not responsible for your decisions. It is your free will alone that deprives you of happiness." She picks up the wooden spoon, shoving it into the batter. "And if you think I'm being harsh, talk to your dad about it. You have no idea how much you've wounded him."

But he *can't* talk to his dad, because Dan Brother is never home. Since that fated dinner, he stays at the church after work, or makes house call after house call, coming home only after everyone is in bed. Dinners used to be full of chatter. Now it's the scraping of silverware and the occasional home-work discussion, with an empty chair at the end of the table.

"I'm sorry," he tells her, ever the repentant son. Without question, he knows her anger comes from the intensity of her love. *Imagine*, he thinks, *worrying that your family would be separated from you for eternity. Imagine truly believing that God loves all of His Children, except when they love each other the wrong way.*

To think God loves the trees, his brain paraphrases from a book he read once, *but condemns that blossoming thing they do in spring.*

Sebastian circles the center island, moving closer. "She really was bringing something for the class."

"I thought you were done with that."

"I need to critique one of the manuscripts Mr. Fujita hasn't read yet." None of this is an outright lie.

"But you're not seeing him again? Or talking to him?"

"I haven't talked to him in weeks." This part is also true. Sebastian has stayed away from the school, away from any place they went together. He hasn't hiked. He wants to tutor but knows the temptation would be too strong; it'd be too

353

easy to stop by his house again, wait for him outside of class.

He doesn't even have any old voice messages left. He deleted them only minutes before his father confiscated his phone.

"Good," she says, visibly calmer. She unplugs the mixer and begins to scrape the side of the bowl, scooping batter into waiting baking cups. "You owe Mr. Fujita for everything he's done, so you can read those books for him, if you have time. You have your meeting with Brother Young and the last of your interview requests to complete." His mom is happiest when she has a list of things she can check off, delegate, and organize, and Sebastian lets her, even if it's the only way she'll talk to him. "Finish your obligations, and then, please, let's move on."

Together, Brother Young and Sebastian kneel on the floor and pray that Sebastian can be strong, that he can become an example again as he goes out into the world, that he can still make some good out of all of *this*.

He can tell Brother Young feels better when they stand, because he has that look of a man who has done something meaningful with his day. He embraces Sebastian, offers his ear anytime, tells him he's proud of him. He says it with the wizened clarity of a much older man, but he's only twenty-two.

If anything, once the elder leaves, Sebastian feels worse.

354

Praying is a reflex, a ritual, a part of him—but it doesn't hold the same promise of relief it used to. Dinner is called, but Sebastian isn't hungry. Lately, he eats because depriving his body seems like one more sin, and the cart is nearly toppling with them as it is.

In his room, the laptop hums quietly on his bed. He powered it up as soon as he was alone—nearly an hour ago—and has slowly watched the battery die down. The pattern is becoming a calming ritual: The screen dims with sleep, and Sebastian smooths a finger across the trackpad to wake it up again.

There's a new folder on the desktop labeled AUTO-BOYOGRAPHY, and it contains the only file he's interested in reading, but he can't manage to do it. In part, it's the anticipatory ache he knows will only get sharper as soon as he starts reading. But also, there's something fascinating about how organized and clean Tanner's Seminar notes are. The folder holds a number of versions of the document, all clearly labeled, with dates. He had photos of Sebastian too, labeled

SEBASTIAN SOCCER 2014

SEBASTIAN SOCCER 2014.A

SEBASTIAN SALT LAKE TRIB

SEBASTIAN PUB WEEKLY 2016

SEBASTIAN DESERET NEWS 2017

So there's the catch. This book is the key to get inside

Tanner's head. The vain side of Sebastian wants to get into that space more than he's ever wanted anything, to see every overanalytical detail. The rational side of Sebastian realizes it's no closer to the real Tanner than he is now, or ever will be again. Is the torture worth it? Wouldn't it be better to delete the folder, thank Autumn, and have her pass along a verbal message to Tanner? Something genuine and final, that can't be printed and passed to him silently across the dinner table—like his father did with all of his texts and e-mails?

Without his noticing, the room has grown dark again. Sebastian slides his fingers across the trackpad and squints into the brightness. His hands shake as he clicks on the icon, and the screen fills with words.

It opens with a boy and a girl, a dare, and crumbs on a bed.

But where it really begins is with a double take and the words "His smile *ruins* me."

Sebastian reads through most of the night. His cheeks, at some points, are wet with tears. Other times, he laughs—honestly, he's never had so much fun as he did falling in love with Tanner. He follows them up the mountain, remembers that first kiss. He sees the way Tanner's parents worry—Jenna's early warnings now seem nearly prophetic.

He watches Tanner evade the truth, keep Autumn in the dark. His pulse pounds in his ears as he reads about the noises they make, of fingers and lips and hands that skim lower.

He falls in love under a sky full of stars.

The sun starts to break, and Sebastian stares at the screen, eyes blurry. Other than standing to plug in the laptop, he hasn't moved in hours.

He sucks in a breath, feeling hollow but jittery, unmistakably elated. Terrified. His family will be up soon, so if he's going to do something, he needs to go before anyone sees him leave. He could simply call Fujita, explain the personal nature, suggest a grade.

His muscles protest as he gets to his feet and disconnects the cord, reaches for the laptop, and slips out the door.

TANNER

Tanner stares at the computer screen. Blinks.

His mom leans forward, squinting. "What are you looking at?"

"My grades."

She lets out an excited "Ooooh, they're up fast!" and then grabs him around the shoulders, squeezing when her eyes make it down the entire list.

Not that it matters. He's already packing up his room, preparing to take the battered Camry and drive to LA. But the grades, they aren't terrible. The A in Modern Lit wasn't a surprise—he skated through that one. Calc, too. The rest are pleasant discoveries, but not altogether shocking. But an A in the Seminar, and he never even turned in the book.

On autopilot, he reaches for the phone, dialing the school office.

"Mr. Fujita, please?"

The head secretary Ms. Hill's voice comes clear through the line: "One second."

"What are you doing?" His mom leans around, trying to catch his eyes.

He points to the *A*, right in the middle of his screen. "This doesn't make sense." In fact, it feels almost wrong, like he's getting away with the kind of mild crime Autumn always seems to accuse him of. It's one thing to charm; it's another to receive a stellar mark without even completing the one assignment worth a majority of his total grade.

A new line rings once, and again. "Hello?"

"Mr. Fujita?" Tanner fidgets with the sleek, black stapler on his parents' desk.

"Yeah?"

"It's Tanner Scott." There's a pause, and it's weird how meaningful it feels. It makes anxiety bubble up in him. "I just checked my grades."

Mr. Fujita's gravelly voice seems even coarser over the phone. "All right?"

"I don't understand how I got an A in your class."

"I loved your book, kid."

Tanner pauses. "I never turned in the book."

The other end of the line goes quiet, almost as if it's been cut off. But then Fujita clears his throat. "He didn't tell you? Ah, crap. This isn't great."

"Tell me what?"

"Sebastian turned it in."

Tanner squeezes his eyes closed, trying to figure out what he's missing. "You mean the first twenty pages?"

"No." A pause. "The whole thing."

He opens his mouth to respond and can't think of a single word.

"It's great, Tann. I mean, I have thoughts on edits, because I can't help myself, and your ending sucks, but at the time, how could it not? Overall, I sincerely enjoyed it." He pauses, and in that time, Tanner is unable to figure out what to say.

In the past, when he's read the words "my thoughts are reeling," the idea of that just felt overblown. But right now images are on a loop, a flickering filmstrip: his laptop in his drawer; the words "I'm totally gay" on a page; Sebastian's face just before he fell asleep on the couch beside him, satisfied, cocky, also, a little shy; the deteriorating, half-assed ending to his document.

"Maybe 'enjoy' isn't the right word," Fujita is saying. "I hurt for you. And him. I've watched this story unfold so many times, I can't even tell you. I'm glad the two of you have worked things out."

Fujita pauses again, and it seems like this would be a good time for Tanner to say something, but he doesn't. Now he's stuck on *I'm glad the two of you have worked things out.* Bewilderment is the predominant emotion. He hasn't spoken to Sebastian in weeks.

"What?"

360

"But I think you did something here," Fujita says, ignoring this, "showing him your heart. I think you truly did. And your voice is alive. I knew you were writing, but I didn't realize you were *writing*."

This conversation has officially gone too many steps past where Tanner last understood what the hell was going on. His laptop, as far as he knows, has been safely planted in his dresser along with socks, some shin guards, and a couple of magazines his parents can't track on their magic software.

Tanner stands, jogging upstairs to his room. On the phone, Fujita has gone quiet.

"You okay over there?"

Tanner rummages in his drawer. His laptop is there. "Yeah. Just . . . processing this."

"Well, if you want to come down sometime this summer and talk through my notes, I'd be happy to. I'll be here finishing things up for the next two weeks or so."

Tanner looks out his window at the street, at his Camry parked at the curb. How crazy would it be to just show up at Sebastian's house? To ask him how he got a copy of his book, how he managed to get it into Fujita's hands?

Reality sets in and panic starts to climb up the back of his neck. Sebastian *read* it. The whole thing.

"Tanner? You still there?"

"Yeah," he says, voice cracking. "Thanks."

"You headed to the signing later?"

Tanner blinks out of his daze. His upper lip is damp now; his whole body is on the verge of a frantic, feverish shiver. "The what?"

"The signing, down at—" Fujita pauses. "What am I thinking? Of course you aren't. Or, are you?"

"I honestly have no idea what we're talking about."

Tanner can hear the creak of Fujita's desk chair as he shifts. Maybe he's sitting up, paying attention now. "Sebastian's book came out yesterday."

Time seems to slow.

"He's signing at Deseret Book over at University Place, at seven tonight. But I don't know whether to expect you there." An awkward laugh and then, "I hope you come. I hope this goes the way it does in my head. I need an end to that story."

Autumn climbs into the car. "You're being oddly broody and cryptic. Where are we going?"

"I need best friend powers, activated." He leaves the car in park at the curb and turns to face her. "I don't know how it happened, but Sebastian turned in my book to—"

One look at her complexion—splotchy pink, awareness dawning—and he knows.

He isn't even sure why it didn't immediately occur to him. Maybe he liked the image that a heroic Sebastian would climb in through his window, dig around in his drawers for

362

the laptop, copy the file over, and ride on his loyal steed (his bike) to school to turn in the manuscript and save Tanner's ass. But of course the more banal explanation is at play: Autumn. She read it. Gave it to Sebastian as a bit of a *Look at this broken soul. You did this, you monster*, and boom. Sebastian's guilt overtook him, and he couldn't let Tanner fail.

He did it out of pity.

Tanner deflates. "Oh."

"You're telling me he *turned it in*?"

"You're telling me you didn't know?"

She leans in, her expression urgent. "I didn't know he gave it to *Fujita*. I swear. I just thought he should read it. I thought maybe *he* could grade it. He had my drive for about a day, and then he gave it back."

"That's a pretty big decision to make for me."

"I was emotional," she says, only mildly remorseful. "And your book was awesome. It was a crazy time, okay?" She grins. "I'd just lost my virginity."

Tanner laughs, playfully pinching her leg. At least that much has returned to normal in the past few weeks. And in truth, Autumn gets as many free passes as she wants these days. Despite the return of easiness between them, he still isn't entirely comfortable holding her feet to the fire.

"Well, I got an A," he tells her. "And the world didn't end. Still, I can't imagine what it took for him to do that. Fujita knows now, obviously." It's been a couple of weeks since school ended. Maybe everyone knows. Or maybe Sebastian took three steps backward, right back into the closet. "Sebastian's book came out yesterday, and he's signing at the Deseret down on University."

Autumn's eyes widen with thrill as she understands what they're doing in the car. "We *aren't*."

"We are."

The line begins in front of the store and snakes around, outside the strip mall and down University almost half a block. It reminds Tanner of the airport when there are mobs of people waiting at the baggage claim for their missionaries coming home. When the Mormons come out, they come out *en masse*.

Tanner and Autumn tack themselves onto the end of the line. It's early June, and the wind is dry and hot. Other than the mountains, which jut straight up from the earth, the city feels unendingly flat. It isn't, not really, but it has that same low-expectations vibe, the bland urban design to an unambitious town.

A tiny thrill builds in Tanner's stomach, spreading warmth outward. He's going to miss Autumn, but he'll be near the ocean again.

A man in a short-sleeved plaid shirt approaches. His left arm holds a stack of at least ten books. "Are you here for the signing?"

Tanner nods. "Yeah."

"Did you bring a book, or are you purchasing here?"

Autumn and Tanner exchange an unsure look. "Buying here?" Autumn wagers.

The man hands them each a book from the dwindling stack in his arms and peels two Post-it notes from the top of a pad. Tanner nearly laughs. They're blue, just like the ones holding all his angst and love and melodrama.

"Put your names on these," the man says. "It will make it easier for Sebastian to personalize it when you get up front."

A rope tightens around Tanner's chest, and Autumn lets out a tiny groan of sympathy.

"After it's signed, you can pay at the register." It would never occur to the staff that someone might be handed a book and take off without ever going inside.

The man leaves, and Autumn turns to him, clutching her copy. "This is weird in so many ways."

"Yeah." Tanner stares at the novel in his hands. On the cover is a fiery landscape—a burnt valley, mountains still alive with green, looming over the encroaching flames. It's beautiful. The colors are rich, nearly three-dimensional. A cloaked boy stands at the foot of a mountain, holding a torch. At his feet, the title rises from the paper in thick foil.

FIRESTORM
Sebastian Brother

The title doesn't have any meaning yet to Tanner. Maybe it never will. The idea of spending—he flips to the back—four hundred pages with Sebastian's creative brain seems nearly unbearable. Maybe someday, when he's moved on and this all just seems like a tender bruise in his history, he'll open it up, look at his name scrawled generically there, and actually be able to appreciate the story between the covers.

"No, I mean, this is weird for *me*," Autumn says, breaking into his thoughts. "I can't even imagine what it's like for you."

"I'm starting to wonder what the hell we're doing here. This could be a disaster."

"You don't think he half expects you?"

Tanner gives it some more thought. He hasn't tried to contact Sebastian, not since the brush-off e-mail. No doubt he thinks Tanner will just disappear. He probably should just disappear. "No."

She points ahead of them, down the block. "Well, we are conveniently close to the Emergency Essentials store if you need anything."

"That is such an LDS thing to have in a town," Tanner mumbles.

Autumn doesn't argue. They stare at the strip mall sign, with the three largest businesses advertised in bold letters: Deseret Book. Emergency Essentials. Avenia Bridal.

"This is all very LDS," she agrees.

"Do you miss the church?"

She leans into him. Her head barely reaches the top of his shoulder, so when he puts an arm around her, she tucks neatly beneath his chin.

"Sometimes." She looks up at him. Anyone watching would think they were a couple. "I miss the activities and that certainty that if everyone is happy with you, you're doing everything right."

Tanner wrinkles his nose at her. "Gross."

"Exactly," she says, patting his chest. "That's exactly my point. Sebastian wasn't doing anything wrong with you."

He looks around meaningfully and lowers his voice, "So we say."

This time Autumn whispers. "You aren't wrong to be here."

The line starts to move, and Tanner's stomach drops. *Aren't* they wrong to be here, at least a little? If this isn't the definition of blindsiding, it's awfully close. Yeah, Sebastian and Autumn went behind his back to turn in the book, but this is public. Sebastian will have to keep it together. Tanner will have to keep it together.

He takes the pen from Autumn's hand when she finishes writing down her name and writes his own. He doesn't do it to be cheeky; he does it out of practicality: It's entirely possible that Sebastian will be too flustered to remember how to spell T-a-n-n-e-r.

The line moves slowly. Tanner imagines Sebastian behind

a counter or a table, charming everyone who comes through.

His stomach growls, and the sun hangs low in the sky before giving up and diving below the mountains. With the sun gone, the air cools down for the first time all day.

Autumn swats a mosquito on his arm. "Okay, let's go through this."

"Go through what?"

She gives him a concerned look. "What you're doing here."

He takes a deep, sharp breath. "I'm just going to thank him for what he did—he'll know what I mean—and wish him good luck on his tour, and his mission."

"That's it?"

"That's it."

She stretches, kissing his jaw. "You're sweet."

"You're a menace."

"At least I'm not a virgin menace anymore."

The people in front of them turn around, eyes wide in scandal.

Autumn lets out a faux-mortified "Oops."

Tanner ducks, trying not to laugh. "One of these days, that joke is going to land very, very badly."

"That was pretty close."

They're almost to the door now, and can see inside that the line goes only about fifteen more people before it reaches the end. Sebastian.

Tanner can't see him, but he has a front-row view of the odd, jovial vibe. The roomful of men in suits, women in dresses, celebratory cups of punch. There's a table with cupcakes and veggies with dip off to the side. Someone made a cake. Not only is this a signing; it's a launch party.

Sebastian's parents are there, talking in a small half circle to a woman with a name tag and another person—a man in a suit and tie. Autumn steps inside, and Tanner follows, holding the door for the person in line behind him. The door knocks into a display table, and at the sound, Dan Brother looks up, smiling on instinct, before his expression turns stony.

It hadn't occurred to Tanner that he would see Sebastian's parents, that they would recognize him, that they would associate him with the cancer infecting their son. But of course they do.

"And *there's* the dad," Autumn says, nodding to Dan across the room.

"Yeah."

Sebastian's mother looks up at Dan Brother to gauge his reaction, as if seeking guidance. After a pause, they both manage to shift their expressions back to neutral.

Autumn tucks her arm through Tanner's. "You okay?"

"I want to leave. But it's too late."

It *is* too late. They're two people back now, and Tanner can see Sebastian. He gets an eyeful of him too, wearing a neatly pressed blue dress shirt and dark tie. His hair is shorter.

He's wearing his mask of a smile. But even in this LDS bookstore, behind a wall of LDS people, he still looks like the guy on the hike, the guy eating Chinese food, the guy on the hood of the car.

Then Sebastian looks up and sees who is next in line, and the mask crumbles, for just a second. No—longer. It's a double take, and it's so achingly familiar.

Tanner steps up, holding his book out. "Hi. Congratulations."

Sebastian's jaw tics, and he clears his throat, brow furrowed. "Hi." He looks down, pulling Autumn's book closer, slowly peeling the Post-it from the front. "Um . . ." He exhales, and it trembles its way out of him. He clears his throat again, flipping the book open to the title page, lifting his pen with a shaking hand.

Autumn looks frantically back and forth between them. "Hey, Sebastian."

He looks up at her, seeming to blink into focus. "Autumn. Hi. How are you?"

"I'm good. Leaving for Connecticut in a couple weeks. Where's your first tour stop?"

"After this? I head to Denver." He ticks off the cities robotically: "Portland, San Francisco, Phoenix, Austin, Dallas, Atlanta, Charleston, Chicago, Minneapolis . . . um . . . Philadelphia, New York, and then home."

"Wow," she says. "That's insane."

Sebastian lets out a dry laugh as he signs her book first, writing a simple *Good luck at Yale. Best wishes, and thank you, Sebastian Brother.*

He hands Autumn her book and then pulls Tanner's copy closer. After a brief scowl at the Post-it note, he balls it up in his fist and drops it into the trash can at his feet.

Tanner has been quiet for a few seconds, and Autumn gently elbows him in the side. *Say something,* she mouths.

"I came to say thank you," he says quietly, hoping he's out of earshot from the people around them—specifically, Sebastian's parents. Sebastian stiffens, and focuses on whatever it is he's writing. "For what you did. I'm not sure I understand *why* you did it, but I'm grateful."

"Thank you so much for coming tonight, Tanner," Sebastian says magnanimously. Having recovered his composure somewhat, his voice projects out beyond the protected space of the table.

The tone is so sickeningly false that Tanner nearly laughs. Finally, he meets Sebastian's eyes again, and it's devastating. His voice may have recovered, but his eyes haven't. They're tight and shiny with tears.

"Oh my God, I'm sorry," Tanner says quietly. "I shouldn't have come."

"Are you a fan of the fantasy genre?" Sebastian's voice is still forcibly bright. He widens his eyes, working to pull the tears back inside.

This hurts them both, and now Tanner feels like a monster. "I hope your book tour is amazing," he says, not bothering to carry on the other side of a fake conversation. "I hope your mission is too. I leave for LA in August, but call me anytime." He gives one final glance up. "Anytime."

He takes the book from Sebastian's hand without even looking at it and turns, leaving Autumn to pay inside. Tanner pushes through the crowd and back out onto the street, where there is oxygen, and space, and a complete lack of dancing, lake-in-the-sun eyes staring up at him.

Being on book tour is like being able to breathe again. There are no chaperones or parents. There is no church.

Not that his mom didn't try to tag along. He's not sure if it was seeing Tanner that instigated it or just last-minute mom jitters, but she'd e-mailed his publicist two days before he was scheduled to leave. Thankfully, his publicist had explained that flights had been purchased and accommodations booked, and unless his mom was prepared to book cross-country flights and hotels for a thirteen-city tour, there just wasn't time.

Sebastian has traveled outside of Utah for school trips and family vacations, but never like this. His publishing house arranges a car and driver to pick him up from the airport and drop him off at his hotel, he has a handler to get him to and from events, but the rest of the time is his.

His next signing is in Denver, and though it's obviously not as big as the one back home, it's still pretty crowded. There are only a handful of empty chairs during his talk. What a surreal awareness to catch, like a whiff of something delicious, that the strangers in this room even know who he is.

The line is mostly girls, but there are a few guys scattered in. Sebastian knows Tanner isn't coming, but it never stops the way his pen runs off the page at the sound of a deep voice near the back of the line, or his eyes snap up in the hopes of a head of dark hair above the crowd.

Sometimes he can't believe Tanner was actually there. His parents certainly didn't want to acknowledge it. There was no one he could turn to after Tanner and Autumn left to ask, "That was Tanner, right?"

He'd wanted to tell him how much he loved the book, how reading it had changed something inside him, and how he'd printed it out the very next morning, knowing he'd take it on tour with him. But he couldn't, not there. He hadn't wanted Tanner to leave, but he had nothing articulate to say because the words "I miss you" were shoving their way to the front, boisterous and shrill.

It's the *missing* that keeps him up at night—in Denver, in Austin, in Cleveland—and that's always when he reaches for it, searching through his bag to pull out Tanner's book. He can open it anywhere—page twenty, page eighty—because on every page he'll find a love story that shines a light into the dark, dusty corners of his self-loathing, that remind him something *did* happen, that it was real. And it was right.

Sometimes he thinks about what he wrote in Tanner's

copy of *Firestorm*, and wonders whether Tanner even opened the book to see it.

▲

Yours always,
Sebastian Brother

Sebastian is hit with a wall of heat as he steps out of the Salt Lake City International Airport, and wishes he had changed out of his shirt and tie before leaving JFK.

"I can't believe you got to go to New York," Lizzy says, clutching a small glittery Statue of Liberty to her chest. She's back to her old self, and it makes him wonder whether it's because everyone expects he's back to *his*, too. "Was it as cool as it looks on TV?"

"Cooler." He wraps an arm around her shoulder and pulls her in, pressing a kiss to her hair. It was nice to get away, but he can't believe how much he's missed her. "Maybe we can go there sometime," he says. "When the next book is out."

Lizzy pirouettes her way along the crosswalk. "Yes!"

"If Lizzy gets to go to New York, then I think we should go to San Francisco and visit Alcatraz. Did you go *there*?" Faith asks, looking up at him.

"I didn't, but I saw it from the pier. My handler took me to dinner at this seafood place, and we walked along the water. I didn't know you wanted to go or I'd have sent you a picture. I think I have one in my phone."

Faith forgets any possible insult when Sebastian scoops her up to carry her over his shoulder. Her delighted squeal is deafening in the cement parking structure.

Mrs. Brother unlocks the doors, and the question sits like a stone in Sebastian's chest. "Dad and Aaron couldn't come?"

"Your father took Aaron along to a couple of house calls today, but he said he'll see you at dinner."

Sebastian spoke with his dad a handful of times over the last two weeks, but there's a knee-jerk reaction to him not being here. His father's absence from this return is a heart-beat in the tip of a cut finger. He feels it so acutely, so constantly, because it's *wrong*.

Fortunately, he doesn't get to dwell on it because as soon as Lizzy sings that dinner is a surprise, Faith—unable to keep the secret any longer—shouts, *"It's pizza!"*

Lizzy clamps a hand over Faith's mouth and delivers a loud smooch to her cheek. "Way to blow the surprise, dweeb."

Sebastian leans forward, helping Faith with her seat belt. "Pizza for *me*?"

She nods, her giggles still muffled behind the weight of Lizzy's hand.

Sebastian loads his bag into the back.

"And before this one blows it," his mom says, buckling her seat belt as he climbs into the passenger seat. "There's something else." She grins over at him. "I sent your papers off."

He nods, giving her a pleased smile, but words don't immediately come because the wind has been quietly knocked out of him. Time away was good. He misses church, and the kinship of being surrounded by like-minded people. He misses Tanner, too, but knows the mission is still the best path for him.

It's just that he thought he would send off his mission papers himself when he got home. He'd hoped sending them off himself might solidify the decision, make it real and set his path in motion.

Her grin slips, and he realizes she's been anxious about telling him. She was worried she would get this exact reaction—uncertainty.

He does everything he can to wipe it from his face, replacing it with the smile that seems to move across his mouth with the reflex of an inhale. "Thanks, Mom. That . . . makes things so much easier for me now. One less thing to worry about."

It seems to have done the trick. She softens, turning back to the wheel. They drive down the ramp, navigating the maze of construction cones as they go. Pulling up to the kiosk, she slips her parking stub into the machine and turns to him. "I was wondering how you'd feel about doing it with everyone together."

"Do what together?"

"Opening your letter." She turns back to the kiosk to pay, and in that ten-second reprieve, Sebastian struggles to bury the panic that follows the reality of those three words. She means his mission call.

A voice in the back of his head screams *no*.

It's like living with a split personality, and he closes his eyes, inhaling slowly. It was so much easier to be away. The impending mission was palatable from a distance. The constant imposition of his mother, the weight of expectation—coming back home is overwhelming even ten minutes in.

He can feel the engine rumble and realizes she's done paying and they're moving forward. When he looks over at her, her jaw is tight, eyes hardened.

Sebastian feigns a yawn. "Oh my gosh, I am so wiped. Yeah, Mom, that sounds amazing. I assume Grandma and Grandpa would come too?"

Her shoulders relax, smile returns. "Are you kidding? They wouldn't miss it for the world."

An hourglass has been tipped over in his stomach, pouring lead. He takes a shallow breath.

"But I don't want Sebastian to leave again," Faith calls from the backseat. "He just got home."

"He wouldn't leave yet, honey," his mom says, meeting her eyes in the rearview mirror. "Not for a couple months."

Sebastian turns and gives his baby sister an encouraging smile, and he can't even explain it, but he has the urge to reach for her, pull her to him. *Two years.* She'll be almost thirteen when he gets back. Aaron will be learning to drive, and Lizzy will be ready to start college. He's homesick and he hasn't even left yet.

"So you'd be okay with that?" she asks. "It wouldn't be too nerve-racking to have everyone there?"

Sebastian leans his head against the back of the seat and closes his eyes.

Heavenly Father, please give me strength. Give me the wisdom I need, the surety of decision. I'll follow wherever you lead me.

"I think it's a great idea," Sebastian whispers. "It sounds perfect."

The plus side to being gone was that his problems seemed a lot smaller from far away. The feeling isn't real, and he realizes it as soon as he walks into his house—surrounded by familiar sights and sounds and smells. Reality comes crashing back.

He's just put his suitcase on his bed when there's a knock.

"Can I come in?" His dad peeks his head around the partially closed door. "I see our world traveler is back."

"Yeah. And exhausted."

There was a tentative cease-fire when the book came out and his parents were able to see the pride of the entire community focused on Sebastian. But he hasn't had much time alone with his dad in months, and Dan Brother's presence in

Sebastian's room makes the space feel claustrophobic.

"You have plenty of time to rest up before dinner," he says. "I just wanted to bring you this." He hands him a stack of mail. "And I wanted to welcome you home. We're very proud of you, son. I know you had a rough patch, and it's made me prouder than you can realize to have witnessed you rise above it all, and be stronger for it. 'Adversity is like a strong wind: It tears away from us all but the things that cannot be torn, so that we see ourselves as we really are.'"

Sebastian frowns, trying to recognize the Scripture. "I don't know that one."

Bishop Brother laughs, and looks at Sebastian with fondness. "Arthur Golden, *Memoirs of a Geisha*."

"Okay, yeah, I would never have gotten there."

The laugh deepens, and his father's eyes shine. "I guess I'll leave that one out of Sacrament next week." He turns to leave before stopping near the door. "Oh, and your mom said there was something in there from Mr. Fujita." He nods to the stack of mail in Sebastian's hand. "Might be your last paycheck, so don't wait too long to open it."

"I'll go through it after I unpack."

When his father leaves, the air slowly drains from his lungs. He closes his door completely and crosses the room to unpack. Toiletries, sweaters, suit, jeans. Underneath is the copy of Tanner's book he'd printed and taken with him.

The pages are worn, there's a grease stain on the front from a restaurant in Denver, and the edges are curled in the upper right corner where he would flip through with his fingers as he read. Although he's probably read the entire thing at least ten times, after the first read, he never started at the beginning. He would flip through and stop, reading from whatever point forward he chose. Sometimes he would start while Tanner was clothes shopping with his mom and Autumn. Other times he would open to the section at the lake, and *faggot*, and Tanner's mortifying exchange with Manny.

But being far away from home made him feel removed from *this*, too. His problems at home might not be real, but if they weren't, that meant Tanner wasn't real either. He didn't have any photographs of him, but he had this book.

Sebastian takes the manuscript and slides it behind his headboard before opening the envelope from Fujita.

Dearest Sebastian,

I hope this letter finds you many books lighter, and many adventures richer. I wanted to update you on our mutual friend's manuscript. I'm not sure if you've spoken to Tanner, but he knows how I came into possession of his

novel. He called when grades were
posted, certain I'd made some kind
of mistake. I was happy to inform him
that I had not.

I've been working with him on revisions,
and encouraged him to make significant
changes. Not changes to the subject
per se, but seeing as how I think
he could really have something here,
I suggested changing the names
and characteristics of the two lead
protagonists, along with any other
identifiable details. I've been in
contact with a handful of editors, and
there's a possibility the Seminar could
be two for two. We would, of course,
consult you first.

My deepest gratitude, Sebastian, for
your bravery. I wish you well. You are
an exceptional human, with depth and
heart. Don't let anyone—or anything—dim
that light inside you.

Sincerely,
Tim Fujita

Indeed, behind the letter he finds his final check, and Sebastian sends up a silent word of gratitude; when his parents ask about it later, he won't have to lie.

Staring down at the paper, Sebastian understands his mom's urgency in sending his application off. Fifteen minutes and he's right back where he started, missing Tanner with an intensity that has every muscle poised and ready to propel him straight out the door.

It's too much to imagine Tanner's book being published, and so he pushes it away, suddenly grateful he'll be gone again soon, maybe out of the country. Far enough that he can outrun the ache and the temptation to see him again, just once, and tell him everything.

The next weeks move in a time warp. House calls with his father, mowing lawns for everyone and their grandmother, helping families move. Sebastian barely has time to dig behind his bed every night and read a few pages of Tanner's book before his eyes are pulled closed by total exhaustion.

The letter, his mission call, arrives on a Tuesday, and the envelope sits on the kitchen counter, untouched, for four days. His mother's family is flying in from Phoenix. His great-grandmother is due to arrive from St. George by five. A dozen friends and family are driving down from Salt Lake, and countless others are coming from just down the road.

By three his mother has tiny armies of appetizers laid out on baking sheets. Pot stickers, quiches, mini Frito pies, and—to the side—a huge vegetable platter. Faith and Lizzy are in matching yellow dresses. He and Aaron wear identical navy suits.

His hands shake. His jaw is tight from clenching it. They all pace, make small talk, wait.

Tanner's voice is a soft, teasing loop in his head. *If you hate this so much, why are you doing it?*

The answer is easy. When he thinks of being gone, he relaxes. When he speaks to God lately, he feels better. It isn't the mission or the faith he's unsure of. It's the weight of his parents' shame and the pressure of their expectation.

He walks, heart on fire, to the kitchen. "Dad. Can I take the car for a few?"

Bishop Brother looks up, eyes concerned. "You okay?"

"Nervous," he says honestly. "I'm fine. I just . . . I need to go down to church for ten minutes."

His father likes this answer, cupping his shoulder in a palm and squeezing with a gesture of solidarity before handing over the keys.

Sebastian means to go to church, he does. But instead, he turns left, not right, drives straight when he should turn, and eventually finds his way down the NO ACCESS dirt road. He parks there, dragging a blanket from the trunk and staring up at blue skies, trying to remember the stars.

It isn't the same out here now. For one, it's sweltering; the air swarms with mosquitoes. The second difference—the absence of a long body beside him—is even more notable. He gives himself ten minutes, and then twenty. He tries to say good-bye to Tanner, but even when he closes his eyes and asks God for the right words, for the spell that will unlock his heart, they don't come.

Sebastian learned on tour that one of the responsibilities of being a published author is having social media. He has accounts, but they remain largely inactive, in part because the temptation is so great.

He's resisted so far, but lying on the hood of his car, he finally caves and opens Instagram, searching for Manny's name. Scrolling down his list of followers, he finds what he's looking for: *tannbannthankyouman*.

A laugh tears out of him.

Tanner's account is unlocked, and Sebastian presses his thumb to the profile image, expanding it. It's a terrible idea. He knows it. But when Tanner's face pops into view, his heart seems to fill with warm water, pressing everything else aside. It's a picture of Tanner holding an enormous pink flower. It obstructs half of his face, but his eyelashes seem three-dimensional. His eyes are luminous, hair shaggier than the last time he saw him, mouth curled into that singular, joyful smirk.

Tanner's Instagram feed is even more addicting than Sebastian expected: a picture of him in the backseat of his car, pretending to strangle his father from behind. A picture of Hailey, fast asleep beside him, with the caption, I NEED AN ALIBI #NOREGRETS. A picture of a hamburger, some terribly fake aliens, Tanner's Camry parked at a curb in front of a building called Dykstra Hall, and then—Sebastian nearly sobs audibly—a photo of a smiling Tanner standing in an empty dorm room, wearing a UCLA shirt.

Sebastian's thumb hovers over the "like" icon. If he touched it, Tanner would see. Would that be so terrible? Tanner would know he was thinking of him. Maybe in time they could even follow each other, keep in touch, talk.

But this is where Sebastian gets into trouble. In his head it never stops at talking. It goes to phone calls, and meeting up, and kisses, and *more*. Because even now, as people are probably arriving at his house—all of them here for *him*—he's *still* thinking of Tanner.

In a few weeks, he'll receive the Melchizedek Priesthood, and after that he'll go through the Temple, receive his endowments—and he's thinking of Tanner. He tries to imagine wearing his garments—something he's looked forward to his whole life—

And he can't breathe.

He's gay. He'll never be anything else. Tonight they'll all be waiting for Sebastian to give his testimony and speak on how full of joy he is that he's been called to spread God's word wherever He's chosen to send him, and he doesn't even know where he fits into God's word anymore.

What is he doing?

As he goes inside his house, his mouth waters—it smells like food. His mom comes up, gives him a squeeze and a cookie.

She looks so *happy*, and Sebastian is about to ruin everything.

He clears his throat. "Hey, guys." Not everyone is here yet, but the important ones are. Five smiling faces turn in his direction. Faith tugs at her dress, straightening proudly when he looks at her. He remembers what it feels like, to be little like that and watch someone as they're about to open their letter. It's like sharing a room with a celebrity.

His heart splinters. "You all look so nice tonight."

His mom moves to stand near the dining room table. Her apron says KEEP CALM AND SERVE ON, and all he can think about is Tanner's mom and her rainbow apron that embarrassed her son, and what Sebastian would give to have a parent who accepted him for what he was, no matter what.

"Sebastian?" his mom says, taking a step closer. "Honey, are you okay?"

He nods but feels a sob rise in his throat. "I'm sorry. I'm so . . . so sorry. But I think I need to talk to Mom and Dad for a few minutes alone."

I made a joke the other day on the phone to Autumn: I don't know which is worse, Provo or Los Angeles. She didn't get it, and of course she didn't because she's living in an idyllic Connecticut wonderland, wearing elbow-patch sweaters and knee-high socks. (She is; don't kill the fantasy.) LA is great, don't get me wrong. It's just massive. I grew up near San Francisco, so I know big cities, but LA is a different thing entirely, and UCLA is a city within a city. From above, Westwood Village is this dense network of arteries and arterioles within the huge LA vascular system, sandwiched between Wilshire and Sunset. It took about three weeks here before I stopped feeling like I was drowning in an urban ocean.

Mom, Dad, and Hailey drove out here with me in August in what I think we would all describe as the worst road trip in the history of time. At various points, I'm sure we each prayed for the zombie apocalypse to wipe out our loved ones. Bottom line: Hailey does not do well in confined spaces, Dad drives like a blind grandparent, and none of us agrees on music.

Moving on: Orientation was a blur. There was a lot of training on how not to be a rapist or die of alcohol poisoning, both of which I think we can agree are good things to cover. We heard about the honor code—a quaint, well-intended suggestion compared to the iron-clad monstrosity imposed at BYU. Three weeks later and I'm not sure I remember what's even in it, because clearly no one listened.

I was assigned to live in Dykstra Hall, which apparently isn't bad because it was renovated a few years ago. But given my lack of any previous experience in the matter, I can only say: It's a dorm. Twin beds, separate bathrooms for males and females, with a long row of showers on one wall and a long row of toilets on the other. Laundry rooms. Wi-Fi. My roommate, Ryker, is easily the wildest person I've ever met. It's like the universe said, *Oh, you want to leave Provo for something a bit more lively? Here you go*. Bad news: He parties pretty much constantly and reeks of beer. Good news: He's hardly ever here.

We don't need to declare a major until sophomore year, but I'm pretty sure I'm going premed. Who knew, right? The science programs here are great, and if I minor in English, it's a great balance course-load-wise. Look at me, being proactive.

Science was an obvious choice, but I think we all know I can't move too far away from English, either. One, because Autumn has trained me so well, it would almost be a waste to leave that behind. But two, writing tapped something in me

I didn't know was there. Maybe something will actually happen with this book. Maybe it won't and I'll become inspired again and write another. Whatever. Writing is a tie—however tenuous—to him. I can admit now that I need that.

He's still there in nearly every step I take. At the first party I went to, I played the social game and met a couple of people, had some beers, flirted here and there, but went home alone. I wonder when I'll be past this constant ache and actually want someone else. There have been situations where I think, *If it weren't for Sebastian, I probably would have hooked up tonight*. But I want *him*. As crazy as it sounds to think this book is only for me—especially after everything—it feels safe to say it here: I haven't given up hope. His reaction to seeing me in the bookstore has stuck with me. And he drew a *mountain emoji* in my book. He loves me. I know he does.

Or, he did.

And being here is different more than just on the scale of the city; no matter what's happening in the rest of the country, LA is a gay-friendly town. People are out. People are proud. Couples of every combination walk down the street holding hands and no one even blinks. I can't imagine that happening on the average street in most small towns, definitely not in Provo. Mormons are generally too nice to say anything to your face, but there would be a gentle gust of discomfort and judgment carried on the wind.

I don't even know where Sebastian ended up going on

his mission, but I'm worried about him. Is he having fun? Is he miserable? Is he stuffing a part of his heart into a lockbox just to keep the people in his life happy? I know he can't be contacted, so I'm not texting or e-mailing, but just to release the pressure valve in my chest, sometimes I'll type something up and send it to myself so at least the words can get out of me, stop stealing my air.

Autumn told me that his mom was going to host some public Facebook party for the letter opening, but I couldn't stomach it. I assumed Autumn lurked on there, following the action, but she swears she has no idea where he ended up. Even if she was lying, though, I made her promise not to tell me. What if he's in Phoenix? What if he's in San Diego? I wouldn't be able to keep from driving there and trolling the neighborhoods for Elder Brother, the hottest guy alive, with his floppy skater hair and white shirtsleeves, riding a bike.

Sometimes, when I can't sleep and can't stop thinking about everything we did together, I imagine giving in and asking Autumn where I can find him. I imagine showing up wherever he is, seeing him in his missionary uniform, and his surprise at seeing me there. I think I'd make the trade: *I'll convert, if you'll be with me, even in secret, forever.*

The first weekend in October, I call Auddy like I always do: at eleven on Sunday. There's always the pain at first, the stab wound inflicted by the familiar pitch of her voice. Oddly, even as hard as it was saying good-bye to my folks at my dorm, saying bye to Autumn was harder. In some ways I hate that I didn't tell her everything sooner. We'll have other safe places, but we were each other's first safe space. No matter what we say or what promises we make, it changes from here on out.

"Tanner, oh my God, hang on, let me read you this letter."

This is honestly how she answers. I can't even reply before she's already put the phone down, off—I presume—to retrieve Bratalie's latest manifesto.

Her roommate is a total drama queen, actually named Natalie, who leaves passive-aggressive notes on Autumn's desk about noise, tidiness, the lack of toothpaste sharing that should occur, and the number of dresser drawers Autumn is allowed to occupy. Fun fact: We are also pretty sure she masturbates when she thinks Autumn is asleep. This isn't related to anything, really, but I found it genuinely fascinating and required a lot of detail before I would agree with the theory.

Her phone scrapes across a surface before she returns with a bright, "*Ohmygod.*"

"A good one?"

"Maybe the best so far." Auddy takes a breath, laughing on the exhale. "Remember how I told you she was sick earlier in the week?"

I vaguely remember the text. Our box gets pretty busy. "Yeah."

"So, it's related to that. Okay. 'Dear Autumn,'" she reads,

"'Thank you again for bringing me breakfast the other morning. I felt so sick! I feel like such a jerk for saying this—'"

I laugh incredulously, anticipating where this is headed. "Oh my God."

"'—but I can't stop thinking about it, so I just need to get it out. The fork and the plate were both dirty, with crusty stuff. And then I thought, *Did Autumn do this on purpose?* I hope not. I know I can be fussy sometimes, but I want us to be as close forever as we are now—'"

"Wow, she's *delusional*."

"'—so I thought I would simply ask. Or maybe I just wanted to let you know that I knew, and if it was intentional, that was sort of nasty of you. Of course, if it was an accident, just ignore this. You're so sweet. Xoxo, Nat.'"

I scrub a hand over my face. "Seriously, Auddy, find a new roommate. She makes Ryker seem mellow."

"I can't! From what I've seen of others changing roommates, it's so much drama!"

"*This* isn't drama?"

"It is," she agrees, "but there's an element of the absurd to it too. It's objectively fascinating."

"I mean, I get her letter about cracker crumbs. I've been warning you about this for years now. But a dirty fork and plate when you're bringing food to her sickbed?"

She laughs. "It's as if she doesn't eat at the dining hall. The dishes are all pretty sketchy."

393

"How dare they! Don't they know they're *Yale*?"

"Shut up. How's LA?"

I look out my window. "Sunny."

Auddy groans. "Good weekend? Anything interesting?"

"We played Washington State yesterday, so a bunch of us went to the game."

"Who would have pegged you as a football fan?"

"I wouldn't say *fan* so much as *aware of the unspoken rules*." I lean back in my desk chair, scratching my jaw. "A few guys over in Hedrick were having a party last night. I went with Breckin." My first and closest friend so far, Breckin escaped a small town in Texas, and by some strange coincidence is (1) gay and (2) Mormon. I couldn't make this up if I tried. He's also smart as hell and reads almost as voraciously as Autumn. I'd have a crush if my heart wasn't already taken. "Pretty fun day. I don't know. What'd you do?"

"Deacon had a race yesterday, so we did that."

Deacon. Her new boyfriend, and a deity on the rowing team, apparently.

There is a small curl of jealous heat there. I can't deny it. But mostly, he sounds like a pretty cool guy. He's Irish, and totally infatuated with Autumn, so I already like him. He even texted me last week to ask me what I thought he should get her for her birthday. Recruiting the best friend: smart move.

"I miss you," I tell her.

"I miss you too."

We exchange Thanksgiving travel details, promise to talk next week, and ring off, with love.

For about fifteen minutes after we hang up, I feel blue.

But then I see Breckin in my doorway with a Frisbee.

"Which one this time?" he asks.

Thanks to a pitcher of vodka tonics and a *Breaking Bad* marathon one night in my room, he knows everything.

"Both of them."

He waves his Frisbee. "Let's go. It's nice outside."

There have been a few moments in my life when I think I've felt a higher power at work. The first was when I was six and Hailey was three. It's my earliest clear memory; I have fuzzy ones from before it, of throwing pasta or staring up at my ceiling at night while my parents read me a book, but this was the first where every detail seems to have been tattooed in my mind. Mom, Hailey, and I were in a T.J. Maxx. The racks were rammed so close together and stuffed with clothes, it was nearly impossible to pass between without rubbing against something woolen or silken or denim.

Hailey was being playful and silly, and hid a couple of times in a rack Mom was sorting through. But then she disappeared. Completely. For ten minutes we ran around yelling her name with increasing hysteria, digging through every rod, shelf, and rack in the store. We couldn't find her. We alerted the saleswomen, who called security. Mom was hysterical.

I was hysterical. I'd never done anything like it before, but I closed my eyes and begged—not a person, not a power, maybe just the future—that she was okay. Only a few weeks before, I'd learned the word "kidnap," and it seemed to rewire my brain so that I viewed everything through the lens of a possible abduction scenario.

I felt better when I said it over and over—*please let her be okay, please let her be okay, please let her be okay*—and maybe that's why it always made sense to me later, when Sebastian said he felt better when he prayed. I knew I was helpless, but it still felt like my good intentions had power, that they could change the trajectory of whatever had happened to my sister.

I'll forever remember the calm that washed over me. I kept chanting it to myself, and went and hugged Mom while the saleswomen ran around hysterically, and my calm transferred to her, and we just stood there, breathing in and out and silently believing that she was nearby somewhere while security barked orders through their walkie-talkies and the saleswomen checked every back room. We stood there until Hailey popped out of a dusty clearance rack in the very back of the store, wearing an enormous, proud grin and yelling, "HAILEY WON!"

There have been other times too. The feeling that there is someone warning me away from the ocean on a day the beach is eventually closed for dangerous riptides. The soothing relief of being so upset about something and, in an instant, being able to stop looping through the catastrophic scenarios and breathe in and out—wondering what it was that put the spiraling panic on hold and reminded me to unwind. Sometimes they're small moments, sometimes they're big, but I've always felt they were just part of being human, of being raised by thoughtful humans.

Still, *being raised by thoughtful humans* doesn't explain what happened that Sunday afternoon. Breckin and I went outside, Frisbee in hand. It was amazing out—seventy-four with no wind, no clouds. The weird marine layer that hovers until lunchtime had evaporated, and the sky was this unreal blue, the kind every tourist notices and mentions. Breckin's bright green Frisbee cut through it, back and forth between us. We dodged people on the lawn, apologizing when the Frisbee landed at someone's feet or—once—hit their shin. We started with the sun to our left, but as we threw, and chased, and caught, I ended up with the sun directly in my eyes.

I'm probably romanticizing it now—in fact, in my more atheist moments, I *know* I'm romanticizing it, though in other times, I'm less sure—but in hindsight, I see the pattern of our game as this looping, meticulous Spirograph. With each of Breckin's throws I caught, I shifted in a matter of precise degrees: ten, fifteen, twenty, thirty, until I had rotated exactly ninety degrees from where I began.

Everyone has a gait, as unique and recognizable as a fingerprint. Sebastian's gait was always upright, unhurried, and careful: each step as even as the one before. I knew his shoulders—wide, muscular—and the way his head sat on his neck—chin up in a sort of graceful bearing. I knew that he walked with his right thumb tucked loosely into his palm, so that it always looked a little like he was making a fist with his right hand while his left hand hung at his side, relaxed.

And there he was, but backlit. None of his features were visible, just his walk, coming toward me.

Breckin threw the Frisbee, and my wide, searching eyes caught the heart of the sun, and the disk sailed straight past me.

When the bright spot finally dissolved from my vision, I looked past Breckin again. The figure was closer now, but it wasn't Sebastian after all. It was someone else with great posture, chin up, a loose right-handed fist.

A close match, but not him.

I remember learning in biology in eleventh grade that the neurons that signal pain, called C fibers, actually have some of the slowest-conducting axons. The sensation of pain takes longer to get to the brain than nearly any other type of information—including the conscious awareness that pain is coming. The teacher asked us why we thought this might be evolutionarily advantageous, and it seemed so simple at the time: We need to be able to escape the source of pain before we're debilitated by it.

I like to think this is how I was somehow already braced against the pain of realization. In this case, the blinding sunshine reached me first, warning me of the painful signal ahead—hope. Reminding me that of course it couldn't be Sebastian. I was in *LA*. He was somewhere else, gathering souls. Of course he wasn't there.

He is never going to be here, I thought. *He is never coming back.*

Was I okay with it? No. But missing him every day for the rest of my life was still easier than the fight Sebastian had: to stuff himself inside a box every morning and tuck that box inside his heart and pray that his heart kept beating around the obstacle. Every day I could go to class as exactly the person I am, and meet new people, and come outside later for some fresh air and Frisbee. Every day I would be grateful that no one who matters to me questions whether I am too masculine, too feminine, too open, too closed.

Every day I would be grateful for what I have, and that I can be who I am without judgment.

So every day I would fight for Sebastian, and people in the same boat, who don't have what I do, who struggle to find themselves in a world that tells them white and straight and narrow gets first pick in the schoolyard game of life.

My chest was congested with regret, and relief, and resolve. *Give me more of those*, I thought to whoever was listening—whether it was God, or Oz, or the three sisters of Fate. *Give me those moments where I think he's coming back. I can take the hurt. The reminder that he's not coming back—and why—will keep me fighting.*

I picked up the Frisbee, tossed it to Breckin. He caught

it one-handed, and I hopped side to side, elbows out, reenergized. "Make me run for it."

He lifted his chin, laughing. "Dude, watch out."

"I'm good. *Throw it.*"

Breckin jerked his chin again, more urgently. "You're going to hit him."

Startled, I tucked in my elbows, wheeling around to apologize to whoever was there.

And *he* was there, maybe two feet from me, leaning back like I might in fact elbow him in the face.

Losing control of my legs in an instant, I sat ass-down on the grass. He wasn't backlit anymore. There was no halo of sun behind him. Just sky.

He crouched, resting his forearms on his thighs. Concern pulled his brows down, drew his lips into a gentle frown. "Are you okay?"

Breckin jogged over. "Dude, are you okay?"

"W-w-w—" I started, and then let out a long, shaking exhale. "Sebastian?"

Breckin slowly backed away. I don't know where he went, but looking back, the rest of it was just me, and Sebastian, and an enormous stretch of green grass and blue sky.

"Yeah?"

"Sebastian?"

Oh God. The sweetly cocky grin, the joke everyone can be in on. *"Yeah?"*

400

"I swear I just imagined you walking from clear across the quad and thought God was giving me some life lesson, and not twenty seconds later you're standing *right there*."

He reached out, took my hand. "Hey."

"You're supposed to be in Cambodia."

"Cleveland, in fact."

"I didn't actually know. I just made that up."

"I could tell." He grinned again, and the sight of it set about building a scaffold around my heart. "I didn't go."

"Shouldn't you be in Mormon jail?"

He laughed, sitting down and facing me. Sebastian. *Here.* He took my hands in his. "We're working out the details of my parole."

The banter fell away in my head. "Seriously. I'm . . ." I blinked, light-headed. It felt like the world was too slowly coming into focus. "I don't even know what's going on."

"I flew to LA this morning." He studied my reaction, before adding, "To find you."

I remembered the day I found him outside my house, flayed by his parents' silence. Panic crawled up my neck. It was my turn to ask, "Are you okay?"

"I mean, LAX is sort of a nightmare."

I bit my lip, fighting a grin, fighting a sob. "I'm serious."

He did a little side-to-side nod. "I'm getting there. I'm worlds better seeing you, though." A pause. "I missed you." He looked skyward, and then back at me. On their return trip, his eyes were glassy and tight. "I missed you a lot. I have a lot of forgiveness to earn. If you'll let me."

Words were a jumbled mess in my head. "What *happened?*"

"Seeing you at the signing really threw me. It was like being shaken awake." He squinted from the sun. "I went on my book tour. I read your book almost every day."

"What?"

"It started to feel like a new holy book." His laugh was sweetly self-deprecating. "That sounds crazy, but it did. It was a love letter. It reminded me every day who I am and how much I was loved."

"*Are* loved."

He inhaled sharply at this, and then added, voice quieter, "A few weeks after I came home from New York, my letter came—my mission call. Mom planned this huge party. There were probably fifty people coming to our house, more waiting to watch on Facebook."

"Autumn told me. I think she watched it, but I wouldn't let her tell me anything."

He swallowed, shaking his head. "We didn't do it in the end. I told my parents that night that I didn't think I could go. I mean," he amended, "I knew I could talk to people about the church, and my testimony, and what Heavenly Father wants for us." He bent, pressing his mouth to my knuckles, eyes closed. It felt like worship. "But I didn't think I could do it the way they wanted: tied off from you, and them, and trying to be someone I'm not."

"So you're not going?"

He shook his head, his lips brushing back and forth over the back of my hand. "I withdrew from BYU too. I'll probably transfer somewhere else."

This time, hope beat every other reaction to the punch: "Here?"

"We'll see. The advance on my book is giving me some breathing room. I have some time to think."

"What about your family?"

"It's a mess right now. We're working our way back to each other, but I don't know what it will look like." He tilted his face up, wincing. "I don't know yet."

I want this burden, I thought. And maybe that's what just happened. Maybe I earned it. I want to be at least partly responsible for showing him that what he might lose is outweighed by owning his life, completely.

"I'm not afraid of having some work ahead of us."

"I'm not either." He smiled up at me, bared his teeth against my hand, and with his playful growl, blood rushed hot to the surface of my skin.

I took ten seconds, eyes closed, to calm down. Breathe in and out, and in and out, and in and out, and in and out.

And then I leaned forward, pouncing, tackling him. He fell backward in surprise, and I landed on top, staring down at his wide, sparkling lake-eyes. My heart pounded against my breastbone, pounded against his, banging on the door to be let in.

"You're *here*," I said.

"I'm here." He looked around where we stretched out on the grass, instinctively hyperaware. Not a single person was paying any attention.

So he let me kiss him, just once. I made it a good one, though, offering up my bottom lip.

"*You're* here," he said. I felt his arms slide around my waist, hands linking at my lower back.

"I'm here."

ACKNOWLEDGMENTS

It isn't necessarily fair to expect authors to have only one "book of their heart," but it is true that if we had to choose, *Autoboyography* would claim that tender spot.

We started talking about this book years ago; Christina worked in a junior high counseling office in Utah, and saw teen after teen coming through who honestly believed, devastatingly, that their parents would probably rather have a dead child than a gay one. As a woman who grew up bi in the queer-friendly world of the Bay Area, Lauren felt a social obligation to reach out to teens whose experiences weren't as easy. We did a great deal of research before we began drafting, including taking a trip to BYU and Temple Square with our dear friend Matty Kulisch. By the time we actually sat down to write Tanner's story, it nearly came out as a single typed stream.

For the push and encouragement to WRITE THIS BOOK, we love you, Christopher Rice, Margie Stohl, and Cecilia Tan. Thank you for the support and enthusiasm and the wisdom. And in addition, Chris, yes, we are writers, but we will never be able to express what it felt to read your notes after you finished. The time and thought—and amount of YOU that you put into that critique letter—was without question the most generous act we could imagine, and we are forever devoted to you.

Dahlia Adler, thank you for reading the first draft of the manuscript, for the back-and-forth, for being open to all questions—even the stupid ones, though you'd never call them that. You are a true gem to your author peers, and we hope you know how grateful we are for what you've given us.

Kiersten White, your feedback was stunning, and your blurb still makes us cry. Your esteem here has meant the world to us; thank you endlessly. Candice Montgomery, Amy Olsen, and Tonya Irving, thank you for taking time in your busy lives to read this, to give us thoughtful feedback, and to be the vocal cheerleaders you have been for so long now.

Our team holds strong for this, our eighteenth book. Erin Service, you are what keeps us sane. Adam Wilson, your eyes and hands steer this ship, every time. Holly Root, you are more than our rock, you are our gravity. Kristin Dwyer, you are the glue and the heart. Our families have seen us rabid for this project from the second it began and are as excited for it as we are; we are lucky, lucky women. Zareen Jaffery, thank you for working to make this manuscript stronger, for loving these boys the way we do. And thank you to everyone at Simon & Schuster Books for Young Readers for working to get this book into readers' hands.

Last but most important, these final words of thanks:

Anne Jamison, none of this would have happened if you hadn't talked it out with us, pushed us to make things harder for our boys, to embrace reality and angst. Thank you for connecting us with Matty, for always making time for us—dare we say "for taking the time to shepherd us"? WE DARE.

And to Matty . . . What can we say here that isn't better saved for the time we can hand you the hard copy and lose our minds together? This almost feels like too public a space for sharing something so personal, but the three of us know how our lives have changed from this experience. We love you massively. Thank you for all of it, for every perfect, honest, loving second of that first trip, and every other one we will take together.